The unicorn-like ... where he lay in the mid-morning shade ... the bonsai trees. Ky-Lin sprang upright, thinking for a moment that the Blue Mountain had erupted again, but recognised immediately that the noise came from the harsh, cacophonous voices of the dragons. They were clearly upset.

He did a quick transformation, desk-ornament size to pony size and trotted along in the afternoon heat, his hooves throwing up little puffs of dust.

As he neared the Blue Mountain, he heard a sudden clatter of leathery wings above. Claws seized his shoulders and he was borne upwards into the air with a whoosh! and a sinking lurch in his stomach. He saw the plain beneath him disappear with alarming speed.

One of the dragons had pounced on him and was carrying him higher and higher towards the northeast, but to what purpose? Was he to be dropped from a great height, to be smashed to smithereens? Made into a snack for the dragons' dinner? But perhaps they had something less violent in mind.

The next moment they started to drop like stones. Beneath them the black maw of the mountain rose up with frightening speed: a dark blot, an inky puddle, an ebony lake—the mouth of Hell itself!

The dragon braked sharply at the last moment, then did a neat landing in the middle of a circle of six scaly others, dropping Ky-Lin unceremoniously to the ground.

All the dragons were hissing. They were not amused. . . .

BAEN BOOKS by MARY BROWN

The Unlikely Ones
Pigs Don't Fly
Master of Many Treasures
Strange Deliverance
Dragonne's Eg

DRAGONNE'S EG

MARY BROWN

Copyright © 1999 by Mary Brown

A Baen Books Original

Baen Publishing Enterprises
P.O. Box 1403
Riverdale, NY 10471

ISBN: 0-671-57810-3

Cover art by Bob Eggleton

First printing, June 1999

Distributed by Simon & Schuster
1230 Avenue of the Americas
New York, NY 10020

Typeset by Windhaven Press, Auburn, NH
Printed in the United States of America

This is for you,
Sam,
with my special love!

Acknowledgments

My thanks as usual to my husband Peter, whose patience appears to increase as mine decreases!

Thanks also for the support of the "Baen Family" always there if needed.

Last, but not least, as a reward for his persistent interest, I shall dedicate this book to Sam, my own "Beau Thai". . . .

BOOK ONE

"Where there's a Will there's a Way"
—William Hazlitt

Chapter One

Birthday Girl

"Please, Miss! Ern's 'avin' a fit again . . ."

Birthdays shouldn't be like this, I thought savagely as I squeezed along the narrow row between the desks to where Ernest was jerking uncontrollably. I held him tight for a moment, glad to see that he hadn't bitten his tongue; as his spasms lessened and he started to snore I scooped him up in my arms and carried him out of the class, down the corridor and into the kitchen, where there was a pallet in a corner for emergencies. I stripped off his soiled pants, chucked them into a bucket and rinsed them out, my nose wrinkling as I draped them over a fireguard to dry.

Ellen turned from the stove, where she was stirring the soup.

" 'Im again? Just cover 'im up, I'll keep an eye on 'im." The smell of the soup made my mouth water. On the table the bread was already sliced. Ellen saw my face.

"All counted out, miss—but come 'ere . . ." She

3

took a knob of crust from the side and dipped it into the soup. "Careful, it's 'ot!"

And absolutely delicious. I crammed it into my mouth all at once, in danger of choking.

"Thanks, Ellen. Only an hour to go . . ."

"Thank God it's Sat'day!"

"Amen to that!"

As I made my way back to the classroom, making sure no crumbs would betray my scrounging and wiping my mouth on one of my second-best handkerchiefs, one used to mop up childish tears, snot or blood from cuts and grazes, I reflected that I should have a full two hours extra this afternoon to celebrate my twenty-first birthday.

School was from eight in the morning till six at night, Mondays to Friday, but on Saturday we broke two hours earlier. Fine in summer, but in winter it made little difference, the nights closing in early. Just two hours longer shut away in my room, a smoky little fire in the grate; just two more hours mending or trimming or studying. Once a week I would call at the local lending library, but I read so fast and so voraciously that I had to ration my pleasure to an hour a day. One penny a week was all I could afford, this being the going rate for borrowing.

I preferred to save a penny or two here and there and browse through one of the second-hand bookshops. This way I had built up my own little library: by now I had some of the novels of Mr. Dickens, Miss Austen, the Misses Brontë, Mrs. Gaskell and Mr. Thackeray, a Treasury of Poetry, the collected Histories of Mr. Shakespeare and *The Commonplace Cook*. This latter I could not really put to the test, as the fire in my room would only hold one pan at best and cooking in one's room was discouraged, but if some day I had a home of my own I should, theoretically, have knowledge enough to produce good, nourishing meals.

In the meantime I, like pupils and teachers alike at the Reverend Ezekiel Moffat's Charity School, lived on just that: the posthumous generosity of our founder. Founded sixty years ago in the early 1820s, the worthy minister had envisaged saving the souls of London's poorest children with his four "R's": Religion, Reading, 'Riting and 'Rithmetic. His daughters, who now ran the school, had added another "R": Refreshments.

For many of these children of the streets the food they received at school was their only sustenance. On arrival each child was given a slice of bread and dripping and a drink of milk and water. At lunchtime there was a bowl of Ellen's soup and another slice of bread and at hometime a slice of bread and scrape and another drink of milk and water. We teachers shared the same diet, which made the twenty-six pounds a year we received go a little further. It meant I only had to buy supper during the week, and could spoil myself on Saturday nights and Sundays.

Still, ten shillings a week didn't go far. Four shillings a week for rent, plus a penny for hot water. One penny a day for the emptying of my slop bucket. This last was definitely worth it, not having to tramp down two flights of stairs to use the revolting, fly-infested privy in the backyard. That made five shillings and four-pence. Three-pence for laundry, a penny for the library, which left four shillings and four-pence for everything else, which included clothes, coals, sewing materials and ribbons, soap and, of course, food.

At present I was managing to save one shilling a week towards the cost of material for a winter dress and new boots, and another shilling went into the Co-operative Bank. Then there was the collection at church on Sundays and a penny for the Missionary Fund, which left me two-pence a night for a meat pie or a couple of sausages. This week I had bought wool to knit mittens and a muffler for the winter,

but I had the princely sum of nine-pence left with
which to indulge myself tomorrow.

In the fine weather I would make a packed lunch
and take it out into one of the parks, but when it
was wet or cold on Saturday nights I would visit the
butcher for a couple of chops, then the greengrocer
for potatoes and some apples or an orange, plus a
loaf from the baker and perhaps a chunk of cheese
from the grocer. Saturday night was cheapest too, as
all was closed for the Sabbath, and the later you
went, the better the bargain.

Back in the classroom my pupils were in disarray.
Obviously those who could had scratched their ver-
sions of "Cat, Rat, Mat, Hat, Sat" onto their slates,
and were now teasing one another, throwing things
or fast asleep. I hurried over, apologising to Miss
Hardacre and Miss Hepzibah Moffat for the possible
disruption of their Middle and Senior classes, clapped
my hands for order, tapped a few heads with my
ruler and hurriedly wiped the blackboard with a
damp cloth and substituted "Dog, Log, Hog, Bog,
Fog" for the earlier words. I then moved down the
aisle, praising where I could, as blame was no use
with these deprived children.

Some of them were patently ineducable, others
would never get further than adding the simplest of
numbers and writing their own names, but there
were exceptions, like Jude and June, half-caste brother
and sister who held the glimmerings of something
better. These two now presented me with "The Cat
sat on the Mat" and "The Cat in the Hat" respec-
tively. Next term I would recommend them to Miss
Hardcastle's Middle Class, who were now monoto-
nously reciting their seven times table.

Having all three classes in the same room was difficult at the best of times, but usually two were either
writing or listening so we teachers didn't have the
added strain of shouting above each other.

Of course there were always more girls than boys. As soon as they were old enough the latter were out on the streets for their parents, thieving, running errands or, if they were lucky, 'prenticed out to coal merchants, chimney sweeps, dockers, lightermen or costers. The girls, if they were presentable, usually ended up on the streets at puberty or helping out in laundries or cookshops. We did have some successes: some of the children had been properly placed, boys to printing presses and the retail trade, even one to the Christian Church; the girls out as milliners, seamstresses, nursery governesses or placed in respectable households. But these alas, were few and far between.

I had been here in London for three years now. My parents had died within a week of each other of a low fever while I was still at boarding school. We had never been well-off—it was said my mother had married beneath her to a humble watch-maker and repairer—but they hadn't stinted on my education, more than they could have afforded; but once all debts had been paid and most of the furniture sold from our rented cottage, I found all I had was enough to keep myself for six months, a few sticks of furniture and fond memories of a pretty, merry mother who was a hopeless housewife, and a gentle, retiring father who waited for work rather than seeking it out.

So, Miss Sophronisbe Lee would have to find a situation, fast, but for an unattached girl of nineteen with no special skills and only the recommendation of her headmistress to back her applications it wasn't easy. At first I was picky, answering only those advertisements that appealed to me, but as time passed I grew more desperate as most of my applications were either unanswered or were curt rejections, the general consensus being that I was both too young and too inexperienced.

So I no longer applied to those advertisements for

a "genteel children's governess," or "Lady F. requires
experienced ladies-maid," rather was I driven to reply-
ing to seekers of companions for the elderly, or
housekeeper in a "large and boisterous household."
These came to nothing as well, if you discount an
interview I actually undertook with hope concerning
a "disabled gentleman" requiring a young lady for
reading aloud, writing letters and other "light duties."
Unfortunately he was not too disabled to chase me
all over his study and he made it very clear what the
"light duties" would entail. . . .

This went on for nearly three months until I had
almost decided to apply for a straightforward domes-
tic post, when I had an unexpected bonus. One of
our neighbours had paid a visit to an aunt in London, and brought back a morning paper which contained ten suitable posts. Although the paper was a
few days old I answered all the advertisements
eagerly, then sat back and waited. And waited.

Of the ten, four never answered, and I had five
replies turning me down, but the last letter was different. This was from the headmistress of a Charity
School offering a teaching post. "Young person, male
or female, to teach class of five- to eight-year-olds in
poor district. Wages: twenty-six pounds per year.
Some food supplied. Only serious and dedicated
applicants need apply." Her advertisement had been
last on my list because of the low wage, but somehow the tone of the letter I received fired me with
an uncharacteristic enthusiasm.

"*I note that your qualifications are more than adequate
for our Junior Class, but you must realise that the possession of knowledge is not, in itself, the only requirement
in a good teacher. It also involves patience, a liking for
your pupils and, above all, the art of communication.*

"*You are young, but that cannot be held against you:
you will not have had time to form bad habits or hard
opinions. I note from your headmistress's recommendation
that you have a mind of your own and are not afraid*

to express your views: I prefer this attitude to that of a milksop-miss.

"*If you decide to take the post you must be prepared to live in an insalubrious district and deal with children who are poor, ill-clad, unwashed and often apathetic. The position is not an easy one, but it might well prove rewarding if you manage to improve the lot of only one of these deprived children.*"

So, my youth and inexperience didn't matter! Even my assertiveness was accepted as a sort of virtue. Was I patient? I thought so. Could I like the unlikeable? Probably—after all, children were children the world over. Could I communicate? Definitely!

And so, a fortnight later, the remaining sticks of furniture sold, apart from my father's comfortable wing-chair, my mother's writing desk and embroidered footstool and a mantel-clock that I had had in my bedroom since I was a child, I took the stage to London and a new life.

And here I still was, nearly three years later.

Perhaps if I had had the faintest idea of just how tough those years were to be I would not have come, but, perversely, I was glad I had. Financially I was badly off; I lived in squalid conditions and probably didn't eat enough healthy food, and the teaching was mind-blowingly monotonous and unrewarding. It seemed my nostrils were always full of the smell of unwashed bodies, urine, chalk, smoke and fog.

Against all those was the plus of living in London itself. It was a wondrous, vibrant city, full of museums, galleries, ancient monuments, theatres, parks and beautiful churches, all of which fed the hunger for beauty and learning which I hadn't realised had lain dormant in me for so long. The fantastic wonders of the Crystal Palace, the military bands, the Palace with its changing of the guard, the gaily dressed people, the shops crammed with goodies—

Of course there was the other side as well. London

was like a beautifully dressed woman with dirty underwear. Horrendous slums, depraved and deprived
lower-classes, running sewers, a pall of choking smoke
most of the year; the blind, the crippled, the lame
begging on every street corner and the prisons full
of debtors, thieves and worse.

But these three years had toughened me. I was
now far more self-reliant, realising just how sheltered,
pampered and protected I had been as a child. Now
I believed I knew far better how to extract the best
from the simplest of pleasures. I also realised how
our little school shone out like a bunch of bright
weeds against the dull poverty around us.

Only one in ten of our little charges really benefit-
ted from the education we offered, but at least they
were off the streets, were fed, warm and, if necessary,
clothed. Miss Moffat and her sister were adept at vis-
iting some of the better neighbourhoods, especially
if a child in the household had died, and begging for
charitable cast-offs. Most of the bereaved were only
too glad to be rid of unpleasant reminders. Otherwise
we took advantage of any scraps of cloth we managed
to gather and cobbled together what we could. Every
Christmas and Easter each child was presented with
a bright new penny, (birthdays being out because few
of the children knew their birthdate), and at the New
Year there was a bag of sweet biscuits.

The headmistress and her sister were as unalike in
appearance as could be. Miss Moffat was tall, slim and
severe-looking; Miss Hepzibah was small, round, wore
wire-rimmed glasses, and sighed a great deal: Ellen
told me she had been disappointed in love. There was
one other member of their household: Madeleine, a
remarkably quiet and composed young lady of about
nineteen who filled in as a teacher when necessary,
and was apparently adopted by the Misses Moffat as
a baby. When I expressed to Ellen my admiration for
their generosity, she shrugged her shoulders.

"There's some as would say they didn't have much

choice," she said, and left me to work it out for myself. I guessed Madeleine must be at least a distant relation, for she bore a remarkable resemblance to a younger Miss Hepzibah. . . .

There was a bustle at the back of the classroom and every childish head turned to where Ellen was carrying in the cauldron of lunchtime soup. She was followed by Madeleine with a tray of bread and a bundle of spoons. Next came the enamel bowls and a bucket of soapy water and a rag, for every child had its face and hands washed before eating. I slipped out to the kitchen to check on little epileptic Ernest, and found him already seated at the kitchen table with soup and bread. On the way back I passed Miss Moffat, who gave me a nod before striking the brass gong outside the classroom to signal luncheon, a sound quickly drowned by the scrapes of chairs and stools, excited squeals and the rush of feet as the children formed into class lines. As usual there was much pushing and shoving, seeming that every second without food was life-threatening, but the routine was well established, and as soon as Miss Moffat entered the room and called for order she gained it within a half-minute.

Madeleine wiped hands and faces, I handed out bowl and spoon, Ellen ladled out into the former and Miss Hepzibah and Miss Hardcastle doled out the bread. The children went back to their desks to eat, before returning their bowls, having their hands and faces wiped clean again and escaping to the yard at the back for a half-hour, to play tag, leapfrog, Fairy Footsteps or Hopscotch and visit the privy.

Then, and only then did we teachers repair to the kitchen to eat our luncheon and toast our toes, with the added bonus of a cup of hot, strong tea to follow. This was also the time when we discussed any especial problems with the children; those who needed extra clothes, who appeared to be sickening

for something or who showed signs of maltreatment
or abuse.

This half-hour always whizzed by, and today the
children were even more difficult to control, but this
was usual on a Saturday. My class were supposed to
be doing the simplest of simple arithmetic, but even
the effort of adding one and one together seemed
beyond them, let alone two and two. At least three of
them were fast asleep, heads on desks, and the rest
of them were either yawning or wanting to pick a fight.

The classroom seemed to be getting darker and
darker, although it was only the first of October.
Glancing up at the long windows, so high up they
had to be opened (rarely) and shut by a hooked pole,
my heart sank. So far autumn had been bright and
fairly sunny, but now the first yellow wraiths of fog
were rubbing against the grubby panes. It seemed
I shouldn't be spending my afternoon tomorrow after
church strolling in the park. At least I had a good
book to read: I had re-borrowed Miss Anne Brontë's
Agnes Grey from the library. A failed governess maybe,
but in the end she had gained her man.

Of course I had to enjoy her final success vicari-
ously, for I had never had even the sniff of a proper
suitor. One couldn't count the boisterous schoolboy
who had tried to steal a kiss on my fourteenth birthday, nor yet the young curate with the sticky-out ears
who was always begging me to come and see his
pressed-flower collection. In London the pattern had
been the same. I discouraged the approach of strangers, and the only man of my acquaintance had been
the student on the floor above at my lodgings. According to my landlady he originated from Dublin, in
Ireland, and he certainly had the gift of the charm and
volubility of his race, and he insisted on writing me
reams of doggerel which he shoved under my door
nearly every day. I ignored his knockings—no visitors
after six o'clock, no gentlemen in ladies' rooms and
vice versa—and either returned the "poems" the same

way they had come or, if I was feeling particularly
vicious, they were useful for laying the fire.

But this was not the limit of his attentions.
Although he never did nor said anything improper,
and hardly spoke at all except for the conventional
greeting now and again, he seemed to shadow me
everywhere. He peered over my shoulder at the
baker's, the grocer's shop and the butcher's; he was
in the seat behind me at church; he checked on my
choice in the library; he was behind me in the park,
at museums and galleries, and he even peered
through the railings when I was ushering the children in and out.

Then, after some three months he disappeared,
owing my landlady for the last two . . .

I jerked awake. Goodness, I was succumbing like
my pupils to a Saturday afternoon lethargy! I looked
around to see what had disturbed me and saw that
the door to Miss Moffat's private apartment was
open, and Miss Moffat was beckoning Toby (one of
our successes: it was he, the youngest member of our
laundress's family, who usually escorted me home)
from his place in the top class. Of course everyone
stopped whatever they were doing to listen to the
exchange, although the actual words were inaudible.

I tapped my ruler on the desk. "Come, children:
anyone who has finished please bring your slate to
me . . ."

I looked up. Twelve- or thirteen-year-old Toby was
threading his way through the desks, heading straight
for me! What could he possibly want? What dread
rule had I broken that the headmistress needed to
see me urgently at three o'clock on a foggy Saturday afternoon?

"Miss Sophy?"

My throat was suddenly dry and I swallowed convulsively. "Yes, Toby?"

"Miss Moffat asks that you 'tend her in her office, most
partickler. Seems there's a gennulman to see you . . ."

Chapter Two

The Bequest

How often do the most innocent among us imagine themselves guilty! During that long walk from my desk, through the crowded classroom and down the corridor to Miss Moffat's study-cum-sitting-room I felt I was experiencing all the terrors of Mr. Sidney Carton on his way to the guillotine, the voices of the children, the chant of the mob—

Yet what could I have done? My thoughts rushed around like a rat in a maze, seeking some explanation and finding none. And who was the gentleman who wanted to see me? Was he from the police? Had someone I knew done something dreadful? Could it be a forgotten creditor of Papa's?

I could feel my heart beginning to race, my whole body to tremble, and it was only when I raised my hand to knock on Miss Moffat's door that I remembered to discard the half-sleeves I wore to protect me from chalk-dust and pat my hair into some sort of order, though as I had inherited Mama's unruly curls it was merely a case of tucking them hastily into my snood.

I could no longer put it off; whatever lay on the

other side of that door I would face with my head held high—so high, I fact, that when I knocked briskly and walked in, not waiting for an answer, I remembered too late the tatty rug that lay just inside the door, a trip-trap for the unwary.

Miss Moffat rose from behind her desk. "Watch where you put your feet, child! And please straighten your collar."

I rose from my knees, smoothing down my skirt, cursing under my breath at my clumsiness.

"Sit here, beside me."

It wasn't only the chill in the room that had me clasping my hands tightly in my lap—there was a perfectly adequate fireplace, but to Miss Moffat winter only began with the first snows—no, it wasn't the cold, it was the figure lurking in the shadows whose face I couldn't see that had me trembling.

Miss Moffat addressed the shadow. "Please be seated, Mr. Swallow," indicating the Windsor chair across from her. She turned to me. "This gentleman is from the firm of Goldstone, Crutch and Swallow of Lincoln's Inn. He has a legal matter to discuss with you." She half-rose from her chair. "If you wish I shall leave you to—"

"Oh, no, please!" I clutched unthinkingly at her sleeve. "I should much prefer you to stay." This although the ogre of the shadow proved to be only a slight, middle-aged man with a bald head and half-glasses. He sat down, laid a bundle of papers on the desk and cleared his throat.

"This is she?"

Miss Moffat leaned back in her chair, patting my arm reassuringly. "Yes."

He coughed, rearranged his papers. "Well, Miss Laye—"

"Lee," I corrected automatically.

"Of course, of course . . . Miss Lee. I am here to reveal some of the terms of our client's Last Will and Testament. I say 'some,' because a part is left for you to discover." He shuffled the papers again. "I must say it has taken some time for us to discover your whereabouts, as the private detective who was hired to trace you is—was—behind bars. A matter of a small debt which we were obliged to disburse, as the gentleman was a trifle obdurate in the matter of your address until we had—ah!—freed him."

Client? Will? Private detective? Prison? It sounded as though I was caught up in some travesty of a novel, a combination of Mr. Dickens and Mr. Conan Doyle. Miss Moffat saw my bewilderment and patted my arm.

"Mr. Swallow," she said. "You have me a trifle confused and, I believe, Miss Lee even more. Do we have a name for this client of yours whose Will you are executing?"

The solicitor looked faintly astonished. "Of course. I assumed—that is I believed—that Miss Lee would know of whom I spoke."

"No," I said. "I'm sorry, but I haven't the faintest idea."

He smiled, but it was a thin smile. "Perhaps I had better begin again. . . ." He extracted a document from the heap in front of him. "I have here the Death Certificate of one Algernon Charteris Lyle, the eminent archaeologist, who died some six weeks ago and is buried in the local village church . . ." He looked at me expectantly.

I shook my head. "I know no-one of that name."

His eyebrows shot up. "Mr. Lyle of Hightop Hall in Dorset? I speak of your uncle, Miss Lee!"

My uncle? But I hadn't got an uncle. I said so. "I'm sure my father . . ." I faltered. Wasn't Lyle my mother's maiden name? I was sure now that I had seen it on my parents' wedding certificate, which I kept with other important papers. But my mother had never mentioned that she had a brother, never talked about her family at all. I searched my memory; hadn't she once handed Papa the newspaper, remarking: "Read that article, my dear: it seems our Algy is making quite a name for himself . . ." Papa had said: "Not enough to seek out his relations," and Mama had said quietly: "You know how they felt about us—" but Papa had interrupted: "Not in front of the child, dearest . . ." and that had been that.

"Was he my mother's brother?" I ventured.

"Exactly!" He rubbed his hands together, as if I had got ten out of ten in some obscure test. "I gather your mother's family were not without some standing in the county of Dorset, but when their only daughter ran off to marry a humble clock-repairer—" he contrived to make it sound a profession slightly lower than that of refuse-collector "—they cut her off without a penny and broke off all further communication."

"I'm sure she didn't mind!" I said hotly. "My parents were devoted to one other! We didn't have much money but we were a very happy family. And Papa wasn't just a clock-repairer: he was a qualified watch-maker, with letters after his name!"

"He was also, I believe," said Mr. Swallow, "of Eastern origin?"

I was silent. I saw Miss Moffat glance sharply at me and then look away.

"My father's true name was Henry Li," I said at last, spelling it out. "His mother was French, his father Eurasian. His parents settled in Switzerland after they married, and that is where my father learned his skills. When his parents died he decided to try his luck in England, where he changed his name to Lee by deed-poll." I turned to Miss Moffat. "I'm sorry, ma'am. Perhaps I should have told you. It wasn't a deliberate omission, I've grown up with the knowledge all my life."

"It would have made no difference," she said firmly. "It must be interesting to consist of so many cultures. For myself, I have always had an interest in the East . . ." She recalled herself, to glare at Mr.

Swallow. "But I do not see what this line of questioning has to do with the matter in hand."

"I apologise for any embarrassment," he said. "But I believe it to have relevance. During their lifetimes, Mr. Lyle's parents forbade him to communicate with his sister, for this very reason. It seems they were somewhat . . ." He hesitated.

"Prejudiced," supplied Miss Moffat.

"Precisely. While they were alive our client respected their wishes, but with their deaths he made enquiries and was satisfied that your parents were reasonably well off and happy with the birth of a daughter. He purchased Hightop Hall the better to house the many artifacts he brought back from his travels and these were added to over the next few years as his activities were extended." He coughed, and shuffled the papers again before continuing.

"Unfortunately he contracted malarial fever at one stage, and once at home recuperating suffered a mild heart attack, which gave him cause to re-assess his future. He decided to leave your mother a small legacy, but when he tried to contact her he found both your parents were dead, Miss Lee, and that you had moved to London, address unknown. He commissioned us to search for you, but we had no success." He sniffed and glanced around the rather shabby little room. "Obviously we were looking in the wrong places.

"As his health worsened he decided to take matters into his own hands and advertised for a private detective, payment on results. In this he had greater success, as the young man was quite enterprising. He has a very—persuasive—way with him, and once he had ascertained from one of your former neighbours that you had applied for various posts from a particular newspaper, and the approximate date thereof, it did not take him long to narrow down the search. To cut a long story short, he not only found you, but furnished your uncle with such precise details of your looks, character, likes, dislikes and situation, that he immediately added a codicil to his Will." He extracted a paper from the heap. "I must say we found it a trifle unusual . . ."

Unusual? The whole matter was unbelievable from my point of view. During the last half-hour not only had I found—and lost—a forgotten relative, it appeared I had also been left a legacy! I could not mourn a man I had never known, but I could be grateful that he had tried, at the last, to make up for the prejudices of his parents. Mama would have been comforted to know that her "Algy" had thought about her at the end, and that he had also considered his niece. I wanted to know what my uncle had looked like, his manner, but now was not the time for questions: Mr. Swallow was still talking.

" . . . insofar as it is incomplete. I am not in possession of the full facts, as I believe your uncle has left you a choice. There is a letter awaiting your perusal at Hightop Hall, and I have moneys here for you to travel there and read the same. So far, his instructions to us are clear. So is the fact that he has left you the contents of a small, locked cabinet in what was his study. I have the key here." He handed it to me. "All the rest of his artifacts have been left to various museums, his books, writings and manuscripts to his Cambridge college." He paused and cleared his throat again. "Although his housekeeper and her husband have been left a small legacy, I cannot promise you that you will have much money as your lot. During his last years he lived on his capital and the house and grounds grew more and more neglected, although the Hall itself has not suffered any structural decay.

"So, do not expect to live in luxury. I suggest you keep your present post for the time being, travel to Dorset to see what is in your uncle's letter, then decide what to do next. You will give her permission to take the trip, Miss Moffat?"

"Gladly. The child has taken no holidays since she has been with us, except for the usual weeks at Christmas and Easter, and of course her post will remain open." She said all this, but she knew the real reason I had taken no leave was because (a) I needed the food and (b) I had nowhere to go. She turned to me. "Take all the time you need. Your wages will still be paid, and Madeleine will cover for you."

"Then when will you be ready to travel, Miss Lee?"

I thought rapidly—everything was happening so quickly. Still, the sooner the better. I glanced at Miss Moffat. "Monday?"

She nodded.

Mr. Swallow shuffled his papers together for the last time. "In that case I will have one of our staff down there to meet you and help out if necessary. We shall reserve a seat on the train and arrange for a carriage for the last part of your journey. Our representative will reside at the local inn and you may do the same, or stay at the Hall if you prefer. I will telegraph the housekeeper to expect you. All costs will be borne by your uncle's estate.

"If you would call at our offices in Lincoln's Inn at nine-thirty on Monday morning—number 22A—we shall have all ready for you."

We shook hands—his were clammy and cold—and Miss Moffat escorted him out. Through the open door I could hear the clatter of nailed boots as the last of the children made their way home, and the noises from the kitchen as Ellen cleared all away for the weekend. Through the net curtains behind the desk I could see the fog thickening.

I glanced at my fob-watch: five minutes past four. An hour and five minutes and my life could have changed completely.

I leant back in my chair. It had all happened too quickly for me to grasp the implications. Sure, I knew what I had to do next, how and when, but it just didn't add up to anything concrete. My mind and body were still attuned to a Saturday at the school; time now I went home, did some shopping on the way, picked up my laundry, lighted my fire, collected my hot water and had a wash, ate my supper, did some mending and then relaxed with my library book before undressing and going to bed. Tomorrow, Sunday, my best dress and church. Perhaps a walk in the afternoon, a visit to one of the parks, a halfpenny ride on one of the open-top horse-drawn trams . . .

I realised I was trying to push my new knowledge away, instead of both accepting it and trying to make sense of it. The fact was, I was afraid. So far there had been so few changes in my life—going away to school, the death of my parents, finding this post in London—that I was ill-equipped to deal with sudden advances or retractions. It was only now that I was beginning to realise what a rut I had got myself into in the last three years; well, here was a situation I had been forced into and I felt the first stirrings of anticipation. Perhaps this was the beginning of something new and exciting—

There was a knock on the door and Ellen brought in a tray of tea.

"Miss Moffat said as 'ow you'd missed your bread and jam you might like to join 'er in a cuppa. She'll be back in a minute, just locking up." She hesitated in the doorway. "She said as 'ow you're off on Monday to look at your uncle's place and might not be back. Just like to say as 'ow we'd miss you. And if you ever need a cook, I'll be there like a shot." She slipped out the door, then poked her head round it again. "Young Ern 'as gone off with 'is sister, but master Toby says as 'e'll wait in the kitchen to see you 'ome . . ."

Dear Toby! Like the rest of my laundress's children, he was not certain which of his various "uncles" was his father, but he was no worse for that, being one of our most promising pupils, determined to better himself. Realising that my lodgings were within a stone's-throw of the laundry, he had offered to show me a quicker way home.

This had opened my eyes to the darker side of the city. Narrow alleys with houses leaning crazily in all directions, gutters running with ordure, shouts, screams and rantings from behind open doors with no hinges; windows nailed up with sacking; beggars with no hands, no legs, no eyes. Rats as big as cats scuttling in and out of the heaps of refuse, some of which latter came alive as we passed, gnawed fingers grabbing for my skirts, Toby's ankles. We crept through the filth of courtyards where dogs prowled and snarled and fought and copulated and half-naked children played listlessly with rags and pieces of string. We passed low taverns, stinking of sour beer and wine and the sweet decay of vomited gin, men and women staggering out, their faces bloated and blotched, swaying and falling into the gutters. We went by the painted women, some not even yet women, but boys and girls no older than Toby himself. Lines of people waited for the pawnbroker to open for the evening so they could "pop" their few possessions from one week to the other. Flies fastened on our hands and faces, greedily seeking salt; we stepped aside for the rag-and-bone man with his cart: rags for paper, bones for glue, bottles for reuse. The night-soil people never came here and slops thrown from the windows stained the house-fronts and caked the cobbles.

The sights, the sounds, the smells, all combined with the thick, murky air, revolted me: it was like a walk through Hell. But Toby walked through it all with the assurance born of familiarity. With him I was safe. He knew the streets and many of the people, warning off the urchins who would have crept up behind me to snatch at my reticule, bonnet or even cloak. I saw that he carried a small sharp knife, besides the short, weighted stick stuck in his belt. After that first time I never wanted to tread that way

once more, but he persuaded me every now and
again. I never came to any harm, and gradually he
introduced me to his especial friends: the old-clothes
dealer, Simeon, whose face reminded me of the illu-
strations of Fagin in "Oliver Twist"; Pegleg Pete, a
crippled ex-sailor, who hawked matches; Old Nell,
who had a houseful of felines, spending whatever she
earned with the cat's-meat man; Sal, a prostitute
whose moneys kept not only herself but her three
young siblings and an invalid mother and my
favourite, little Em, a crippled child with the sweet-
est singing voice I had ever heard.

This night, with the fog closing in, we would go
by the longer route. I decided that supper would be
a celebration, not only for my birthday but also for
my uncle's legacy, whatever that might be, and that
I would invite Toby to share it with me.

Miss Moffat came back and shut the jingling bunch
of keys away in her desk.

"Well, that's that for a couple of days," she said
briskly. "Pour the tea, child, while I wind the clock.
It only needs attention once a week, and Saturday
is as good a day as any other . . ."

I poured out the way Mama had taught me: milk
first, the first cup for the guest, second for the host,
in case the tea grew too strong. This was never a
problem with Miss Moffat's tea; Ellen brewed it as
she liked it, pale and straw-coloured. I picked up the
tongs and added the rare pleasure of two lumps of
sugar to mine. The headmistress drew the drugget
curtains, turned up the lamp, accepted her cup and
saucer and took a couple of sips before seating herself in the chair next to mine.

"Well, this afternoon was a surprise, wasn't it?"

"Yes, ma'am. I'm afraid it hasn't quite sunk in yet."

"No more it will child, until you find yourself on
that train on Monday morning."

"I've never travelled on a train . . ."

"Then you have both a treat and an experience

in store! I well remember the first time I travelled so . . . The speed! Why, we must have reached at least thirty miles per hour! The worst things were the smoke and smuts and the hardness of the seats . . . Make sure you visit the Ladies Room at the station before you board the train: there is nothing worse than travelling in discomfort. Try and find yourself a 'Ladies Only' carriage: you will be safe from tobacco smoke and any unwelcome attentions."

"But surely, ma'am, no gentleman would venture to light a pipe or cigar in front of a lady without first requesting permission?"

She sniffed. "Once upon a time, yes, but times are changing, and not for the better." She leant over and squeezed my knee. "Besides, if you are in a 'Ladies Only' you will feel less inhibited when you unwrap your sandwiches or pie."

I was becoming more and more bewildered. "I shall need to take food with me?"

She nodded. "It would be wise. You will probably have just a crust for your breakfast, then you will have to walk to Lincoln's Inn. From there I presume they will provide transport to the station, but you will have to wait for the train. It is possible, I believe, to obtain a cup of tea there, but you will still have a long journey ahead. I cannot see you arriving at your final destination much before the middle of the afternoon, and who knows then what comforts, or lack of them, will await you? You would not wish to arrive in a distressed or fainting condition, would you?"

"N—no," I said. "Thank you for your advice, ma'am. I shall certainly take some refreshments with me. May I pour you some more tea?"

"Thank you. And please help yourself. I think we should try Ellen's seed-cake as well . . ."

Another cup of tea and two slices of cake later I felt far more relaxed. As I put down my empty cup and saucer she leant forward once more and squeezed my knee again, quite hard this time. "Have you given thought to what you will do in the future?"

"I suppose—I suppose it all depends on what is in my uncle's letter." I faltered, feeling uncomfortable all of a sudden.

She released her hold. "Of course. But if you find only a small amount is involved—will you consider returning here?"

"Of course," I reassured her. "In spite of everything, I have still enjoyed my time here. And I should miss the children sorely—"

"And us?"

I puzzled. "I don't know Miss Hardacre very well, but Ellen is a dear! Miss Hepzibah and Miss Madeleine are always very pleasant and you have shown me every consideration—"

Suddenly she stood up and loomed over me, her shadow huge on the wall, then she bent forward and cupped my face in her hands. "I should have realised where you got those eyes from," I thought she said, but couldn't be sure, because the blood was beating so strongly in my ears. She bent closer: she smelt of stale powder. Without any warning she kissed me full on the lips, as my mother might have done, but this wasn't a motherly kiss.

I pulled my head away and stumbled to my feet, knocking over my chair. When I had righted it and turned back, hoping my cheeks were not as flushed as they felt, Miss Moffat had her back to me, fiddling with something on the mantelpiece. Her back was very straight, but I noticed that the hand I could see was trembling. Her voice, however, was as firm as ever.

"Ask Ellen to collect the tea-tray, will you?"

Chapter Three

Journeying

I was so busy puzzling over Miss Moffat's uncharacteristic behaviour on the way back to my lodgings, that it wasn't until we were nearly there that I realised that Toby had hardly uttered a word. Normally he was that delightful mixture of child and young adult which comes at the onset of puberty; one moment he would be darting ahead, leaping up to pull a leaf from a tree or somersault over some railings, the next he would engage me in serious conversation, asking impossible questions like "What does the Prime Minister *really* do?" or "Does the Queen wear a different pair of shoes every day?" or even "How far is it to the Moon?"

Very often I was stumped for a sensible answer. He was a naturally inquisitive child with an affectionate nature, though I sometimes wondered whether this had anything to do with the fact that he always managed to coax a sausage or pie from me on Saturdays . . . Not ever by direct asking, but the wistful face and appreciative thanks always touched my heart.

Being the youngest in the family at home he ran

errands and delivered the laundry. His two eldest sisters were married and the younger two worked with their mother, although one was crippled. Of his brothers, one had run off to sea and the other was serving three years for assault. The "Missus" of his mother's title was purely a courtesy one. She had a fancy for soldiers and sailors: easy come, easy go. This I had learned from Ellen, who was expert at putting two and two together.

All the children had been to the Charity School at one time or another, but Toby was the only one to have shown any aptitude. He could read and write, although the latter was largely phonetic. He wrote as he spoke with all dropped or substituted aitches: "Hay" was " 'ay"; "afterwards" was "halfterwoods." His arithmetic was exceptionally good, in fact he was way ahead of his teachers, and used the abacus with bewildering speed.

But this afternoon there were no questions, no skipping ahead, no jumping the piles of leaves that swirled with every passerby. The fog didn't seem to be getting any thicker, but the gas-lamps had a smoky nimbus and people loomed up in shadowy insubstantiality to disappear again almost immediately, and the cries of the street vendors and the rattle of wheels had a muffled quality.

I tried to make conversation, but there was either no response, or he replied in monosyllables. As we reached the turn to my lodgings I fumbled in my purse and extracted a three-penny bit.

"Here, Toby, this is for my laundry. Don't bother to bring it back for a couple of hours, but when you do please tell your mother I would like your company for a while as escort. Clean face and hands, please!" I patted him on the head. "And please try to look a little less miserable! It's my birthday today . . ."

He looked up at me, his expression unreadable. "Happy birthday, Miss."

The clock of St. Michael and All Angels church

nearby struck five. "Well then . . . See you about seven. Do you want to borrow my lantern?"

He shook his head and darted away. I made my way up the steps to my lodgings, still wondering what had upset him. Once in my room though, I was too busy to dwell on a mystery which was probably just a storm in a teacup anyway.

Putting on my apron I lighted the candles, laid the fire, collected yesterday's ashes in the coal-scuttle, put two weeks' rent in my pocket and went downstairs to find my landlady.

Explaining that I would be away for a few days due to the death of a relative, I also added that if I decided to stay longer I would send for the rest of my belongings, and arrange for their transportation. To this end I would give her two weeks' rent, the second in lieu of notice if I did not return. She was full of questions of course, but I pleaded distraction and escaped upstairs with my ration of coals and the promise of hot water within the hour.

Once swept, dusted and polished I looked around my little room with an affection of sorts I had not known I possessed. After all, it was the only place I could call home, and the unknown was always daunting. For three years, not altogether easy ones, this place had been my refuge. Over there was the bed with the patchwork quilt I slept under; there was the rickety table where I ate my meals; there was my mother's desk where I wrote up my diary, there was the window-sill where crumbs were placed for the hungry London sparrows and over there was the little shelf where my books were placed, next to the hooks for my clothes.

Books! What in the world would I have done without the escape they offered? My imagination had soared away from the confines of four walls—into the marshes with Hereward, fleeing the destruction at Pompeii, crusading with Ivanhoe, tasting the quieter gossip at Cranford, or enjoying the ecclesiastical

in-fighting at Barchester . . . How often had I wished
I had been a part, a real part, of the stories I read!

I gave myself a mental shake. After all the adventures I had yearned for, what was I doing clinging
to a dingy little room, when on Monday my whole
life might change!

Come on, young woman, I told myself. Today is
your birthday, your coming-of-age. Tonight you will
take Toby out for supper, a treat for you both. In
the meantime go out and buy something you want—
not something you need—find an extravagance.

Three-quarters of an hour later I returned with
bread, bacon, pies and two oranges for Sunday, and
my birthday presents to myself: a bottle of shampoo
scented with orange-flowers and a bar of soap to
match, rare luxuries, and two second-hand books:
"Our Mutual Friend," by Mr. Dickens, and "Westward
Ho!" by Mr. Kingsley. I should take them both with
me on Monday. I had also bought some sprigs of
rosemary and lavender to pack amongst my clothes,
and had withdrawn all my savings. Not that I had any
intention of spending them, but they might be useful in an emergency. I could always put them back
afterwards—after *what* I wasn't quite sure.

My hot water arrived, I had a thorough wash, put
on a clean white blouse and sponged my dark-blue
skirt and cloak and polished my boots. Then I pinned
two rosettes of white ribbon to my bonnet. Mama
had taught me the importance of matching the
colours of my dress discreetly, without drawing undue
attention to it. "A lady is not known by her dress but
by her manners," was one of her favourite sayings.

I peered at myself in the scrap of cracked and
blotchy mirror above the mantelshelf, holding my
candle close, but my face looked mysterious, far away.
Without conscious thought I tried to focus my eyes,
which had apparently inspired Miss Moffat to such
uncharacteristic behaviour, but they looked exactly
as they always had to me. Greeny-hazel, with thick

black lashes—perhaps it was a slight tilt upwards at the outer corners that had intrigued her? Papa's eyes had had the same tilt but his eyes had been dark brown.

I shivered of a sudden and slammed the candle down, wax dripping into the hearth. Rubbing my mouth I tried to wipe away the memory of that kiss, unasked and resented. Would it happen again if I returned to the school? I hoped not: there had been something unsettling, wrong about it.

Footsteps on the stairs, stumbling a little in the dark, and a knock on the door. I opened it and there was Toby, my escort for the night.

Only he didn't look as if he was going anywhere. Thrusting the bundle of laundry into my arms he turned to go, face dirty, hair uncombed.

"Toby! What's the matter?"

"I'm not coming!" Tossing the laundry onto the bed, I seized his arm and drew him into the room.

"What do you mean, you're not coming? Won't your mother let you?" I laughed. This was incredible! He must know I intended to feed him and he was always hungry.

"Just why don't you want to come? Are you ill? I thought we could find somewhere pleasant to eat and—"

"And *I* thought you were my friend!"

"Of course you are my friend. Why should you think otherwise?"

"Because you're goin' away, that's why! And you're not comin' back neither, only you won't admit it. You're not just cel'bratin' your birthday, if that's what it is, you're cel'bratin' goin' away! And you didn't even tell me!" He looked as if he was about to stamp, throw something or burst into tears, and I didn't want him doing any of these.

"Toby! I'm surprised at you. That's one of the reasons we are going out tonight, so I can explain, just to you. Instead of waiting to hear what I have to say, you've obviously listened to some half-heard story from Ellen, who—"

"I listened! I listened at the door when you were with that lawyer fellow—"

"You shouldn't eavesdrop! It's wicked, and—"

"But that way at least I knows what's goin' on! Didn' hear it from anyone else. Straight from the 'orse's mouf.'"

I thought for a moment. "And did you hear my conversation with Miss Moffat later?"

He shook his head. "Saw me in the corridor, she did, an' sent me back to class."

"Then you didn't hear her ask me what I had decided to do in the future, and whether I had thought of returning?"

He shook his head again.

"Mr. Swallow said my uncle left very little money, did he not? Well, when Miss Moffat asked whether I had thought of returning, I told her it all depended on what I found when I went down there, and what was in my uncle's letter. So, what's the problem? Come on now, pull yourself together. I shall probably be back within the week."

"If'n you say it like that . . . Cross your heart and hope to die?"

I obliged. "Now then, what about that chop-house round the corner?"

"Nah . . ." He shook his head dismissively. "Ma does their linen, and I gets to see the food. Cat's meat. Flies all over." He brightened. "Tell you what: I know of a place 'bout quarter-mile away. Nothing posh, but the grub's good an' you gets value for money. Maggie May's. You game?"

"Maggie's" proved to be an Irish quarter-mile distant: more like a half. The fog was thickening, but Toby had the lantern and guided me safely enough, though I near jumped out of my skin when a bell clanged at my elbow, but it was only the muffin-man, wooden tray on his head, ready to cry out his wares.

There were few people about, and we passed the chop-house I had suggested with only a small sigh of regret from me, for Maggie's sounded much more fun. It was.

We descended steep steps to a basement lit by oil lamps, with a large open hearth at the far end. It was warm, smoky, but cosy. Being early to dine, not long after seven, there were few tables occupied, these by quiet, respectable-looking people. Looking more closely at my surroundings I saw the floor was of worn, well-scrubbed red tiles, the walls were distempered white, and it would seem that none of the tables or chairs shared a common origin, although the former were spread with clean and cheerful red gingham cloths and starched napkins.

A small, round woman wearing a large white apron came bustling out from the back.

"Why, Master Toby! How nice to see you . . . And you have brought a lady-friend with you!" Her black eyes, darting from one to the other, had probably summed us up correctly even before Toby introduced me as his teacher, whom he had brought here for her birthday treat.

" 'Cos you makes the best 'n' freshest food in Lunnon," he added.

She wiped her hands on her apron. "Well, that's very kind of you, Master Toby. We shall have to make sure we live up to your recommendation, shan't we?" She led us over to a table in an alcove near the fire, where it was warm enough for me to discard bonnet, cloak and gloves. "Now, what can I get for you? My standards are up on that blackboard over there: tripe and onions, steak and kidney pudding, mutton with caper sauce, rabbit pie, liver and onion sauce, stewed eels, and a treat from India, vegetable curry. What do you say?"

"Rabbit pie for me," said Toby, "Though the tripe and onions sounds great . . ."

"Leave it to me," she said and turned to me. "And

how about you, miss?" She looked at me speculatively. "I can tell you aren't a tripe and onions lady, nor yet one for eels . . ." The very thought of either put me right off. "If you don't mind waiting a little while, I'm sure I can come up with something to suit," and off she whisked back to the kitchen, her large apron spreading like the sail of a ship.

Five minutes later a serving-maid brought a bowl of tripe for Toby and some toast and paté for me, accompanied by a large jug of lemon-barley water.

"Starters," she announced.

The paté was delicious, with a hint of brandy behind the chicken liver base. My first hunger sated, I glanced around the restaurant once more. It was filling up nicely; some single gentlemen, married couples, a pair of lovers and at least two families. Nobody seemed to mind the mismatched furniture nor the odd pairings of cutlery.

Toby followed my gaze, scooping up the last of his sticky, glutinous tripe with a slice of bread. "Mostly clerks as come here," he said. "They finishes late, and it's a good place to bring the fambly. Mrs. May does the cookin' and her daughters wait on. Mr. May works at the docks; good man, but a bit dumb. She's the one as keeps them all goin'. Used to work as cook to a titled gent till 'e went bankrupt."

But bankrupt her dishes certainly were not. Toby's rabbit stew came with carrots and turnips and I was served with a mouthwatering plate of Beef Wellington, the pastry light and flaky, the meat pink and tasty, the mushrooms complemented by the tender French beans served as my vegetable. We both finished with apple pie flavoured with cloves and cinnamon and dressed with a rich custard. It was probably the most delicious meal I had had in years, and much cheaper than I had expected.

A satisfactory end to a very odd day.

Chapter Four

The Journey

After church the following day I started my packing. There was probably no need to parcel everything up, but even if I were to be away only a couple of days, my belongings would be safer packed away. So, into my father's old cabin trunk went my clothes (what there were of them), the patchwork quilt, spare bonnet, best boots and linen. In the tray at the top went writing materials, sewing things, books and the gold-rimmed, rose-patterned cup and saucer that had been my mother's favourite. I strapped up the trunk and labelled it, then also labelled the writing-desk, chair and footstool.

My dirty linen would go to Toby's mother on Monday, for return on Wednesday, and I prepared a label for that as well. I would travel in my working clothes, but in my travelling valise went clean underwear, night-dress, dressing-gown, slippers, washing things, an apron and my best blouse, skirt and jacket, plus the two books I had not yet read. It was so heavy by the time I had finished, I was glad I would be met at the other end.

I broke off to eat bacon sandwiches for lunch, and

34

later warmed a pie for my supper, with an orange with each meal, but the time went so swiftly that it was after seven before I asked for hot water, one lot for washing my hair with my new shampoo, the other for an all-over wash. It seemed years since I had seen a proper bath-tub.

I asked the landlady to call me at six, plenty of time to clear out the grate, bundle up the washing, take it to Toby's mother, Mrs. Jugg, buy fresh bread and ham for sandwiches, plus a couple of bottles of ginger beer.

I had thought I would spend a sleepless night, worrying about the morrow, the future in general, but surprisingly I slept like a top, was ready in plenty of time and was five minutes early at the offices of Messrs. Goldstone, Crutch and Swallow of 22A, Lincoln's Inn.

Mr. Swallow was waiting for me.

"Ah, Miss—er—Lee. All arrangements have been made. You will catch the ten-thirty train from Waterloo, which will arrive at three at Deepling Crossing. There, our representative, Mr. Cumberbatch, will have arranged transport to Hightop Hall. The caretaker and his wife have been advised of your travel plans, and you will stay at the Hall until these matters have been—ah—sorted out satisfactorily. Mr. Cumberbatch will stay at a nearby hostelry, to be contacted when you are ready for your next move."

He handed me an envelope. "In here you will find your ticket and some travel expenses." He shook my hand. "I wish you luck, Miss—er—Lee."

Outside the office, treading through the fallen mulberry leaves, I opened the envelope. Inside was a first class ticket for a "Ladies Only" compartment and twenty bright shillings. A fortune! There were no cabs in Chancery Lane, so I crossed to Kingsway with better luck.

At the station there was over an hour to wait, so I bought a buttered scone and a cup of coffee, all

the while marvelling at the great glass and stone
edifice, echoing with the huff and puff of the
engines, the shriek of whistles, the clatter of the hurrying passengers, the call of the newsboys and the
announcements, through a megaphone, of arrivals
and departures.

The air was thick with that rotten-egg smell that
seemed characteristic of steam engines, and the
ground strewn with debris, amongst which pigeons
and sparrows rooted for crumbs. I hesitated over buying a newspaper, but decided I had been prodigal
enough. Besides, I had my books in my valise to read.
After checking the platform from which my train left,
and confirming the time, I retired to the Ladies
Room, remembering Miss Moffat's advice and visit-
ing the washroom.

In spite of all this the time seemed to be crawl-
ing, not helped by the fact that I was checking my
fob-watch every three minutes, or so it seemed. The
waiting-room was nearly full; a woman with two
grown daughters, a market-lady with two baskets of
eggs, a severely dressed, thin woman with a satchel
full of leaflets and another reading from her Bible.
Small children ran around, whining at the delay,
eager to escape and look at the engines.

Eventually, with still twenty minutes to go, I
decided to see if my train was at the platform. It was,
and a helpful guard showed me the way to my compartment and indicated my reserved seat, a corner
one facing the engine. No-one had briefed me as to
tipping, but he seemed grateful enough for the penny
I offered.

It was all more comfortable and clean than I had
expected from Miss Moffat's reminiscences, but perhaps she had not travelled first class. My seat was
well sprung, there was a sunblind at the window and
a small upper window that could be slid open. I put
my valise on the netted shelf above my seat, took off
and folded my cloak and adjusted my bonnet in the

mirror opposite. Then I sat back and watched the
passengers hurry past my window; all shapes and
sizes, men, women and children, laden and unladen,
purposeful or hesitant, smart or shabby. Seeing the
numbers, I was glad I had the luxury of a reserved
seat.

In the event I was joined only by two nuns and
a languid lady with a lorgnette, who shut her eyes
and apparently dozed off as soon as the train started.
The sisters meanwhile occupied themselves with their
rosaries and reading their psalters, so I was not
obliged to even open my mouth during the whole
journey.

I had thought I would treat myself to a chapter of Mr. Dickens and one of my sandwiches, but
I was too engrossed in the journey. The speed, the
smooth motion, except when we passed over points,
the ever-opening vistas of town and country that
flashed past the windows entranced me, punctuated
as they were by the chuff-chuff of the powerful
engine and the diddly-dee, diddly-dee of the wheels
on the tracks.

Once we had crossed the slow-moving Thames and
cleared the smoke-grimed tenements of south London we emerged into a world I had almost forgotten: the green and pleasant land of rural England.
I had not realised how much I had missed the fields,
trees, streams and cattle that were so much a part
of my childhood. I found my hands were clenched
in my lap and I was filled with nostalgia as at one
moment we plunged into a cutting with bosky woods
stretching up on both sides, their leaves turning red,
yellow and brown and fluttering down in the wake
of our passage. Then we would have a straight run
through fields bisected by neat hedges in which
brown and white Herefords grazed or ponies galloped
away, pretending panic at our passage, their tails held
high.

There were long, low farmhouses, sheep dotting

their fields; over there they were burning the stubble, smoke mushrooming up and drifting away north with the breeze; here they were already ploughing, the patient Shires straining against their collars as the straight furrows grew behind them.

Sometimes we rode high on an embankment, the sun throwing our shadow like a toy train onto the fields on our right. Now and again I would catch a glimpse of a stately home, in white or yellow stone, usually set on a knoll and backed by carefully cultivated woods. These set me to wondering what my uncle's house was like. With a name like Hightop Hall it ought to be grand enough, and at least I would be spending a couple of days there in greater luxury, I hoped, than my London lodgings.

This was a stopping train, as opposed to an express, and we halted at every station, from those that serviced small towns to those that were only to offload milk-churns for a farm across the fields. I kept careful count of the number of stops, as Mr. Swallow had written in pencil on my ticket that mine was number sixteen.

Deepling Crossing, when it came, was just another halt, and I was the only one alighting or getting on, and I felt rather lost as I watched the train puff its way round the curve and disappear.

I looked about me. The downside platform on which I stood had no exit and was backed by fields. Across on the upside however there was what looked like a ticket booth, a gate and a lane leading away into the distance—but no sign of any transport. I glanced at my watch: the train had been on time, but perhaps punctuality in this part of the countryside was more lax. After all, even in these advanced times, many people didn't own a timepiece of any kind, in or out of the home. Farmworkers relied on light and dark in the passing of the seasons, those in towns or villages on the striking of the church clock.

No point in just standing around. I walked to the end of the platform where it sloped down, crossing the line carefully in case another locomotive appeared suddenly, and walked up to the ticket booth, checking on the way that "Deepling Crossing" was clearly painted on the signs on both platforms: right place, right time.

I tapped on the closed shutters of the ticket booth, but there was no answer. I tapped again, a little louder this time—still no reply. I walked around to the back—but there was none! It was just a three-sided shelter, containing a stool, a broken clay pipe and two or three ancient ticket stubs: obviously the ticket-collector didn't have much call for his services.

I walked over to the wicket gate and peered down the lane: still no sign of transport. Well, I could wait a little longer, but after a half-hour pacing the platform, I began to feel worried. I decided the best thing to do was have something to eat, because I was feeling distinctly hungry. I took the stool out of the booth, found a patch of sunshine and sat down to enjoy half my ham and chutney sandwiches, washed down by one of my bottles of ginger beer. I could have eaten the rest, but thought it wise to keep them for emergencies—like the non-appearance of any form of welcoming party.

By the time an hour had passed since the arrival of the train—during which time two expresses had roared through the station, one up, one down, causing me to shrink back as I was buffeted by their passage, I had decided that enough was enough. There was only one way out of the station so I would walk in that direction, to meet whoever had been sent out to fetch me.

I returned the stool to the booth, picked up my valise, opened the gate and walked out into the lane. I then decided it would be wisest to relieve myself before anyone turned up, found a gap in the hedge and a nettle-free patch, a lesson I had learned early

as a child when running around the fields and lanes,
too far away from home to seek our bathroom.

Thanking the good Lord that I was wearing my
stout boots, kilting up my skirt against the dust in
the lane and picking up my valise I started off again.

The lane wound and turned on itself, obviously
following some long-forgotten sheeptrack, and as I
walked, changing my increasingly heavy valise from
hand to hand, the land rose and fell on either side.
I passed the entrance to two farms, but the houses
were so far down the access roads that I didn't dare
risk asking for directions or aid, in case I missed my
intended transport. I passed a couple of cottages too,
but one was derelict, and the other housed a zany
old man who apparently had never heard of Hightop
Hall.

At last I came to a cross-roads. There was a sign:
to the left DORCHESTER THIRTY-SIX MILES. To the right
just the one word: LONDON. Putting down my valise,
I stood irresolute. Left, right, straight ahead? I
looked at my watch: four o'clock, two hours since
I had alighted from the train. Spreading my cloak
out on a grassy bank, I sat down to review the
situation. Here I was, apparently miles from anywhere, it was October, night would be descending
soon, and—

Cartwheels? I stood up and peered across the road
to the lane's continuation and slowly a cart came into
view, the driver and horse looking half-asleep, their
heads nodding in unison.

Springing to my feet I ran across the road and
waved my arms frantically to halt the cart. The driver
hauled on the reins and the cart came to a stop: "JOS.
CARTER. CARRIER" I read on the side. Breathlessly I
asked if he knew the way to Hightop Hall.

He looked at me suspiciously, then nodded.
"Yerss."

"Is it that way?" Pointing back the way he had
come.

"Yerss."

"How far?"

"Depends . . ."

"On what?"

"Whether you takes the high road or the low road."

"Which is the quickest?"

"High."

"How far that way?"

"Ten mile, give or take."

"Do you know where I could get a lift?"

For the first time he seemed to look at me properly. "You wanting to go there?"

I could have screamed. "Yes, I do. Urgently. It was my uncle's house."

His face brightened. "You be Miss Lee?"

"*Yes!*"

He scratched his head. "Be you sure? You supposed to be at the station—sent to meet you, I was." He scratched his nose this time. "Why bain't you at the station?"

I explained, as patiently as I could. "I thought I would be met by a young gentleman from London—did he send you instead?"

He nodded.

"Didn't he tell you the time of my train?"

"May have done. But I be a carrier. Old Nan, she wanted that chair delivering from her daughter's. Jones wanted them stores early. Got to keep in with the regulars . . ." He pursed his lips. "You coming then?"

The cart turned as slowly his conversation had been, and as cautiously. There seemed to be no attempt to help me up, so I hoisted my valise aboard and climbed into the back via a wheel and a flurry of petticoat. Not that the driver took the slightest notice. I settled myself on a pile of dusty sacks and off we went. After a few miles we turned off the lane into another, even narrower.

I tapped him on the shoulder. "Is this the high road?"

He shook his head. "The low."

"But I thought you said the other way was shorter!"

"And so 'tis. Horse prefers this way . . ."

After that I gave up, ate the rest of my sandwiches and drank the other bottle of ginger beer and even dozed a little as the miles slipped away with the creak of wheels and the clop of hooves. Two hours later I woke with a jerk as the cart pulled up.

"Are we here?"

"Yerss."

I lowered myself and the valise to the ground. The sky was already glooming over and the wind had turned chill.

"That'll be five shillings, miss."

"I beg your pardon?"

"Five shillings to the station and back."

"But you didn't—" I caught myself in time. "Didn't the young gentleman from London pay you?"

He shook his head. "Said it was up to you. Said you'd have money."

I had been caught napping, literally. A good job Mr. Swallow had been generous with my travelling money. I paid the carrier and he trundled off down the lane.

I turned to survey my temporary lodgings. Open double gates, a small lodge, and a weed-infested driveway that led through tumbledown parkland uphill towards—

The most hideous mansion I had ever seen.

Chapter Five

Hightop Hall

It looked as though three different houses had been welded into one.

In the centre was what must have been a perfectly pleasant Queen Anne three-storey home. Red brick, with a grey slate roof, it was approached by a shallow set of steps leading to double doors. Two large windows on either side of the door indicated perhaps a withdrawing room and dining room, and behind these would be morning room, study, music room and, attached at the back, the kitchens and dairies. Above, on the first floor, were slightly smaller windows, bedrooms, I guessed, and dressing rooms. Above these were eight dormer windows, like surprised eyebrows, which would be for the servants. So far, so good.

But look to the right and the whole aspect changed. Sir Walter Scott would probably have approved of the grey stone castle, complete with towers, turrets and battlements, that was attached to the main building. Not on the grand scale maybe, but nonetheless this modern copy was

utterly incongruous among its older settings. There
was even a round tower. . . .

If that was not bad enough, then glance to the left.
On the other side of the main building was what
looked like a white stone Regency town-house, whose
front door was approached by a pillared portico like
a temple. Again, on its own it would not have been
out of place, but the two-storey building, pleasant
enough of itself, only served to accentuate the horrendous amalgam of the whole.

I stopped first at the lodge, of course, but the
shutters were down and there was no answer.

My heart sank, nevertheless I trudged up the long
drive, hoping against hope that it would be better
inside. But the windows gazed back at me blankly,
and on either side what must have once been attractive parkland was full of tall grass, rank weeds and
neglected trees. The only sign of life anywhere was
a thin plume of smoke rising from one of the chim-
neys on what I had already mentally christened "The
Temple."

At last, cold, out of breath, I stood in front of
the doors of the main house. There were door-
knockers of greeny-tinged brass lion's heads, and a
bell-pull to the right. I hesitated, then knocked first.
No answer. I knocked again and used the bell-pull
for good measure. Still no reply. Then I noticed,
stuffed into the left-hand lion's mouth, a scrap of
paper. Pulling it free, I studied it by the failing
light.

"Miss Lee," it read. "Please go to the other door
on the left." That must be the front door to the
Temple. Well, at least someone was expecting me!

Picking up my valise I scurried across the front
of the main house, my bonnet flapping in a sudden
quixotic wind. It felt like rain, too.

Arriving at the other door I was grateful of the
shelter of the portico as I searched for a knocker,
but there was none, so I thumped on the door with

my gloved hand. I waited a moment and thumped again, and less than a minute later I heard bolts being withdrawn and the door swung open to reveal a middle-aged couple carrying candles.

"Miss Lee? Come in, come in, you must be perished!" The woman drew me in, relieved me of my valise, which she handed to her husband, then preceded me down an unlit corridor towards an open door at the end. "You are late: we were expecting you much earlier."

I explained as best I could, and the woman tut-tutted. "You were picked up by that lazy, good-for-nothing Josiah? I'm surprised the lad from London chose him . . . But of course he has been finding the cider at the inn a trifle heady, so I hear. Sooner he gets back to where he came from the better!

"Now, miss, if you don't mind the kitchen I can have you warm and fed in a trice. If you wish to wash up, here's a candle, and it's the second door on the left out the back."

I recognised the euphemism, and was glad to relieve myself and wash the grime from hands and face. Returning to a roaring fire, I found my bonnet, cloak and gloves put away neatly.

"Thank you, Mrs . . . Er?"

"Early. They calls us Early and Late, Bill and me, 'cos I was Lattey before we was wed." She obviously expected me to laugh, so I did. "Now, miss, here's a mug of mulled ale. Do set yourself down by the fire and I'll have something for you to eat in a minute."

Mrs. Early bustled about, laying a place at the scrubbed pine table, lighting a couple of oil lamps and stirring the contents of various pots and pans, while her husband brought in more wood to replenish the fire, till I had to draw back my chair to avoid getting scorched. He filled a copper with water—which I guessed would be for washing—smiling and nodding all the while, but speaking only in monosyllables.

As people they were physically alike; medium height, round and rosy-cheeked with smooth dark hair. Their only real difference, apart from being opposite sexes of course, was the volubility of the one and the taciturnity of the other.

I liked them both immediately, and never had cause to change my mind.

I sat down to a simple but tasty repast: julienne soup, cottage pie and peas and blackberry tart and cream. As I ate the housekeeper bombarded me with questions about London: was it as big as they said, the largest city in the world? How many people lived there? Was the weather any different? (She had heard about the fogs). Did lots of titled people live there? Did they eat different food? What did the river Thames look like?

I answered as best I could, but once I had finished my meal I was caught out by a half-stifled yawn. She noticed at once.

"Well now, my poor dear, here's me rattling on and you must be fair wore out! I thought as how you might like a warm bath before you goes to bed, so Mr. Early will carry up some hot water while I shows you where everything is." She lit two candles and handed me one. "There's more in the bedroom and a fire lit too. Now, if you'll just follow me?"

Leading me up a flight of stairs that curved onto a landing above, she opened the second door on the left. "This whole part of the Hall was once the nursery wing, but when your uncle bought the place he decided to use it as the guest wing, being small and easy kept up and warm." She moved into the room and lit candles on the mantelshelf, above a cheerful little fire, and on the bedside table. "Had some peculiar ideas your uncle did; liked nothing better than to sleep in a blanket outside on the hill: said it reminded him of abroad. No wonder he was always getting the shivers!"

I wanted to ask her more about him, but she was still rattling on.

"Your bed has been warmed, but I'll put in another stone. I'll draw the curtains—there'll be rain before morning, Mr. Early says." She suited the actions to the words, then opened a commodious wardrobe. "This is for your clothes. Hangers on one side, shelves on the other." As if by magic her husband arrived with my valise, although I thought my poor possessions would be lost in that piece of furniture. "There's your dressing table. Bath, commode, wash-bowl and hot-water jug are next door, first on the left." She bustled about, turning down the bed, putting more wood on the fire. "Will a call at eight in the morning suit? I'll see there's hot water for you next door.

"Now, don't you worry about a thing. Sounds as though Mr. Early has filled up the bath. If you want us, we're downstairs, left off the kitchen. Tomorrow I'll show you the rest of the premises."

"My uncle left a letter—"

"Everything's in the study across the landing, which used to be the day-nursery. Best leave it till morning when you're refreshed. I'll show you then. Now, anything else you need?"

After they had gone I unpacked my valise, put away my belongings and ventured into the bathroom next door, where I found a large, enamelled bath half-full of hot water, plus two jugs of cold, towels and soap.

Shedding my clothes I climbed in gratefully to soap and soak, until I felt my eyes closing.

Back in the bedroom I set my mantel-clock above the fireplace where I could see it; this was one of the things I couldn't have left behind, even for a couple of days. It had been a gift from Papa for my fifth birthday and was set with miniatures of my parents in the stand.

I drew back the curtains and pulled up the sash window; outside it was raining softly and the air was full of the sweet smell of wet earth and decaying leaves. The fire had sunk to a red glow. I blew out the candles and groped my way back to the high double bed and climbed into the starched linen sheets smelling of lavender. My toes found the renewed and wrapped stone hot-water bottle; I remembered, just in time, to say my prayers, and fell asleep before I could form another thought. . . .

I was awoken by the curtains being drawn back on a sunny morning.

"I left you for an extra half-hour as you were sleeping so sweetly," said Mrs. Early. "I see you're like your uncle in preferring an open window. . . . Hot water's ready next door. I took the liberty of laying up in the kitchen as it's warmer, but if you prefer to eat alone I can bring you something to the study next door?"

I assured her that the kitchen was fine. Had I really slept for twelve hours? It must have been the first time in memory.

"Afterwards I thought you might like to take a walk around the grounds with Mr. Early, and I could take you round the rest of the Hall before lunch, then you could have the afternoon to yourself, to see what your uncle left you . . ."

It all sounded fine to me, and as any dissent would probably have prompted Mrs. Early to further vociferous efforts, I agreed readily enough.

Breakfast was oatmeal with cream and sugar—how long it was since I had had porridge!—bacon and mushrooms, toast and marmalade and a pot of strong tea.

Afterwards I donned boots, cloak, bonnet and gloves and prepared to follow Mr. Early around my uncle's demesne. He started at the back door to the Temple, which led out to a cobbled yard. To the left were greenhouses and a well-cultivated kitchen-garden, and beyond that a stand of firs and pines, sloping down towards the road, to what must be the western end of the property. Good for both firewood and carpentry.

Turning towards the back of the main part of the house, I noted that there were still onions, broccoli, cabbages, sprouts—these waiting for the first frosts—carrots, turnips and swedes ready to be harvested in the kitchen garden. Beyond was an orchard, blessed with apple, plum and cherry trees.

At the back of the main house were the stables, empty except for a pony for the all-purpose trap, but a score of chickens pecked among the cobbles, and a half-dozen ducks doused their beaks in the pond at the rear. Farther on was a herb-garden, still cultivated, and the remains of what had been an ornamental garden surrounded by a neglected box-hedge, where tangles of late-blooming roses rioted amongst dead-headed phlox, delphiniums, oriental poppies and michaelmas daisies.

Behind the Castle part of the property was what once had been a shrubbery, and sprawling bushes of rosemary, sage and lavender. It should have been sad amongst all that neglect, but it wasn't. Nothing was actually dying away, all was still living and lusty. The soil was obviously fertile, and I longed to be amongst the most neglected: pull up the weeds, prune the roses, trim the shrubs. . . .

With goats and sheep to crop the grass, which would mean milk and cheese, this place could be almost self-supporting. A couple of bee-hives, perhaps, some pigsties and a stretch of potatoes—

Mrs. Early came out to call us into luncheon, mutton and caper sauce, with a milk pudding to follow. It had taken longer than I had expected, that exploration of the grounds, and I hadn't yet seen the interior of the rest of the house. Time seemed to whiz by, far faster than it had in the metropolis.

After luncheon Mrs. Early suggested that she show me over the rest of the Hall while it was still light enough to dispense with candles. The full tour took two hours.

We started in the Temple: across from my bedroom was the study, and farther down the corridor two more guest rooms. Downstairs, apart from the kitchen and Mr. and Mrs. Early's rooms, there was a sitting-room, dining-room and morning-room. A nice, comfortable home for a couple with two children . . .

The rest was very different.

The main house was very much as I had imagined: withdrawing-room, dining-room, morning-room, library, music-room and a small ball-room on the ground floor, plus the outhouse kitchen and dairies. There was also a cellar with empty wine-racks. On the first floor six bedrooms, two dressing-rooms, two bathrooms, and in the attics accommodation for a staff of at least twelve. A large house for a large family fond of entertaining.

As for the "Castle"—small, odd-shaped rooms, unexpected steps and stairs, low ceilings, slit windows, a superb view from the battlements and a baronial hall that could have seated a hundred, complete with a minstrel's gallery! Children would love it; their imaginations would run riot, and scrambling up and down inconvenient turret stairs would be an added bonus. A perfect place for a school, I thought. Or an orphanage . . .

The houses, apart from the Temple, were sparsely furnished. A few tables and chairs, including a vast table in the "baronial hall" to seat at least sixty, and a couple of dozen decrepit beds, wardrobes and dressers.

"Nothing left of any value," said Mrs. Early. "All the good linen, pots and pans, carpets and rugs, china and cutlery went to where you is staying now. The curtains in the rest of the place fell to shreds, and he sold the silver and gilt. Said he didn't need it no more."

I think the most incongruous items in the whole of the main house and the Castle were the artifacts, labelled and wrapped, that were still waiting to be collected. In the hall of the main house were row upon row of Greek statues, Roman mosaics, Egyptian mummies, Sumerian stone friezes, European arms and armour, Mayan idols, French tapestries, German carvings, Italian glass, Celtic crosses, Russian icons, coins from around the world, and the housekeeper assured me that this was only the remnants of my uncle's collection, still waiting to be collected. In the bookless (sad!) library were scrolls, manuscripts and stacks of papers. Everything was neatly labelled.

"He wanted everything to be catalogued," said the housekeeper. "Right down to the smallest item. Although he collected all his life, and took great pleasure in his collections, spending hours just looking at a statue or a piece of writing, after he became ill for the first time he had a change of heart. He said things like what he had collected weren't just for one man, they should be shared by everyone. That's why he sent a lot of the stuff back to where it came from, if they had museums and things to put them in. Rest goes to museums and libraries here. This lot is the last waiting to be collected.

"You seen enough, miss?"

I had, indeed! My feet ached, my head buzzed and I felt as though I had spent three days in one of the London museums without a way out. How could anyone have spent most of his life collecting avenues of stones, miles of statuary, piles of papers and heaps of coins? I would be glad when they were all gone and the house was empty again. At least my uncle had had the sense to realise that history belonged to everyone—but then I realised that thinking like this I was treating the place as my own, not as something that would probably be sold under my nose.

Back again at the Temple, Mrs. Early ushered me upstairs to the room my uncle had used as his study in his last few years. A large, square room facing

southwest, with blue Chinese-patterned wallpaper and
a Chinese carpet to match. To the right a bright fire
burned in the grate and opposite the door a long,
now-darkening window looked out on pastureland
and the pine wood. Immediately to the left was a
long, low map-chest; on the left wall was a curio
cabinet, the one I presumed my uncle had left me.
The centre of the room was filled with a pine table
about six feet square with two chairs, and over by
the fireplace was what looked like a comfortable
Windsor rocker, with cushions whose colour matched
the curtains, a burgundy that contrasted pleasantly
with the blue and white of the wallpaper and carpet. An empty bookshelf occupied the left-hand side
of the fireplace.

On the mantelpiece was a large manila envelope . . .

"Why don't you slip out of that skirt and blouse
and put on your dressing-gown?" suggested the housekeeper. "I'll wash the blouse and iron it in the
morning, and sponge the skirt at the same time. It's
heavy with the dirt from outside and the dust in, I
can see that. I'll bring you a tray of tea, and you can
have your supper up here later. That way you can
have the evening in peace to read your uncle's letter."

A half-hour later, two cups of tea, muffins, egg-
and-cress sandwiches and fruitcake eaten and drunk,
I took down the envelope from the mantelpiece,
snuggled up in the rocker, opened the seal and
started to read my uncle's letter.

Chapter Six

My Uncle's Letter

At first it was difficult to follow the crabbed, small hand that helter-skeltered across the pages, but I took it slowly and methodically, realising that my uncle had probably written it during his last illness.

"My dear Niece," he had written. "It is one of my regrets that we shall never meet, although I have the advantage of knowing a little of what you look like, and also have an idea of your disposition."

Out from the letter fell a small pencil sketch. No way was it me—I thought I recognised a copy of a soap advertisement that graced the hoardings in London, but the girl had my curly hair, large eyes (even to the tilt) and wide mouth.

"As far as I can see, you have inherited your mother's hair, short nose and mouth; the rest must come from your father. I have had nothing but good reports of you. My solicitors wasted six months trying to discover your whereabouts and I had almost given up hope, when I saw an advertisement by a fellow calling himself the head of a Lost-and-Found Bureau. I had him visit me here and was both

surprised at his youth and charmed by his manner,
which was obviously his intention.

"However I decided to give him a try, though payment was to be by results only—I have often found
this is efficacious, especially when hiring porters,
guides etc. abroad. To cut a long story short, the
young man found you through a combination of
common sense and good luck far sooner than I had
hoped. During this time I suffered another heart
attack and realising that the next would be the last,
I paid him for finding you and suggested another
payment for sending me a detailed report as to your
character, disposition and interests.

"You must forgive this second-hand snooping, but
I felt there was such a short time left to decide
exactly how to dispose of what little there is left. I
learnt of your poorly paid post, your earnest
endeavours with the children and your especial care
of a young boy called Toby Jugg—why do parents not
think harder before they burden their children with
names that will invite derision? I say nothing of the
name you were burdened with, you notice! I was told
of your scrimping and saving, your regular attendance
at church; I was also given a list of your reading
matter, and the museums, concerts and galleries you
attended. All of these I thoroughly approved of—even
down to your regular feeding of the sparrows on your
window-sill!"

I put down the letter in bewilderment. How on
earth could this person he hired have found out all
this—even down to the sparrows? I got up to stretch
my legs and to both pull the curtains and light the
oil lamp on the table; candles, unless right at one's
elbow, are not ideal for reading. It must have been
difficult for Miss Austen and the Misses Brontë, I
reflected. I put a couple more logs on the fire, and
the pine spat and crackled cheerily.

I moved over to the table to continue reading.

"I am of the opinion that you have inherited the

courage and love of life that characterised my dear
sister and also the patience and attention to detail
that must have contributed to your father's success
as a watch-maker, and probably both a compassion
and love of learning that has nothing to do with
either.

"But I digress. This letter was meant to explain
why I have been so dilatory in contacting my only
surviving relative. Let it be said here and now that
I was weak not to stand up to my parents, and initially it was pure escapism that made me choose a
life abroad, but gradually I became absorbed in
exploration, and discovered a real affinity for the
objects I excavated, so much so, in fact, that collecting rapidly became an obsession that took over my
life, even after the hold my parents had over me was
loosed by their death. *Mea culpa!*

"It was only after my bout of malaria, which recurs
even now, and the first heart attack and consequent
enforced convalescence, that I began to see how self-
ish my life has become. Of course some of my work
has been worthwhile, especially the research, but a
great deal has been downright stealing, the theft of
historical objects that rightfully belong in their countries of origin. So I determined to return the majority
of the artifacts from whence they came, but where
this was either unwise or impracticable, I would leave
them to museums here, so that they might be enjoyed by all. Research material and papers go to my
old college, in the hope that they may inspire future
students to follow my profession, albeit with a greater
sense of responsibility.

"Part of my regret, as far as you are concerned,
is that all that travel and acquiring of artifacts have
left me with very little money, and during these last
few years I have been living on my capital. My solicitors inform me that once the last artifacts have been
shipped, funeral expenses paid, an annuity (which
they richly deserve) left to Mr. and Mrs. Early and

their own charges disbursed—avoid solicitors like the plague, Niece, if you can: they will bleed you dry!—there would be only the Hall and less than five hundred pounds left. And if they say 'less,' then that is exactly what they mean.

"And now I come to the nub of the matter. There remains in my estate four or five hundred pounds and the Hall. I offer you a choice. You may either take the money and walk away to, I hope, a better life, in which case the solicitors have instructions to sell the Hall to endow an archaeology scholarship at Cambridge, or you may inherit the Hall and do with it what you please. In this case the moneys awaiting will be used for you to undertake an expedition very dear to my heart, which I am now too old and ill to contemplate. This latter choice will not be easy, but I am convinced that if any woman can do it, you can. If you decide to take the money I shall not blame you, but give it to you with my blessing. If that is your decision, inform the solicitors and it is yours at once. However if the other alternative has any appeal please read—carefully—the rest of this letter . . ."

I sat back in my chair. Four or five hundred pounds was a fortune! I could give up work, rent a small cottage and even afford a cleaner. . . . Or, if I went back to work, I could buy some decent clothes and find a better position. Whichever way, the money would last for a long, long time—at least ten years. I found I was smiling with relief and pleasure; how very kind of my uncle!

But he had mentioned an alternative: something about an expedition? Although I was sure I had made up my mind, I owed it to him to at least read on.

"Ah, I see you are either not satisfied with a little security, or else are filled with a natural curiosity in that you continue with this letter. Good. I should tell you that I hate to leave any matter unfinished, and there is one problem I have been unable to solve during my lifetime. If I may beg your indulgence to explain further?

"I visited many out-of-the-way places in my journeys, but it was on a routine stopover in Venice that my curiosity led me to visit a local auction, the contents of a crumbling palazzo that was being pulled down to make way for a more modern building. There was little to attract my attention, except for a box of miscellaneous items, amongst which was a rather fine blue glass vase. I already possessed one, so bid for the box, paying less than a tenth than I thought it worth.

"I caught the transport I was awaiting, leaving the unopened box in store, and almost forgot to retrieve it when I returned some three months later, and did not fully examine it until some year later, when I finally returned here. The blue Etruscan vase joined its sister—they are some of the few items I kept: you will find them in the morning-room downstairs. Most of the rest of the items I threw out as chipped, broken or worthlessly modern, but right at the bottom I found a package wrapped in an old cloak. It contained a round object like a small cannon-ball, a crumbling bundle of manuscript, an ivory figurine of some age and a twisted piece of horn.

"At first I could see no connecton between the disparate objects, but a closer scrutiny revealed that around the round object was wrapped a piece of material which read: 'This be Dragonnes Eg.' Of course I treated this statement with the scholarly contempt it deserved, but by now I was intrigued enough to examine the manuscript more closely. I found it was written in a kind of mediaeval shorthand, but once I had cracked the code I found it contained the remnants of an interesting tale. Remnants only, alas, because many of the pages were wormeaten or had fallen into dust, or the poor ink used had faded beyond deciphering.

"That part I could translate contained the story

of a brave young woman who undertook some sort of pilgrimage, firstly to find a husband, and then trace her lover, who, according to the story, was a dragon-man. According to the narrative she covered many hundreds of miles in her searching and the story is unfinished. I dismissed it as pure fiction at first, but when I had finished the translation, with its sorceries and magics, talking animals, shape-changing and flying pigs, I found many of the details as to places—a desert I recognise, towns that still exist miles from anywhere, rivers and mountains that are readily identifiable—so convincing that the writer must at least have visited these places.

"A couple of scraps of map accompanied the manuscript, and these I have redrawn. My translation together with these and what remains of the original are locked away in the cabinet to which you have the key."

I glanced across at the cabinet; the key was in my reticule and I was dying to open it and take a look, but I would see what else my uncle had to say first.

"I could not immediately see any connection between the four objects in the bundle, but then I recalled mention of an 'Eg'—the product of a liaison between the heroine and her dragon-lover—being stolen. There was also mention of a 'Unicorn's ring' and a shape-changing creature called 'Ky-Lin,' a mythical creature from the Buddhist religion.

"Once I realised, however, that whoever had collected these articles believed in their being kept together because of their relevance, I examined them more closely. I weighed and measured the so-called 'Eg'—typical mediaeval phonetic spelling—then attempted to break it open or crack it, but it resisted all my efforts. One thing I did notice was that it was not as cold as stone. It seemed to hold the same warmth as of that fossilised resin, amber. The little ivory figure is exquisitely carved, obviously Chinese, but shows no sign of the "life" attributed to it in the manuscript. As for the twist of horn, presumably meant to represent the so-called 'Unicorn's Ring,' it would fit none of my fingers nor those of Mr. and Mrs. Early.

"So I put this puzzle to one side for two or three years, occupied as I was with other matters. When I returned to it, of a mind to retain the manuscript and the figurine and dispense with the stone and the twist of horn, I made a startling discovery. On picking up the stone it felt heavier and larger than previously. Unwilling to trust my senses, I checked both weight and size against my earlier notes, and indeed, if I had calculated correctly initially, the stone was not only four ounces heavier, it was also two inches larger!

"Now I am not a superstitious man, any more than other scientists, but here was something strange. I was due to travel to the Valley of the Kings, a journey I could not delay, but as soon as I returned I again weighed and measured the stone, to find it had gained another couple of ounces and another inch in diameter. This time there was no mistake, no miscalculation, which I had rather hoped for as a rational explanation. And it was still relatively *warm*. . . .

"I wonder if you can have any idea of the turmoil this discovery threw me into! Here was I, a dry-as-dust scientist without an ounce of imagination, forced to re-evaluate all my previous theories as to the state of the universe! At first I clung desperately to the theory that what I held was merely some large reptile egg, of a species as yet unknown, but yet was not a dragon a reptile? Was there some truth in the manuscript? Were the times so different then that what we now dismiss as sorcery and magic did exist? I am no longer sure of just how true scientific facts are: all I am sure of is that something mighty strange is going on. I have left a list of measurements of the egg—or stone, who knows?—in the cabinet, together with the measuring instruments, and I'm willing to wager you will find an increase.

"Explain it I cannot, except that I do now believe that the object will not get any rest or fulfilment until it is returned to the place from whence it was stolen. Perhaps it will hatch out into something so incredible that our modern, nineteenth-century minds cannot encompass it.

"If I were still alive and well I would make this my last expedition, but, as you will realise as you read this, I am not. I would ask that you, my niece, might undertake this task. An arduous and tall order, I agree, but as I said before, I cannot bear unfinished business. If you do decide in favour of this suggestion, then the moneys you may receive as a lump sum will have to be used for travelling expenses, especially as someone from the solicitors' office would have to accompany you, and I would wish the young 'detective' who found you to travel with you as well, as extra protection.

"I have another, more quixotic, condition: that this expedition must be completed within a calendar year. So, my dear niece, you have a choice: either accept what little moneys I have left, or embark on an adventure you may never forget. It is up to you, but before you decide I would ask that you read my transcripts, look at the maps and examine the contents of the cabinet. Also remember that if you do succeed you will receive Hightop Hall, to do with as you will. Hideous, I agree, but it would make a good school or orphanage . . ."

Strange . . . exactly what I had thought.

"When you have read the transcript, then read the last pages of this letter—"

There was a tap on the door.

"Suppertime, Miss Lee," said Mrs. Early. "Hope I'm not intruding—goodness me, you've near let out the fire!" Rapidly she laid the table from a tray she had brought with her, then poked and coaxed and replenished the fire till it was once more a cheerful blaze. "I'll be up with the soup in a moment—"

"Don't go, Mrs. Early." I hesitated. "Tell me—you knew my uncle for—how long?"

"Thirty-five year," she answered promptly. "Not to know him as we did when he moved here, but I went as under-housemaid to his parents when I was thirteen, and have been with the family, as it were, ever since. Mr. Early was gardener's boy when I first met him, and—"

I tried to stem the flood. "What I really wanted to know was what he was like as a person—"

"Just you wait one moment . . ." She clattered away down the stairs to reappear with a magazine, which she opened at a well-thumbed page.

"See this? It were a sketch some artist did for a posh magazine, and it's him to a T!"

I must confess I had expected a tall, burly man, with probably a full beard, but the reality was quite different. He had been clean-shaven and balding. In the drawing he looked nervous and had his hands clasped behind his back. The man I was looking at was unused to the niceties of social life and preferred objects to people. No, not preferred: felt more comfortable with. A lonely man . . .

"Would you say my uncle was an imaginative man?" I asked, handing back the magazine. She looked puzzled. "I mean, was he easily persuaded into believing superstitious tales, for instance?"

She shook her head vigorously. "Quite the opposite, miss! Very sceptical, he was. Never took nothing for granted. Always weighing and measuring and labelling things. Liked everything just so, he did." She paused. "Only time I ever saw him upset was over something in that cabinet; something about measurements that weren't as they should be. Even had us trying to put some old bit of horn on our fingers to prove something or other, but it didn't work." She paused again. "Come to think of it, it was that time he asked us if we believed in magic. Strange, coming from him . . ."

"And what did you say?"

"Said of course we didn't; after all, that's what he wanted us to say. Not true, of course; anyone who lives on or near the land knows all about witches and such, though he never noticed the hag-stones as are hung near the back doors, nor that the nearest trees are rowans . . . Still, him being so generous and all, couldn't destroy his beliefs. Why, if I was to tell you that Mr. Early and I were courting for twenty years before he asked us here, and that he not only attended the wedding but gave us the gift of a full twenty pounds to set ourselves up with, well then you'll know that—"

There was another knock on the door and Mr. Early came in with some more wood. He nodded to me and spoke briefly to his wife. "Tatties is done," he said.

This signalled the end of Mrs. Early's reminiscences, and the appearance of supper: tomato soup, cutlets, roast parsnips and potatoes and a helping of local cheese and biscuits to follow. When she came up to clear away the dishes she brought me a hot toddy, and asked if her husband should bring up my bathing water in a couple of hours. I looked at my watch: eight-thirty.

"That'd be fine, thank you." A couple of hours should be long enough to read my uncle's transcript, but I must admit it was with a rapidly beating heart that I fetched the key to the cabinet from my reticule and fitted it in the lock.

It turned easily and the door swung open. There were two blue-velvet lined shelves. Picking up the lamp from the table, I peered inside. On the top shelf was a bundle of papers in a leather folder, a small curiously carved creature and a twist of horn. The lower shelf held a box of hard, dry vellum, some measuring instruments and a large, round object that glinted in the lamplight.

This must be the fabled "Dragonnes Eg" that had so perplexed my uncle. I touched it gently—as he had said, it wasn't cold like stone. I wanted to pick it up, test its weight, but decided that first I would read the transcript, so I took the folder back to the table, turned up the lamp, put another log on the fire and settled down to read.

As my uncle had said, it was an intriguing story. As I sipped my toddy, redolent with cloves and cinnamon, I followed the adventures of a girl called Summer who left home when she was orphaned to find a husband, but it seemed she found everything but; it pictured her with a magic ring, which enabled her to understand the speech of animals, but it didn't stop her from ambush, ghosts, starvation and a flying pig. Much of the story was missing apparently, but my uncle had tried to make her journey clear through mediaeval France, then a series of petty kingdoms. The first part ended with reference to a "dragon lover."

There was more in the second part of the narrative. Apparently the girl decided to pursue her missing dragon lover, accompanied by her dog, also mentioned in the earlier narrative. She travelled many miles towards a fabled Blue Mountain, where she hoped to find her lover. On the way (this bit wasn't quite clear) she produced a small dragon's egg. She found her lover, but the egg was stolen at the last moment by Ricardus, one of her companions, only to be returned on his death to a merchant in Venice who had inherited Summer's memoirs. What happened to her afterwards wasn't clear either.

I sat back in my chair.

Of course the whole thing was ridiculous! Dragon lovers, flying pigs, talking dogs . . . And yet while I was reading it I had almost been persuaded that it was true. I shivered, and noticed the fire was nearly out. I could hear Mr. Early clumping upstairs with the first of my hot water. Hastily I returned the transcript to the cabinet and locked it. Time enough to examine the other objects tomorrow, when daylight would show everything in its true light, I hoped. In the meantime I looked forward to a good night's sleep . . .

Which I didn't get.

All night long I tossed and turned, dreaming of dragons: tiny ones scurrying about the carpet, medium ones stalking the corridors of the Hall and large ones landing on the roof—

And all of them crying with one voice: "Bring us back our egg!"

Chapter Seven

More Revelations and a Visitor

I had asked Mrs. Early to call me at eight-thirty, and at a quarter to nine I was seated in the kitchen, gritty-eyed and pale of face, tackling kippers and toast. It was a big pot of Assam tea which finally pulled me round, that and a brisk walk as far as the orchard, where I finished off with a Cox's Orange Pippin.

Back to the study, where a fire was already blazing. Once again I opened the cabinet; first I looked in the box where what remained of the original manuscripts were housed, taking care not to handle the pages too harshly—even as I looked they seemed that they were crumbling away before my eyes. It was a miracle they had lasted this long, anyway. If my uncle were right, some six or seven hundred years!

I put my uncle's letter and his transcript on the table and looked at them again, paying attention now to his footnotes, where he had identified various

towns and places, and glancing at the maps he had
drawn to interpret, as far as he could, the route the
girl Summer had taken.

It looked an awful muddle, with a lot of guesswork
thrown in. . . .

Now for the egg—or whatever it was. I had forgotten to pack my shawl, but I went and fetched my
cloak, so it wouldn't roll around the table. I made
it a kind of nest, then went to take it out of the
cabinet. It was far heavier than I had imagined. I had
never seen a round egg before, though I understood
the ostrich and most reptiles preferred this shape,
but as far as I knew those were all white in colour,
whereas this one was definitely a greyish colour with
a metallic sheen and little sparkly bits that caught
the light.

Back to the cabinet to get the measuring calipers
and the scales, with the measurements my uncle had
already made, some dozen in all. Luckily the basin
for the scales was round, so the egg wouldn't tip. I
looked at the last figures my uncle had quoted for
weight and width and decided to work from those.
Not that I expected any increase in either, but at least
it would set my mind at rest. Dragon's egg, indeed!
First the weighing . . .

Some ten minutes later I sat back in my chair, my
hands trembling. Somehow, in the six months since
my uncle had last recorded his findings the what-ever-
it-was had gained a full seven ounces in weight and
an inch in width!

What was this—this *thing* that sat on the table in
front of me? I found I was pacing around the room,
my arms wrapped tightly around my chest. How
could something like that grow larger by the month?
Nay, the day, the hour, the minute? My heart was
pounding, my mind racing. Perhaps the scales and
the calipers were wrongly set, perhaps my uncle's figures were fictional, perhaps I was hallucinating,
perhaps . . .

But I ran out of perhaps, which were getting more ridiculous by the moment, and calmed down a little, just enough to decide to examine the other objects in the cabinet. Forget about the Thing for a while.

First I lifted out the yellowing ivory figurine and examined it closely. It was obviously meant to represent some sort of mythical being, for it contained elements of more than one creature. A horse or deer, buffalo, fish? For sure it had never walked the earth in that guise! But then, hundreds of years ago, who could have imagined an elephant, giraffe or kangaroo? But no, this was definitely from the imagination.

Next I went back to the cabinet for the scrap of material that was supposed to be from the horn of a unicorn, another mythical beast. An insignificant scrap it was too, almost transparent in its triple curl. I put it down next to the Thing and the little figure. Now I had all the pieces of my uncle's puzzle together with the story they were supposed to come from, but what to make of it all?

I touched the "Eg" again and noted its warmth, I turned the figure this way and that; I picked up the ring once more—

There was a sudden knock on the door, I started, and the ring I was holding in my left hand slipped out of my fingers and dropped over the middle finger of my right. Mrs. Early came in, looking flustered and wiping floury hands on her apron.

"You've a visitor, miss! It's that young gentleman"—she said the word as if it were a bad taste in her mouth—"from London as is staying at the Lamb and Flag in the village. The one from your uncle's solicitors . . . D'you mind if I bring him up? There's no fire lighted downstairs, 'cept in the kitchen."

I was about to say that would be fine, when said young gentleman appeared in the doorway behind her, followed by an angry-looking Mr. Early.

"Wouldn't wait," he said tersely.

"It's all right, Mr. Early," I said. "Come in, Mr . . . ?"

"Cumberbatch, Claude Cumberbatch. Junior clerk in the offices of Goldstone, Crutch and Swallow of Lincoln's Inn." He presented me with a card. "And you must be Miss Sophronisbe Lee." Without a by-your-leave he dropped into the chair opposite mine and gazed around the room. "Servant's quarters?"

"Not exactly, Mr. Cumberbatch." I tried to control my temper: he was probably younger than I was. "I find it most congenial . . ." His expression indicated that it wasn't the sort of place he expected to be received in. "And now that you have finally found me . . ." I paused to let that sink in; after all I had arrived two days ago and had not had so much as a message. " . . . may I offer you some refreshment? A cup of tea, perhaps?"

"Oh, I think something more lively than that, miss! Tea is for old biddies. Let's see, does this establishment boast a bottle or two of sweet sherry?"

I shook my head, just in time to see Mrs. Early nodding hers. I glanced at my watch. "I feel that eleven in the morning is a trifle early for spirituous liquors—"

"Oh, maybe for school-mistresses, but for us men of the world . . ."

I glanced at Mrs. Early: perhaps she had something in mind. From her smug expression I realised she had.

"Perhaps the young gentleman would like to give me his opinion on some rather strong turnip and ginger wine we have been saving for special guests? With some salted biscuits, of course . . ." It must be poisonous! "And you Miss Lee? China, or Russian with lemon?"

"China if you don't mind. And a couple of your sweet cakes, please."

While she was gone Mr. Cumberbatch—what a mouthful, I thought—got up and wandered round the room, peering through the window, poking the fire, gazing into the cabinet, setting the rocking chair tipping back and forth, fingering the velvet of the curtains. He then sat down again and poked the Eg with his finger, setting it into a dangerous wobble.

"Be careful!" I said sharply. "I don't want it to roll off!"

"No problem, miss!" He reached out his hand for the ivory figurine, but I was there before him. Somehow I didn't wish him to touch it; I was glad I had the twist of horn on my finger temporarily—he would probably have snapped it in half.

I studied him as he sat in his chair, cracking his bony knuckles. He was probably in his late teens or early twenties, thin almost to the point of emaciation, with a pasty complexion and straight fair hair, rather greasy, worn long down to his collar. He had pale blue eyes, a large Roman nose, a lot of teeth and a rather weak chin. In fact his facial structure was that of someone you might see in one of the *Punch* cartoons as representing the last scion of a degenerate aristocracy. His voice would have betrayed him, however: it held decided echoes of the East End of London.

He was dressed in the latest fashion of high collar, tight jacket with checked waistcoat, baggy trousers and pointed shoes and even wore a pair of the hideous yellow gloves that were all the rage, but his linen wasn't the freshest and from where I sat I could smell the scent of the tavern: greasy food, stale ale, whisky and tobacco. Indeed right at that moment he extracted a leather pouch from his pocket, pulled out a cheroot and lit it with a vesta, which he threw at, and missed, the fireplace. I rose immediately and opened the window then crossed to his side, took the cheroot from his fingers, and tossed it on the fire.

"You didn't say you didn't want me to smoke! Cost me four pence—"

"And you didn't ask!"

Luckily for us both Mrs. Early knocked with a tray of tea and little sponge cakes for me, and a jug and large wineglass plus a plate of salted biscuits for our guest. "Let me know if you want anything else, miss . . ."

What she really meant was that it was unorthodox for me to receive a gentleman in my rooms, but that she would be handy (probably just outside the door), ready to rush in and defend my honour . . . I hadn't the slightest doubt that that would be unnecessary.

Claude Cumberbatch filled his glass to the brim and took a long draught. There was a peculiar expression on his face when he put the glass down, and he took a hasty mouthful of biscuits.

I was letting my tea brew. "To your liking, Mr. Cumberbatch?"

"Er . . . Very unusual. I've never tasted anything quite like it . . . Home-made, I venture to guess?"

"Certainly. Not for the faint-hearted, I agree, but excellent for warding off the chills of inclement weather. It is, of course, a man's drink. Another glass? Do help yourself." I poured out a cup of tea and sipped it.

"Was there some especial reason you wished to see me, or is this just a social call?"

"Huh? Oh, yes." He fumbled in his pocket. "Got— got a 'munication from the firm s'morning." He was already slurring his words, to my delight. That wine must be strong! He slurped another draught. "Want to know when—when you're ready to go back—back to Lunnon . . ."

"Who said I wished to return to London?"

"Well, you must: no—no-one in their ses-, sesnes, would want to live in the w-wilds . . ."

"I do have a choice, Mr. Cumberbatch."

He finally produced the letter, all crumpled, and waved it at me with a shaking hand. "It says—Mr. Swallow says—as the most 'venient train would be twelve-fifteen on Friday, or ten-thirty Sat'day. Take a trap from the inn . . ."

"Sure you wouldn't prefer the carrier?" I couldn't keep the sarcasm from my voice, but he didn't notice.

"Oh, no, far too s-slow. Never get there . . ."

"Does Mr. Swallow say anything else?" From where I sat the letter looked at least two pages long.

"No, no, no . . . Just some 'structions for me. Private . . ."

He filled his glass from the jug, draining it down to the last drop. "Goo' stuff this . . ."

"I'm sure it is," I agreed, "Now, as to the letter of Mr. Swallow's—"

But he wasn't listening; in fact he wasn't hearing anything at all. His head was down on the table, his hands hanging loose to the floor and he was snoring heartily. I rose to fetch Mr. Early to dispose of him, but decided that Mr. Swallow's letter came first. As I scanned the first few lines it occurred to me with a certain surprise that even a few days ago I wouldn't have dreamed of reading someone else's correspondence. But things had changed dramatically, and this concerned me and my future life, so blow the conventions!

The letter read as follows: *"Mr. Cumberbatch, as our representative I ask that you visit Miss Lee, enquire as to her health and well-being, and assure her that if there is anything we can do to facilitate her enquiries, to let us know. I do not expect her to be precipitate in her decision, as I judge her to be careful in her considerations. Please inform her that her employer, Miss Moffat, is happy for her to take as much leave as she wishes. If for any reason, she wishes to visit London before she has made up her mind, please inform her of the times of the trains, buy her a ticket, and escort her to the station. Please assure her of our best attention at all times."* It was signed in an indecipherable squiggle.

So much for being expected to accept my uncle's offer of cash and return to London the day after tomorrow! Just because Claude Cumberbatch couldn't stand the countryside, I was supposed to fall in with his plans and return him to London!

I stuffed the letter back in his pocket and went downstairs to find Mr. and Mrs. Early, suggesting they dump him just outside the gates to the Hall, but Mr. Early harnessed the pony to the trap, saying he would deposit him with the landlord of the Lamb and Flag.

"Punishment enough with the head he'll have on him," he said, in a rare burst of confidence and volubility. "Yon's strong stuff."

Mrs. Early arranged that, not to waste the journey, he could bring back various items she was short of: sugar, flour and oil. "And you'll be needing a new yard-broom and a bag of nails," she reminded him.

When they had gone she suggested that I take a closer look at the rooms in our part of the house. "There's some nice bits and pieces, and they'll all be yours if you decide to take on your uncle's dare."

"Dare?"

"Well, it's like that, isn't it? He did talk to me a bit, you know. About that Egg-thing. Wanted it to go back to where he thought it belonged. I expect it worried him because it didn't fit in with all his theories; men like him always like things neat and tidy." She paused. "You don't have to say, miss, but I reckon as how he's given you a choice: take what money's left and the Hall's sold, or try and take the thing back to Chiney, or wherever, and get the Hall when you gets back."

I didn't deny it. "Put like that it isn't much of a choice, is it?" I said with a smile.

"I agree, but not the way you think. I reckon it depends on the person. Were I your age now, knowing what I know, I wouldn't hesitate. But thirty years ago I would have chosen different. Then I was just an under-housemaid, glad for a roof over my head, reasonable food, a small wage and a day off a month. If then someone had suggested I give it all up and

travel abroad—me, who hadn't been farther than
twenty miles from here in my life—and get my own
cottage if and when I returned, I'd have turned it
down flat. I'd have taken the money."

She looked at me shrewdly. "Circumstances is different, but the situations much the same, I'd say. As
I said, depends on the person concerned . . . Now,
shall we take a look at the rest of this place properly?"

The remainder of the floor I was on consisted of
bedrooms, adequately if sparsely furnished with beds,
wardrobes, chests of drawers and dressing tables, with
bright rugs on the polished floors; a large window
at the end of the corridor gave a good light.

Downstairs it was different. The fanlight above the
front door threw bars of sunshine across the black-
and-white tiled floor and a couple of small sidetables
were bright with vases of autumn leaves. The first
door on the left revealed a pleasant dining-room,
mainly in blue, down to the seascape over the side-
board and the Passion-Flower patterned crockery and
china candlesticks. "Your uncle said all the furniture
in here were by a man called Chippendale," ventured
Mrs. Early. "He preferred it to the modern stuff." So
did I.

The next room on the left was the morning-room.
Here the emphasis was on the colour green with a
couple of touches of dark blue—I noted the Etruscan
vases on the mantel. The room was still full of the
morning sunshine, with its two tall windows facing
southeast; two small sofas, half-a-dozen chairs, a gam-
ing-table, two pretty landscapes and plenty of room
for a writing-desk like my mother's.

Across the corridor was the withdrawing-room, this
in rose and green. Longer than the other two rooms,
it had a fireplace at either end. One half was obviously meant for cosy relaxation by the fire, with sofas
and occasional tables, and the other for perhaps
cards or even dancing, for there was a piano and two

card tables with chairs. On the walls were a dozen gold-framed prints of those deliciously scented French roses, and over both the fireplaces, in rose-veined marble, were large, ornamental Italian gilt-framed mirrors, which made the room seem even larger than it was.

The last room was smaller than the others, but was fully shelved, except that on one wall hung a huge oilcloth map of the world, pierced by a multitude of coloured mapping pins.

"This is where your uncle kept his books and manuscripts," said Mrs. Early. "That map on the wall showed all the places he'd been. In his last illness he had a pallet bed brought in here, because he found the stairs difficult. Liked to lie and look at the map, he did." And the map should be kept right there, I thought, a fitting memorial. But it would be nice to fill the bookshelves once again, and my father's wing-chair would do well beside the fire . . .

There was no carpeting in here, apart from a Persian rug by the fireplace, and the polished wood flooring was echoed in colour by the table, leather-seated chairs, curtains and copper candlesticks.

"Did he die in here?" I asked, noting that the pallet had been removed.

"Oh, no. He died outside, up on Bracken Hill. He would have wanted it that way. Mr. Early found him up there, one day when he missed luncheon. All peaceful he looked, like he'd fallen asleep on a pleasant dream," and her eyes filled with tears, which she mopped with her apron.

I was most impressed with the arrangements at the Temple: as I had thought before, it would be ideal for a small family—but I must stop mentally furnishing it with my own bits and pieces, I told myself, because I most certainly would not be staying!

As soon as Mr. Early returned we had luncheon—toad-in-the-hole, minted peas and gravy, with apple crumble and custard to follow—and as it was a sunny afternoon I took another walk around the grounds, kicking up the piles of leaves like a child in a park, the scent of a bonfire Mr. Early was tending tickling my nostrils with its evocative scent.

After tea I did some necessary darning, only noticing as I finished that I was still wearing the ring. I tried to pull it off, but it wouldn't budge. I even used soap, but it stayed just where it was, on the middle finger of my right hand. Actually I didn't mind it being there at all; it felt warm and comfortable. It would have been nice if it had been gold, or contained a precious stone, but I had never had a ring before and was pleased to see that if I looked closely there were little sparkles of colour in it, rather like an opal.

I had supper with Mr. and Mrs. Early in the kitchen, and went upstairs again determined to make a "Pros" and "Cons" list so that I would be absolutely certain I had made the right decision to take the money my uncle had offered, rather than attempting that ridiculous expedition, but I got no further than the headings on a sheet of paper before I found myself yawning prodigiously.

Country air was very enervating, I decided, as I put the Eg, figurine and transcript in the cabinet, locked it but left the key there. I asked for hot water and a half-hour later was tucked up in bed with one of Mrs. Early's hot toddys. I read the first chapter of *Westward Ho!* but couldn't keep my eyes open any longer. Blowing out the candles I laid my head on the pillow and slept dreamlessly.

Called at eight-thirty, refreshed and hungry, I ate my breakfast hurriedly then went upstairs, determined to concentrate on my listings. I got out the Eg and placed it on the cloak once more, then reached inside the cabinet for the ivory figurine—

It wasn't there!

Chapter Eight
Pros and Cons

I couldn't believe it! It couldn't just disappear like that! Frantically I searched the cabinet again: the manuscript in its box, the transcript, the egg—they were all there, and the ring was on my finger. Could I have left it on the mantelpiece, the shelves, the table or one of the chairs? I knew I hadn't, yet I searched the whole room methodically and even went into my bedroom in case I had left it in there.

Mrs. Early had lived up to her name and the study had been swept and dusted, yesterday's ashes removed, a bright fire was burning and the wood-basket had been replenished. The cabinet had been locked, but I had left the key there. Was it possible the housekeeper had removed the figurine for cleaning? It seemed extremely unlikely, but I must ask—

Could there have been a stranger in the house? I remembered young Cumberbatch's visit: could he have . . . ? But no, I distinctly remembered refusing to let him touch it. And I was still convinced that I had put it away last night, safe and sound.

I crossed to the door, but as I opened it I heard a faint rustling noise behind me. I stopped, listened. There it came again. I looked back across the room—no, it must have been the fire crackling, a log falling . . . I heard it again, and for one wild moment thought I saw a corner of the curtains twitch, as though a mouse had run behind it. Or a rat . . . It twitched again—that did it! I didn't mind mice, but rats (and cockroaches) were right off my list of tolerances.

I raced downstairs and flung open the kitchen door.

"Mrs. Early! Mrs. Early . . ." She was kneading dough on the marble slab. "Do we have rats in the house? And have you seen that little ivory figurine? It's gone missing. I just thought . . . you might . . ." I sat down heavily at the kitchen table, my heart pounding. "And have there been any strangers in the house? I mean, in this part of the Hall? Or could they have got in from another part?" I was trembling.

She smacked her hands together to rid them of the flour, rinsed them in a bowl of water on the side, then wiped them on a cloth. "Now, Miss Lee dear, just start again, tell me what's the matter . . ."

So I tried to be coherent and rational. I explained how I had found the figurine was missing, and as I had left the key in the lock overnight, wondered if she or her husband had removed it for cleaning? She shook her head. I asked, had anyone else been in this part of the house? Again she shook her head. I explained that I thought I had seen the curtains move, but everything I said made the whole thing sound sillier and sillier. I sounded like a hysterical female of the worst kind.

But she didn't laugh at me. Instead she opened a cupboard and put a glass of sweet sherry in my hand.

"Now, sip this down, Miss Lee, and calm yourself. . . . We neither of us ever touched nothing

of your uncle's, unless he asked us particular. That
answers your first question. As to others in the Hall,
the only strangers, apart from that lawyer fellow
yesterday, have been those packing up and remov-
ing the artifacts, and then we always keep the door
from the Hall through to here locked, as it is today,
as is the front door. Back doors bolted at night,
otherwise there's always one of us in the kitchen.
That's number two. As for rats or mice or anything
else like that, I pride myself there's nothing in this
part of the house like that."

I sipped the sherry, already feeling better. "Sorry,
Mrs. Early, but it was a bit of a shock to find it
missing."

"Not to worry. Howsomever, we'll take a besom
up there and if there's anything or anyone as
shouldn't be, they'll get short shrift. As for the ivory,
it's probably fallen down behind something . . ."

Once upstairs she attacked the curtains, but there
was nothing there. She turned to the cabinet. "Now
show me exactly where you put it."

I pointed to the top shelf, but I saw it even before
she did. Not on the top shelf but the bottom, next
to the manuscript. And I knew, I *knew* I had searched
that shelf!

"Why, there it is!" She picked it up and handed
it to me. Even as I took it in my hand I knew it had
changed. It was surely nearly twice as large as before.
"You must have misplaced it." She smiled at me.
"Well, all's well that ends well, that's what I say!
Luncheon at the usual time?"

I sat at the table in the study. On the table was
the Eg, the ring was on my finger, the ivory in my
hands, and I was looking at each in turn.

Here was a mediaeval round-shaped object, warm
to the touch, that kept on growing; a ring that
wouldn't come off, reputedly part of a mythical
Unicorn's headgear, and an ivory figurine that dis-

appeared and then reappeared, larger than before. And all this was somehow tied in with my uncle's wish that I return this egg to wherever it was supposed to belong. Against all this was the attractive alternative of taking whatever money was left and abandoning all these strange objects to their fate.

All except the ring: it still wouldn't budge. . . . And yet I liked the feeling if it on my finger. I would have preferred to find out what the egg contained, although I didn't want a baby dragon deposited in my lap, and the ivory looked friendly. . . .

I had never been abroad and there would probably never be another chance, unless I settled down and took a post as a governess who took children to a place like Brittany for the summer, or perhaps worked for a family who wanted a chaperone for their daughter at a German spa.

Stop daydreaming, I told myself severely: you're not likely to do better than the Charity School, although with the extra money you could live far more comfortably.

Right. Pros and Cons. I drew out a sheet of paper, took ink and a pen. I made two headings: Plan A, take the money; Plan B, take the Eg back. Then I subdivided each into two sections, for and against.

I started with Plan A. Immediate money, which would either keep me a lady of leisure for a few years, or supplement any income I received for longer. Either way, freedom from penury for a while. So much for the pros. I turned to the second column and tried to be fair. How long would the money last? Would it be so little, after all, that I would have to go on working, whether I wished to or no? What if I became ill or crippled? Then came a line which seemed to write itself: Did I really want the rest of my life to be so dull, predictable, plain *boring*? I looked down at what I had written: was my life dull and boring? It certainly wasn't now.

I thought back on my life at the Charity School.

Life had been ruled by the seasons, although the
same lessons came round time and time again. Only
the children had been different, but not much. Different faces, different names, but the same poverty,
apathy and hunger, the latter not for knowledge, only
Ellen's soup.

I did love London, however. Apart from the
museums, galleries, parks, libraries, concerts, churches
and buildings, there was the teeming life and the
magical way everything changed with the seasons.
Spring, with its hope; crocuses springing through the
grass in the parks, the glorious scent of violets and
narcissi in the baskets of the flower-sellers, the first
house-martins swooping over the rooftops and the
urgent chirp of nesting sparrows—in such a season
it was torture to be shut up in school all day. Then
came summer with roses falling over the railings of
the houses and the welcome warmth; but summer
could also be over-hot, dusty and sticky, with the
smell of sewage and rotting food percolating even to
the schoolroom—in such a season it was torture to
be shut up with the smells all day. Autumn was crisp
and colourful with falling leaves, the scent of bon-
fires and blowy skies. On those days I longed to
escape the confines of the school: torture to be shut
in all day. Winter could be cold, foggy, with frost and
snow, but still there was the comfort of a warm fire,
the taste of roast chestnuts from the corner vendor
and the lights and celebrations of Christmas. In such
a season it was torture to be shut in all day. . . .

I couldn't remember thinking like this before. I
don't believe I had ever analysed my feelings in this
fashion—perhaps deliberately. Maybe I had been afraid
of admitting to myself what I really felt like, because
I couldn't change my situation, so would have to
accept it without whining to myself that I wanted
something different. Of course my work was worthwhile, and I knew I did it to the best of my ability,
but I now knew it wasn't the only thing in the world.

Had I always been so fond of my freedom? I had loathed the restrictions of my boarding-school, though I had submitted in order to please my parents. At home I had been happy enough, although I was always escaping to the woods and fields, or into other worlds with my books. Our village, Ditchling in Sussex, was pretty and friendly enough, but sometimes I had stood at the crossroads and watched the Brighton express coach go thundering past, or its counterpart stop at the inn to let its caped and crinolined passengers alight for refreshments before the continuation of their journey to London, I had often wished I could just jump aboard and leave everything behind, to glimpse what lay over the hill. . . .

All this had nothing whatsoever to do with the lists I was trying to draw up, I told myself. A little boredom and frustration are common in every life. Security, and perhaps to be needed, that was what mattered. I looked at my watch: time for luncheon.

Afterwards I decided to walk off a little of the pork, stuffing and applesauce by strolling the couple of miles or so to the village. The first building I came across was the Church of the Good Shepherd, where I ventured in to pray for guidance and leave an offering in the box near the door. The church was obviously old, and owed much to the trade in wool, judging from the carvings in wood and stone. There were some pretty stained-glass windows, all reflecting Christ's life as the Good Shepherd.

The village itself held little to speak of: the Lamb and Flag, a butcher's, chemist, grocer, and green grocer, ironmonger's, general store and forge. I bought some black darning wool for my stockings at the store, but was careful to scurry past the inn with my bonnet pulled forward, as I had no wish to encounter Mr.Cumberbatch.

I dawdled on my way back to the Hall, collecting brightly coloured sprays of berries to put in the study, so the sky was already darkening as I reached the driveway, but I noticed that Mr. or Mrs. Early had hung a lantern by the front door of the Temple to light my way: it was almost like coming home.

I drank a late cup of tea in the kitchen, put my berries in a glass vase, went upstairs and placed them on the mantel, then settled down with my list of pros and cons. I had put a sheet of paper with Plan A on it aside as completed, but as I glanced at it I noted that I must have added something I didn't remember to the "cons" side. "How can I find true fulfilment if I stay at home?" I must have written it, because it was in my handwriting—but it wasn't my style.

I decided not to worry any further about it, but to concentrate on the pros and cons of Plan B, the expedition and the chance of inheriting Hightop Hall. I picked up my pen, wiped it with the pen-wiper, dipped it in the ink-pot and hesitated, then under "pros" I wrote: "Foreign Travel." After another two minutes: "I like the place." Another minute: "It was what my uncle really wanted," and lastly: "It would make a pleasant school or orphanage."

Unfortunately the "cons" column was far easier to complete. Never been abroad before, didn't know where to start or whether the money would last out, women just didn't go on expeditions, I would have to suffer the proximity of two people I didn't know, I only had a year in which to do it . . . Besides which there weren't any such things as dragons or unicorns, so what was the point? I finished with what I should probably have started with: even if I succeeded, I wouldn't have enough money to keep up the Hall. It would have to be sold; a pity, but there it was.

I sighed and laid down my pen. There, it was easy enough to make a decision if one was logical and systematic about it. Better safe than sorry.

It was now Thursday evening—I had been here three full days!—and I decided I would write a letter to the solicitors later tonight and get Mr. Early to deliver it to Mr. Cumberbatch tomorrow. If a reply was received in time, I could travel back to London on Saturday, otherwise it would have to wait until Monday. I hoped so: I rather fancied a few more days being cosseted in what was, to me, the lap of luxury.

I wondered what would happen to the Eg? I had already decided to take the ivory with me—it would look nice on my mother's writing-desk, and the ring seemed to be a fixture. I would throw away the original manuscript, but keep the transcript and read it again one day, for fun. The Eg? Perhaps I could take it down to the beach at Brighton, where my parents had taken me as a child, and roll it down the pebbles into the sea. Or I supposed I could give it away—but who would want something that looked like a cannon-ball, was warm to the touch, and kept on growing?

I decided I would have supper in the kitchen with the Earlys, so I could quiz them about their memories of my mother, but I wouldn't tell them of my decision to take the money until tomorrow or the next day.

They both remembered my mother as a harum-scarum, pretty girl with a mind of her own, easily bored and with no mind to her lessons. Apparently my maternal grandfather was much like my uncle, a recluse, and it was my maternal grandmother who ruled the roost. She was fond of entertaining, was highhanded with the servants, a stickler for routine and a strict disciplinarian with her children, which didn't suit my mother.

"First chance she got, she was off," said Mrs. Early.

"You mean—when she met my father?"

Mrs. Early nodded. "He came to the house two, three times to do a routine check on the clocks. There must have been—oh, twenty or more in those

days. The usual clock-minder fell ill, and your father
happened by chance in town at just the right time.
Nice young man. Only saw him twice, quiet and
respectful. But your mother fell for him head over
heels, she did. He stopped at an inn nearby, and
turns out later she let herself out of the house several times and met Mr. Lee outside.

"Your grandmother was fit to turn purple when
she found out and shut your mum up in her bedroom, and kept the key under her pillow. This went
on for three weeks, and all the staff were real sorry
for the poor lass. Your father was dismissed on the
spot and she tried to persuade your grandad to put
a whip across his shoulders. Luckily for your father
your grandad believed it was six of one and a half-
dozen of the other. Perhaps he knew his daughter
better than most gave him credit for . . .

"And then one day your mother disappeared."

"Disappeared?" This was all news to me. My parents had never discussed their earlier life in front of
me. They were absorbed in each other, so in love,
even after all those years, that even I felt sometimes
excluded.

"Yes, disappeared as though she had never been!
Your gran paid her a visit before breakfast, to give
her her usual lecture, unlocked with the only key, and
found her daughter gone! You can imagine the state
she was in! Everyone was questioned, but had she
not had the only key I think she would have dismissed us all. Then she got a note from your mother,
signed in her married name of Lee. Not that we
would have known about it but that she screwed up
the letter and threw it away, and one of us, er—found
it."

"What did she say? How did she escape?" I was
on the edge of my seat.

"Seems the two young lovers were more resource-
ful than we thought. Your mother knew that your
gran would blame everyone but herself, so she

explained how it was done. She had torn a petticoat
into strips and attached it to some ribbons, so she
could lower it out of her window at night and
exchange letters with her lover, your father. He told
her what to do: save some candlewax and keep it soft,
and when your gran came in to lecture, take a quick
impression of the key, which she always left on a side-
table. She lowered the wax out of the window, your
father had a key made and hey presto! They were
away!"

I leant back in my chair. My parents had been so
inventive, so daring. But it was difficult to think of
them as a pair of star-crossed lovers.

Was I lacking in their initiative, I wondered as I
went upstairs again? Surely not, I thought as I replenished the fire, just because I had chosen security over
speculation. I must write to Mr. Swallow at once
before I was tempted to change my mind.

I took a fresh sheet of paper and dated it. "For
the attention of Mr. Swallow," I wrote. "Dear Sir,"
but then I noticed something out of the corner of
my eye. The ivory figurine had gone missing again!

I looked under the table, back in the cabinet, on
the shelves, behind the curtains but it wasn't there.
I sat down again at the table. What in the world was
happening? I glanced at the papers on which I had
written my pros and cons and suddenly was on my
feet, my hand to my mouth.

On the sheet of Plan B where there had been a
long list of cons, there was now a mess of spilled ink.
On the left, against the few pros, had been added
a couple of lines in flowing capitals: *"YOU WILL
HAVE HELP, YOU KNOW."*

Chapter Nine

Ky-Lin

I didn't scream. I didn't faint. I didn't panic.

I could have done all three quite easily; why didn't I? Perhaps because I was too frozen with shock, perhaps because a curious calm seemed to be descending around me, which appeared to emanate from the ring on my finger. I looked at it. It was more sparkly than ever and seemed to be throbbing a little, in time with my heartbeat. Then I looked again at the mess of spilled ink and those alien words in an alien hand and I suppose at that stage I wasn't really surprised to see that they were fading even as I watched, and now were gone.

Even three days ago I would have been utterly fazed by all this, but I felt my whole life was changing by the minute and that shortly I shouldn't be surprised if someone told me that the earth was flat and the moon was made of green cheese. Perhaps that is why I found myself talking to something that couldn't possibly be there.

"All right," I said. "Fun's over. Come out, come

out, wherever you are . . ." It was like being back
at the Charity School again, looking for some child
who had hidden rather than return home.

There was a pause, a log settled on the fire; I went
and put on another, and returned to the table.

"I'm going to close my eyes," I said, "And count
to ten, slowly. When I open them again I expect
everything to be back to normal. If so, I won't take
any more action. But if it isn't, and there's a coach
or train tomorrow, then you won't see me for dust."

"That would be a great pity," said a tiny but perfectly clear voice, (in my head, of course), "after all
the trouble we took in getting you here in the first
place."

I closed my eyes, and kept them firmly shut. Of
course! I told myself, there's a perfectly simple
explanation to all this. You had a good supper of
chicken and stuffing, stayed on to hear Mrs. Early's
reminiscences of your parents and fell asleep as soon
as you started your letter to the solicitors. You are
dreaming now, but in about half an hour Mr. Early
will be bringing up your hot water and Mrs. Early
your toddy. You can go on dreaming until then, so
why not enjoy it? See what happens. Play along.
People this room with elves and fairies. Let yourself
go. Pretend this is a palace and you the princess. Fly
out of the window—no, *not* a good idea, what if you
were sleep-walking?

"I'm going to start counting now," I said. "One,
two—"

"Buckle your shoe . . ."

My eyes snapped open, then I closed them as
quickly. If it came to playing games, then I could play
with the best.

"Three—"

"What will you see?"

"Four—"

"Knock on the door."

"Five, six—"

Silence. Then: "Do you really want things as they were?"

"Of course! Have you any better suggestion?"

"Yes," came the tiny voice. "Open your eyes and see things as they could be."

I considered, my eyes still shut. "No. Four, five—"

"Look alive! You've already said that . . . Just try. It can't hurt. Stop counting and open your eyes."

"I'll open my eyes when I've finished counting, and not before."

"And you want your dull, lonely, cramped, circumspect life to continue as it was?"

My eyes flew open. "It wasn't—isn't—dull and circumspect! Who are you to judge, anyway?" I shut my eyes again. "Five—"

"You've said that."

"Right!" I was getting distinctly annoyed. "Six, seven, eight—"

"It could be too late . . ."

"Rubbish! Nine—"

"Rise and shine!"

"Ten!" I opened my eyes, expecting to see everything as it had been before I started dreaming. Some dreams you can control, make them turn out the way you wish, and at first sight this looked like one of those, but, unfortunately, it held one or two surprises. The ring pulsed on my finger, the Eg glowed in the lamplight, and the pros and cons lists were as they had been originally. And there, in the middle of the table was the missing ivory figure—

Only it wasn't. It was neither ivory nor a carving. It was alive! There might have been a superficial resemblance to the original figurine but it *was* only superficial.

About the size of a clenched fist—my fists were clenched right at this moment—it had the body and hide of a deer, the hooves of a horse, antennae flicking back and forth on either side of its mouth, a mini-horn in the centre of its forehead and a long

and sumptuous buffalo's tail, with a large plume at
the tip, almost as big as itself. This was now waving
back and forth like the tail of an annoyed cat.

But it was the colour that was the most arresting.

Legs and tail were dark grey, it had a bright yellow belly, the antennae were pink and the hide on
its back bore various shades of blue, purple, brown
and rose. The plume of its tail was the brightest of
all: crimson, green and gold.

"Who on earth are you?"

The creature regarded me with bright, brown eyes.
"I am a Ky-Lin."

The name sounded familiar, though for a moment
I couldn't place it. "What's a Kiling?"

"Lin. Ky-Lin." He nodded. "I am in the transcript
your uncle made. I am a mythical creature, if you
prefer it that way. My Master is the Prince
Siddhartha, whom men call Buddha, and I come
from China. When my Master graced the earth with
his presence he had a group of my brethren as his
companions, his disciples, his bodyguard. We were
trained by him to respect life in any form, right down
to the ant in the grass, the grass itself. We were
taught never to injure or kill anything living, however insignificant it might seem to be . . ." He broke
off and coughed delicately. "Might I trouble you for
a bite to eat? My throat is rather dry after all these
years . . ."

What did you give a creature like this in your
dreams? I glanced around wildly. "I'm afraid I only
have—er, ink or water in that vase. Or a bit of—
candle?"

The creature shook its head. "Not really sustaining . . . Now if you would lift me up onto the
mantel—no, better still, if you would bring the vase
down onto the table, then I can break my fast."

I went over to the mantel and fetched the vase
containing the sprays of berries and watched, fascinated, as the creature chewed the pulp from the hips,

haws and blackberries as if they were manna from
heaven, though I noticed he spat out the seeds tidily
onto the piece of paper I had intended writing to
the solicitors on.

He saw my look. "I am leaving the seeds so that
you may sow them in the garden tomorrow, to make
other plants."

If he imagined I was going to—but he obviously
did. Better humour him. "But of course. Would you
kindly tell me what you are doing here, after all these
years?" Thousands, if he really had anything to do
with the Buddha.

The creature hesitated for a second. "There is
always one bad apple in the barrel. My companions
attained Nirvana, but I wasn't good enough. I was
careless and broke some of the rules: truth was, I
liked the world and wanted to stay in it. My Master gave me a chance to expiate my sins by helping a young girl called Summer to attain her Quest.
After that I thought to have rest, but received a message that my task wasn't done. You could call it a
piece of unfinished business, I suppose: Summer's
egg must be returned to the dragons." He put his
head on one side. "And you are the person to do
it."

"Rubbish! I'm not the only person in the world!
What you need is an experienced traveller, someone
like my uncle was—"

"What we need is you!"

"Why *me*? And who's 'we'?"

" 'We' is me, the Egg and the Ring." He pushed
the rejected seeds into a neat pile, fluffed out the
plume on his tail and sat down on his haunches. "If
you had a little patience, I'll tell you how we all fit
in. Firstly, I accompanied young Summer to the place
this is destined to go, so I know the way—"

"But that was *hundreds* of years ago!" I was glad
to note that, although this was all a dream, I was
answering logically.

"Years, your years, mean nothing to such as we. We are all some centuries old."

"But why does the Eg have to go back right now, after all this time?"

"Because, after lying dormant for many, many years, it has started to grow, and this means it will soon be ready to hatch. If you have read your uncle's transcript you will know that this egg is the product of a liason between Summer and her dragon-lover, and that she and Jasper, for that was his name, took the egg to the Blue Mountain, where the remnants of the dragons live, to trade it for a promise that Jasper might retain his human shape during Summer's lifetime. As you also know, it all went disastrously wrong when the egg was stolen at the crucial moment. Summer lost her life, together with that of her lover, or so I believe, and the dragons lost their egg. If they know where it is, and that it is about to hatch, then they will come to find it, and that cannot be allowed to happen . . .

"Er . . . Could you possibly tip the vase a little? I find that talking after all this time is thirsty business . . . Thank you."

"You say you know the way, but there are maps . . ."

"I can grow larger, large enough to carry burdens on my back. I speak all the tongues known to man, and eat and drink very little. I also know the places to avoid, the dangers one might come across."

"In that case," I said frivolously, "you and I and the Eg could set off tomorrow, and you could carry us there and bring me back in a week or so!"

He shook his head. "It would take far longer than that . . ." Didn't he have a sense of humour? "Besides, you forget we have to take someone from the solicitor's to ensure fair play, and that young detective as well."

"And if they took one look at you," I said, "either large or small, they would swear off spirituous liquors forever and refuse to go anyway!"

"Not necessarily. I can change in a few seconds— or at least I will be able to after a little more practice; more than a few years in any one shape and one grows somewhat stiff."

"Have some more berries," I suggested.

"Not at the moment, thank you. I have had an elegant sufficiency."

"This size-changing—is that how you disappeared yesterday?"

"Of course. When I opened the cabinet—metal-bending is one of the things one learns early on—I found difficulty in the latter stages of the change. That is when I had to whisk behind the curtain and you found me resembling a rat. So, regress again and back to the cabinet."

"But I looked all over for you!"

"Down and around, yes, but not up. I was on the ceiling."

"Oh." There was no answer to that. I went back to the beginning again. "But why especially me? I know my uncle had this bee in his bonnet, but—"

"Because you are the Chosen One: the Ring-Bearer." He sounded as though that explained everything.

"This? This tatty bit of horn?" I held up my finger.

He looked scandalised. "That's not just a 'tatty bit of horn,' as you call it! That is a precious sliver from the horn of a fabulous Unicorn, who lived over a thousand years ago, and sacrificed his immortality for a love you couldn't hope to comprehend! He left behind the Ring to future generations to use for the good of the world. It has been passed down from generation to generation. Summer used it on her travels, and when she had no further use for it she left it in my safe-keeping. And the next wearer is you."

"But anyone could wear it—"

"Your uncle couldn't, neither could the house-keeper or her husband. The Ring chooses its own wearer. If you don't believe me, try and take it off."

"I can't. It seems stuck."

"Exactly!"

"What do you mean?"

The Ky-Lin sighed. "As I intimated, the Ring only fits those it has chosen. You could offer it to anyone in the world, of any race, colour or creed, large or small, male or female, fat or thin, young or old, and the Ring would still discriminate. I have no idea why it chooses whom it does, but it selects that person who is most fitted for the task to be undertaken. And it has special properties, you know."

"Such as?"

"It can warn you of danger. It can calm you down, make you think logically. It conserves your energy, keeps you young. Most and best of all, it allows you to communicate with the animal world. And if you weren't wearing it now, you wouldn't understand me."

I looked at it with more respect. I believed what he said—one did in dreams. Magic ring . . . "Does it do anything else? Can I have three wishes, for instance?"

He looked disgusted. "You're not being serious!"

"Oh, I am! This is the best dream I've had in *ages!*"

He bounced over the table towards me. "You're *not* dreaming! Listen to me. Everything points to you being the one to return the Eg. Your uncle bought us all at auction, in a lot I had taken care to be included in. Although he wasn't the one we looked for, he translated the manuscript and realised we should all be kept together. *He* couldn't solve the problem, but something told him you could."

"But he didn't even know me! How could he expect me to do what he could not?"

"I don't know. Perhaps because he knew and admired your mother's—his sister's—spirit of adventure. Perhaps because he knew your father must have had special qualities to keep her happy all those years.

Perhaps because he liked what he heard when he had
you investigated." He hesitated. "Perhaps just because
you were family . . ."

Footsteps on the stairs, the clank of a bucket. Mr.
Early bringing up my hot water. I gathered the papers
on the table together, the sheet with the seeds on
top, turned up the lamp, put away the pen and ink.
In came Mrs. Early with my hot drink. She glanced
at the table.

"Been busy, miss?"

I was awake again, and yawning. "I think I
dropped off for a while," I said. I picked up the Eg
and the ivory and put them back in the cabinet,
locking them in and putting the key in my pocket.

The following morning I checked the study before
I went down to breakfast. Mrs. Early had cleaned,
dusted and laid the fire, but everything else was as
I had left it. Even as I checked, I had allowed myself
to acknowledge that I had almost been persuaded by
that dream last evening to believe I had held a
conversation with a small creature with a colourful tail
called a Ky-Lin, and that I wore a magic ring that
allowed me to talk to animals . . . How ridiculous!
I looked for the seeds, but they had gone, of course.

I decided to try out the ring on the kitchen cat,
a fat, lazy creature who spent most of its time by the
fire. "Good morning, cat! How are you this morning? Caught any mice lately?"

The cat stared hard at me, as well it might, then
stomped off, its tail twitching irritably. So much for
magic rings, I thought triumphantly. So much for
dreams . . .

"Anything special to do today, miss?"

I shook my head. "Nothing planned, Mrs. Early."
I peered out of the window. "Looks like a nice day;
I might go for a walk, to clear my mind."

"Good idea, miss. Nothing like fresh air, your uncle
used to say. They are coming for the rest of the

statues and papers today, so I've got two girls from the village to give everything a good scrub now the place will be empty. Would you mind cold cuts for luncheon?"

"That'd be fine . . . Tell you what: I could take out a picnic, like I used to do in London. Some sandwiches and lemonade, perhaps."

"No sooner said than done, miss! I'll have a basket ready for you."

I went upstairs to change into my serviceable boots, to hitch up my skirts some two inches higher and collect my cloak. No need for bonnet or gloves, as the sun was shining and there was little wind. I decided I would explore the pine wood and search for mushrooms in the pasture behind the Hall. I would take *Westward Ho!* with me and read of the further adventures of Amyas Merion. I would have a day in which I worried about nothing, put letters and decisions to one side. I would just be holidaying . . .

Picking up my book and giving it a hug in anticipation of the pleasure it would bring, I crossed over to the study, just to make sure everything was as it should be before I left for the day. Downstairs I could hear Mrs. Early giving instructions to the village girls, with much clanking of buckets; Mr. Early had gone out to the orchard earlier to prune the cherry trees, and no-one, apart from Mrs. Early's cleaning, had been upstairs, not even the cat, which made it all the more frustrating to find that someone—or some*thing*—had ripped all my papers to pieces; pros and cons, the start of the letter to the solicitors. Torn them all into bite-sized pieces and scattered them on the neatly laid fire, and that since breakfast!

Running back into my bedroom and snatching the key from from my reticule, I went back into the study and opened the cabinet. Inside all was as it should be, but I was so angry that I picked out both the Eg and the ivory and dumped them on the table, shouting: "I've had enough of all this! You're mine to dispose of as I will, and that is exactly what I am going to do!"

And with that I picked them both up again and, wrapping them in my cloak, stormed down to the empty kitchen, snatched up the picnic basket and set off past the kitchen-garden and orchard, feet stamping so hard on the path that I saw Mr. Early suspend action with the pruning-shears and scratch his head in puzzlement.

I set off to climb towards the back of the wood, but before long I was hot and sticky, so I transferred the ivory and the Eg, which seemed to weigh a ton, into the corner of the picnic basket, taking care not to squash the sandwiches.

The wood was stifling. Inches of dead pine-needles hindered my feet, red squirrels dashed the branches overhead, chattering angrily at my intrusion, and the trees only offered intermittent shade from the bars of suddenly hot sunshine that struck down on my bare head, so that I felt sick with heat.

At last I broke through into the open, and I saw ahead of me to the right a bracken and gorse-covered hillock. It could have been part of the grounds of the Hall or not, but at that stage I didn't care. I climbed a stile, ripping my skirt as I did so, struggled a few yards up the hill and then sat down, exhausted. The head-high bracken, with its fusty-dusty smell and autumn russet dress almost met over my head and golden gorse was still a-buzz with bees . . .

I lay back and closed my eyes. "Kissing's out of fashion, when the gorse is out of bloom," I recited sleepily, relaxing at last, with only the hum of insects and the plaintive cry of a curlew to disturb my rest.

I don't know how long I slept, but when I looked at my watch it was a quarter to midday, and for a moment I felt disoriented. Then I remembered where I was and what I had to do. Struggling to my feet I hitched up my skirts into my belt, picked up the basket and started to climb the hill again, hampered by the strands of bracken. At last I reached an outcrop of rock near the top, which I though would serve my purpose.

I undid the straps to the picnic basket and there was the Eg, glinting in the sunshine. I hesitated for only a moment, then picked it up, still marvelling at its weight and warmth, and then deliberately let it tumble from my hands down the hill, where it cut a momentary swathe through the bracken before the reddish stems closed behind its path. Something stabbed at my right hand, but I ignored the sting— a mosquito, perhaps, or more likely a midge, this high up.

"Goodbye and good riddance!" I called out after the vanished Eg. "Hatch your dragon out here if you feel like it! I'm not travelling half round the world just for you . . ." A flock of pigeons flew overhead, probably from some stubbled field, the clap-clap of their wings disturbing the air with a momentary chill.

I paused for a moment, then picked the ivory figurine from the basket. "And as for you . . . !" But words failed me. "Just disappear from my life, that's all!" and with all my strength I hurled it away, till it disappeared into the heart of a distant gorse-bush. There was another stab on my right hand. If I climbed right to the top of the hill the insects probably wouldn't bother me so much.

Once there I found I was looking down on the back of Hightop Hall. The stick-like figure in the kitchen-garden must be Mr. Early, and way down the drive I could see two horsedrawn pantechnichons apparently carrying away the last of my uncle's artifacts. A plume of smoke rose from the kitchen chimney, but that was the only other sign of life. I opened my book, but the sun hurt my eyes, and my stomach felt empty, although it was only twelve-fifteen.

I felt better for doing as I had, of course I did, so why did I feel so—so empty?

Of course it couldn't be guilt, could it? I had done nothing to feel guilty about, had I? Absentmindedly I opened and ate my sandwiches: home-boiled ham with mustard, egg and pot-grown cress, late, sweet tomatoes, an apple and a slice of plum cake. I finished with a drink of lemonade, but after it all I still felt empty, and everything seemed to have tasted the same. I must have been sickening for something.

I looked for mushrooms, but only in a desultory fashion, and found none. Afterwards I left the basket and my book at the top end of the orchard and walked down the drive, turned left and walked until nearly sundown. Once back I retrieved the basket and went towards the kitchen door. Two pigeons were cooing to one another on a corner of one of the outhouse roofs; they glanced at me as I passed.

"C-r-oo-l," said one.

"Th-r-oo them away," said the other. "S-a-a-a-w her . . ."

I dropped the basket onto the cobbles.

Chapter Ten

"Repent Ye . . ."

I heard the tinkle of broken glass as the basket hit the ground, but it scarcely registered. I stared up at the pigeons—ordinary grey ones with the sheen of green on their necks, dark bands across their wings—as they strutted above my head. They nodded to one another, fluffed up their feathers, nothing more.

I stooped to pick up the basket, then it came again.

"Croo-oo-ool," came the soft voice. "Too-oo-oo coo-oo-l for the Eg."

I was trembling violently. Now I was hearing voices! As if in answer the ring on my finger started to throb. I looked down at the ring, up at the pigeons, remembered a flight of them passing over when I threw away the Eg into the bracken. Could it . . . ? No, it couldn't. But the Ky-Lin had said . . .

There was no-one about, no humans anyway. "Right," I said out loud to the birds. "If you're so clever, just tell me exactly what I'm supposed to have done?"

"Yoo-oo-oo-oo know," crooned the pigeons. "Yooo-oo-oo knoo-oo-w!"

It was true! Either that or I was mad or dreaming. I pinched myself: no dream. And I didn't think I was mad. Then all that fantasy the other night must have been true. That little creature that called itself a Ky-Lin must have been speaking the truth.

To say that I was devastated was an understatement. I was terrified, exhilarated, awed and humbled at one and the same time. Being a logical girl, or so I believed, I had accepted fairy tales as just that: pretty fiction. To suddenly find that there was another dimension demanded a tremendous leap of faith, a conversion into the suspension of disbelief.

I needed to give myself time to think; routine things first. I picked up the basket and took it into the kitchen, emptying it carefully on the table. The glass tumbler was broken, as was the plate. I wrapped these carefully in the sandwich paper and put them on the draining board. Luckily the stone lemonade bottle was intact. That, together with the knife used for paring my apple, I placed in the sink, and the apple peel on the fire, remembering too late that Mr. Early might have used it on his compost-heap.

So far, so good. I was calmer now. Perhaps I should put the kettle on the stove and make myself a cup of tea. Mrs. Early should be back soon, and—

The kitchen cat walked past, her tail in the air. "Murderesssss!" she hissed.

I sat down at the kitchen table and burst into tears.

After a lonely evening, trying to read and failing, and a restless and disturbed night, I awoke the following morning with stomach pains. Of course I knew what it was, the curse of all women, but this time the gripes were worse than usual, so much so that I declined breakfast, but once Mrs. Early had found out what was the matter she insisted I spend the rest of the day in bed, with hot stone bottles, a drop or two of laudanum and a light diet.

"Used to suffer the same way myself, miss, and in those days there was no excuse for not carrying on with your jobs. Swore that if I ever met someone the same, I'd treat them different."

No point in telling her that this didn't happen every time, that I believed in my heart that it was some kind of retribution for my doings of the day before. But of course she didn't know the Eg and Ky-Lin were somewhere out on the hillside, open to all the vagaries of the weather. Now I really knew what it felt like to feel guilty!

And it didn't help that the sermon the following morning appeared to point directly at me: "Repent ye, for the Kingdom of Heaven is at hand . . ."

We went to church in the trap, tying the pony to the rail outside. The church, probably Norman in origin, was comfortably full, but to my surprise the churchwarden led us to a private pew near the front, which had belonged to my uncle. I saw many of the congregation turn to each other and murmur as we took our places. I was wearing my best skirt and jacket in navy blue, and had trimmed my bonnet with black rosettes and ribbons in deference to the mourning for my uncle. Once the service started I was soothed by the familiarity of the words, and comforted by the sunlight striking through the stained-glass windows and casting patterns of soft reds, greens and blues on the aisles. These did much to soften the harshness of the half-hour sermon, which seemed to strike at the root of my guilt, and I found myself wriggling uneasily.

Once the service was over, as was the custom, those in the closed pews at the front left the church first. Most of the congregation was soberly and sensibly dressed, with the odd coloured ribbons or checked jacket, but the party I now saw for the first time might have been dressed for a garden party or a wedding. As they passed our pew there was no disguising their curiosity. They stared quite openly. A middle-aged couple, two somewhat older, two young men, three young ladies, followed by probably a ladies' maid and a governess, all looked at me as if I were an exhibit in a sideshow.

Only a week ago I would have blushed and lowered my gaze; today as my uncle's representative I returned their gaze steadily enough, inclining my head infinitesimally in acknowledgement of their interest. Mr. and Mrs. Early and I were a were a few paces behind their party as we moved towards the church porch, so I was in a perfect position to hear the following exchanges; there was no attempt to lower their voices.

Taller of two young men: "Quite a nice-looking gel, wouldn't you say, Mater?"

Mother: "Passable, I suppose, if you like that somewhat sallow complexion. But remember, she hasn't two farthings to rub together. From what I heard, her uncle left her penniless."

Smaller young man: "Have to sell up, I suppose. There's a nice piece of rough shooting at the back."

Older man: "Reasonable stand of timber, too . . ."

Father: "We'll see, we'll see. Shouldn't think she'll quibble over a price."

One of the girls to the others: "My dears, did you see that *awful* bonnet? And she was wearing *boots* . . ."

By now I was crimson with both embarrassment and anger, conscious that everyone within earshot must have heard. How dared they!

But Mrs. Early was whispering in my ear. "Take no notice, miss. Both families made their money in trade, and can't keep staff above a week or so."

But unfortunately that was not the point. They had the money, so believed they could behave as they wished. One thing was for certain: if ever I was in a position to have any say in the disposal of Hightop

Hall, then the very last people to be allowed to bid for it would be the people who had behaved so condescendingly.

I needed a diversion. "Will you show me where my uncle is buried?"

Mrs. Early led me down a side-path in the churchyard to a secluded spot shaded by an ancient yew tree. Here were no urns, vaults, stone angels, crosses with wreaths or elaborate railings; just a green mound, the turves beginning to knit together, and at their head a curiously shaped slab of stone, rather like a broken tooth. It was streaked and striated with green, and could have been malachite. On its surface were some deep indentations, which if looked at from a certain angle could have formed a cross. Inset in the stone was a small bronze plaque bearing my uncle's name and dates of birth and death, nothing more.

Mrs. Early considered it, her head on one side. "I'm getting quite used to it, but it looks—looks . . ."

"A bit pagan," I supplied with a wry smile.

"I'm sure that was the word I was looking for," she agreed. "Brought that stone back from his travels, he did, many years ago. Set it up against his bedroom wall and said: 'That's my headstone, Mrs. Early. I expect the vicar will object, but that's what I want. You can see it bears the symbol of the cross.' Morbid I thought it was, having it there, and I couldn't dust it without a shiver. Looks better in the open."

As it was still fine I elected to walk the couple of miles home—strange, "home" was now its name in my mind—and I picked sprays of hips and haws and a twist of Old Man's Beard to replace those depleted by Ky-Lin two nights ago, and put them in a silver-rimmed glass in the centre of the study table, before changing into my working-clothes for Sunday lunch.

"Rain later," said Mr. Early, coming in to wash his hands. "Wind's getting up. Cold snap coming—more berries'n usual."

I hoped the rain would hold off until I had done what I had to do.

I found I had a good appetite from my walk back, and tucked into a typical Sunday luncheon: Brown Windsor Soup, roast beef and horseradish sauce, Yorkshire pudding, roast potatoes, gravy, boiled cabbage and carrots, with apple tart to follow.

As I climbed upstairs I could hear the wind getting up: I must hurry. Putting on my cloak and boots, I decided against a bonnet, "awful" or not—it would probably blow away in the wind. I should be gone at least a half-hour, so decided to check that the fire in the study was made up before I left.

But this was not the first thing I noticed. To my utter astonishment there, on the table, finishing his second rose-hip and fishing out the seeds and laying them out in a neat row with his delicate antennae, was Ky-Lin!

"Absolutely delicious!" he said enthusiastically. "How nice of you to think of me. Someone threw out the last lot of seeds, but we will save these to plant when we go out—"

I rushed forward and picked him up, hugging him fervently. "You came back!"

"Of course. I—"

"You knew I would come and look for you, didn't you?"

"I knew you were very upset—"

"I was all mixed up! I didn't realise that what you had said was the truth—about the ring and the Eg. But then I heard . . . How did you get back, anyway?"

"Pigeon Post. This morning . . . Er, do you think I might get down? I'm afraid I'm not used to being hugged."

I apologised and set him back on the table. "But how did you get up here?"

"The pigeons dropped me off—literally—in the stable-yard and the cat gave me a lift upstairs, carrying me as she would one of her kittens. A little hazardous . . ." A tiny forked tongue came out and flicked fastidiously over his hide.

"I was coming to find you before it started raining," I said. "You and the Eg." I explained how I had become convinced he had been telling me the truth about the ring. "I felt—sort of guilty. I shouldn't have lost my temper. So you needn't worry, I'll make sure you and the Eg find a safe haven, wherever and whenever."

He looked inordinately pleased. "I was sure you would decide correctly," he said. "I must thank you in advance."

I waved away his thanks. "Please don't do that: it may take some time to get you both settled."

He nodded. "Then shall we go and pick up the Eg before the weather worsens? I know exactly where it is—I watched over it in my larger guise last night."

I tucked him in my cloak till we were away from the hall, then he sat on my shoulder as I climbed the hill.

"Exactly how big can you grow?"

He considered. "About pony-size, maximum. Normally I travel round as small as I can, and in the most convenient material: ivory, stone, wood, amethyst—I have been all those."

I couldn't think of anything to say. If he were to be believed—but why not? Everything he had said so far was apparently true.

"Here we are," said Ky-Lin.

I lowered him to the ground and he darted off through the bracken. As I followed I noticed he avoided actually touching living growth, just jumping from pebble to bare earth to stone. I stooped down and picked up the round Eg and examined it as best I could.

"It hasn't come to any harm, has it?" I asked anxiously.

Ky-Lin waved his tail dismissively. "Take more than

a roll down a hill and a night in the open to harm that. Whatever is in there is well insulated. Your uncle tried to break it and crack it with a hammer, but it wasn't hurt."

By the time we reached the orchard the rain had started to fall, and Mr. Early was so busy fetching in the last of the wood and Mrs. Early the washing, that neither of them noticed that I was carrying something in my cloak, so I had time to arrange everything nicely on the table in the study, including paper, pen and ink, before Mrs. Early came in with my tray of tea. Even Ky-Lin had reverted to his ivory shape, but as soon as she had gone I was witness to a remarkable transformation.

First his outline seemed to blur and soften, then expand. For a moment it trembled on the brink then suddenly his head, then his body, emerged from its covering like a chicken from its egg. Last of all were legs and tail; he was having trouble with his right fore-leg however, which initially seemed reluctant to grow as long as the others but finally, after an all-over shake, all the pieces came together.

"Getting better," he said. "Only twenty-five seconds."

"Would you like a sip of tea, after all that exertion?"

"China?"

"Lapsang Souchong."

"A sip would be nice."

I let it cool in the teaspoon before I offered it to him, then watched as the forked tongue, each side working independently, emptied the teaspoon without spilling a drop.

"What do you eat and drink at home?" I asked.

"A little rice every now and again, cheese, nuts, windfalls—that sort of thing. We Ky-Lins are not allowed to eat flesh or pluck anything that is actually growing."

"And can you fly?"

He shook his head. "We leave that to creatures like the dragons, among us so-called mythical creatures. They fly, we don't; they eat meat, we don't; they collect treasure on earth, we don't; they are aggressive and unforgiving, we are not. Different outlook. Different life-style."

He hesitated, then continued. "But I'm afraid I can't tell you much more about them than that. I have seen them flying in the distance, usually at night, although they normally keep away from human habitation. I think that nowadays they are afraid that with all the modern ways you humans have developed for killing, they may one day become targets themselves. While once they were fearsome enough to terrify whole towns and villages, their shape and brain-size hasn't developed from what you would call their 'prehistoric' days, whereas you humans have changed with the times." He added, "I've never seen one close to, nor do I wish to, and I believe their language is incomprehensible."

"Then why . . . ?" I hesitated.

"Did I become involved with the Eg? I thought I had explained. First, it is Summer's egg: unfinished business. Secondly, I volunteered. Unofficially, of course. Besides, it's an egg, not a dragon—yet." He sat down on his haunches. "And now that the explanations are done, hadn't we better get to work? You'll need paper, pen and ink."

"What for?"

"To plan our strategy, of course. Better to have it all written down. And then there's the letter to your solicitor—"

A step outside, a tap at the door, and Mrs. Early entered, carrying a small packet wrapped in oilskin.

"I'm sure I don't know what that young gentleman is about, sending young Jem from the inn out in this weather! Like a drowned rat he is, and told he's to wait for an answer!"

"What is it?"

"A letter from that Mr. Hamperhutch, the one from the solicitors!"

I opened the letter. "*Miss Leigh,*" it read. "*Today is Sunday, and tomorrow will begin the second week you have sojourned at Hightop Hall. May I remind you that your stay was only intended for you to confirm the acceptance of the moneys left by your uncle. My employers await your decision with some impatience, in order that they may arrange your return to London. If you will do me the honour of inscribing a few lines to the effect of your intent, I shall ensure that the letter leaves on the stage in the morning. Your humble servant, Claude Cumberbatch.*" Hmm, a bit more polite than the last. But there was a postscript. "*PS: If you would be kind enough to give the boy, the bearer of this, a couple of pence, I should be obliged.*"

"The cheek of the man!" I crumpled the note in my hand angrily, then thought for a moment. "Mrs. Early, the boy—would you see he dries out by the fire, please? And perhaps a glass of your raspberry cordial and a slice of cake . . . Any chance of the rain slackening off?"

"Mr. Early says perhaps a half-hour or so, though it'll be back before morning."

"Then I shall write an answer to this immediately!"

As soon as the door closed behind her I drew a sheet of paper towards me, grabbed a pen and opened the inkwell, to see out of the corner of my eye what had been an ivory figure a few minutes ago, turn once more into a living creature.

"Right, Ky-Lin! Just for that young man's impudence I shall stay until Saturday at least!"

He looked flabbergasted. "But we can't possibly be ready by then! It'll take at least a fortnight longer!"

I turned to him, puzzled. "To do what?"

"To get ready to take the Eg back to China, of course . . ."

Chapter Eleven

Surprise, Surprise!

I paused, pen in hand, not quite sure I had heard correctly. A large blob of ink spoiled the first page.

"*What* did you say?"

"I said we would need more than a week to prepare for the journey."

"Which journey?" But even as I asked, I think I knew the answer. Another, smaller drop of ink fell on the paper. The earth and the moon . . .

"The one we were talking about earlier," Ky-Lin explained patiently. "You said you were prepared to do your utmost to get the Eg and I back where we belonged. Remember?"

I recalled saying something to that effect, but he had interpreted it quite differently from my meaning: I had meant him to understand that I would find somewhere nice for them to settle down in, *not* take them all the way back to China!

"But I didn't mean—"

"No, of course you didn't realise how much there was to be done. You will have to resign your post at

the school—that letter can be written tonight, together
with the one to the solicitors. They will have to arrange
for your bits and pieces to come down here, and of
course find a member of their staff to accompany us,
to make sure we actually carry out our quest."

"But you don't understand—"

"Of course I do! Anyone in your position would
be a little apprehensive about the journey. But we'll
have a good look at the maps, and don't forget I
speak most of the languages and can guide you over
the last part easily."

"But I haven't said—"

"That you'll need new clothes? That's another
thing we must arrange. At this time of the year, for
the first part of the journey at least, you will need
much warmer wear. And of course we don't know
how soon that mysterious young detective your uncle
used to find you will take to reach us."

"But—"

"No, of course I will travel incognito, at least until
and unless the others will accept me. I can travel
quite comfortably in one of your pockets. A nice, new
travelling jacket should have plenty of those for a
compass, chocolate and Ky-Lins!" And he wagged his
tail at his own bit of alliterative nonsense. "Oh, and
you must get a passport."

I laid down my pen very carefully and sat back in
my chair. I had run out of buts or, more correctly,
knew whatever I said, Ky-Lin would chirp in with
some enthusiastic idea for the promulgation of the
journey. *His* journey. Not mine.

I knew very well I was being manipulated; I also
knew that I had very little chance, apart from fleeing into the night and seeking Mr. Cumberbatch's
unwilling protection, of getting out of this. And even
then the mythical creature would probably reassemble
itself into a pony and come galloping after me, or
grab the attention of a passing owl and get there
before I did.

At the beginning of the afternoon I had been fully determined to go back to London, resume my post at the school until I could find something better, invest my uncle's money and live a more comfortable life. But there had been my sense of guilt, exacerbated by that uncompromising sermon; I had been really happy to see Ky-Lin again, to the extent of an uncharacteristic hug; I had been upset by the odious conversation I had overheard at church about the proposed disposal of the Hall, which I now realised I was very fond of, and the final straw had been Claude Cumberbatch's letter.

Crumpling up the spoiled sheet of paper I got up and tossed it onto the fire, then crossed to the window, pulled up the sash and leaned out to smell the resin from the rain-soaked pines. Crossing back to the table I pulled out a fresh sheet of paper, wiped the nib with the pen-wiper and dipped it into the ink.

"Right, Ky-Lin, you win!" I said. "First the letter of resignation. Want to dictate?"

An hour later, with both letters written, I realised that this was what I had wanted all along: a clean break, a new life, the spice of adventure. I felt myself grow stronger and more positive with every line I wrote, as if a weight had suddenly lifted from my shoulders. I remembered a game we had played at boarding-school: you put your arm straight down against your side, then leant against a wall, pressing the arm as hard as you could for three or four minutes, then stepping away. Your arm rose into the air of its own volition, like magic.

My spirits were rising, just like that arm, so when Mrs. Early arrived to inform me that the rain had stopped and to collect the tea-tray, I was able to greet her with the sort of smile I hadn't felt like giving since I arrived.

"I have two letters here, Mrs. Early. Please give

the boy this six-pence for his trouble." I knew that she would puzzle over the addresses before she handed the letters over, so I thought I would anticipate any confusion. "This one is to my previous employer, announcing my resignation, and the other is to my solicitors, asking them to forward my luggage from my former lodgings and advise me as to what arrangements need to be made before we set off."

Her face lighted up, then she frowned. "You're not stopping then, miss?"

"For a while—until we are organised. By the way, sometime in the next week or so there will be two gentlemen staying here, the ones who are to accompany us—er, me."

"You're going to take that stone ball all the way back to Chiney? Well, I never . . . Not that I thought you wouldn't, mind. And then you'll come back here and make this place something to be proud of. Heaven be praised!" And she meant it.

"What do we do now?" I asked Ky-Lin, once she had gone.

"We wait," he said, "We wait . . ."

In the meantime there was plenty to do. I sent off for catalogues of men's and women's travel-wear, and with Ky-Lin's help picked out stout, high-laced boots, thick gloves, leggings (!), a leather cap with ear-flaps, warmer underwear, a money-belt, a man's tweed jacket (small size) and a wicked-looking "hunting-knife." I didn't dare ask what that was for. From another catalogue we picked out a warm blanket, which I sewed up to form a sort of sleeping bag— we were going to sleep in the open? And a light-weight haversack.

All these items were, of course, cash on delivery, but I was relieved when Mr. Swallow paid us a visit in person on Thursday. I wouldn't have wanted to pay for all those items out of my own money.

I was pleased to be able to receive him in the morning-room, with a bright fire blazing and a vase of autumn leaves on the games-table. He raised his eyebrows at his surroundings, obviously impressed. Mrs. Early brought in sherry and sweet biscuits, and as he sipped and nibbled, and confirmed that he didn't need accommodation as he had booked into the inn for the night, I could see that he was revising his opinion of me.

He produced a folder full of documents, brushing the crumbs from his waistcoat as he did so. "I have here your uncle's instructions if you were to choose his alternative plan—which action on your part Miss, er, Lee, I must admit, rather surprises me—and he confirms that he wishes the expedition outward to be completed within one year. The time of your return is immaterial." He managed to make the latter sound unlikely.

"On the outward journey I should budget for one pound per day. There are moneys for outfitting included. Any moneys not used can be utilised for your—er, return." He consulted his papers. "I have contacted a certain—er—Mr. Danny Duveen, whom it was your uncle's wish should accompany you. I gather you will be able to accommodate him? I believe he is out of funds again."

I nodded. "We have room enough. What about your own representative?"

He seemed faintly embarrassed. "We are having, ah, a little difficulty in choosing the right candidate, I am afraid. But I expect to confirm the position as soon as possible." He shuffled his papers together. "When he—this person—arrives, he will bring the moneys with him, together with a receipt, of course, and his luggage. I can also confirm that your own personal belongings will be dispatched by train tomorrow and I have arranged for them to be picked up at the station and transported here—"

"Not by the village carrier, I hope!"

He raised his eyebrows. "Why, yes. Our Mr. Cumberbatch assures us he is an excellent man."

"Excellent, nothing! He is lazy, idle and forgetful! Can't you find somebody else? Or at least hold back my possessions until we find alternative transport?"

He shook his head. "Firm arrangements have already been made. The luggage will have left your lodgings long before I can contact anyone to stop it. Can you not find someone to accompany him and make sure he is on time?"

"What about Mr. Cumberbatch?"

He looked embarrassed again. "He has already returned to London, I'm afraid, as his presence here was no longer required."

I thought for a moment. "What time does the train arrive? Is it the same one I travelled on?" He nodded. "Wait a moment, please . . ." I went and had a quick word with Mr. Early, who seemed glad enough to oblige, then returned to Mr. Swallow. "Please ensure that the carrier is here at ten-thirty in the morning. Mr. Early, the housekeeper's husband, will accompany him to the station, making sure he is on time for the train and that the luggage is properly taken care of. Do I have to pay him again?"

"But I understand that Mr. Cumberbatch . . ."

"Then you understood wrong." I rose to my feet. "And now, if there is nothing else? Mr. Early will drive you back to the village."

"It has been a pleasure to do business with you, Miss—er—Lee." He stood up to shake hands. "I must also say that I would not have believed at our initial interview that you would have the determination and will to undertake this task, although I know your uncle had great confidence in you."

I was flattered. I had always thought of myself as something of a mouse. True, I had tackled the hard work and poverty in London pretty well, but what choice had there been? Come to that, what choice had I had here? I thought there had been, but what chance did I have against a magic ring, a close-to-hatching dragon's egg, and a fast-talking, persuasive, wily little Oriental creature of myth?

"Thank you, Mr. Swallow. I am grateful for your help. If—if our expedition proves a success, I presume you will have the papers ready to sign over Hightop Hall to me?" Nothing like sounding confident.

"Of course." He bowed. "I look forward to your return, Miss—er—Lee."

That evening Ky-Lin and I pored over the maps I had taken from my uncle's map-chest: Europe, Russia, Northern China.

"Is this the way you went with Summer?"

He shook his head. "Our way went further south. She travelled from Venice, through Turkey and Arabia into Persia, which is where I picked her up. We then used a caravan route through Northern India and Southern China, across the Gobi desert, then up the Altai Mountains to there—" He touched the map with his hoof. "All modern names, of course. Then, many of them were different, together with the boundaries. Of course, then time didn't matter: now it is of the essence. I suggest the northern route will be quicker."

"But—at this time of year—won't it be colder?"

"Probably; that's why I suggested the warmer clothes. But if we initially use the rivers—Rhine and Danube and across the Black Sea to Georgia and the Caspian, then we can cross the Khirgiz Steppes and bypass the Gobi: the Desert of Death they called it in those days—it will be cheaper. We can use commercial barges up the rivers. The only alternative . . ." He hesitated.

"Yes?"

"The way your uncle would have taken. Straight by ship to India, then north by camel-train. It would be quicker and infinitely more comfortable but we couldn't afford it."

Then that's out, I thought disconsolately. I looked at the mileage graphs at the bottom of each map, measuring them off a thousand miles at a time against my thumb joint, and—

"It must be five or six thousand miles!" I gasped.

"Double that," said Ky-Lin. "We're not flying, you know."

Double? That would make it twelve thousand miles! It wasn't possible! I couldn't do it! Nobody could . . . The dismay must have shown on my face, for Ky-Lin plumed his tail reassuringly.

"We *can* do it. Just about . . . Don't worry, girl. But from now on, until we leave, I want you to practice walking in your new boots, with a rucksack weighted with stones on your back. If you do that, it will be easier when the time comes."

"*Walking*! I thought you said we were travelling by river!"

"Have you ever found a river that you only had to step across to find another? There will be travel between all the waterways and beyond. If we can't find wheeled or animal transport, then we walk, and we carry our food and belongings with us."

"It's all right for you!" I burst out. "You're going to end up being carried in someone's pocket!"

He waved his tail. "When the time comes I shall do my part, I promise you."

"All right! I understand you will translate, guide and advise us, but what about the hard slog we shall have?"

He was silent for a moment, then: "Please put me down on the floor near the window and stand back . . ."

I did as he asked. For a moment or two nothing happened, then I saw something I would not have believed had I not seen it. Turning from mouse-size to rat-size was one thing, but what Ky-Lin managed was incredible. His outline became cloudy and there was a sort of creaking noise, followed by some popping ones and he grew up in size, first one leg and then the other; a thickening of the body, enlarging of the head, and finally his tail shot up into the air, the plume larger than ever, and his outline became clear and distinct.

I stepped back, suddenly scared. He was now as pony-sized as he had once boasted.

"Hey, there, don't be frightened!" His voice was the same, although it had deepened in tone. He stepped towards me, and his hooves clicked on the wooden floor, the plume of his tail swishing back and forth, creating a current of air that brushed me like a caress. "You see? If necessary I can carry burdens as great as any human. As I said, if we have to walk then I will do my share."

I opened my mouth to say something, to apologise, when we both heard footsteps in the corridor outside: Mrs. Early with my hot toddy!

"Open the window!"

I rushed to do his bidding, there was a hiss like air escaping from a balloon and a flurry of curtain and Ky-Lin had disappeared.

Mrs. Early bustled in, setting my hot toddy on the table by the maps. "Been plotting your journey, have you? Many's the time I'd see your uncle with not only the table but the floor covered with— Why! You've got the window wide open! It's raining again and you'll catch your death in that draught! I know your uncle was one for fresh air, but enough is enough . . ."

She began to cross towards the flapping curtains, but I stopped her.

"It's all right, Mrs. Early. I opened the window because some smoke blew back into the room. I'll close it in a minute."

"As you wish. Mr. Early will be up in a few minutes with your hot water . . ."

As soon as she had shut the door behind her I

rushed over to the window to find a diminished-to-
his-normal-size Ky-Lin shivering on the window-sill.
Lifting him inside I pulled down the sash and put
him down on the rug by the fire to dry out. I was
trying hard not to laugh, he looked so bedraggled.

"Here, have a sip of my hot toddy . . ."

He did, then pulled himself together in a small,
dignified way. "I bet you would fare no better if you'd
been out there in the rain, and had to change back
so quickly . . . Yes, thank you, another sip or two
would be most welcome!" A long drink. "Er, this *is*
alcohol-free, I suppose?"

My luggage arrived the next day, mid-afternoon.
Jos. Carter, Carrier, came trundling down the drive
with Mr. Early next to him in the front seat. The men
carried my mother's writing desk into the morning-
room, where it was unwrapped and polished by Mrs.
Early. My grandfather's wing-chair went into what I
had christened the library, where it received the same
treatment from the housekeeper. The books went into
the study, and my trunk into the bedroom, where I
unpacked what little I had and put it away into the
wardrobe and chest of drawers. The patchwork quilt
I spread over my bed, bringing a bright patch of
colour to the room.

Mrs. Early commented on what I had brought.
"Two nice pieces of furniture, miss, and the chair
matches the curtains perfectly. Is the quilt your own
work?"

I explained it was my mother's handiwork, and she
was full of praise. "By the way, miss, I've taken the
liberty of putting the laundry basket in the kitchen.
It was that heavy, Mr. Early said, that I thought you
might have something special in it."

Laundry basket? My meagre laundry usually came
in a brown paper parcel. Surely Mrs. Jugg hadn't
wasted one of her hampers, which usually went to
those with a far bigger laundry than mine? And

heavy? I would go down and take a look.

But first I tried out my father's chair in the "library," letting its soft curves and soft cushions wrap me into remembered ease, but suddenly there was a loud scream from the direction of the kitchen.

Rushing down the corridor I opened the kitchen door and found Mr. and Mrs. Early looking at a medium-sized laundry hamper in the middle of the floor.

Mrs. Early was armed with a poker. "It moved," she cried. "I'll swear it did!"

"Saw it too," said Mr. Early, armed with a cudgel.

I gazed in alarm at the hamper, which bore a label addressed to "Miss S. Lee, Hightop Hall, Dorset. By Rail."

Suddenly the whole basket jerked and creaked and we all jumped back. One of the leather straps snapped, and there was a faint groaning noise.

"There's something inside," I said. "Perhaps it's a dog . . ." I was scared stiff, but reckoned we couldn't leave whatever it was trapped in there for ever. Making a quick decision I moved forward and fumbled the other strap free, then moved back quickly.

Mr. and Mrs. Early clutched their weapons more tightly.

"Come out!" I said loudly. "At *once!*"

The lid lifted, fell back, and out of a tangle of laundry stepped—

"*Toby!*" I cried.

Chapter Twelve

Toby

"Toby!" I repeated. "What in the *world* are you doing in there?"

He looked a real scarecrow: tangled hair, tousled clothes, a smeary face, filthy hands—and most of this had come off on my laundry, in which he had been wrapped.

Mrs. Early lowered her poker. "You *know* him, miss?" She made it sound like a crime.

I started to explain, but he turned a pitiful face in my direction and clutched the front of his trousers.

"Wanna piss, miss!"

I snatched at his sleeve, rushed him out into the yard and pointed him in the direction of the outside privy. When he reappeared, looking much better, I hauled him back into the kitchen.

"Would you be kind enough to give him a mug of milk, Mrs. Early?" He downed it in one gulp, sighed, and put the empty mug on the table. "There's more where that came from," I said, "when you have explained yourself!"

"Where'd you want me to start?"

"At the beginning. Just a moment though . . ." I turned to Mr. and Mrs. Early and finished explaining who and what he was. "Not my idea," I said.

"And just look at what he's done to your laundry!" Mrs. Early snatched out the sheets, pillowcases and towels. "Need more than one boil!"

"Right, Toby!"

"Er . . . I ain't et nuffin since—"

"How many times do I have to tell you? 'I haven't eaten anything since . . .' Repeat it after me—and leave out that whine . . . Good. Carry on. You can eat after you have told me why and how you are here. The truth, mind."

I was fiercer with him than usual, largely because his appearance had been such a shock, bringing back the environment I had come from with painful clarity, now when I had decided to give it all up.

He hesitated. "I hid in there because I wanted to be with you. When—when I heard as you weren't coming back—"

"*That* you weren't—"

"That you weren't coming back, I grew desperate. Me Mam's latest—"

"*My*—"

"My Mam's latest hates me, he does. Doesn't want me in the house no more—"

I sighed. "*Any* more. Come on, Toby, you can talk better than that!"

"He told me as—that—I reminded him of a frog. Me—my Mam—was always saying as—that my dad was the best lover she ever had."

I looked at his filthy face. Large, long-lashed eyes, straight nose, determined chin— "You don't look a bit like a frog—or a toad, come to that."

"Not a *frog* frog, a Frenchie Frog. Me—my Mam—let slip he came from a town called Paree."

All Mrs. Jugg's children had different fathers, I

knew that. Beside me Mrs. Early's eyes were like saucers.

"But how did you get in there? And when?"

"Miss Madeleine. From the school, remember? I went and told her everything, how I wanted to be with you, an' all. She went and saw my Mum. My Mum's got the hots for this new fellow—"

There was a gasp from Mrs. Early: such things just weren't mentioned.

"—and she said as it—that it was probably for the best if'n I joined you. For the time being, at any rate."

"But why the laundry basket?"

"Miss Madeleine ain't—hasn't got no—any—money, seeing as—that she's only Miss Hepzibah's by-blow—" Another gasp from Mrs. Early. "—so it was my Mum's idea, to save the fare. Miss Madeleine got permission to check that your things were all packed proper—properly—and she shut me in and labelled me this morning before they came to take everything to the station."

I wanted to laugh, but kept my voice severe. "And how do I know all this is the truth?"

He fished about in his pockets. "Got a letter from Miss Madeleine."

Taking the crumpled envelope I opened it and rapidly scanned the contents. It seemed that Madeleine Moffat had hidden depths. Not only did her letter confirm all that Toby had said, but she added a few details about Toby's new "uncle" that Toby would never have told me, which also made me glad that he was away from home. She hoped I could find him a good position, suggesting that he deserved it and would benefit from further education. She closed by regretting she had not had the chance to bid me farewell, and wishing me well in my new life. In a hastily written postscript she added that she had taken over my position at the school, "Although I shall not, of course, be receiving any wages!"

So here I was, a sort of surrogate aunt, charged with finding Toby a secure position and a temporary home, on top of everything else I had to think about! I looked at the filthy, forlorn-looking boy and felt a rush of sympathy. It must have been quite an experience, being humped and bumped around on carts and trains, upside down or right way up, without food or water and never even sure if he were going to arrive safely.

"Does he stay, miss?"

"For the time being, Mrs. Early, until we can find him a suitable position. I realise this will mean extra work for you—"

She shook her head. "Think nothing of it. Just a bit more food on the stove, for I'll bet he has an appetite . . . And if I might suggest it, he could do with a bath!"

He certainly could. It was warm in the kitchen, and even where I stood I could smell the unwashed children stink of the school . . .

But Toby had turned to me in something like terror. "A barf? I ain't 'ad a barf since Gawd knows when!" Obviously the very thought had washed away any attempt at correct speech.

"Now listen to me; you came here uninvited and I could send you straight back to London, if necessary in custody. Don't think I'm not pleased to see you, but if I let you remain, then you must do exactly what I say, is that understood?" He nodded. "Now, Mrs. Early will give you something to eat—" Indeed, she was already ladling soup into a large bowl. "—And then you will have a bath, as she suggested. I myself bathe every day, and I shall expect you to do the same. Understood again?" He nodded once more, as if he couldn't trust himself to speak. I realised he must be feeling that perhaps he had made a mistake in leaving home, so I softened my tone and added: "And as soon as Mr. and Mrs. Early have dealt with you, you can come upstairs and we'll have a talk by the fire and tea and cake."

The housekeeper cut a large hunk of bread and set that and the soup on the table, pulled up a stool and motioned Toby to eat. He needed no further invitation. He fell on the food like a starved dog, and ate as untidily, stuffing the bread into his mouth until his cheeks bulged, and slurping the soup noisily. I opened my mouth to remonstrate, but behind his back Mrs. Early shook her head, conveying without words that she understood his hunger. He was obviously in good hands.

"I'll send him up when he's ready, miss. Don't worry, he'll be all right. And if you hear a noise or two, just ignore it. I doubt he's seen soap and water in a good while . . ."

So I ignored the yells and screams I heard some time later, as I brought Ky-Lin up to date with what had happened.

"I shall be curious to see your little friend . . ."

But I don't think either of us was prepared for what came up shortly after Mrs. Early's tea-tray, now with a bigger tea-pot and two large slabs of cake.

"Mr. Early will be up with him in a minute, Miss," she said without preamble. "We had to burn his clothes, they were that flea-ridden. Once the eggs get into the seams, there's nothing else to do." She looked uncharacteristically hot and bothered, with wisps of hair escaping from under her cap. "So, begging your pardon, we've put him in one of your uncle's old nightshirts, not having anything else to hand. Your uncle wasn't that tall, but the garment reaches his ankles, and we had to stuff the slippers with paper. He wouldn't wear the combies . . ." She turned to go, then came back and lowered her voice. "Thought you might like to know: poor lad was covered in bruises and two burns. Not where they would show, mind. Reckon it's a good thing he's away from all that."

Poor Toby! But I had expected as much from Madeleine's letter.

She turned to go again, but hadn't quite finished. "By the by, the nightcap was your uncle's too, but we thought it best to cover his head against the cold. It was the lice as well, you see . . ."

I didn't immediately, and it was only when Mr. Early ushered the boy in a couple of minutes later that I realised the extent to which he had been "done over," as he would have put it.

I had always seen him as a healthily tanned, curly-haired boy with a ready grin, but what I saw now was someone I hardly recognised. A thin pale-faced lad with freckles on his nose, wearing an absurd nightshirt and a nightcap with a bobble on the end, shuffling across the floor in over-large slippers. His eyes were big, dark-rimmed and frightened.

"Toby? Come and sit down and let me pour you some tea." He smelt of good, strong carbolic soap, and even his bitten nails had been scrubbed clean. "My word! I hardly recognised you. It's nice to see you so—so clean and tidy! Aren't you glad to get rid of all that London dirt and grime?"

He looked at me resentfully, his lower lip trembling, then suddenly snatched off the nightcap, to reveal that they had shaved him completely bald. "Just look what they done to me hair! Bald as a coot, I am!"

"It'll soon grow back," I soothed, even as I tried to hide my dismay at the loss of his normally luxuriant mop. He saw my expression and flushed angrily.

"See? You don't like it neither! Looks like a freak I does, a bloody freak!"

"Toby! Don't swear—"

" 'Nough to make a saint swear!" I heard a tiny snigger from the hidden Ky-Lin. "You ain't never 'ad your 'ead shaved, 'ave you? Bloody cold it is too: you'll 'ave me catch me death!"

"Oh, come on," I said placatingly. "I think it makes you look sort of—sort of *distinguished*. Like one of those marble busts we saw in that museum once, remember?" For sometimes I used to take him with me on my expeditions in London.

"They was wearing stone wigs," he said disgustedly. "And I ain't wearing no wigs, stone or otherwise. Right fright I'd look!"

I forebore to say that he looked a "right fright" at this moment. Leaning forward I touched his skull; it was strange to study the true shape of the head, so often hidden by hair, with its unaccustomed slopes, furrows and hollows. I examined my own head later, discovering for the first time my own bumps and lumps. Phrenology was an emerging science, I learned.

"Listen, Toby! Once your hair grows back—and it will, and quickly too—there'll be no more lice, no more nits, no more scratching. Doesn't that make any difference?"

"Not when you're as bald as an egg! Not when folks are goin' to look at you as if you came from a freak show! Not when the wind is whistling past your ears fit to freeze off your balls!"

"Toby!" I expostulated, though I was grinning inside, and there was another snigger from the hidden Ky-Lin. "That's enough of that! Tomorrow I will have you kitted out properly in the village, including a nice cap to hide your baldness. Now, drink your tea and eat your cake and I'll show you where you will sleep."

He ate his slice, and mine, and drank three cups of tea, with six lumps of sugar in each. Afterwards he looked much better, with a flush in his cheeks and a sparkle in his eyes.

I leant back in my chair, waiting till he had finished, initially loath to spoil his mood, but it had to be done.

"Look here,Toby, at the risk of repeating myself, I didn't invite you here, and I'm afraid you have come at rather a busy time as I shall be going away on a long journey very soon. Before I go, however,

I shall find you somewhere to live and, hopefully, some job or other to keep you busy. However, if I agree to take on the responsibility of doing this, you must promise to behave yourself, and keep your bad language to yourself. Understood?"

He nodded, and I relaxed. Not for long.

"Reckon I'll go with you, miss."

"Oh, no you don't!" I said. "This is nothing to do with you. I'm not taking you on an expedition to China!"

"Chiny? Must be a third of the way across the world!" His eyes were now dangerously bright. " 'Member that map we had in the classroom?"

Indeed I did. Probably about six feet by four, a Mercator projection, it was primarily meant to glorify the British Empire, with all the red bits showing that we seemed to have conquered half the world. Actually its most useful function was to hide the badly stained plaster of the wall, for as a map it was pretty useless. The greasy brown oilcloth had dimmed so that the red was pale pink, the blues and greens and yellows all dulled to a sort of dun colour, smearing the world into an ancient hoarding, rather than the bright tapestry it should have been.

"Used to look at that map all the time, miss, 'specially when the lessons were boring. I was nearest, see. Got to understand what the different shapes were: ours looking like a little old lady in a bonnet riding a pig to market; Italy like a posh boot, kicking little Sicily, France and Germany big squares—and Chiny and Roosia so big they could swallow up 'most everybody else, 'cept the triangle of India. And the rivers, miss! Like wriggly worms, they was—sorry, were—so it must take a long time to travel along them, though it looks shorter in a straight line . . ." He ran (temporarily) out of breath. I was fascinated; I had never heard him so animated, and had no idea he was so keen on geography—unless of course he was making the whole thing up in order to impress me and book his place on our expedition. If so, it was a very adroit performance, especially as it seemed to be spontaneous.

"I never knew you were so keen on maps and things," I said carefully.

"Oh, yes! I used to look at Miss Madeleine's sometimes when she took over if Miss Hardacre were—was—off. She's like you, buys books second-hand, but they got maps mostly, and plants and animals. Helped me make up my mind what I'm goin' to be: a 'Splorer."

"An explorer?" Small chance, Toby, I thought. You need to have a private income for that sort of thing.

"Yes, however long it takes. Reckon I could get a job, save a bit, then volunteer to join an expedition. Cook, carrier, collector—whatever, till I gets—get enough to strike out on me—my—own."

In spite of my misgivings, I was impressed. If his actions matched his determination, then he would succeed.

"China is out of the question, I'm afraid, but tomorrow or the day after I'll tell you where I'm going and why. It's quite a story . . ." I doubted he would believe it though. "Ah, here's Mrs. Early to tell us supper is ready . . ."

After seconds of mince and dumplings and treacle tart, I gave him a candle and showed him to his bedroom, explaining that I was just across the corridor, and introduced him to the commode in the bathroom.

"No guzunder?"

"No . . . ? Oh, I see. No chamber-pot! Relieve yourself now, and I'll see you into bed."

I could see he was overawed by his bedroom, with its spruce single bed and the fire that had been lighted to air the room. He allowed me to tuck him up, but when I turned back to say goodnight I saw he was out of bed and standing on the rug.

"What's the matter?"

"It's so *clean*, miss! And—and too *quiet!*"

"Rubbish! You'll soon get used to it. If you are going to be an explorer you have to get used to anything, and this will then seem like luxury. Blow out the candle and go to sleep . . ." A little harsh, perhaps, but it wouldn't do to accept everything he said at face value.

When I got back to the study Ky-Lin was nibbling at a couple of hazelnuts which I had collected for him earlier.

"Well, what do you think?"

"Not bad at all. A *little* more time in the sun, perhaps, but nice and sweet just the same . . ."

"No, not those. Toby!"

"We can take him with us," said Ky-Lin. "He's a likely lad."

"We can do no such thing! He's only a child."

"He's a bright thirteen- or fourteen-year old, and a trip like ours can only be good for him. Who else at his age and background gets a chance to travel like that? Where else would he hear different languages and have the chance to observe other life-styles? How do you know that the expedition wouldn't be an inspiration for him to follow his dream of being an explorer? Would you deny him all that?"

Put like that I was behaving like the classic wicked stepmother, denying a deserving child the chance of a lifetime because I was too protective, couldn't be bothered, didn't want the responsibility, saw too many drawbacks.

"He's not very strong." I said weakly. "It's a long way . . ."

"He's tougher than you think. You are a model for the sort of woman he has never known before. I think it would do him more harm if you leave him behind. Don't forget you are the only secure point he has in his life at the moment. One day he may go back to his own family, but from what the housekeeper said he's better off here for the time being.

The boy needs affection, praise, most of all to feel
he's needed. Here's your chance to make something
of him; a year or so travelling could make all the
difference. He's at a difficult time of life physically,
too, just growing up. The discipline of a long trek
will add muscles and inches, just wait and see." He
paused. "I don't say there won't be moments when
we shall want to throw him over the moon, but I still
think it's worth it. Besides," he added slyly, "how do
you know you will get on with your other travelling
companions? At least you know Toby will be on your
side . . ."

I had lost, and I knew it. "What about telling him
everything—including you?"

"The sooner the better," he said briskly. "Save me
all this chopping and changing. Er . . . could you
possibly find some more of these splendid nuts
tomorrow?"

I bathed, then sat up and read for a while before
seeking my bed. I decided to check on Toby before
I turned in, but was horrified to find his bed was
empty. Rushing down the stairs to find Mrs. Early,
I collided with her at the bottom. She had her finger to her lips.

"Hush, Miss . . . Just take a peep at this." She
opened the kitchen door quietly and I peered in. At
first I could see nothing untoward and then I glanced
at the fire: there, wrapped in one of the blankets
from his bed, the cat cuddled to his chest, was Toby,
fast asleep on the rug.

Mrs. Early had a smile on her face. "Reckon a soft
bed and being on his own is something he'll take a
time to get used to. Don't worry, I reckon he'll do
just fine!"

Chapter Thirteen

Educating Toby

In the morning I had to deal with an increasingly impatient Toby, forced by his lack of clothing to stay indoors, but Mrs. Early had given me an idea. I asked her to look out all the clothing my uncle had left, and she produced woolen shirts and sweaters, tweed jackets, caps and leggings, mufflers, gloves, shoes, a double set of underwear still in its tissue paper, handkerchiefs (ditto), and a lined cloak.

"I gave all the well-used materials worn next to the body—socks and underwear and such—to the Church for the poor, after I'd washed them," said Mrs. Early.

"You did right," I told her. "And you may do the same with those shoes and gloves, but I think we can make something of the rest for the lad." And after a tape-measure and a list for Mr. Early, he set off for the village and returned before luncheon with boots and felt slippers, socks and mittens for Toby, plus the village seamstress. She spent the afternoon, with Mrs. Early's help, cutting and snipping and sewing and altering. Although Toby was two or three inches shorter than my uncle, width-wise they were about the same, so it was only a case, for the most part, of shortening sleeves and hems and lifting waist-lines. They also made a good job of altering the caps to fit, so that by dark Toby had a full set of clothes. The seamstress took the rest back with her to alter at home, promising to return them by Monday.

Toby was as pleased as Mr. Punch, and strutted around in his finery, trying to catch glimpses of himself in any mirror he could find, but insisted on wearing his caps back-to-front, with the brims at the nape of his neck.

"All the fashion in Lunnon," he said. "Wish me mates could see me now!" He wanted to rush out straightaway and parade himself but luckily it started to rain.

He ate like a horse at all meals, but was reluctant when reminded about his daily bath.

"I had the scrub to end all scrubs yesterday! Why, I'll bet I lost most of my skin as well, see, I'm a diff'rent colour! Me—my Ma didn't believe in baths. Laundering, yes; bathing, no. Why, I might even shrink! Clothes do, sometimes . . ."

I had to smile. "Toby, people don't shrink from bathing! Don't you see, if you hadn't had a good scrub you would have dirtied the sheets on your bed and the nice clothes you're wearing? Just like you ruined the laundry in the hamper . . . I can't tell you how happy I am to at last have the stink of London out of my nostrils, and don't have to look for fleas or lice anymore. And you look and smell so much nicer now!"

He looked at me, then grinned, a smile that was both cheeky and endearing at the same time.

"Just testing . . ." He thought for a moment, then added: "Thanks for the clothes, and for letting me stay," and gave me a quick, embarrassed hug. Which was enough to forgive him everything—for the time being.

The following day being Sunday I was in two minds about taking Toby to church with us, guessing that the only previous religious teaching he had received were the prayers and Bible readings we had had at the school, but he seemed to think it was natural to accompany us. I told him he must sit quiet, listen to the sermon and behave reverently through the prayers and lessons.

"Din' I sit quiet for five years in that school? Din' I listen to every—well, nearly every—word that was said? Did I ever not behave myself?"

He was right. Many of the children that had a spark of life left in them, apart from eating enough to keep them alive and wearing enough to keep them warm, became bored and restless. Toby had been less trouble than most, because we had all given him books to look at and extra work to do; the others wanted to be entertained, rather than providing their own amusement.

In any event he behaved himself perfectly in church, absorbing the ritual bowings and scrapings only a half-second behind, following the prayers and lessons in the prayer-book I lent him, and singing the one hymn he knew lustily. This week the snobbish families weren't present—perhaps they had satisfied their curiosity the previous Sunday—so we were greeted with friendliness untainted with condescension.

Toby and I decided to walk back to the Hall and, freed from the restrictions of the service, he reverted to pure boy. He kicked at the heaps of leaves, whistle-copied the song of a robin, hunted the hedgerows for old nests, while I picked some more bright foliage and lingered here and there to find some more hazelnuts for Ky-Lin. I hoped it would be sooner rather than later that he revealed himself to the boy, because it was becoming increasingly difficult for us to find time on our own to plan our journey.

After luncheon it started to rain again, so I took

Toby on a tour of the rest of the Hall to keep him
occupied. Now all the rest of my uncle's artifacts had
been removed it was possible to appreciate just how
much space there was. Our feet echoed on the bare
wooden floors, on marble tiles, clattered up and
down endless stairways. We went, on Toby's insis-
tence, from cellar to attic and back again. Not that
the place was entirely empty; ordinary, plain tables
and chairs, a few bedsteads, cupboards, wardrobes
and chests had been left behind, as were some
threadbare rugs and runners and a pile of moth-
balled blankets.

He was enchanted with everything. Watching him
dash about I realised what little space he had had in
London, just tramping the same streets day after
day. To be sure there were parks and grassy spaces
in town, but he had never been encouraged to use
them, except when he rarely accompanied me on a
picnic, and in the large buildings like museums he
had to behave sedately. Here he romped on the way
back from church and was now behaving as if he
were attending a party. Although the place was as
clean as Mrs. Early and her girls had been able to
get it, he still managed to end up happily grubby.

As we went back to the door leading into the
Temple and tea, he slipped his hand into mine.

"You know what, miss? I reckon as this place would
make a wonderful holiday home for poor children—
or even an orphanage . . ."

After tea I pretended my eyes were tired, and had
him practice his reading by telling me a couple of
stories from my *Fairy-Tales by the Brothers Grimm*. He
seemed to enjoy "Rumpelstiltskin" best. After supper
we had a hand or two of cards and I sent him to
bed at half-past nine, with a length of string, to
practice some cat's cradles I had shown him.

I settled down with Ky-Lin, tracing-paper and one
of the more detailed maps to plot the first part of

our journey. We decided to take the railway to the coast, first ascertaining where we would get a ferry across to Holland, travelling on deck as it was cheaper, and then to the mouth of the Rhine where it debouched into the sea and on by barge or boat to southern Bavaria and then cross overland to the Danube in order to continue our journey eastward.

I had the tracing-paper in place, cut into strips like the old-fashioned ones, where you only concentrated on the bit you wanted to travel, with Ky-Lin holding down the farthest end with his hooves, when there was a light tap at the door and Toby entered.

"Couldn't get to sleep, miss: reckon it was those apple dumplings we had for supper. Can I come in for a bit?"

I glanced at Ky-Lin, expecting him to have changed into a figurine; instead he was just the same, except that he was perfectly still. He winked at me.

"You can come in for a few minutes," I said. "Kindly shut the door."

He sat down opposite me, and I could see he was about to ask about the maps, but then he caught sight of Ky-Lin.

"Gosh, miss, you've got a cuddly toy! Where'd you get him from? Never seen one like that before . . ."

"And you aren't likely to. This—this is a representation of a creature who comes from China. In the mythical past he and his brethren were guards and guides for a holy person called the Buddha. Part of his teaching was that you could be reborn again, depending on the way you lived this life, and that every living thing was trying to do the same. In other words even the smallest living thing is trying to better itself, and you must never destroy anything alive, plant or animal. A fly can be reborn as a bird, from there to a rabbit, and thence to a man . . . But if you are bad, then you regress."

"So you don't stamp on an ant in case it's on its

way up . . . I see." He leant forward. "Can I touch it?"

I glanced at Ky-Lin: another wink.

"Yes, but gently. He's fragile."

Toby reached out his right index finger and stroked it down Ky-Lin's spine. He drew it back, a look of surprise on his face. "Why, he's quite warm!"

"Yes."

"But toys aren't warm . . ."

"Well, he's not exactly a toy—"

As if in answer Ky-Lin winked at me again, then proceeded to act exactly like a mechanical toy. He made a whirring noise, then rose on his haunches to all four hooves, swung his head from side to side, then stepped slowly and jerkily round to face Toby, this time nodding his head, then sat down on his haunches again.

Toby's eyes were as round as the saucer-eyes of the first dog who guarded the treasure in the fairy tale, and he must have been holding his breath, for he let it out in a great sigh and a low whistle.

"Woweee! He's like those mechanical toys we saw in that museum once . . . Must be worth a bundle!"

"Irreplaceable," I agreed, trying not to giggle. "As far as I know, he's the only one left in the world."

"Did your uncle bring him back from his travels?"

"Yes, together with a couple of other things that I have inherited. Tell you about those in a minute."

He nodded towards Ky-Lin. "Does he do other things too?"

"Loads!" I was enjoying this and, from the look of it, so was Ky-Lin. "What would you like him to do?"

"Er—turn a somersault?" He put out his hand. "Hadn't you better wind him up again?"

"No. He goes for quite a long time without— without any external influences, don't you, Ky-Lin?"

The little creature nodded, obliged by starting his

whirring noise again, and turned a grave and well-controlled somersault. Then he executed a pirouette and fluffed out his tail to its fullest glory.

Toby clapped his hands, then frowned. "But how do you tell him to do these things? How did he know to do a somersault next?"

"Ah, that's part of his magic!" Ky-Lin sank back on his haunches, making a noise like a coiled spring running down.

Toby said: "You were going to tell me about the other things your uncle left? Are they toys as well?"

"No, definitely not." I looked across at Ky-Lin who gave me an almost imperceptible nod. "Listen, and I'll tell you a story." I fetched the manuscript out of the cabinet, where I had kept everything since Toby arrived, and gave him a potted version of Summer's story, explained about my uncle's will and told him of the choice I had made. He didn't seem at all surprised.

"Just what I would have decided, miss. Where's the egg then that we're taking back to Chiney—er, China?"

"The Eg *I* am taking back to China . . ." I brought it out of the cabinet and laid it on my shawl on the table.

"Does that do tricks as well?"

"Not as such, but it is growing larger every day, it's warm, and my uncle believed it holds something living. He also couldn't smash or crack it, so it is somewhat unusual. Pick it up . . ."

He did, although it was heavy, and examined it carefully, rolling it around in his hands.

"It *is* warm . . . So that's what a dragon's egg looks like." He turned a puzzled face towards me. "But there aren't any dragons, are there, miss, so how can that be a dragon's egg?"

"Most people would say there wasn't such a thing as a Ky-Lin, but there he is on the table." I took pity on him. "No, I didn't believe in dragons or Ky-Lins

or magic either when I first came here, but I have
a more open mind now. Circumstances have forced
me to reconsider, put it that way. My uncle didn't
believe either, but he changed his mind."

Toby continued to examine the Eg, shaking it,
scratching it with a bitten nail, even touching it with
his tongue. He held it to his ear, and suddenly his
face lit up.

"You're right! It *is* alive!"

"What do you mean—alive?"

"I can hear something inside. A soft, kind of flut-
tery sound. Listen!" He handed it to me, but I could
hear nothing. "Can't you hear it?" I shook my head.
"Well, I can! It may not be a baby dragon, but there's
something in there, sure as—sure as eggs is eggs!"
And he laughed at his own joke.

"That settles it," said Ky-Lin unexpectedly. "He
comes with us."

Toby stopped laughing and looked at me. "What
did you say?"

I shook my head. "Nothing. Not a word."

"Somebody said something . . ." He picked up the
Eg, listened. "Not this." He looked at Ky-Lin. "Does
he talk as well?"

"Sometimes . . ."

"Can you make him speak?"

"He speaks when he wants to—but only to me."

"Why?"

"Because I have a magic translator."

He was silent for a moment. "Where's the key?"

"What key?"

"The one to wind him up."

"There isn't one."

He frowned. "Then how do you make him work?"

"*I* don't. *He* does . . . Watch . . . Now you see
him—" I covered Ky-Lin with my hands and willed
him to change back to his ivory shape, which he did
in about ten seconds: "—and now you don't." I parted
my hands and there was the figurine.

Toby picked it up, looked at my hands, under the table and examined my sleeves.

"All right: where's he gone?"

"He's there." I pointed to the ivory.

"You're joshing me! It looks a bit like him, but it ain't him. That's not alive like he was. That can't move."

I sat back. "Don't be too sure! All right, Ky-Lin, show him!"

And in front of Toby's astonished gaze the ivory turned back to the "live" Ky-Lin, slowly and carefully, like a conjurer explaining a trick.

For a moment or two Toby was dumb, then: "If'n I hadn't seen it with my own eyes . . . Guess I'll believe anyfink now." He rose to his feet and bowed reverently as if he were in church.

"Tell him not to be an idiot," said Ky-Lin. "Tell him also that we are taking him with us."

I translated, and Toby's face lit up like an instant lamp. "I'm going with you? Gee-golly-gosh-an'-green Gorgonzola!" He jumped to his feet and did a little jig round the room. "Thank you, thank you, thank you!"

"Tell him the terms and conditions," said Ky-Lin, and I translated as he told me.

"Ky-Lin says I have to tell you that we have a long and difficult journey ahead of us. There will be two other companions with us, as yet unknown, and you will have to fit in with them. It will be well over a year before we return, if we're lucky. There will be dangers to face and it is not a task to be undertaken lightly. If you wish to change your mind about coming, no-one will blame you . . ."

"No way! I'm coming! I'll do anything, just anything! I'll carry the egg all the way to Chiney—China! I'll . . . I'll . . ."

"All right, that'll do! Come here and sit down." This was me talking. "Now, you said you would do exactly as you were told?"

"Yes, miss! Whatever you say . . ."

"And I say bed. Now. Immediately!"

"A little help," said Ky-Lin, and he bent forward and blew gently into the boy's face. "A little Sleepy-Dust . . ."

Within seconds Toby's eyes were drooping, and three minutes later he was in bed and sleeping soundly.

"Another of your tricks," I remarked to Ky-Lin as I fished a handful of hazelnuts out of my pocket.

"Thank you. Nothing special," he remarked modestly. "The Sleepy-Dust I mean, not these excellent nuts . . . I didn't want the lad to get over-excited."

"I hope you know what you are doing, taking him with us."

"So do I," he said. "So do I . . ."

The following morning Toby, clean, fed and shining, came and asked me if he could take Ky-Lin for a walk.

"Oh, I don't think that's a very good idea . . ."

His face crumpled. "But he *asked* me!"

"He did?"

I fetched the figurine out of the cabinet.

"But he hasn't been out of here today. How could he?"

"He asked me—sort of in my mind. Out loud in my mind. Honest!"

"He's right," said Ky-Lin, coming to life again. "I didn't know, however, whether he had understood."

"But what do you want to do?" I asked, the tiniest stab of jealousy prickling. After all, he had never asked me to take him out.

Toby answered for him. "He wants to practise," he said, frowning to himself. "He wants—he wants . . ." and he held his hands out in front of him like a fisherman demonstrating his catch. "He wants to practise growing big."

Ky-Lin nodded at me. "The boy's a natural. If we

go up Bracken Hill, then perhaps I can get rid of this stiffness. I'm afraid I'm a little rusty, as you would put it. And if you would ask the boy to look out for a few nuts or berries?"

"Right, Toby." I described where he was to go, and the search for food for Ky-Lin. "Blackberries—you know what they look like—and haws and hips. Dark red smaller ones, and large orangey ones." I had a good idea. "As it's a fine day, how about me asking Mrs. Early to make up a picnic basket, and I'll join you at lunch-time?"

So, later in the day, after a morning mending, sewing and making lists, I walked up through the bracken with a basket filled with cold egg and ham pie, Russian salad, cheese and onion pasties and Conference pears, with a flagon of ginger beer.

When I reached the top of the hill however, there was no-one to be seen. I was sure, however, that I had heard a giggle from Toby as I climbed up, so I sat down and let the breeze cool my cheeks and ruffle my uncovered hair, content to await whatever surprise was in store. I didn't have to wait long. There was a sudden war-whoop and onto the rocks over my head sailed a pony-sized Ky-Lin with Toby on his back.

They teetered for a moment on the summit, then Ky-Lin gained his balance.

"Great, ain't it?" said Toby, slipping off Ky-Lin's back. "What's in the basket, then?"

Ky-Lin folded himself down to a reasonable size, and we all tucked in, Toby and I with the hamper, Ky-Lin with an assortment of nuts, fruit and berries Toby had provided. I was just packing the hamper with the empties when Toby said: "I wonder who came in the carrier's cart . . ."

"When?"

"When you was climbing the hill. Came down the drive with a couple of people in it, and now there's smoke coming out of another chimney. Look down: you can see it from here . . ."

"Could be our fellow-travellers," said Ky-Lin to me.

"I'd better go see," I said. "Toby, bring back the picnic basket," and gathering up my skirts, I ran back down the hill, to find a flustered Mrs. Early in the kitchen, her mouth drawn down, brewing a large pot of tea.

She didn't wait for my questions.

"Two of them. Says they're the ones what's going with you. Their luggage is in the hall. Shall I make up the other two bedrooms?"

"I'd better have a word with them first . . ."

"Doubt whether you'll be best pleased," she said, looking more disapproving than ever. "Not what I'd have chose myself . . . I lit a fire in the morning-room. You want me to bring the tea in there?"

"Yes, please . . ." I couldn't understand her ill-humour, until I tidied my hair, changed into slippers and walked down to the morning-room and opened the door.

Then I understood part of her temper immediately.

Chapter Fourteen

Unwelcome Guests

"Mr. Cumberbatch!" I was aware I was repeating myself, but I couldn't help myself. And after I had thought to get rid of him forever, here he was turning up again like the proverbial bad penny!

"Your servant, Miss Lee." He rose from the fireplace, where he had been warming his hands. "I have here a package of money and a letter from Mr. Swallow." He handed them over. Taking a paper-knife from the writing-desk I slit the letter open.

It read, after the usual salutations: "*I am sending you Mr. Cumberbatch to accompany you on your journeys, on behalf of our firm, under your uncle's instructions. I have decided to send him as the other members of our firm are more advanced in years, and he is both young and fit. I might add, however, that he is unwilling to undertake this task, but I hope he will become reconciled as time goes on. We have equipped him as well as we could for his travels. He carries with him the moneys for your journey, which I must ask you to receipt as provided.*

"*He will be accompanied by the private investigator*

143

*your uncle also insisted upon, a Mr. Danny Duveen. He
has been provided with moneys for his travelling outfit."*
He ended up wishing us well.

I put the letter and the packet of money down
carefully on the writing-desk, realising that I was pro-
longing the moment when I would have to turn
around and face my unwelcome fellow-traveller. He
didn't want to go, and I didn't want him either! What
a pickle . . . I couldn't imagine a more dreary companion: dreary and useless.

Mrs. Early provided the diversion I needed by
bringing in a tray of tea, so I was able to greet him
pleasantly enough, offer him a cup of tea and assure
him his room would be ready as soon as possible.
All this while I had half an eye on the other occu-
pant of the room, seeming intent on examining one
of the prints on the wall. He was wearing a heavy
caped coat reaching almost to his ankles, as if he
wasn't very tall. I wasn't sure whether his turned back
was indicative of boorishness, politeness as I spoke
with Mr. Cumberbatch, or shyness.

"Did you both have a pleasant journey?" I asked,
preparing to pour the tea.

"Not particularly. Dem' smoky carriage and the
dem' carrier was late—"

"Mr. Cumberbatch: we do not use language like
that in this house, nor will I tolerate it on the journey. You are not in the office now."

My other guest clapped his hands as he turned
round. "Well said, Miss Lee, well said! I always say
you have to watch your mouth in front of the ladies,
so I do!"

I nearly dropped the milk jug.

"You! What on earth are you doing here?" The
man who now faced me was even more familiar
than Mr. Cumberbatch: it was the importunate
young "poet" who had lived for a while at my
lodgings, and who had both pestered me with his
poems and followed me round wherever I went.

What was his name? Random, that was it: Richard Random.

He came forward, flung his coat off over a chair and extended his hand.

"Hello again, Miss Lee! Danny Duveen at your service . . . Mine's two sugars and only a splash of milk."

"But—but you're Richard Random!"

"Was, Miss Lee, was! That was only an alias, if you know what I mean. In my line of work it is essential that you move along and leave no clues behind you. So, the name changes with the job, and so do the disguises. If you had any idea how hard it was to write that dreadful doggerel! I did say two sugars, did I not?"

So this was the man on whom my uncle had depended for his report on me! And I had always thought it was my hidden attractions . . . I had to admit he had been both clever and persistent. As for "disguise," he looked little different: unshaven, untidy, unruly black hair falling over his forehead, very blue eyes. His clothes, too, had seen better days. They were decidedly grubby, ill-fitting, a little out of date, with a compensating touch of the exotic: a multi-coloured scarf, a sporty yellow waistcoat, a green handkerchief hanging out of one pocket, a flashy red-stoned ring. He looked as if he had rummaged very quickly through Old Sol's second-hand clothes shop, or was about to take his turn at a provincial music-hall, singing Irish ballads.

Still, it had been my uncle's wish that he accompany me, and at least he had more spirit than the lack-lustre Claude. Meanwhile the tea was not getting any warmer, so I lifted off the cosy and poured to suit them both; it didn't surprise me one bit to find that Claude preferred his very weak with no sugar.

Mrs. Early tapped at the door to inform me that fires had been lit in the bedrooms, and was the luggage to be taken up?

"Please. Have you seen Master Toby?"

"He's in the kitchen with us, miss."

"Would you have him join me in here? And we will have supper in the dining—room at seven, if that is not too inconvenient?"

"No trouble at all, miss. I'll have hot water sent up to the gentlemen's rooms a half-hour before."

In came Toby a couple of minutes later, obviously having been taken in hand by Mrs. Early, for his hands and face were clean and his hair combed.

"Gentlemen, I would like you to meet Toby, my ward. He will be accompanying us on our travels. Toby, the gentleman on my right is Mr. Cumberbatch from the solicitor's office, the other—"

"But I know's him!" cried Toby, pointing at Danny Duveen. "He came round my ma's a couple of times, asking all sorts of questions 'bout you! He's just a snooper, miss!"

"And your ma sent me away with a flea in my ear, didn't she Toby me boy? Or rather a soapy fist round my head . . ."

"Only after you kicked over a bucket of lye!"

" 'Twas an accident, me boy, a pure accident! Tripped up over the damn' thing, didn't I? Could hardly see a hand in front of my face, down in that steam-filled basement you call a laundry—"

"Mr. Duveen! Toby! That'll do . . . And my remarks about swearing to Mr. Cumberbatch apply equally to you, Sir! Is that understood?"

"Slip of the tongue, Miss Lee, slip of the tongue . . . Won't happen again, I assure you!"

Now why was I so certain that it would?

Supper was an uncomfortable affair. In spite of the fire the room was chilly through lack of use, and although I was used to correct table manners, it was obvious my two guests were not, and their sloppiness affected Toby. Not only was he overawed with the formality of the room, the best china and cutlery, the attempts at polite conversation, he was also thrown by the fact that both men picked up their chicken bones and chewed them, quite contrary to the instructions I had given him only a day or two since, that one only picks up the bones of game-birds.

As a consequence of all this he managed to slurp his soup in one of the many silences, spilled his gravy on the cloth as he was pouring it, one of his roast potatoes shot across the table and onto the floor and he ate it instead of leaving it, he forgot and tried to eat his peas off his knife, so that by the time we came to the tapioca pudding he was too disheartened to choose five of the stewed plums to go with it, to make sure he was the "Rich Man," living in a mansion this year and clad in silks although that game he had always enjoyed working out.

Not that the conduct of the other two was any better. Claude's manners showed some promise, although using his cheese knife to pare his nails was an excruciating sight and he drank his wine in great gulps as though it were water or ale. Danny insisted on second helpings, and left half of them; he kept his elbows on the table and his cutlery at either side of the plate and talked with his mouth full. They both belched.

At the end of the meal I rose to my feet and surveyed the debris.

"Right, gentlemen! Pigs usually eat from troughs, but I will be lenient and elevate you to the kitchen from now on! I cannot have you setting my ward a bad example. I will ask Mrs. Early now to serve you tea or coffee in the morning-room, and will expect you for breakfast—in the kitchen—between eight-thirty and nine. Goodnight. Come, Toby!"

And I swept out leaving them looking as though lightning had struck.

The following morning Toby and I enjoyed our breakfast of porridge, bacon and eggs, toast and

marmalade in peace and warmth. Afterwards we went
up to the study and I taught him a little more about
the maps we would use, and he helped me with the
tracing. I had asked Mrs. Early to light a fire in the
morning-room and left a message for Claude and
Danny that I would meet them there at eleven for
coffee. I learned later that Claude turned up for cold
porridge at nine-forty-five, and Danny didn't appear
at all.

At eleven-fifteen I was still waiting for them to
appear, seething inside, but when they eventually
arrived I saw at once what had held them up. They
were unshaven, apologetic and obviously under the
influence. Either one or both had bottles in their
rooms.

I took the cold coffee back to the kitchen, ordered
some more, extra strong, and left Mrs. Early with a
special directive. The coffee sobered them up a little,
but as I tried to explain our expedition, even showing
them some maps, I might as well have been talking
to my five-year-olds at the School. At last I gave up,
instructing them both to take a walk to the village
and back to "freshen up" (though I didn't mention
the fact that I knew they had hangovers) and
instructed them to return in time for luncheon.

This was a big mistake.

Neither of them turned up for the meal, and it
was growing dark by the time they staggered up the
drive, full of song and strong ale. It was no use rep-
rimanding them, they were past it, so I asked Mr.
Early to "escort" them up to their rooms, supperless,
making sure there were chamberpots under their
beds. He was to call them at seven-thirty in the
morning, informing them that there was plenty of
hot water for bathing and shaving in the bathroom,
and that they were expected to be down for breakfast at eight-thirty prompt.

That morning we all breakfasted together. A
couple of pale, shaky, but clean-shaven young men

spooned down their porridge with little enthusiasm
but the kedgeree went down better and by the time
they reached the toast and the second pot of tea was
on the table, they were at least communicating, even
if it was only "pass the butter/any more toast/where's
the sugar/another cup of tea" type of speech.

After that it was a lot easier as they apparently had
very little spare cash left, and the stores of liquor they
had brought with them rapidly diminished. The
instruction I had given Mrs. Early on that first morning was to examine their luggage—snooping perhaps,
but I was a young woman on my own, charged with
leading an expedition with two unknown men as my
escorts, and no chaperone. So it was up to me to
find out as much as I could about my erstwhile companions before we started.

It appeared that Claude's luggage, apart from a
couple of bottles of sweet sherry, was of the conventional sort—well-worn but clean and mended underwear and a couple of rather threadbare suits. He
obviously was a mother's boy, because his pocket-
handkerchiefs were embroidered in blue with his
initials, a jar of menthol and eucalyptus cream and
another of corn-cure were wrapped in tissue, there
were lavender sachets and a silver-framed photograph
of a beaky-nosed matron, the spit of her son. The
travelling clothes the solicitors had provided were
adequate, though when I checked them later with
him, it was obvious he needed stronger boots and
a travelling cape.

Danny Duveen's luggage, such as it was, was a different matter altogether. While Claude's clothes and
effects were in a battered but well-polished suitcase,
Danny only possessed a crumpled cardboard case
which, according to Mrs. Early, contained the sum
total of six whisky bottles, three empty, three full,
two dirty shirts and some unmentionables, also filthy,
two electro-plated hip-flasks (empty), a packet of what
appeared to be recommendations for jobs, all in the

same hand, two marked decks of cards and another envelope of what Mrs. Early described as Dirty Photographs in capital letters and a reddened face. (For the record I examined these later and can only report that I had a good laugh.)

What Mrs. Early appeared to be most shocked about in Danny's luggage was not the dirt or the photographs, but the lack of nightshirts: apparently it was a crime above all others not to go to bed decently clad. I forebore to tell her that I had done just the same in those stuffy August nights in London when the only relief was to cast everything off and open the window to one's nakedness.

So. Claude was more or less provided for, apart from stronger boots and a cloak, but Danny had nothing, as far as I could see, and was probably a con-man, a gambler, fond of the bottle, had little use for hygiene, and was not above indulging his lower tastes with a little wishful thinking.

I discussed all this with Ky-Lin, who had met both Claude and Danny, via Toby's pocket, a couple of times. He was the one who advised me to treat them as a couple of recalcitrant schoolboys who wouldn't learn their tables, and now advised me to go through what remained of my uncle's clothes for Danny, remarking that he was afraid I would still have to use some of my own money to kit them out.

"Of course," he added helpfully, "if that Irish fellow decides he doesn't want to go, then we can discount him, quite legally, I believe."

No chance.

I had agreed with Claude to furnish him with stouter boots and a cloak and, I must say, he was properly grateful, but when it came to Danny . . .

First of all I asked why he had not come properly equipped and got the sort of answer I expected: no list and no money. "Then what happened to the moneys supplied to you by the solicitors?"

"Oh, that . . . Well now to tell you the truth I

thought those were to sort of set me on me way. Pay off the odd debt or two, you know . . ."

"Instead of which you got drunk as a skunk and gambled the rest away," I said equably.

"How did you—? Oh, come on now, Miss Lee. Darlin' girl, a lad has got to have his bit of fun before going on a life or death expedition, now doesn't he?"

"Not with somebody else's money," I said firmly. "And I am not your 'darling girl': please remember that. And may I ask where your ordinary clothes are? Shirts, suits, shoes?"

He spread his arms wide, with what he hoped was a disarming grin. "In rags or in hock, truth to tell!"

"That's better. I prefer the truth. Now, if my uncle hadn't considered you capable of undertaking this journey . . . You can, of course, back out if you wish to, and no hard feelings?"

He looked horrified. "Oh, no, I'm going with you! Otherwise I don't get—"

"You don't get what, exactly?"

"The fifty quid the solicitors said your uncle promised."

So that was it. Right, Mr. Duveen would get just as much as he deserved and no more. I went through my uncle's belongings once again and found that he and Danny were of a size—had that been an added attraction I wondered—and that I could provide Danny with nightshirts, combinations, shirts, jackets, socks, caps, gloves and even shoes which needed no further alteration and which, luckily, Mrs. Early had not yet passed on. There was even a little-used pair of walking boots. So, in the end, all he would need was a travelling-cloak and, like Claude, a haversack and blanket. I heaved a sigh of relief.

Having sent off for the last of our requirements, I settled back for a few days, with Ky-Lin's help, trying to make our guests better prepared for the journey. By now they were what I would call "house-trained"—in other words they were bathed, shaven, appeared on time for meals, were polite and (more or less) tidy. That they were bored was quite obvious. Neither of them were readers or walkers or naturalists and the idea of helping Mr. Early in the garden was anathema to their town souls. There was no doubt they missed the metropolis. Most of the time they spent playing cards, probably with Danny's marked decks, so Ky-Lin and I decided a little further education was necessary.

One morning after breakfast I brought them up to the study, for a lesson in map-reading.

Their reaction was unexpected.

"What do we need to look at maps for?" said Claude, covering his mouth at the last minute over a tremendous yawn.

"So as you can find your way should we get lost on the way," said Toby, unfortunately catching the yawn and repeating it.

"Why then should we get lost?" asked Danny. "Sure the way is plain enough, is it not?"

I had a feeling of misgiving.

"Tell me," I said. "What have you two been told about the journey?"

Claude was the first to answer. "Mr. Swallow told me that you were taking one of your uncle's artifacts back to where it came from, that you were given a year to do it in, and that I was to accompany you to make sure the conditions were fulfilled."

"Did he tell you where we were going?"

He shook his head. My heart sank.

"And you?" I asked, turning to Danny.

"The solicitors said that I would get fifty pounds for acting as an escort while you went on a journey for your dead uncle."

"Do *you* know where we are going?"

"No, but at least it'll be better than here . . ."

I threw up my hands in despair and even Toby looked disbelieving.

"Mean to say as you two gents don't know we're

walking to Chiney and back with a dragon's egg and
a—" He clapped his hand over his mouth just in time;
I had warned him not to mention Ky-Lin.

"Chiney?"

"I believe the boy means China, Claude me lad,"
said Danny. "Full of little yellow men."

"But isn't that a long way away?"

"Nearer than the other side of the moon," said
Danny. "And they've probably got a decent rail service most of the way."

"I hope it's not too hot," said Claude. "I always
get hay-fever in the summer."

"It's the thought of the rice that's putting me off
right now. I never fancied rice pudding, even with
a dollop of me mam's gooseberry jam . . ."

"Can't you send it by post?"

I decided it was time to intervene, but before I
could open my mouth Toby took over.

"Let me, miss. Reckon I could put it straight and
quicker." And he did. He explained as you would to
under-fives about my uncle's will, got the original
manuscript from the cabinet and briefed them on
Summer's journey and ended by saying that my uncle
believed the Eg, which he also produced, belonged
to the dragons. He ended by dashing Danny's hopes
of a rail service and Claude's of using the post,
explaining to the latter that a dragon's egg was far
too precious to entrust to a postman, and anyway
they probably didn't have them in China.

I couldn't have put it better myself.

They both looked rather white when Toby had finished, though Claude tried a last-ditch stand.

"But there aren't any such things as dragons," he
said. "We all know that!"

"This is what we have all been taught," I said.
"Dragons don't exist and never did. Like fairies, elves,
gnomes, brownies, goblins, trolls, ogres, giants,
witches and wizards. If so, why are there so many
legends, myths, folk-tales? I admit that I now have

an open mind, and an open mind, gentlemen, is what you will need if you are to journey with us!"

"We've come all this way to—to take a lump of stone to China? Was your uncle out of his senses?"

"I don't believe so, Mr. Duveen. As I said, I have an open mind, but certain happenings, which I am not at liberty to discuss, have convinced me that there is more to this 'lump of stone' than we imagine. Besides I am bound to this journey now, else I renounce all hope of inheriting Hightop Hall. So you see, I have a vested interest." Perhaps that would appeal to his mercenary instincts.

It did. "Would there be any treasure at the end of all this? If you're talking about legends, then they all had it that dragons were hoarders of fabulous jewels . . ."

"I doubt it," I said. "I think our rewards will be less substantial. If we succeed, I shall inherit this place; Toby will have had the adventure he's always wanted; for you, Mr. Cumberbatch, this is just part of your job, but it should prove more interesting than sitting behind a desk all day; Mr. Duveen, it means you will be free of debt for the time it takes to get there and back. That should be some incentive." I looked round at them all. "Now, shall we have a look at the maps?"

The next two weeks were pretty hectic. Eventually everything I had ordered came through, including two lengths of lightweight rope, a compass—"In case I'm not at hand all the time," said Ky-Lin—containers for salt, tea, sugar and water and tin plates, mugs and cutlery. It all sounded dreadfully Spartan and rather intimidating.

"Are you sure we hadn't better take a frying-pan and a stew-pot?" I said to Ky-Lin, intending frivolity, but he answered me seriously enough.

"I don't believe we shall need those, initially at least. And in order not to weigh us down too much, I suggest we buy them on the way."

Instead of heavy leather suitcases I had ordered two wicker ones, lined with oiled silk against the rain. They were much lighter, and it was agreed that Claude and Danny would share one, Toby and I the other, keeping items to a minimum, which meant underwear and spare shirts and sweaters, and any personal items we couldn't do without. Toby and I were easy, but the other two quarrelled until the day we left over what they considered essential.

As for the haversacks, it was agreed that Toby would carry the Eg, wrapped as usual in my shawl, and extra towels and toiletries; the men would take the ropes, plus the crockery and cutlery, and I would carry the maps, papers, sewing things and a small pair of binoculars. We also carried a blanket each. I was encumbered with a moneybelt, which I had no intention of handing over to either of the two men, although it was heavy, once I had changed the money into smaller coin.

Strangely enough getting all the paperwork through had been the most difficult. To get passports and all the requisite permissions from the embassies in London had proved frustrating. France, Germany and Bavaria were easy enough, and Russia came through at the last moment, but from China we heard nothing.

The date was agreed, we booked ahead on the overnight ferry to Holland and, through the same firm, a trip by ferry on the first stage of our journey up the Rhine. Mrs. Early packed whatever she could that would last us through at least part of our journey: salt, tea, sugar, dried fruits, shelled nuts, apples, long-lasting fruitcake and parkin, pickled eggs, a tin of cocoa, Liebig's extract of meat, packets of pepper, a jar of ready-mixed mustard, home-made chutney and pickles and a well-smoked ham. By the time these had been distributed between our haversacks, we were all visibly sagging.

That was not all—for the first two days of the

journey the housekeeper had made sandwiches, pies, tarts, cakes, buns and biscuits, and included two large flagons of lemonade and barley water, which meant we had to burden ourselves with a huge hamper as well, but at least it would save money.

Hiring a small carriage from the village we made good time to catch the four-fifteen slow train to the coast, boarded the ferry and settled down on deck later in the evening. Leaning on the rail, I looked back at the lights of the coast and the still-shining blur that I took to be the white cliffs of Dover, a popular landmark.

It wasn't a cold night, nor was there much sea running, yet I had been shivering. I found it difficult to believe that we were really on our way and that here I was taking a trip by sea for the first time.

Toby joined me, and Ky-Lin leapt from one of his pockets to stand on the rail between us.

"Not superstitious are you, miss?"

"Don't think so Toby . . . Why?"

" 'Cos tonight's All Hallows' Eve—Samain, they used to call it."

"A good omen," interrupted Ky-Lin. "That was the night Summer set off on her travels, so she told me . . ."

But in spite of his optimism, I found myself shivering again.

BOOK TWO

"Over the hills and far away."
—John Gay

Chapter Fifteen

Slow, Slow, Quick-quick Slow

I threw my corsets into the upper reaches of the Rhine, and watched them bob up and down in our wake, their strings trailing behind like the tentacles of an octopus.

It was strange to feel a cotton shift next to my skin instead of thinly covered whalebone, even stranger to know I could wriggle about without restriction. I had worn stays or corsets ever since I could remember—probably five or six years old—and the only relief had been at night when I could curl up in my nightdress and rub away the marks left on my skin. But over the years I had grown so used to lacing myself up each morning that it had become as automatic as brushing one's hair or teeth.

I shivered a little—not from cold, for I had plenty of layers of wool on underneath—but from my daring. No lady went around without her corsets. I wondered if that had led to the term a "loose woman."

Toby joined me at the rail, handing me a cup of coffee and a hunk of garlic sausage on rye bread. The corsets were still in sight.

"Cor! Me mam wears them!"

"Those . . ."

"Those, then. Bet they was—"

"Were."

"Were uncomfortable. Pinchy. Me mam was always getting bits of her stummick stuck in the laces . . ."

"Yes, well . . ." I shivered again.

"You chilly, miss? Can't've been that warm . . ."

"No, they weren't. Just feels strange without them."

"Better, I hopes, seein' as they's gone forever. Less you wants to swim for 'em that is."

I gave up trying to correct him. Usually he was very good, but if something unusual happened he tended to slip back into Cockney.

"No, no swimming . . ." I wouldn't have lasted two minutes in that water anyway. Thin sheets of ice broke off against the sides of the string of slow-moving barges as we chugged up the narrowing river, soon to reach the limit of navigable waterway.

It was now mid-December, and we had had a mixed journey. We had slipped easily through Holland, watching the windmills with their slow-moving sails, imagining the flat fields blossoming with tulips in the spring and admiring the ingenious Dutch in their efforts to keep the ever encroaching North Sea at bay. Our transport had been comfortable, with good food and clean linen, but unfortunately that part ended at Koblenz. Apparently the ferry ran no farther at this time of year, a fact that the firm that booked us had omitted to mention.

We complained and protested (through Ky-Lin) that we had paid to be carried farther, but the captain just shrugged his shoulders and referred us to our tickets which only specified transport up the river, "according to the usual rules and regulations." So we would have to find something a lot cheaper, to make up for the money we had lost. Thus the barge we were on now.

We had switched from one mode of travel to another, as and when we could find it, but mostly by river transport, although a couple of times we went along the bank by wagon, cart or stage, rather than waste time waiting for a barge or ferry. The trouble was, it was all too slow for our purpose. True, there was time to admire the wonderful scenery and marvel at the fairy-tale castles perched impossibly high on the cliffs above the river, but I was conscious all the time of how swiftly time was passing.

"We take to the road tomorrow," said Ky-Lin, appearing from my pocket. "Then we should travel faster. Don't give up yet!"

He seemed to be able to read my thoughts, was always encouraging and had been invaluable in translating our wants; he would perch on my shoulder, hidden by scarf, and make my requests in my own voice whispering the reply so only I could hear it! All I had to do was pretend I was talking and try to synchronise my actions. Magic as good as I had ever seen.

Both Claude and Danny, knowing nothing of Ky-Lin, were amazed at my linguistic prowess. Although I was still "Miss," we were now on Christian-name terms. This had come about after we had crossed the English Channel for they had both been as sick as dogs in spite of the calm sea, and all pretence of male superiority went overboard together with their suppers, and "Miss Lee" had disappeared in "Please help me, Miss Sophy!" and "Mr. Cumberbatch" in "Shut up, Claude, it's not as bad as that!" and "Mr. Duveen" became "Serves you right for making such a pig of yourself, Danny!"

"How will we travel?" I asked Ky-Lin.

"Well, there will be some public transport—coaches and the odd railway—but I think it might be better to hire a coach partways."

"But surely that will cost the earth!"

"Not necessarily. Much more convenient and we can travel by a more direct route; there are plenty of posting-houses between here and the Danube, and that is our next target."

It started to snow, great blobs whirling out of the grey sky, and we slipped and skidded on the icy deck as we made our way to our cabins. Claude and Danny were in the saloon, a polite term for the place where we ate as well. They were playing cards, Danny wrapped up to the eyeballs in coat, cloak, scarves and mufflers, while Claude, who seemed to have developed a permanent sniff and a drip on the end of his nose, was complaining bitterly about Danny's winning streak. I suspected that the latter cheated, but there was no way of finding out.

We retired to my cabin, where I continued as best I could with Toby's education, with Ky-Lin's help. He knew more about everything than I did, anyway.

The following day we disembarked at a small town called Schwarzberg, which Ky-Lin said meant Blackhill, after the mountain behind; although it belied its name, being now covered with last night's snow. We visited all the livery stables, but found there was no private transport to be hired, so we repaired to an inn by the quay for luncheon, and to discuss our next move.

Toby was gazing out the window at the barge unloading when he suddenly made a rather crude exclamation, which I didn't bother to try and understand, but obviously he had been struck with some idea.

"Look out there, folks: what do you see?"

"Barges unloading," said Claude, wiping his nose for the umpteenth time. "Why?"

"Yes, but what's waiting to be loaded up?"

Danny craned his neck. "Looks like logs of wood to me . . ."

"Exactly!" Toby was obviously bursting to impart

his theory. "And what did we bring on the way up?"

"Sugar, dried fruit, flour, toys, barrels of wine, hunting rifles and ammunition, thick eiderdowns . . ." I was beginning to see which way his mind was working.

"Exactly," he said again. "Don't you see? They brings up what they needs up here, stuff they can't make themselves, and vikky-verky—sends back their wood in exchange."

"So?"

Toby was still patient. "So, Master Claude, just where does all that stuff from the barge go to?"

"Sure it goes into the shops here, I suppose." said Danny.

"Place ain't big enough. And what about all those parcels and packages they was carrying?" I let him tell it his own way, though by now I was smiling.

"There must be lots an' lots of small towns and villages round here what wants the goods, and someone got to take them there, and that is why we couldn't hire no transport!" He was flushed and bright-eyed. "So all we've got to do is find a carrier who's going our way and beg a lift!"

After that it was easy. Ky-Lin and I found a man who was taking a covered wagon to the next village on our way, staying overnight with his brother, then travelling on to the next town, and was glad of our company, promising to find us overnight accommodation. When we attempted to pay him for his troubles later, he refused, adding: "The more the people, the fewer the wolves," which Ky-Lin and I didn't bother telling the others, not sure whether the wolves he referred to were human or lupine. I did notice, however, that he carried a loaded rifle by the driver's seat. What he did accept, however was the offer of Mrs. Early's empty food hamper, which we still carried with us, explaining that it would be useful for carrying his racing pigeons.

And so it went on. We accepted lifts when we
could, used public transport when there was any,
hired the occasional chaise and were sometimes holed
up for days by bad weather, spending Christmas in
a cheery little inn in a forest and stuffing ourselves
silly with roast goose, sausages, pork and masses of
potatoes: roast, boiled, baked, grated and fried, or
mashed. We also ate vast quantities of cabbage, fermented with white wine, which they called
"Sauerkraut," and of course there were trays of gooey
cakes, sweet biscuits and candies. There was also a
tree, decorated with pretty bows, a custom the
Hanoverian-born Prince Albert, the late husband of
our dear Queen, had apparently introduced to
England.

By the middle of February we were well on our
way, the snows had begun to melt, the going was
much easier and traffic on the roads more frequent.
I was still worried about the money situation, but our
spending had slowed down somewhat. We were all
in good health—thank God!— although Claude still
nursed his perpetual sniffle. Danny still sneaked off
for the occasional drink—I had to give them a little
pocket-money for their regular needs, but while Toby
saved his and Claude spent his on luridly coloured
picture-postcards to send home to his mother or on
throat-lozenges, Danny spent his on strong beer or
spirits.

Nevertheless, both men were improving: Claude
was becoming less stuffy and staid, and Danny could
be the life and soul of the party, if he chose. Toby
was growing and filling out by the day, making a real
bonny lad, and every day to him was a new discovery.

In February we reached Bavaria and the upper
reaches of the Danube, and with the better weather
we made good progress from Neuburg to Ingolstadt,
Ingolstadt to Regensburg, then Straubing, Deggendorf
and Passau. In March we crossed the border into

Austria and really felt spring had arrived. If Bavaria had been charming, Austria was even better. The people were warm and welcoming, indulging in music at the least excuse; pipes, flutes, fiddles, trumpets and drums all sounded from one house to another, and even the school-children carried their recorders to school.

We spent three days in Linz, due to the unwelcome return of late snows, but we took the opportunity to repair our wardrobes: stockings and summer underwear for me, thinner shirts and socks for the men and Toby. As the touring season had now begun, we decided to take one of the tourist boats as far as Vienna, which we had heard was the most beautiful city in Europe.

A tour of the city was included in our tickets, although it passed so swiftly it seemed we were whirled past the fine buildings and statues without a chance to get more than a glimpse, but we did also get tickets to a concert in the evening, dominated by the divine waltzes of the brothers Strauss. Although the favourite was apparently the "Blue Danube"—a misnomer if ever I heard one: it was a sort of brownish-grey—my favourite was the "Emperor" with its full, sweeping tones and at times I could almost imagine being clad in silks and being borne aroud a vast ballroom in the arms of one of the handsome, uniformed officers who seemed to twirl their moustachios on every street-corner . . .

Their uniforms were so figure-hugging, the girls at boarding-school would have gone into swoons over them—

For almost the first time in my life I felt longings of a strange kind, a sort of yearning to be held tight in masculine arms; I wondered if it had anything to do with throwing away my corsets. Did I miss their tight restrictions, or was it more the general looseness of body bringing on a looseness of the emotions?

I subdued these feelings fiercely.

We left Vienna at the beginning of April, and had now been travelling for over five months. I asked Ky-Lin how much farther we had to go. "Are we half-way yet?"

"Well . . . Not exactly."

"But we've been travelling for ages! If we are to get there in time—"

"We will, we will. Up until now we have been travelling relatively slowly because of the terrain. Once we get to the steppes—"

"The what? The stairs?"

"Steppes. With two P's and an extra E. Now we have to get to the mouth of the Danube—perhaps another couple of weeks—then across the Black and Aral Seas—"

"You never told me all that!"

"You saw the maps."

"But—but—"

"You did."

I was silent for a moment. "It—it all looked—sort of smaller . . ."

"Maps usually do."

"But you're sure we're on course?"

"Sure. Sure as I can be . . ."

And with that I had to be satisfied.

Soon after we left Vienna we took to the roads again, traffic being faster and cheaper. We even took advantage of the infrequent railways, although the farther east we travelled, the more primitive they became, with frequent stops and delays, and with the warmer weather they could be stiflingly hot, and the wooden bench seats were exceedingly uncomfortable. If one tried to open the windows to get some air, they either wouldn't open or one got covered in smuts, most of the engines being wood- instead of coal-fired.

We passed through parts of Hungary, Slovakia, Croatia, Romania and Bulgaria with little time to absorb or enjoy the differences in each. The plains of Hungary and Croatia, mountains and forests of Slovakia, Transylvania and Walachia blurred into one another, the only distinctions being the differences of language which I was not clever enough to distinguish between, though Toby apparently could, according to Ky-Lin.

"The boy has a musical ear, and pace intonation and the particular lilt of language means much to those so gifted."

"What language did Summer speak?" I asked on impulse.

He considered for a moment. "Mostly Norman-French, and some Market-Latin, which was of course widely accepted in the west. I helped her with the Oriental languages of course, and she talked to the animals through the Ring which you now wear."

Now that he had answered one question about a person he normally seemed reluctant to discuss, perhaps he would satisfy another. "What was she like?"

"She was a very brave, considerate young woman. Over-impulsive, perhaps, but she was full of ideas, loyal and caring."

I had really wanted to know what she looked like: all females are curious about their predecessors or rivals. "Was she beautiful?"

He wrinkled up his nose, curled and uncurled his antennae. "Beautiful? My Master taught us that all Life was beautiful, from the leaf on the tree to the tooth of a shark. But if you ask me about the length of a nose, the shape of a mouth, the formation of one figure as set against another member of the human race, then I cannot tell you. Could you tell me that one ant is more 'beautiful' than another? No. Another ant is the only one who would know. I am a Ky-Lin, and things like this do not concern us."

He must have seen the disappointment on my face, because he added: "She was about three inches shorter than you"—I was five feet six inches—"but then people were shorter in those days. Her hair was much lighter, and her eyes much bluer and a different shape, too. The formation of your bodies was similar." He thought for a moment. "And she smiled more often than you do."

Was I really that morose? Still, what did I have to smile about . . . Just to please Ky-Lin I essayed a grin, more a stretching of the mouth over the teeth. "That better?"

He shook his head sadly.

Chapter Sixteen

The Suitor

If the so-called Blue Danube was brown, then the Black Sea was definitely blue; dark, deep blue—my paint-box would have called it Prussian. As we stood on the dockside waiting for the ferry to start loading, it was sparkling like a jewel. The sky was clear, except for some small, fluffy clouds, the May sun was warm, and we were all in good spirits. Once we had crossed this sea we should embark into the real unknown. The rest of the journey, apart from a short journey up the Don, would be overland.

The gangplank was lowered and we climbed aboard with the other passengers. Some of them had brought their own food and would sleep on deck, as we had done when we crossed the English Channel, but the cost of a cabin was outweighed by the extra comfort. Or so we thought . . .

We had booked two doubles, Toby and I to share one, the men the other, but when we located them they were far from ideal. They held two, short, tiered bunks, both tiny and hard, with one thin blanket;

there was also a hook for hanging clothes, a hanging lantern and a deeply recessed wash-basin and jug, which looked faintly ominous. A small porthole gave a restricted view, and Toby and I found it difficult to squeeze past each other in the confined space. In the end the one who wasn't washing, changing or looking out of the porthole had to tuck their feet up on one of the bunks.

It was complicated by the fact that there was no room for our haversacks or suitcases, which had to be stored in the hold, so everything we would need for the two days of sailing had to be extracted and stowed away somewhere. The Eg we kept with us, plus night wear, washing-things and our cloaks, but when we went to check on Danny and Claude we found the latter complaining that there was no room for his legs and Danny swearing at his clothes hook, which had just fallen off the wall. On every available space on the ferry were printed, on yellowed, faded paper, in English, French, German and Russian the Rules and Regulations. Breakfast, luncheon and supper would be served in the dining-saloon at—and there was then a list of "bells," which repeated ringing was apparently the way sailors measured their time. Each meal was the equivalent of two shillings per head. No-one was allowed in the engine-room or on the bridge, otherwise passengers were allowed the run of the ship. Canvas chairs were available for those who wished to sit out on deck. In inclement weather all would be expected to remain below, deck-passengers in the saloon. In the case of several blasts from the ship's sirens, we were all to assemble on deck, prepared to board one of the two lifeboats.

From the elevation of the deck we looked out at the calm blue sea, the mountains in the distance, and wondered what all the fuss was about. The weather seemed set fair, the air was balmy, our fellow-passengers seemed cheerful enough and the sailors unconcerned. Rough weather, alarm signals and life-boats could safely be ignored, I reckoned.

"I do hope it won't be choppy," said Claude apprehensively.

"Of course it won't! The sea's like a mill-pond."

"All right for you, Sophy. You didn't get sick last time." The "Miss" had finally disappeared. I didn't mind.

"And you won't this time," I comforted him. "It's all in the mind, you know: *think* sick and you'll *be* sick."

"Up and down, up and down, up and down," intoned Danny mischievously, suiting actions to the words. "Up and down, and—"

"Shut *up!*" said Claude, clutching his stomach.

"Give over, Danny!" I said. "Or you'll catch your-self with your own shenanigans."

"Just listen to the girl! And isn't she catching on to the Irish just like crabs to a piece of bacon rind!" The very mention of food made Claude look anxious again, as Danny knew it would. "Now I remember when I was a wee one, and I had a stomach upset, Mam used to make me sick by tying a piece of bacon rind to a length of string and—"

"Come on Claude," I said firmly. "You can walk me round the deck." I glanced back to where Danny was standing with a huge grin on his face. "Don't forget you will be sharing a very small cabin, and the only toilet is way down the corridor, in case Claude feels . . . unwell."

The smile was wiped off his face as if it had been sponged.

The meals were adequate, if uninteresting, consist-ing mainly of cold cuts, pickles, hard-boiled eggs, black bread and preserves, with weak coffee. On that first day the steamer chugged across a smooth sea, and gradually the coastline receded behind us. Up on deck the engines didn't sound too bad, mainly a sort of throbbing beneath one's feet, but both in the dining-saloon and more markedly in the cabins the constant clatter and thrust of the machines could give the more sensitive a racking headache. Of course we all knew it was only for two nights, but what with the noise and heat below decks and the inconvenience of the tiny cabins by the following morning we were all short-tempered, and the thought of another night in the same conditions was daunting.

At least no-one had been sick . . .

We spent most of the day on deck, enjoying the warmth and sea-breezes. Now at the mid-point of our voyage, there was no sight of land, except for the occasional smudge of smoke, one of which heralded the crossing of the ferry's sister-ship to port of us. There were a couple of small fishing boats in the distance, but the real excitement of the day was provided by the passengers crowding to the rail to watch some great fishes diving and surfacing again alongside, like giant needles tacking the hems of the water. There were eight or nine of them, it was difficult to count, as their black backs gleamed for only a moment before they plunged back down again.

"What are they?" asked Toby excitedly, leaning over the rail so far I felt constrained to grab his belt.

One of the passengers, a well-dressed man with a fair moustache, answered his question, in rather drawly English.

"Why, they are dolphins, my boy, and they are mammals, not fish. They are sociable creatures, and often follow ships in and out of harbour, no-one is quite sure why."

"I wouldn't have expected them here," I said without thinking, realising too late that the gentleman might think me too forward for joining in the conversation without an introduction. "I thought they lived in warmer seas. It must be very cold here in winter."

"Oh, in winter they go back to the Mediterranean,"

said the gentleman, raising his hat politely. "The Black Sea isn't landlocked, unlike the Caspian. To the south it flows out near Constantinople." He bowed. "May I introduce myself? Archie McCall at your service, on leave from my regiment." He didn't say which one. "Just an idle tourist, I'm afraid."

He looked at me interrogatively and although I had no wish to involve us with a stranger, it would have been bad manners not to reciprocate.

"Miss Lee, and my—my brother, Tobias."

He smiled, smoothing his moustache. "On holiday, like myself?"

I opened my mouth to agree, but Toby forestalled me.

"Oh, no," he said seriously. He was still watching the dolphins, but I could see the mischievous look on his face. "We're on a sort of pilgrimage."

"Pilgrimage?"

"Yes. We're going to China with a Buddhist to look for dragons!" And with that he turned and grabbed my hand. "C'mon sister dear, let's see if there are any dolphins on the starboard side!" But once out of ear-shot of the bemused Mr. McCall, he turned on me. "What are you always telling me? Don't never—"

"Ever . . ."

"Don't ever talk to strangers! That's what you've always said, and what are you doin'? Chattin' up the first likely gent who eyes you up!"

"I wasn't 'chatting up' anyone!" I was amazed at his vehemence. "It was you he was talking to, about the dolphins."

"Just an excuse, *sister* dear! He's been following you around looking for a chance ever since we came on board. Last night at supper he was swooning over every mouthful you took."

I was surprised. "I never noticed . . ."

"You was too busy gobbling that cabbage-stuff."

"Toby! I don't gobble!"

"Well, perhaps not. But you know what I mean."

"No, I do *not*! I do not invite attentions from any-one, male or female, and I never have . . ."

And this was entirely true. Not that there had been any males at boarding-school, and when I had come to London to teach I was just another shabby little school-marm who spent nine hours a day in the class-room and the rest either in her lodgings or else in decorous visits to an art gallery, concert or museum, and who would look twice at such? As far as being out alone in the metropolis, I never left the school in the dark without Toby's escort, to dis-courage unwelcome attentions. In the summer I kept to the more populous ways and scurried along with my head down, finding it easy to blend in with my surroundings like the blandest of wallpaper. That was why Miss Moffat's strange behaviour had so upset me.

"Well, this gent's been following us round all day. And he's got his eye on you."

"You're wrong, Toby—"

"No, I ain't! He's comin' over here now . . . You just leave him alone. He's bad news. Don't encour-age him. Don't even pass the time of day . . ."

But I had had enough. I wasn't going to let a child—and that was all Toby was, after all—dictate to me whom I should or shouldn't talk to. I was a responsible adult and could trust my own judgment to choose my own acquaintances. Besides, after the exclusive company of Claude, Danny and Toby, it would be nice to hold a conversation with somebody different. And if he proved to be a bore, then we were reaching our destination tomorrow, and that would be the last I should see of him.

After all, I was free to do with my life as I wished, once this expedition was over. I could marry a tramp, live in sin with an artist in a Parisian attic, join a harem, live as a gipsy, settle down to a respectable spinsterhood. Freedom of choice was an intoxicating thought, so when Mr. McCall approached me again

I accepted the offer of his arm for a turn about the deck, ignoring Toby's furious scowls.

He was an agreeable companion, telling me of his recent trip to Australia, where he had studied closely the strange marsupials—kangaroo, koala, and wallaby that I had seen pictures of, but never come across even in a zoo. He also spoke of the Aborigines, the primitive natives of that continent, but I was rather taken aback by his attitude towards them, dismissing them as feckless, dirty and backward, fit only to be driven away into the bush.

"But surely those people, who were there before the settlers arrived, should be given the consideration they deserve?" I asked rather more warmly than I should. "I myself contribute regularly to the Mission Society, and our members believe most strongly that these children of God—and this includes the native Indians of North America and the Negroes of Africa—should be treated like any other member of the human race. After all, it is only ignorance that restricts them from becoming useful members of society, and ignorance can be cured by education."

"Your sentiments do you credit, Miss Lee!" he declared. "I am amazed that such a pretty and demure young lady should be so emancipated! You are to be congratulated on your humane outlook."

I blushed with pleasure. It was comforting that such a widely travelled gentleman should be willing to listen to my views. I felt quite exhilarated, and glanced up at him with gratitude, being reminded, unfortunately, of Red Riding Hood, for his teeth, when he smiled, were rather large . . . But he *had* called me pretty.

"I am so glad to have made your acquaintance, Miss Lee. It is rare to meet someone who is both charming and erudite."

If possible, my blushes grew even deeper, but I averted my gaze, and hoped my bonnet hid the most tell-tale of them.

"You are too kind, sir. Any erudition I have acquired is entirely due to my profession as a school-teacher, I am sure."

"A school-marm? I might have guessed." I glanced up at his face, fearing disappointment or ridicule, but it was perfectly bland. "But I cannot guess what such a talented young lady is doing so far from home and during term-time too . . . ?"

It was a clear invitation to declare my true mission, but I side-stepped his enquiry with a noncommittal answer.

"Like yourself, Mr. McCall, I am taking some leave."

"With your brother? I believe you have two other companions as well?"

"Mr. Cumberbatch and Mr. Duveen are escorting us, yes."

I was becoming a little annoyed by his questions, but as if sensing this he turned the conversation to other matters. At luncheon I found the attentive Mr. McCall on one side and a scowling and uncooperative Toby on the other, who constantly tried to monopolise the conversation, and when that didn't succeed, exhibited dreadful table manners, for which I had to reprimand him, thus gaining his objective of my attention.

Afterwards Mr. McCall commented on our relationship. "Your brother . . . He doesn't seem—quite in tune with you?"

How to answer this time? "He's . . . he's not exactly my brother. He's my ward, although we enjoy a brother/sister relationship."

"Ah," he nodded. "That explains a great deal. A different upbringing obviously. A special pupil, no doubt?"

I nodded too, and changed the subject. Time for a question on my part. "How long do you expect to be away from your regiment, sir? I do not think you mentioned the name?"

He looked at me and mentioned a town: Aldershot, which he could see meant nothing to me, and then a regiment, which meant even less. Shortly afterwards I excused myself to take a siesta, pleading a poor nights rest, and down below I found a furious Toby drumming his heels on the top bunk.

"I tol' you not to get too friendly with that— that—"

"That'll do! I don't want any of your back-street obscenities, nor do I want any criticism of my behaviour! I do what I please with my life, and I might remind you that you are only here on sufferance anyway!"

To my dismay the child that was still in Toby burst into tears and I moved at once to comfort and hug him, chastising myself for being so harsh and unfeeling. A quarter-hour later we were friends again, but he was still adamant in his dislike for Mr. McCall. We agreed to differ, especially as I reminded him that we docked tomorrow and would probably never see the man again.

"And now you must promise not to spoil the rest of the day with scowls and anti-social behaviour. Understood?"

He nodded, but I wasn't convinced. However he seemed to be as good as his word, going out of his way to be pleasant at supper-time and not making the usual objections when I sent him to have a good wash and bed at ten. As I left Mr. McCall put a hand on my arm.

"A little stroll around the deck later on? We can round off a pleasant acqaintanceship by watching the moon rise . . ."

I demurred. "Such behaviour is not possible on our short acquaintance, Mr. McCall—"

"Miss Lee, we are just ships that pass in the night . . ." Now where had I heard that before? "Why lose the chance to exchange a few pleasantries, an episode to press like a flower in the Book of Life?" He was certainly mixing his metaphors!

I'm afraid he took my quickly suppressed smile as encouragement.

"Come, Miss Lee—Sophy—have pity on a lonely bachelor who desires no more than a pleasant memory to carry back to his exclusively masculine and lonely life in barracks . . ."

At that moment, poised between yea and nay, I was rescued by Danny, who reminded me I had promised a hand of cards, so I had no chance to give Mr. McCall a definite answer. However, several hands into the game, I was surprised to learn that both Claude and Danny had noticed his attentions.

"Shouldn't pay too much attention to that chap," drawled the former, apropos of nothing in particular. "Not the right sort at all. . . . My trick, I believe?"

"Sure and begorra and you're right!" added Danny, studying his cards with a frown. "Wouldn't trust the beggar as far as I could throw him." He had been drinking again, and in consequence was losing. "He's a smooth-talking rogue, so he is!"

"It takes one to know one," I snapped. "My game!" and I threw down the three remaining trumps. "And now I am going to my cabin to read. Goodnight, *gentle*men!" and off I flounced indignantly. First Toby and then them! What right had they . . . If I had stopped to consider I might have realised that they were trying to shield me from any trouble, but I was beyond reasoning. The disadvantage to me lay in the fact that I had had to grow up too quickly, make decisions before I had the experience to judge their effect beforehand, and had mislaid something that was essential to a young woman in my position: feminine caution.

In the cabin Toby was apparently asleep on the top bunk, so I took off my bonnet, shawl and money-belt, loosened my hair and lay down on the bunk, prepared to read another chapter of *Westward Ho!* but after a while the lantern started swaying to and fro erratically and getting up to peer out of the open porthole, the glitter of waves from the navigation lights seemed to be rising and falling more energetically than earlier. Perhaps we were in for a storm.

I could have gone down the corridor to the bathroom and had a good wash, then tucked myself up, but I didn't feel sleepy. In fact I felt more wide awake than I had all day. I shouldn't have had that siesta earlier. Perhaps a turn on deck would settle me down; it would be nice to get a breath of fresh air.

Without trying to analyse my decision or make excuses I picked up my shawl, turned down the lamp and made for the door—

"Where are you going?"

"I thought you were asleep!" I said, nearly jumping out of my skin. "Just for a short stroll on deck, that's all."

"You're going to meet that man!"

"Of course I'm not! I have no arrangement to meet Mr. McCall. You should know me better than that."

I turned to the door again, but there was another voice.

"Be careful out there; the wind is rising and the deck could be slippery with spray."

"I'll be careful," I said. "Thank you, Ky-Lin."

I closed the door, but his voice came muffled through the panelling. "Remember the ring; remember what it tells you . . ."

Why the ring, I wondered, as I walked down the corridor and climbed the companionway to the deck, having to clutch at the rail as I did so. I peered in at the lounge: all was quiet, a late foursome of cards and an old man dozing in a corner the only occupants. No sign of Mr. McCall—not that I was looking for him, of course.

The card-players finished their game, the steward

came round with offers of coffee and brandy, but I declined. A gust of wind rattled the doors of the lounge: if I was to take a turn around the deck, I had better hurry. As I rose I felt a twinge in my finger, and looked down at the ring, so much a part of me now that I scarcely ever noticed it was there. Did that signal mean that I shouldn't go out on deck, or perhaps that I should be extra careful?

No further warnings, so I mentally shrugged my shoulders; just a quick foray. But outside the wind caught my shawl, almost tearing it from my shoulders, and loosened my hair still further so it lost its last pin and streamed back from my face. I made my way to the rail with a shiver, for the air was suddenly colder. Below me white caps were crowning the waves, and the bluff bows of the ferry were throwing up spray as they dipped and rose on the swell. I pulled my shawl tighter and knotted it behind: I had had enough. Sleepy or no, I would be better off in the cabin, but I had to cross a third of the deck to reach the way down and didn't want my hands encumbered.

As I inched my way along the rail towards safety, I found the ring was itching and throbbing on my finger; I paused for a moment to rub my hand against my skirt, and suddenly a pair of arms slid around me from behind, fingers slipped familiarly up towards my breasts and I caught the scent of bay-rum hair oil, brandy and cigars.

"Well met, my little school-marm," said a voice in my ear.

"Mr. McCall! Let me go this instant, sir! What on earth do you mean by this—this extraordinary behaviour?"

Twisting away from his grasp, I tried to reach the doors of the lounge, the nearest refuge, but he caught my arm and dragged me back towards the rail, pressing his body against mine in a most suggestive manner.

"Oh, come on, Sophy! Don't pretend that you don't want this! You've been giving me the nod all day—"

I freed one arm and aimed a slap at his face, which he easily evaded. "Mr. McCall! I demand that you—"

"Call me Archie, m'dear . . ." and he bent his head and attempted to kiss me, but I wrenched my head aside, at the same time trying to push him away, but I had underestimated the strength of a man all fired up as he was. My struggles only seemed to bring us closer together, and I realised that this was exciting him still further.

I opened my mouth to scream, but realised I would have no chance of being heard. By now the cumbersome ferry was rearing and plunging in the increasing storm, the wind was whistling through the wire struts of the rigging, and smoke from the two stacks was being whipped away to starboard. There was a light up on the bridge, but the windows on this side were shuttered and my struggles would not be seen.

How I wished I had never come out here! How I wished I had listened to Toby, Claude and Danny! I knew, however, that this was mostly my fault; I had, however innocently, encouraged this monster to believe I had an interest in him. I had to admit I had enjoyed his earlier attentions, being both flattered and intrigued, stupid, naive young woman that I was! Now all I wanted was to gain the safety of my cabin without harm.

"Leave me *alone*!"

"Oh no, my little temptress! Not now I've got you where I want you . . . You're going to deliver the goods, I promise you! If we go down to one of the lifeboats we'll be nice and snug inside . . . That's right! Give us a bit of a struggle: I like a girl with spirit . . ." As he spoke he was dragging me down towards the stern of the ship, his hands gripping me fiercely.

The ring on my finger was throbbing really hard now, and I remembered Ky-Lin's words: could it help me now, when I hadn't heeded its earlier warnings?

The ship gave a sudden lurch, as if the captain had decided to change direction to ride out the storm, and my attacker and I were both thrown over onto the deck, now slippery with spray. I tried to roll away, but in a moment he had followed and thrown his weight on top of me. One arm was across my throat, near choking me, while his other arm slipped down to my rucked-up skirt and his hand groped upwards. Instinctively I brought a knee sharply into his groin and he rolled off me with a groan and a couple of obscenities.

I tried to get to my feet, but the now-slanting deck prevented this, so I started to crawl towards the rail. To my horror I saw Archie McCall scrambling after me, his face twisted with fury. I grabbed the rail with one hand, but a moment later a fist smashed into my face and I lost my hold. The ship gave another lurch and I found I was sliding under the rail. With scrabbling fingers I tried, terrified, to cling to whatever I could: at one stage I had hold of Mr. McCall's sleeve, but I couldn't hold on. To his credit, once he realised I was in real danger, he stretched out a hand to me, but it was too late.

The last thing I saw before I fell over the side was a night-shirted figure skidding across the deck towards us, and a small object seeming to fly through the air. There was a moment when, my mouth open in a silent scream, I seemed to be suspended in mid-air, then I hit the water with a thump that knocked the breath from my lungs, and I went down, down, down . . .

Chapter Seventeen

Treasure Island

Down, down, down . . .

Down into the freezing, dark water, choking and gasping, mouth and nose and ears full of water, lungs screaming for air, arms and legs flailing, pressure of water and weight of clothes pulling one down still further, the accelerated thump of one's heart-beat—

God! Dear God! I didn't want to die! I went on struggling, not even sure which way was up and which down. Suddenly my head broke through to the surface and I took a great gasp of air, a draught sweeter than any I had ever tasted. Then once more I was beneath the waves, struggling to reach the surface again: another gasp of air and then back, drowning a little more each time, my clothes growing heavier and heavier as I tried vainly to tear them off. I started to pray, hopelessly, then I heard God answer me, a tiny voice in my ear, a voice that transcended even the bubble and pop of water that clouded my hearing.

"Stretch out your hand," said the voice. "And hang on tight!"

The power of prayer! Like a trusting child I did as I was told and found I was grasping a chair-leg. A chair? Out here? I was dead, or dying, or at best hallucinating. I stretched out my other hand and found another leg. A chair, or perhaps a table. Well whatever it was, it was keeping my head above water and I was no longer gasping for breath. Moving forward I got my elbow over the seat of the chair, or the top of the table, whichever it was, only to find that it immediately overturned, and I had to start all over again, having luckily kept a hand on one of the legs—

"Steady on, Miss Sophy!" said Ky-Lin. "I haven't quite got the hang of this yet!"

"Ky-Lin!" I gasped, on a gulp of water. "How on earth did you get here? I thought you were . . ."

"Something else?"

"I thought—I thought you were a chair, or a table." I couldn't tell him about God. "Is it really you? You're all stiff and—and wooden."

"How else could I support you in the water? I'm the wrong shape for a lifebelt . . . Sorry I was so long in changing, but I haven't tried this before. I knew I could change into different materials, I knew I could grow larger or smaller, but I didn't know whether I could combine the two at once. Apparently I can. One lives and learns . . . Which reminds me, if you want to live, because we are getting nowhere right now and you are getting colder and colder, I think we need some outside help. Besides which I think I am getting water-logged. Wrong wood, obviously. Please twist the Ring on your finger and ask for help."

"How? What help?"

"Just do it. We need swimmers, because Ky-Lins don't swim. Come on, before you freeze to death and I forget how to turn back again . . ."

So I moved my hands together on one of Ky-Lin's wooden legs and turned the Ring, with some difficulty because my hands were freezing and swollen. "Help us," I murmured. "We can't swim. Please help us . . ."

At the same time I heard Ky-Lin give half-a-dozen shrill, burbling whistles. I waited for a moment. "What's supposed to happen?"

"Just wait . . ."

It could have been five minutes, it could have been longer and my legs had gone numb and it had started to rain, when the choppy waves around us grew even more disturbed and suddenly we were surrounded by surging bodies and a high-pitched whistling such as Ky-Lin had produced.

"Good," said Ky-Lin. "They heard us . . ."

It was the dolphins, and within seconds I was borne up on one of the backs and surrounded by the others, the air thick with talk I could understand through the Ring.

"Bear her up, brother, she can't swim . . . poor girl, we must help . . . we heard the Ring . . . cannot stand the cold . . . mustn't sink . . . can't catch the ship . . . nearest land . . . the sacred one is with her, keep them together . . ."

I was clinging, spreadeagled, across a hard, thick-skinned back, and rolling up and down on the surface—not always, for sometimes my water steed darted a few feet below the surface, to rise again a few seconds later—but at last feeling safe. It seemed easier, too, to try and ride the back of the dolphin as I would a horse; at least that way I kept my mouth above water most of the time. My ride wasn't helped by the fact that that the other dolphins kept close order, sometimes jostling each other in an affectionate, boisterous way.

But where was Ky-Lin? For a moment I panicked, then there was a small voice in my ear.

"Safe and sound. Don't worry: we are being taken

to the nearest land where we will wait for rescue.
Toby will have alerted the captain to you going overboard, but in this storm he would be powerless to
turn the ship to search for you. But the lad knows
I am with you, so he won't be unduly worried."

Perhaps a half-hour later the dolphins' ceaseless
chatter, and the rhythm of the waves, both changed.
The sea became choppier and shallower and by the
occasional light of a moon that appeared to be racing the clouds I could see a darker blur to my left.
The dolphins stepped up their commentary among
themselves.

"Coming in to land . . . a little to the left . . . watch
the rocks . . . run them up onto the sand . . . gently does it . . . she'll feel heavier as we lose way . . .
touch down!"

My watersteed grounded gently on a stretch of
sand and then wriggled up higher so that I could step
off dry-footed—my slippers had long gone—and I
turned to face my rescuers, now sliding back into the
sea. I knew that if I could understand them through
my life-giving, life-saving Ring, then they would understand me as well.

"My friends," I said, standing as tall as I could in
spite of the shivers and shakes of cold and exhaus-
tion, "I and my friend Ky-Lin thank you for coming
to our rescue. We shall be forever grateful!"

"Grateful . . . grateful . . ." I heard. "The human
is grateful . . . we are grateful too . . . do not often
have the chance . . . most do not understand . . . one
day we will speak together without the use of Rings
. . . we will teach humans how to communicate . . .
we will have the art of healing . . . give us the human
children . . . they will understand . . ."

"I hope that will be soon," I said sincerely. Walking forward into the surf I laid my cheek in turn
against the forehead of each dolphin. "Bless you, my
friends . . ."

One by one they slipped back into the sea, their

bottle-shaped snouts bobbing up and down in a kind of farewell. When they had gone I stumbled back onto the sand and sat down suddenly, thoroughly exhausted, feeling as though I couldn't walk another step.

Ky-Lin came up behind me and nuzzled my shoulder. He was now back to his "living" self, but pony-sized still. "Come on, let's get you off to sleep. We can't do any more till morning."

I allowed him to lead me back amongst some trees, away from the rain, and tuck me up in the shelter of an overhanging rock, after insisting that I discard all my clothes apart from my shift and hang them on an overhanging branch. I was now even colder than ever, my teeth were chattering and I was shivering, but Ky-Lin lay down beside me, and with my back against his stomach, I began to respond to the warmth of his body.

He shifted a little. "Turn your face towards me for a moment . . ."

"Why?"

"Sleepy-Dust."

I turned my head obediently and he breathed into my face and nostrils a scent like that of sandalwood boxes in the sunshine . . .

When I awoke, after a night and half a day of dreamless sleep, I found myself lying on the beach, both warm and dry. The sun was high in the sky, interrupted by a few fluffy clouds, and the breeze came warm from the south. One could not have believed the storm of the night before, except for the debris I now saw cast up on the shoreline. And amongst all this debris was an industrious Ky-Lin, sorting out pieces of jetsam.

He looked up. "Feeling better? I thought you would be better in the sunshine so I rolled you down here. Come and give us a hand: we need some dry wood for a fire."

Between us we built a small cone-shaped heap of
kindling, at the base dried moss and strips of birch-
bark. I sat back on my heels.

"How do we light it? I haven't any vestas."

"The way your ancestors did, of course." He gave
me two differently shaped stones. "Strike these
together till you get a spark, and hold it near the
moss. When it catches, blow it into a flame."

But I was hopeless; if I got a flame, it wouldn't
catch. In the end Ky-Lin sat on his haunches beside
me, forbade me to blow, and got the fire going
almost on his own. Anyway, it was soon blazing away
merrily upon which we had to gather damp seaweed
so that it would give off smoke as a signal.

"What if nobody sees it? What if nobody comes?
What if they think I am dead?"

"Oh, they'll come," he said confidently. "This may
be a deserted islet with no water, but there is far
more traffic across than there used to be all those
years ago when the pirates fought here and people
called it the Accursed Isle."

"Accursed? Then no-one will come, and if they do
they won't pick me up!"

"Course they will! You've only got to run down
to the beach in your shift waving your petticoat and
they'll be queueing up to take us off!"

"How do you know about the pirates?"

"I'll show you." He led me across the islet to a
small cave, and there were the skeletons of two men,
two swords and a dagger.

"Obviously they fought, over what I do not know,
and both died." said Ky-Lin. "But this place is so
seldom visited that no-one bothered to bury them."

"Then let's do it now," I said, and I found a thick
fallen branch to loosen the earth while Ky-Lin's
hooves moved so fast I could hardly see them as he
shovelled out a shallow grave. I had thought I would
not wish to touch the bones, but when it came to
it, it was no different than shifting a bundle of sticks:

blessedly, something inside of me had rendered me numb to the revulsion I had thought to feel.

Once the earth covered them I stuck the swords and dagger in the earth beside. "Shouldn't we say a prayer?"

Ky-Lin nodded. "I shall pray that they may find a better way next time, and you that their sins be forgiven and that they gain eternal rest. Strange, we both wish them well, but in different ways."

We stood silent for a moment, then I asked Ky-Lin how he knew the island was called "accursed."

"Places tell you things," he said. "Stones, rocks, caves, houses can retain an image, a feel, of any unusual action. Some of you humans seem to have a stronger feeling for this: they can sense at once when they enter a house whether it has had a sad or happy past." I nodded: I knew what he meant; my mother used to call it "atmosphere," and I knew now that Hightop Hall had a good one, whatever its past.

As turned to go back I stubbed my toe. "Damn! Er . . . Sorry, Ky-Lin. An echo of Toby, I guess."

He nodded. "Do not forget the boy knew nothing better before. You do. But that must have hurt. Let me see? Ah, a little touch with my horn—so—and it is better." Poking about with a hoof, he unearthed a pouch of shrivelled and dessicated leather. "Open it up, Miss Sophy."

I wrenched apart the stiff ties and tipped the contents out onto the ground. "Pearls? But what strange colours . . ."

Ky-Lin examined them, his forked tongue flickering rapidly over each one. "Fifty. All genuine. All beautiful." He examined the pouch. "And they have not been here that long: perhaps twenty years. So this is not what those two were fighting over. Probably someone hid them where he thought no-one would search."

"How do you know—the number of years? And

why are they such funny colours? Look: black, pink,
yellow, a sort of green . . ."

"I know the years through the decay of the leather
they are in, and also because the colours have not
faded: they tend to fade with exposure and age. The
colours? These are very rare, precisely because of that
very thing. They will fetch good prices. Put them
back into the pouch until we can find something
safer to carry them in."

"We're—we're not going to keep them?" I said,
scandalised.

"Why not?"

"Because . . . because they don't belong to us. The
person who put them there will come back for them
one day."

"Unlikely after all this time. Besides, I have felt
them, and there is no sense of ownership. They are
like goods laid out on a stall, waiting to be bought.
You are very lucky."

I didn't understand how he knew all this, but then
there were a lot of things about Ky-Lin I didn't
understand . . .

We trudged back towards the beach, and by now
I was feeling distinctly hungry and thirsty, but Ky-
Lin pointed out a scoop of rock that held a cupful
of rain water, so at least I slaked my thirst. My clothes
were damp-dry, so I dressed as well as I could in the
crumpled, salt-stained garments. I was just fastening
the buttons on my blouse when there came a shout
from the direction of the beach. I snatched up my
shawl and prepared to run, but there was a hiss from
Ky-Lin.

"Wait for me! And do up those buttons . . ."

He was rapidly shrinking before my gaze, and a
few seconds later was back to his figurine self, which
I picked up and put in my pocket.

"Sorry . . ." I prepared to run again.

"You've forgotten the pearls . . . And when you
get to the beach, stagger about as if you are on your

last legs. I'll do the interpreting: just keep your face turned away."

I did as I was told, trod falteringly towards the fire, which was still belching smoke, and sank to my knees, shading my eyes and staring out to sea in the best "Robinson Crusoe" tradition.

"Don't over-do it," muttered Ky-Lin. "On the other hand they are only simple fishermen, so your histrionics are probably appreciated . . ."

There was much excited jabbering from the boat, about two hundred yards from the shore. I stood up and waved: they waved back. No-one made a move to come nearer and I realised, without Ky-Lin's prompting, that they were superstitious about landing on the islet and also, thanks to the dolphins, I remembered there were rocks close inshore. So I kicked sand over the fire to put it out, and then waded into the sea.

Immediately two men jumped into the shallows and waded to meet me, and in a minute or two I was hauled aboard, showing a deal more leg than I would have wished, to lie on the bottom boards of a boat that stank of fish. Not that I cared: at least I was safe, and by the time Ky-Lin had spoken through me, explaining my dramatic escape from drowning and the dolphins help in guiding me to dry land, everyone's mouths were open in admiration.

I was given bread and cheese, which I wolfed down, and chicory coffee which they brewed on a small brazier on deck. I thought-asked Ky-Lin whether they would take us to harbour and he said they would for a large bribe, which was the way they did things here, and that they had had a poor catch because of last night's storm.

"Promise them what they want, I just want to get to dry land and see the others again . . ."

Dusk was falling as we approached the harbour where I should have docked early this morning, and as we chugged towards land I could see the quayside was lined with people. We were followed by the scream of the gulls chasing our boat, as they did with all fishing boats, and in their exuberance my fisherfolk flung their meagre catch overboard to feathered appreciation.

Once we docked and I was helped up the steps to the quayside, I was met by Toby, Claude and Danny, who hugged and kissed me in a very satisfactory manner. It appeared they had at last persuaded the captain of the ferry to turn back to look for me, but of course he had been unsuccessful. It also meant that they had only docked some two hours earlier, and since then they had tried to persuade a flotilla of boats to go out looking for me.

"Only we didn't have the lingo," explained Toby. "Reminds me: you got you-know-who?"

"In my pocket," I said. "Hush . . ."

Toby had rescued my money-belt from the cabin, so it was easy to pay the fishermen well, and we left them recounting my rescue to the rest of the the townsfolk, doubtless to the accompaniment of free hospitality for many days to come. We found a comfortable hotel where I luxuriated in masses of hot water to wash the salt from my hair and skin, sending my clothes out for laundering.

We took a table downstairs for supper, away from other diners, where we enjoyed kebabs with a fruity red wine, followed by sticky pastries and coffee. I felt we needed a celebration, especially since I now held the secret of the pearls.

I suddenly remembered something important.

"What happened to Mr. McCall?"

The others glanced at one another. "He skipped ship as soon as we docked," said Danny. "Last seen heading for the back streets, sans luggage."

"We tried to hang on to him," said Claude. "But no-one would listen."

Toby thumped his fist on the table. "I knew he was no good from the beginning!"

"All right!" I interrupted. "I should have listened to you all."

"Don't blame yourself, Sophy," said Claude, going pink. "You couldn't have known." He patted my hand.

"We understand," nodded Danny. "Sure we do. Slimy feller like that . . . Takes experience to recognise that sort."

I hid a smile.

I had told the others that the dolphins had guided me to safety, and I hoped the townsfolk would now be more tolerant towards them, but I brought Toby more fully up to date later.

"And Toby," I finished, "just stop me from doing anything foolish like that again!"

Two days later, fully recovered and freshly kitted out, we joined a caravan of travellers moving east. I knew we were starting the second, more wild stage of our journey by Ky-Lin's reminder the day before.

"Time to buy that cooking-pot, I think . . ."

Chapter Eighteen

A Very
Unusual Cat

There were no border guards, no flags, no lines drawn in the sand, no indications whatsoever, but I knew immediately when we left Europe and crossed into Asia. It wasn't that the terrain had changed: for days now we had been travelling through undulating countryside, past pretty little villages, snow-capped mountains in the distance, the forests on either side full with June leaf. Then one morning when the ground grew steeper and the ground stonier and I caught the scent of pines on the warm air I knew we were at last in Asia. To be sure I asked Ky-Lin."To humans the extent of countries and continents are lines drawn on a map," he said, "and as such have little importance. But yes, if you were now standing on a map, you would be in that part which has 'Asia' written on it."

I felt as excited as if I were a real explorer. Not in the sense of being the first in unknown territory, but in the knowledge that everything from now on would be different, my senses bombarded with new impressions: touches, tastes, smells, sights and sounds. So much to absorb, so little time to do it. I didn't keep a journal as such, but I had a small sketchbook in which I did some quick drawings and jotted down anything I wanted to remember: "flocks of small brown birds" I had written at one point; "grasshoppers," "lop-eared sheep" and "woman in red scarf" at others. I just hoped it would all mean something when I looked at it in the future.

I left it to Claude to record our progress, which he did faithfully, every day putting first the date and day of the week, then where we were (if we knew), how far we travelled that day, any unusual incidents, approximately how much we spent, and the state of the weather. He had twelve black notebooks, one for every month we spent away, and this was for the benefit of the firm, to prove we had been there and back. I would have found it all very boring.

We had hired a wagon, a driver and two spare riding horses before we joined a caravan, as I had got very good prices for three of the smaller yellow pearls, and I thought we deserved a little luxury. Ky-Lin advised us to carry our own food, so I had to do a quick mental re-cap of the cookery book I had left behind: not that that prepared me much for the cooking of rice, couscous, dried salted meat and fish, dried fruit and vegetables, nor for the making of unleavened bread. Surprisingly, my best help was Claude, who confessed to a liking for cookery, saying that after his father died and they had been "temporarily embarrassed," he had helped his mother with the cooking.

To my mind this more than made up for his dire performance on horseback. I had ridden as a child, and the small, stubby, hairy horses we had now were not much different from my ponies. Danny, being Irish, had an inborn gift for riding almost anything,

and he showed uncharacteristic patience in teaching
Toby, who was an apt pupil. So three out of the four
of us could ride, which would be necessary on the
next stage of our journey, and I realised we would
have to persist with Claude, who still rode (or fell
off) like the proverbial sack of potatoes—or, considering his build, more like a dislocated skeleton, in
spite of the fact that his feet almost touched the
ground.

We kitted ourselves out for the warmer weather
with leggings, loose cotton shirts and, in my case, a
divided skirt for easier riding. The men had haircuts—
yes, even Toby, whose locks were now almost as long
as they had been before—and I decided on drastic
action for myself. But when I arrived back from the
hairdresser, I was greeted with silence.

"Well?"

Luckily the silence had been of approbation, rather
than otherwise, for they came crowding forward and
touched or ruffled my unfashionably cropped head,
springing already into soft curls. Claude decided it
was sensible, Danny that it didn't spoil my beauty,
and Toby said it suited me much better than those
"dull plaits and buns and things."

It certainly felt much lighter and cooler, and was
far easier to wash and keep clean.

In the sunshine we all wore woven straw hats
against the sun and we only rode early in the morning or towards dusk. At night our wagon-driver curled
up outside, near to his tethered ponies, and Toby did
the same. Danny and I did sometimes, Claude never.
I always seemed to find the ants. Normally we flung
back the front and back openings to the wagon,
making sure it had the benefit of the prevailing
easterlies. Even so, it was rapidly approaching the
hottest part of the year, and we all welcomed the
occasional stream, river or lake in which to cool off,
even fully clothed.

The caravan plodded on, ever upwards, our pace

that of the slowest, those who brought their herds of sheep or goats for sale further on. If we had forgotten anything it would have been provided for, for there were the usual entrepreneurs who took their places in the caravan. One family brought a dry-goods wagon, laden with pots, pans, firewood, rope, boots, blankets, harness, nails, hammers, spare wheels and axles for the wagons and whatever else one needed in that line. Another brought food, including crates of chickens, and a third provided ready-cooked food. And all charged exorbitant prices

What they carried back in return was anyone's guess, but Ky-Lin remarked that there was a profitable trade in opium and also in the handwoven rugs and blankets the tribespeople made.

The countryside through which we passed was completely different from the mostly cosy European villages, hills, woods and forests. Here were vast stretches of open grassland, rippling in the breeze, with mountains dim in the distance. The air was thinner, sharper, more difficult to breathe, and we needed time to become acclimatised. One good thing was that Claude's "hay-fever," or whatever it was, seemed to have dried up.

Sometimes we saw no-one else for days, heard nothing different from the clump of hooves, the clink of harness, the cries of the drivers and herders, the bleatings of sheep and goats, the shush-shush of the wind through the grasses, the twitter of flocks of finches as they harvested seeds and the occasional lonely cry of a solitary raptor, circling overhead. Other days we would pass another caravan on the return journey, or see a group of herdsmen with horses or sheep, or a family trudging in single file, laden with packages and parcels, the men in embroidered felt caps, the women in headshawls or scarves.

We didn't always pass through grassland; sometimes we descended into mini-deserts of rocks and stones, and once or twice into the pleasure of a fertile valley with fresh fruit, grain and meat and the sheer bliss of mountain-cold water. To me the tracks we followed were barely discernible in the now-July grass, but Ky-Lin told me that this was part of the old Silk Road, which every traveller knew well enough from centuries ago.

Sometimes our fellow-travellers took out long, unwieldy-looking guns or even sling-shots to try and vary their diet, but although they sometimes came back with a few small birds, the shy Saiga antelope evaded them, standing on the skyline just out of range.

The weather was warm, sixty-five to seventy degrees during the day, and the nights pleasant, and in spite of my clothing, I was becoming as brown as a gipsy. Once we reached our first sizable town I was determined to dispose of my skirt, much as I had chucked away my corsets, and ride breeched like Toby and the men. No-one would care.

Ky-Lin kept me entertained with reminiscences of his travels with Summer and was the ideal travelling companion: compact, easy to feed and full of stories.

And the Eg continued to grow. . . .

At the end of July we reached our first objective, the town of Azumak, which straddled the most important trade routes for hundreds of miles. There was the way we had come and its continuation east; another road swung north towards the Russias, yet another southwest towards Persia, while the one we wanted went southeast towards the mountains of northern China.

To call Azumak a town was flattering it. True, there was a large market-place surrounded by warehouses, eating-houses, lodging-houses and stables; farther out was a small mosque, ditto a Buddhist temple; there was a tiny Greek Orthodox church and an even tinier Christian shrine, whose wooden effigy was so worn it was impossible to tell whether it was male or female, but the streets of the rest of the town were a hugger-mugger straggle of mud huts, tents, stalls, goat-pens, chicken-houses, sheds, yards and night-soil pits.

We found lodgings in one of the inns facing the square, and it was quite the noisiest location I had ever tried to sleep in. Morning, noon and night there were shouts, screams, yells, the rumble of wagons, the squeak of axles, quarrels, arguments, sellers extolling their wares, drums and pipes—and all this without the bleats, grunts, groans and squeals of the animals. Plus the all-day all-night barking of the dogs . . .

We had no intention of staying in this maelstrom of noise, dirt and dealing, but there seemed to be no choice. I had thought one night, perhaps two, before we found a caravan going our way, but it appeared no-one wished to travel that particular road. The rewards of such travel—opium, silk, jade, mohair, certain herbs and spices—were easily available on the longer but safer and more populous Silk Road, for which caravans were made up every two or three days. Travellers for Persia left approximately every two weeks, for Russia there were few takers except in the fur-trading season.

We—Ky-Lin and I—enquired everywhere, but no-one offered. It seemed so frustrating to have come so far, just to kick our heels. We tried to change our lodgings, but there was nothing better available, although we did manage to change our rooms for those at the back—at a higher price, of course. We had to eat out and this wasn't cheap either, and each day we were spending well over our budget. After three days of this I was beginning to despair, in spite of Ky-Lin counselling patience. He also advised me to use some of the waiting time finding us warmer clothes. This seemed ridiculous with the August heat pressing down on us, but he assured me that now was the cheapest time to buy.

Fur jackets, padded trousers (me as well), fur caps
with ear-flaps, fur mitts and stronger boots, this set
us up, together with the what was left of the winter clothes we had worn last winter through Europe.
For all of this, and for the price of the journey ahead,
it was necessary to sell more pearls, which Ky-Lin
counselled me to bargain for through a back-street
trader, rather than travellers from a caravan. I wasn't
convinced, but after he had taken me through both
options, I had to admit he was right.

On the fourth morning I was thoroughly restless
and decided to take a walk round the market on our
doorstep. I left Claude and Danny over one of their
endless games of cards (on the second night I had
made the mistake of giving Danny and Claude money
to buy their own meal, and they had come home
reeling and reeking of some rot-gut called arrack, or
something like that, were thoroughly sick, which
served them right, and stank of anise for twenty-four
hours afterwards, so now we all went out together,
or not at all). Toby had set off with Ky-Lin in his
pocket, having perfected the art of Ky-Lin speaking
through his mouth, Ky-Lin doing the prompting by
little nudges in his pocket. So, although Toby couldn't
understand anything, Ky-Lin could report back to me.
I rather suspected Toby's first call would be at the
camel-lines outside the town. We had both seen a sad-
looking specimen in a zoo in London, and a string
of them on the skyline while we were in the caravan, but he was always fascinated by the varying
animals and birds we came across.

The market was its usual crowded, smelly, noisy
self. Jingling the few loose coins in my pocket, for
I had no intention of buying anything, I wound my
way past the fresh food stalls—meat, vegetables, fruit—
to the dry goods—fish, rice, beans, sultanas and raisins—then to the salt and spices. Next came the sweet
things: sugar, honey, cakes. On to the cloth: silk and
ready-made clothes, thread, needles, scissors, tape and

ribbons. Then there were pots and pans and crockery, the latter ranging from the cheapest to the finest Chinese porcelain. One section was devoted to furniture, mostly bamboo and Chinese, and Persian rugs and carpets. Of course there were stalls for the sale of arms: swords, spears, rifles and percussion revolvers. Jewellery, from the exotic and expensive to the cheap and tawdry—I didn't see any pearls as good as mine. Toys for children, wooden mechanical monkeys, dolls with porcelain faces; one stall devoted entirely to soapstone and jade, the latter from spinach through rose to the pale "mutton-fat". I passed quickly through the stalls selling dull things like hides, saddles, boots, baskets, rope and tents, likewise past those selling tobacco, snuff and hashish, and finding a patch of shade, bought a refreshing cup of sherbert, deciding that enough was enough and that the rest of the stalls could hold no further surprises.

I emptied my tin cup and hung it on my belt, to be rinsed when I returned to the inn. We all had one: it was common sense not to share in the cups and ladles supplied by the drinks vendors, especially when one saw the diseases and sore mouths among the population.

Rather than try and battle through the middle of the market, I headed for the side, knowing that two corners would see me back at the inn. Now I was passing those stalls that faced the buildings surrounding the square. These were mostly small, some of them selling second-hand goods. This was the part where one found the bargains, if anywhere, but although I looked at a couple of embroidered purses I had no Ky-Lin to bargain for me.

Now I was at the last corner before the inn and I hastened my step, but suddenly an almighty great racket broke out just ahead to my right. Squealing, screeching, barking, howls of pain and the crash and splinter of wood. Hurrying forward I came across one of those sorry little stalls that sold "pets": mainly exotic birds, but also reptiles and the occasional dog or cat, although these latter were such prolific breed-ers that the streets were full of mongrels and feral cats already that no-one wanted anyway.

It seemed that this stall was one of the typical, cheaper ones: cages of pink-dyed canaries and colourful finches, a few somnolent tortoises, a couple of half-grown Saluki crosses and—a cat? At least that's what it sounded like. Half the cages were on the ground, the birds fluttering up and down, a tortoise lay on its back, claws waving helplessly, and the dogs were barking furiously and straining at their leashes, their fury directed at a creature crouching right at the back of the stall beside a cage whose door had literally been torn off. The animal was spitting, snarl-ing and growling, while the stall-holder was stabbing furiously in its direction with what looked like a small, two-pronged pitchfork, cursing and yelling and out of control.

I became aware that the Ring on my finger was throbbing madly, so much so that it was actually hurt-ing. I was supposed to do something or avoid some-thing, but what? I stepped forward and turned over the tortoise which crawled away to safety, righted the bird-cages, avoided the snarling dogs, but still the Ring hurt. There was a sudden scream of pain from the corner of the stall and the stall-holder had the cat, or whatever-it-was, pinned down beneath the pitchfork, was picking up an iron bar and obviously moving in for the kill.

Without further thought I moved forward and snatched the pitchfork from the stall-holder's hand, and a moment later wrenched the bar from his sud-denly slackened other hand, throwing both to the ground. He raised his fist at me and I stepped back as he picked up the pitchfork again, prepared to have another go at the animal.

I was in an awkward position. I couldn't under-stand him, nor he me, but I knew without doubt that

I was meant to rescue the animal, now growling quietly in a corner and licking at an injured side. It now looked more like a cat to me, although I had had little to do with them, except as rodent-catchers in barns and stables. I wasn't even sure I liked them very much, although I had never really been able to find out. My parents had never considered pets to be essential to a household. I rode a perfectly pleasant pony, the doctor had a snappy little terrier, there was an aloof striped cat next door and my headmistress had a pair of blue lovebirds, but that was it. I had never stroked or cuddled any animal, and when I saw how obsessed their owners became with them, I decided I wouldn't bother to have one. But I wouldn't see one needlessly hurt.

The trouble was, I had only a few coins in my pocket, and nothing else to bargain with . . .

Still, it was worth a try. I tried the universal gesture for money, rubbing my right thumb and first two fingers together and raising my eyebrows interrogatively.

At once his attitude changed. He fawned and chirruped like his birds and burst into a flood of Arabic, putting down the pitchfork and obviously extolling the virtues of his beautiful cat. When he saw I didn't understand he threw in a few phrases of guttural French for good measure. Through this I gathered that the cat was unique and came originally from Siam.

"Look at his princely form, his unusual colour, his thick soft fur, his extraordinary eyes . . ." Words to that effect, but as I could see nothing but a dim form, a snarling row of teeth and a red-eyed glare I took his rhodomontade with the large pinch of salt it deserved. After five minutes or so, a sum of money was mentioned, which was far beyond my reach.

I shook my head and mentioned a sum commensurate with the few coins I had in my pocket—coinages were some of the terms one learned in all languages, and quickly—but he spat in disgust and waved me away. I knew some of the moves and pretended to walk away, waving my hand as though I had no further interest. The stall-holder caught at my sleeve and now his price had halved, though it was still more than I had.

I mentioned the same sum, he held his nose as though I was a bad smell, I pointed to the still snarling cat and the broken cage, as if it was he who had the worst of the bargain; I even poured my few coins into his palm, but I could see it was no use. I knew also that even if I managed to convey that I would bring back more money, he would have lost patience before I returned, preferring to get a good price for an animal for the pot; many people ate dog, cat or even rat, considering them a delicacy.

But there was nothing else I had to offer; I turned out my pockets and came up with a lump of fluff and a length of string. As a last resort I tried the secret pocket I had made in my new leggings and found the smallest pearl I had brought to change yesterday but kept as we had got enough with the other six—Eureka!

With the air of a conjuror I handed it over to the stall-holder who took it as though it would bite, demonstrated its smallness, tasted it with his tongue to see if it was genuine and again shook his head, though I noticed the coins had disappeared and he kept the pearl between his fingers.

At that moment the cat took matters into its own paws.

There was a sudden blur of movement, it sailed past my left ear and a moment later I yelped with pain as a heavy weight settled on my shoulder and several sharp bits dug into my skin as the creature regained its balance and turned around, so that out of the corner of my eye I could see an ear, an eye, a furry muzzle.

The stall-holder moved forward as if to interfere,

but the cat spat and growled so savagely that he retreated, waving his arms and cursing, no doubt glad to be rid of the pair of us at a profit, for that pearl was worth twenty cats and more.

In the meantime I was frozen on the spot. Having only seen the formidable animal growling, spitting and snarling and feeling the weight and the claws—admittedly now sheathed—I was scared stiff the cat would turn on me if I so much as shifted an inch. I had such a picture in my mind of its savage aspect and menacing growls, so that when it started to purr against my ear I at first thought it was the prelude to imminent attack.

However, just in time I realised the Ring was no longer throbbing, rather was it exuding a kind of soothing warmth. So when the creature rested its head against my cheek and a cold nose tentatively touched mine, I felt I had fulfilled the Ring's intention in freeing the creature. I moved slowly and gingerly away from the animal stall and made my way down the alley towards the inn, a little bowed under the weight. Coming to a wall a little higher than I, I patted the top invitingly.

"Here you are, pussy-cat. Now you are free to go." I was glad there was no-one to hear. "I expect you can catch plenty of mice and—and things. Off you go now, and keep away from cages . . ."

I had thought it would understand, at least in part, through the Ring, but it was obviously deaf or something; it just settled down closer on my shoulder, purring more loudly, its tail tapping gently on the back of my shoulder, as if to say: "Keep on going . . ."

Of course! It was probably hungry. Well, I could probably get something for it at the inn. Reaching the courtyard I stepped over to the outside stairs which led to our rooms, ignoring the curious glances of those who always haunted the place, squatting around a small fire or leaning against a wall in the shade. I walked up the stairs very carefully, so as not to jolt the cat from my shoulders, or have his claws digging in once more.

Reaching my room I first opened the shutters then moved over to my pallet, sitting down gingerly. At last the cat cooperated, leaping down onto the blanket and licking a paw.

"I'll go and get you something to eat," I said, feeling foolish. "A little fish and a drink of milk, perhaps . . ."

I had my hand on the latch when I heard a quiet voice behind me.

"Not raw, if you don't mind. Lightly poached with a sprig of tarragon, and water, not milk . . ."

Chapter Nineteen

An Addition and a Subtraction

I whirled round, convinced someone was playing tricks: Toby, perhaps, hiding under the bed or perched on the roof outside, but the cat and I were alone, and the former had its attention firmly fixed on the other paw. I shook my head to rid it of the cobwebs. All this had been too much; it was just an accumulation of stress, that was all. I was thinking for myself, not the cat. I wouldn't eat raw fish, so obviously I had arranged a recipe in my mind and spoken it out aloud. But the voice hadn't sounded like mine. . . .

I went down to the kitchen with a few coins in my hand and arranged for the fish and tarragon. I drew a fish in the dust on the floor, mimed the filleting and picked a few leaves of dried tarragon from the selection hanging from the rafters. I then pointed to the pan and water, and supervised the poaching, indicating when I considered it done. By

then I was so hungry myself that I bought a leg of
chicken and ate it on the spot.

Opening the bedroom door the cat leapt off the
bed and advanced to meet me, tail held high and
gently waving. I set down the dish on the floor and
removed the cover, the enticing smell making my
mouth water.

"It's hot," I said unnecessarily, for the poor thing
was obviously deaf, like all blue-eyed cats, but it had
the sense to sit back and wait for the steam to dis-
perse. Risking scalded fingers I knelt down and
examined the fillets, pulling out a couple of bones
that had been missed and discarding the tarragon.
"There, nothing left to choke on. I'll put some water
in the cover . . ." Stop talking to yourself, Sophy!

After a couple of minutes it started to eat, delicately: a gourmet rather than a gourmand, obviously.
As it ate I had leisure to study it more closely. It was
completely unlike the chunky tabbies, gingers, blacks,
black-and-whites and tortoiseshells I had seen in
England, nor had it the snub-nosed appeal of the
Persian. Neither did it resemble the shabby alley-cats
we had come across abroad. For a start he was much
bigger and undeniably elegant, slim and streamlined,
with a pointed muzzle and long ditto tail, this last
with a tiny kink at the end. His colour was the most
striking, of course, dark chocolate at the extremities
and a cream body. Without touching him I could see
that the fur was dense and soft. His claws looked
shorter and blunter than most cats, but it was those
beautiful blue eyes that I found the most appealing;
not a dark blue, rather that translucent pale blue of
the tiny flowers we used to call "babies' breath" when
we were children—pity about the deafness. Then I
noticed that his ears flicked back and forth from
every noise outside, and I wondered . . . perhaps he
spoke some strange tongue that was not transmitted
through the Ring.

Finished, he drank deeply, gave me a glance as if

to say "thank you" and leapt back onto the bed to give himself a thorough wash from head to toe, wincing a little as he licked his side, where I could see the skin had been broken, probably by that wretched pitchfork. I put the dish, cover and bowl on the rickety table under the window. I was deathly tired after my expedition, but the bed was occupied, and I didn't want to risk those claws, remembering what I had seen earlier.

"Er . . . Could you move up a bit? I'd like to have a rest." But how could I expect it to understand?

"Sure," said the cat in my sleepy head, moving to the foot of the bed, and without thinking any further I lay down and immediately fell asleep.

"What on earth is *that?*" asked Toby, bursting into my room, but as the answer was perfectly obvious he didn't wait for one but instead launched into an enthusiastic account of how he and Ky-Lin had found a man willing to guide us to his brother's village, some one hundred and fifty miles on towards our destination, and that his brother would be sure to take us the rest of the way.

"Apparently the guide has goods to deliver to his brother, knows where he can hire half-a-dozen ponies, and Ky-Lin says—at least I *think* he says—he nodded anyway and only did a bit of the bargaining—that the price was reasonable. What do you say to that?"

"I say you've done a wonderful job," I laughed giving him a hug. "Both of you!" For of course it had been Ky-Lin who had found the man and done the bargaining through Toby's mouth. "When do we start?"

"Tomorrow at dawn," said Ky-Lin, jumping from Toby's shoulder to mine. "We meet him outside town at the beginning of the track south-east. Each of us will have a pony, and there will be two for transporting our food and blankets and clothes, etc."

"Well, we'd better get going, then! We have to get packed, buy some food and—"

"And I'm *starving*!" interrupted Toby. "Haven't had anything since breakfast . . ."

I discovered I was starving too, and went down the corridor to rout out Claude and Danny. We partook of a hasty meal of fried fish, meat and rice, then set out to do the serious shopping: firewood, rice, salt, oil, dried meat, fish, vegetables and fruit, and extra water-bottles. What with packing and organising, I completely forgot about the cat, though when I at last returned to my room at about nine that night I felt an uncomfortable pang to find that he had gone through the still unshuttered window. He had chosen his freedom. I just hoped he would be all right.

Ky-Lin had already hidden under my pillow, so I took down the dirty dishes to the kitchen and had a quick wash under the pump in the yard and then sought my bed, where I had no trouble falling asleep.

To be awoken by a thump in the middle of my stomach.

"Ouch! What the hell . . ." Sophy! Language . . .

"Sorry! Missed my footing . . ."

Voices in my head again. I turned over and looked at my fob-watch by the moonlight coming in through the open window. Three A.M. At my feet the cat had curled himself up.

"Thought you had gone . . ."

"Just exploring . . . And using the usual toilet facilities. May I ask you a favour? I am afraid that my side is quite painful. I would not wish it to become infected."

I stumbled out of bed and lit the lamp, still convinced I was dreaming, but then one did strange things in dreams. Like talking to injured cats. I dampened one of my diminishing store of clean handkerchiefs and bathed the contusions on the cat's ribs. The skin was broken, weals breaking out on the surface where the fur had been torn away.

"There . . . That better?"

"Let me," said a voice from my pillow. Ky-Lin spoke to the cat. "If you will allow me?"

In my increasingly confused dream the cat nodded, and Ky-Lin moved down the bed and touched his little pink horn to the cat's side. Immediately the skin seemed to heal, the swelling going down.

"Thank you, Sacred One . . ."

"No problem," said Ky-Lin. "And now let's get some sleep. We have a long day ahead of us tomorrow." He blew out the lamp and lay by my pillow, while the cat curled up at my feet again. I slept without further dreams until Ky-Lin nudged me awake just before dawn. We had paid our dues the night before so started to carry our luggage down the stairs and into the street, where it piled up formidably. Toby and the others were to carry it down to our rendezvous, but it took three journeys, and a sleepy sun was reddening the grey dawn as we finished loading our ponies, Mustaq, our guide, muttering at our tardiness.

Even though it was so early, people were already stirring, and I paused to pick up some savoury pancakes from a yawning stall-holder. On either side of these alleys bedding was already being hung out to air on the balconies, cooking fires being lit, sleepy children carrying buckets to the nearest well, bundles of rags coming to life again as vagrants and beggars.

Juggling the hot pancakes in my hands, I saw that the cat was following me. It wasn't coming with us, that was for sure, but it was probably hungry. Carefully I dissected the coolest of the pancakes and laid it on the ground.

"There you are, pussy-cat; goodbye and good luck!" and off I trotted to join the others and hand out the pancakes. The guide provided us with some revolting coffee, which wiped any lingering sleep from anyone's eyes. I was just shortening my stirrups ready to mount, Danny having already lengthened Claude's, who was looking extremely uncomfortable and quite precarious, when I felt a nudge on my right leg. Oh, *no!* Not the cat again!

"Shoo!" I said. "Go away! Look I gave you something to eat, your hurts are better and cats fend for themselves."

"Just a moment," said Ky-Lin from my pocket, which he had swapped from Toby's a few minutes past. "How many are we, counting the Eg?"

Peculiar question, given the circumstances. "Er . . ." I counted on my fingers. Me, Toby, Ky-Lin, the Eg, Danny and Claude. "Six. Why?"

"Summer had seven with her on both her first and second journeys, at least for part of the time. So did the One before her, but that was a long while ago. But the Ring remembers."

And as if to echo his words, the Ring gave a tiny, painless throb.

"You mean that seven is a lucky number?"

"It is considered to be so by some."

It was now obvious which way the conversation was leading. "You want us to take the cat?"

"My wishes have nothing to do with it. I was just trying to remind you of your options. I neither want you to ignore the obvious, nor to make a decision you might later regret. I also believe you should not pass up on any luck that comes your way."

I thought about it. It had been the Ring that had urged me to rescue the cat, and I had to admit it had been no trouble. But it couldn't run behind a horse—

"It can perch quite comfortably on the the pony carrying the luggage," said Ky-Lin, reading my thoughts for the umpteenth time of our acquaintance. I looked down at the subject of our conversation, and a pair of beautiful blue eyes gazed back at me.

"I won't be any bother," it said, quite clearly.

"I thought you couldn't—didn't—"

"He was shy," said Ky-Lin.

When we rejoined the others the cat leapt gracefully onto the back of the luggage-carrying pony and settled down, wedged comfortably between the haversacks.

"Is he coming with us?" asked Toby.

"I suppose so."

"What's he called?"

"Cat," said Danny.

"Tom," said Claude, accurately.

"No," said Toby. "He deserves better than that. He's very beautiful—no, I suppose you would call it handsome for a boy."

"Beau," I said. The cat raised its head and looked at me.

"Near enough," it said, and settled down again. So Beau-cat he became, fulfilled his promise of being no trouble, and was seldom far from my side when we were on the ground.

So off we went into the unknown, through the undulating steppes, always tending higher and higher. Sometimes we rode through grass as high as the horses withers, and other times over stony ground, and I would have been lost in five minutes, but Ky-Lin assured me we were headed in the right direction.

We progressed more or less uneventfully. I cooked for us every night, leaving enough cold for breaking our fast and a lunch-time snack with, as I said before, the competent help of Claude; he seemed to be a loaves-and-fishes man—able to make a little go a long way. Having watched the sort of herbs our earlier fellow-travellers had gathered, I was able to vary the taste of the ubiquitous rice and couscous a little. This was nothing to the spicy smells that our earlier guide, Mustaq, conjured up, although when I begged a pinch of his mixture, it nearly burnt the roofs off our mouths.

At night he erected a kind of tarpaulin for us, and we slept on the ground, wrapped in our blankets and

with our cloaks for pillows. It was the first time I
had slept on bare ground and I'll swear that every
pebble and stone in Turkestan, or wherever we were,
was digging into my hips, spine and shoulders, but
after the first couple of nights I became used to it,
having the sense to clear the space and scrape out
a small depression before I lay down.

I must admit that I was intrigued by the sight of
the night-shirted men, for they bore no resemblance
to the statues and paintings of gods and athletes I
had seen in various art galleries and museums in
London. When we had travelled earlier in the wagon,
there had been a blanket slung between them and
me, but now it was amusing to see the stratagems
they underwent when they were changing: hiding
behind the pony-lines, running off a couple of hundred yards and crouching down or doing as we used
to do at school—undressing under our nightgowns.
They were not as adept at this as I was . . .

Of course many of the workers we had passed in
the fields, and some of the herdsmen also, wore the
minimum of clothing, merely a brief loincloth, but
this seemed normal and natural in the native population—but Claude and Danny had such skinny
shanks! And without regular exposure to the sun,
these limbs looked like white pipe-cleaners, especially
Claude's!

The village we were headed for was some hundred
and fifty miles distant and we reached it in just over
a week. All the while we were gradually climbing, so
gradually that sometimes it wasn't until we stopped
for a meal or overnight camp and looked back the
way we had come that we saw how far we had
climbed. Now we could see the mountains we were
aiming for; just a bluish suggestion on the horizon,
but day by day gaining shape. Ky-Lin reckoned we
had about another five hundred miles to go before
we found a suitable pass though the mountains,
which sounded pretty daunting, especially as we were

well into September. Now that we were that much higher, the grass was not as tall, which made the going easier for the ponies, and we were instead passing through mini-meadows of blue, yellow and white flowers, dancing in the perpetual easterlies.

We spent two days in Mustaq's brother's village because, like many other horse-owners, their ponies grazed well away from the village and had to be rounded up. In the meantime we were lodged at one end of a smelly stable, divided from the sheep and goats by only a wooden paling. We ate well, though: pancakes, unleavened bread, cheese, lamb kebabs and spicy fried vegetables.

Mustaq's brother, Makub, was as like his brother as could be: small, dour and uncommunicative, with the same droopy moustaches. With the help of Ky-Lin we agreed a price, half down, the other half when we reached the mountains.

I bought provisions, though of course the price was much higher so far from a town: more rice, oil, dried meats and vegetables and fruit, firewood, plus some hard and rather smelly cheese. The poor pony carrying the food looked swaybacked by the time we had finished, but we knew these foods would have to last us three weeks at least, till we got through the mountains, as there were no more settlements on the way.

We made good progress during the next few days and Ky-Lin whispered that we had covered at least a third of our journey to the mountains.

The ground was becoming more broken up, and several times we crossed small gullies and streams, and even came across the odd tree. On the evening of the fourteenth day since we had left the village, our guide, Makub, suddenly became more convivial, and suggested he join us for supper, bringing a couple of spicy dishes to serve with our rice.

I didn't entirely trust this sudden change of heart,

and something—perhaps it was the Ring—warned me against his food, and more particularly against the flask he offered round afterwards. I couldn't consult with Ky-Lin, as he had crept off some time before to forage for some fallen seeds he had seen earlier, but it was with a sinking heart that I saw even Toby take a draught from the flask, although he made a face and refused more. When it came to my turn I merely raised the flask to my lips and pretended to swallow, out of courtesy, but to my dismay Claude and Danny set to with a will until the flask was empty. They then broke into raucous song, music-hall ballads with dubious lyrics, some decidedly risqué, and I regret to say even Toby joined in.

It was very late when I managed to get them to bed and by then was exhausted myself and could only give the returned Ky-Lin an abbreviated version of what had happened. I fell asleep to the sound of loud snoring which drowned out the more pleasant sounds of the night.

It was still dark, though dawn wasn't far away, when I was awoken by a panicking Toby.

"Sophy, Sophy, wake up!"

I rolled over. "Whassa matter?"

" 'E's gorn!" It must be bad: he was back to Cockney again.

"Who's gone?"

" 'E 'as. The guide! I went out there to be sick, 'cos me stummick's fair terrible, and there's nothin' an' nobody there. There's nothin' but us! The dirty git's run orf with everythin'! Ponies, gear, the lot!"

Chapter Twenty

On Our Own

I tried to spring to my feet but fell to my knees, tangled in my blanket. Furiously I scrabbled free and went out into the pre-dawn, the skies already paling and the stars fading one by one. Toby was still retching, but Ky-Lin and Beau-cat were anxiously awaiting me. I gazed around: nothing. Toby was right. Makub had left us and taken everything with him. Even the Eg . . . A thief in the night.

What on earth were we going to do? Without food, water or transport we would surely perish, and even if Ky-Lin could guide us back to the village it was doubtful if we could make it. Besides which, the object of all this journeying had gone: without the Eg, what was the point of going on? I sank to my knees in despair, but there was a nudge from Ky-Lin.

"Get dressed," he hissed. "Quick as you can. Wake the others if you can, but I doubt it."

The first quickly done, the second impossible. They lay there and snored and snored and snored, and no amount of shouting, shaking or even kicking

made the slightest bit of difference. I ran out of the
shelter again to find Ky-Lin rapidly changing into his
pony-size mode, as always in fits and starts, ending
with the last shortened foot and a crumpled ear.
Beau-cat was watching impassively, but Toby was still
retching. Ky-Lin finished "changing" and briefly
touched Toby's stomach with his horn.

"That should make it better . . . Tell him, girl,
to stay here and get the others on their feet—if necessary drag them over to the stream and dunk them
in it."

"What's the matter with them?"

"A powerful drug in that flask he gave them. The
food was probably contaminated as well. You and
Beau here had neither, which is why you are well
enough." He paused. "Well, come on then . . ."

"Come on where? What are we going to do?"

"Go after him, of course! Climb on to my back
and hang on tight."

"But we'll never catch him! He's been gone five
or six hours. He must be at least twenty miles away!"

"With eight ponies? Probably only five or six.
Come on, we're wasting precious time."

In fact it was a good ten.

Toby had had the dubious pleasure of riding Ky-
Lin before and enjoyed it—I say dubious, because he
wouldn't touch a living organism, so the progress was
a hair-raising behind-bumping teeth-jarring nightmare—but to me it was an experience I preferred to
forget, especially as Beau-cat had decided to accompany us, and was clinging on for dear life to the back
of my (luckily) thick jacket. True, when we came to
suitable stony ground Ky-Lin trotted instead of
bounding, but when he finally drew to a halt I slid
off his back, groaning and aching in every joint.

"Hush!" said Ky-Lin. "He's not far away. . . .
Where does it hurt?"

"Everywhere," I groaned, but quietly. Even the ces-
sation of movement was a treat.

"Sorry," he said. "But if we had left it any longer or been any slower he would have gone too far, and we must retrieve the Eg, or else I will entirely forfeit my time in Nirvana. Lie still." And quickly and expertly he dabbed me with his little pink horn, and immediately I felt better. Beau-cat seemed all right, although he was carefully straightening his claws to their correct alignment.

"Thanks . . ." I stretched and wriggled about a bit and discovered I was still in one piece. I started to get up but Ky-Lin stopped me

"Stay down. I told you he isn't far. Move forward to that large rock over there and take a quick peep."

By the time I reached the rock I had already seen the plume of smoke over to our right and when I cautiously raised my head I could see that Makub had built a small fire in a little dell, having tethered all but his own pony to a lone tree nearby.

"He reckons he's safe," breathed Ky-Lin in my ear. "What with the drug and the distance."

"What are we going to do? He's got a gun."

"Come back a bit and I'll tell you." Obediently Beau-cat and I followed him until we were out of earshot of the guide. "Now listen you two—"

I pointed at Beau-cat. "Will he understand?"

"We are both animals—" He stopped. "On second thoughts, put your Ring-finger on his collar—"

"He hasn't got one. A collar, I mean."

"Just because you haven't seen it, doesn't mean he hasn't got one."

I pushed my fingers into the soft fur around Beau-cat's neck and, sure enough, I could see a tatty brass-coloured chain, studded with green glass stones. I thought it might be too tight, but my finger fitted quite easily underneath.

"Now listen, and listen carefully, because we haven't time to go over it more than once. He will soon have finished his coffee . . ."

And he told us what we had to do.

❖   ❖   ❖

We didn't get back to the others until the sun was on its way down. What with rounding up the ponies, who had panicked, broken their halters and were anything up to a mile distant, and indulging ouselves in a scrappy meal, plus walking the beasts back, I wasn't surprised to see Toby had come a couple of miles down the track to look for us.

He was overjoyed to see us again, mounted one of the ponies and listened intently as I told him of our successful foray. He declared it was better than a play, but added: "Won't you have to tell the others about Ky-Lin now?"

I looked across at Ky-Lin, who was trotting, pony-size, among the other steeds.

"Well?"

"Probably as good a time as any. It would have to happen sooner or later, anyway. I'll stay behind while you explain, otherwise they'll probably die of fright. Break it to them gently; at least now there are no other humans around."

Claude and Danny were in a sorry state. They were still stumbling around half-dazed, alternately clutching at their heads and their stomachs. While Toby hobbled the ponies, ensured the Eg was safe, and looked out some rations, I built a small fire and heated up couscous and vegetables, telling the two disgraces to go down to the stream and not to return until they were sober, clean and presentable. This took some time, but eventually they returned as the moon rose and accepted a small bowl of food and drank water.

"Perhaps that will teach you to be a little more abstemious," I said severely. "You could have died, you know."

"I shall never, ever again touch strong liquors," said Claude. "Not ever." And as far as I know, he never has.

"What was it?" asked Danny. "Food poisoning?"

"Man poisoning. Makub was going to abandon us, steal our ponies and make his way to the village, where he probably had an arrangement with his brother to take our belongings back to town and sell them. He's probably done it before, on the less-frequented routes."

"You mean—he meant us to die?" asked Claude.

"Well, with no food and no transport, what else?"

Toby looked at me and I nodded. "Tell us then, dear Sophy, how you managed to get the horses back . . ." This we had rehearsed.

"Well," I started, "I couldn't have done it without the help of my friend Ky-Lin . . ." I turned my head and called out into the darkness. "Are you there?"

And out trotted Ky-Lin into the firelight.

A quarter-hour later, when Toby had found Claude cowering a couple of hundred yards away and I had caught up with Danny, and persuaded the pair of them that there was nothing to fear, I introduced them to the mythical creature, explaining that Toby had known about him from the beginning.

"And there were none of your stupid hysterics from him," I added. "Toby took him for what I said he was: someone sent to help us. And before you ask, my uncle bought him many years ago. If you remember I told you part of Summer's story, and he, Ky-Lin, accompanied her on part of her journey and was there at the inception of the Eg we are here to return."

I wasn't sure whether they were listening to me properly, and I must admit that a Ky-Lin by the fire in all his shimmering glory was a sight to behold.

"I might add," I said, "that he can also change his size. That is why you have not seen him before. He has usually been either in my or Toby's pocket. Show them, Ky-Lin."

Obediently, slowly, carefully he shrank back to dog, cat, rat, mouse size and scuttled across to my side.

"See?"

Claude and Danny scrambled back to their places by the fire.

"But how do you'se two understand each other?" asked Danny, a question I had been dreading.

"We have a necessary bond," I said carefully. "A sort of built-in interpreter." I was unwilling to explain the Ring fully, even to Toby. "Now would you like to hear how we beat Makub at his own game?"

"Er . . . You don't have one of your headache powders left, do you?" asked Claude.

As it happened I did, and dosed them both, before settling down to tell them of our Marvellous Adventure.

I explained Ky-Lin's plan to make the thief believe he was surrounded, which meant that we three had to move to different points, and then one by one make as much noise as possible. Beau-cat screamed as only a full-blooded Siamese cat can (which I admit made me jump out of my skin), I was to yell the Arabic for thief, something like "Harami!" then move a hundred yards to my left and groan loudly like a ghost. Then I was to return to my original position and yell "Thief!" again. And so we alternated, Ky-Lin making a sort of screeching noise like a giant eagle owl. By the time we had done this a half-dozen times Makub had had enough. After the first couple of shouts and yells he had fired his long Afghan rifle, then struggled to tip in more powder and shot, but as it was a muzzle-loader he only got off one more wayward shot before Ky-Lin burst on the scene in all his glory, and Makub took one terrified look before leaping onto his horse and heading north at a gallop.

"Will he get back?" asked Danny.

"Very probably. There is plenty of water, and his horse has grass. Ky-Lin says he will be very hungry . . . Perhaps it will teach him a lesson. Of course he will have a good story ready, telling them how we were ambushed by bandits, and he only just escaped with his life."

"Serve him right," said Claude. "Haven't we got an extra horse?"

"His baggage pony. A bit of food and some items we might use for bargaining, if necessary." I didn't tell them this latter consisted of tobacco, hashish, alcohol, opium and, of course, the rifle and ammunition.

"So, what do we do now?" asked Claude nervously.

"We go on, of course. We have food, transport and Ky-Lin will be our guide. He knows the way."

"Are you sure?" asked Danny.

"Of course," I said. But I wasn't. It wasn't that I had no faith in Ky-Lin's guidance, rather I had my reservations about our endurance. We still had a long way to go.

Ky-Lin guided us a little more east of the southeast we had been travelling so far. Now we were higher than we had ever been, the air was thinner and the dawn and dusk closer together as the year waned. Gradually we were assuming our winter clothes: no more night-shifts, rather sleeping in our underwear. The sun was still fierce at midday but the stars burnt cold at night. Consequently we started off each morning shortly after dawn, rested at midday for an hour, then pressed on till well after sundown.

Ahead of us the mountains reared like fearsome, jagged teeth, their tops snow-covered already, wreaths of powdered snow blown westward from their tips like ladies' shawls in a wind. Already we were near enough to see that the lower slopes were covered with thick pine forests, and could glimpse the glitter of the many small streams that cascaded down through ravines and gullies.

I had to admit we were making good progress, but for the past few days I had the feeling that we were being watched or followed. We had glimpsed a couple of herds of shaggy horses, and once I was sure I had caught sight of a mounted horseman. Both times the

Ring had given a tiny jolt but nothing to suggest that danger was imminent. Beau-cat was also uneasy, his tail twitching irritably every now and again, but Ky-Lin kept his own counsel.

One night before we unfolded the tarpaulin and made a pocket of it on the ground, for greater warmth and protection, I asked Claude, busy making notes in one of his little black notebooks, what date it was?

"October fifth. Twenty-six days to go." I wished he hadn't sounded so cheerful.

Perhaps it was the thought that we only had three weeks and five days to go, perhaps it was because I had indulged myself with some cheese, but that night I found it difficult to sleep. My dreams were snatches of rubbish, and I couldn't get comfortable.

So, shortly before dawn I gave up all pretence at sleep and went and relieved myself, accompanied by an equally restless Beau-cat. We teamed up again on the way back to camp, but suddenly everything changed. The Ring gave an enormous stab, and Beau-cat lifted his head and hissed. "Quick! Run! Strangers are coming . . ." and he bounded away in the direction of the camp to alert the others. But before I had gone a dozen yards or so I was knocked to the ground from behind, my head wrapped in a thick covering and my hands fastened; I was then lifted from the ground and carried away.

Chapter Twenty-one

The Shaman

It was hot and stuffy in the felt tent, or yurt, and the smoke took its time leaving the animal-dung-burning brazier and finding its way out through the small hole in the roof.

My hands had been untied and I sat with Toby on one side, the men on the other and Ky-Lin tucked away in my collar, unseen. There was no sign of Beau-cat, but I comforted myself that of all the seven of us, he was best equipped to look after himself.

We had been given a space, rather like prisoners in a dock, but the rest of the yurt was crowded. Both men and women were dressed alike, in trews, short skirts, thick jackets and caps, the latter rising conically to a point, with embroidered ear-flaps. They were all swarthy, with plaited black hair and slanting eyes, the men with wispy beards and moustaches.

They didn't seem particularly menacing, although all the men wore knives in their belts or stuck in the tops of their high boots. The tent was about fifteen feet wide, roughly circular, and supported on thin wooden poles, and there were already some twenty-five people squatting on either side of us. Directly opposite us was a high stool, painted in bright colours and boasting an embroidered cushion, and the people kept glancing at the open tent-flap then the stool, as though expecting an honoured guest.

All at once there was a loud rattling noise and a thin, ululating cry, midway between that of a strangling dog at the end of its chain and an owl with a cough, and through the tent-flap came one of the tallest men I had ever seen, thin to the point of emaciation. He had to bend his bald head to enter, leaving the beams of sunshine outside to dance with motes of dust and pollen.

Everyone straightened up as he entered, and all talk ceased abruptly. He was dressed in skins and a loin-cloth; around his neck was a rattle of bones, from his pendulous ears dangled the same, and in his right hand he held a staff with a triple row of feathers. His face was decorated with a smudge of blue on both cheeks, a yellow line down his nose and a red chin.

He stood for a moment in the centre of the yurt, then raised his arm and rattled his staff deafeningly. All his people bowed their heads as if in worship, and he took his place on the stool like a king ascending his throne. Unfortunately he smelt like a midden.

"Local witch-doctor or shaman," murmured Ky-Lin in my ear. "Very important. We can ignore all the others. He is the one who will decide what happens to us."

"Is he very powerful—as a shaman?"

"Not particularly. Probably got the job because of his genetic defects—all that height and hairlessness. But don't underestimate his power over his people."

"Then what do we do?"

"First of all we listen. If I am not mistaken he is about to give us all a speech: I only hope his is a dialect I understand . . ."

Right on cue the shaman rose to his feet, pointed a finger at us (all his nails looked as if they had never been trimmed, yellow bits of corrugated horn that spiralled away from his finger-ends like corkscrews) and started off in an accusatory tone.

"Good," muttered Ky-Lin. "The dialect is based on Kurdish, and one I can now understand, although I didn't when I travelled with Summer, to my shame, but I have made myself fully conversant since then . . . He is asking who we are, where we came from, where we are bound, why we are in his tribe's grazing grounds. All this wrapped up in flowery persiflage to impress the rest of them. When he's finished he will invite us to reply, which I will do through you. Keep your head down, then he won't notice we don't synchronise. Tell the others to sit still and not interrupt or look bored."

I watched the shaman working himself up into his final frenzy, bones clanking, eyes rolled up into his head, spittle flying from his mouth. His audience was obviously impressed as he finally sat down, there was a hiss of approval. But he hadn't finished. After a moment to seize his breath, he stood up again, reached into a leather pouch at his waist and threw something into the glowing embers of the brazier. There was a flash and a bang, and a cloud of coloured stars filled the space in the roof of the yurt, to fall back and singe the carpets on which we sat.

We all jumped, except for Ky-Lin.

"Third rate," he observed. "All right for children. Poor quality gunpowder, mixed with sand and grit, and little plugs of barium nitrate. We can do better than that . . . Now it's our turn. Stand up, bow to the shaman, keep your head down, and do a regal wave now and again if I give you a nudge. Just to emphasize a point . . ."

Now Queen Victoria I was not, although I had seen her once driving in a London park with two of her daughters, and her "regal wave" had consisted of a languid black-gloved hand being raised an inch or two and doing a quarter-turn in the air.

"Right," I said. I turned to the others and repeated Ky-Lin's instructions, then rose to my feet. It didn't help that one of them had gone to sleep, but to disguise this I did a little shuffle-like dance turning in a circle before facing my audience. My heart was beating like a captured bird, but after ten minutes and Ky-Lin was still droning away in my voice, I relaxed a little. I mouthed, I nodded, I shook my head, I waved my hands every now and again on cue. As I gained confidence I overdid it.

"Steady on," murmured Ky-Lin. "You'll never make Covent Garden at this rate . . ."

In between "our" speech, he told me what he was saying. We were on a special mission, but had left our trail on purpose to meet the great and fabled horsemen of the Plains, who were in a position to help us, if they so wished.

Of course the fame of the shaman had also preceded him, and we had brought a couple of gifts as appreciation for receiving us so cordially.

"Tell Toby to go to Makub's horse and unearth a packet of hashish—just one, mind—and ditto of tobacco."

After a moment or two of indecision he was allowed to go, escorted of course, and when he returned he reported that our gear had not been touched, but that the ponies had been hobbled and were grazing.

"Good," muttered Ky-Lin. "That means they are still undecided how to deal with us."

To say the shaman was pleased with his gift would have been an understatement. His eyes gleamed, his tall bean-pole body gave a little shimmy, but of course his words were less effusive. He thanked us as if we had merely gifted him a half-dozen eggs, but his fingers were trembling as he pulled out a kind of pipe from his tatty clothing and proceeded to pack it with a lot of hashish and a little tobacco, lit it and puffed contentedly, until the sweetish smell of the drug over-rode all other odours.

I could see the other members of the tribe sniffing appreciatively. Was it possible, I wondered to myself, to become affected by the smoke?

"Very unlikely," murmured Ky-Lin, reading my thoughts again. "But any noxious fumes from that sort of thing can harm others . . . Now I am going to demand breakfast!"

It worked. Ten minutes later we were presented with bowls of a milky porridge, followed by a sort of blood-sausage wrapped in rice-flour pancakes, and bowls of pale tea. Everyone was eating with us, and I noticed their appreciation was expressed by loud belchings.

"Tell the others to copy," said Ky-Lin. "Bad manners not to."

Toby managed well enough, so did Danny, but Claude and I, try as we would, couldn't even manage the tiniest burp. Having been brought up to repress any such manifestation of bodily functions, I found I was now surprisingly embarrassed at *not* being able to!

"Wait for it," murmured Ky-Lin. "First Master Claude . . ." A moment later Claude apparently obliged, looking as startled as if he had sat on a thistle, wondering where the sound had come from. "Yes," said Ky-Lin. "I can throw my voice. Useful sometimes. Your turn . . ."

My expressions of appreciation were more genteel, but still I blushed.

"Now down to business," said Ky-Lin when the debris had been cleared away. "First we'll soften them up with a story . . . Ready?"

He proceeded to tell them the story of the little slave-boy Summer had called "Tug," because she couldn't pronounce his name, whom she had rescued and taken with her on her journeying, until he had been fortuitously re-united with his tribe.

Ky-Lin's account however, differed a little from the fragment I remembered from my uncle's summary. "Once upon a time, many, many moons ago, before your father's father's father's time, a prince was born to your people. At that time your herds stretched from dawn to sunset across the plains and your people were as numerous as the stars in the sky . . ."

The shaman was half-asleep, but everyone else shuffled forward on their heels, and the light from the tent-flap was dimmed as those outside leant in to listen too. It seemed that like children all over the world, there was nothing these people loved better than a story.

"This prince, Xytilchihijyckntug—" There was a great gasp from the audience and several of them nudged each other, so perhaps Ky-Lin had got it right. Even the shaman now had one eye open. "This prince could outrun the wind, outride the greatest horseman in the world, throw a spear farther than the eye could see and charm both men and women with his wit and wisdom. He visited other peoples to bring back to his own people the best of other cultures. He lived to a great age, outliving his three wives and was survived by fourteen sons and seven daughters. When he died it seemed the whole world mourned his passing, for the sun withheld his face for seven days, the moon was veiled, the winds were hushed and the clouds wept for sorrow . . ."

In other words, it rained for a week.

"But the story I have to tell," continued Ky-Lin (and me), "concerns a time when the prince was only a young boy, some ten or eleven years old . . ." And he went on to tell the story more or less as I knew it. How the boy was captured, sold and re-sold until Summer bought him at auction, being the nice girl she was, and how they travelled together until they came across some of his tribespeople performing at a fair, when he went back with them. Not as briefly as that, of course, but with much verbiage and colourful episodes which served to show the young prince's promise, even at that age.

Our audience were quiet as mice, except for now and again a little "hoo!" or "ha!" of appreciation.

There was no mention of the Ring, nor how Tug had repaid his debt by rescuing Summer from jail, instead I heard to my astonishment that *he* had taught *her* his language, instead of the other way round, which is why I could speak it now. Apparently too, Summer had put off her own journeyings in order to return him to his people without delay.

I began to see where all this was leading: the idea of a long-ago debt that now needed repaying—but Ky-Lin was winding up his peroration.

"They finally parted with tears of regret, the prince swearing a solemn oath on the bones of his forefathers that if ever Summer, her heirs or friends needed help from him or his tribe, in the however distant future, that help would be forthcoming. And now," said Ky-Lin simply, "we are here to collect the debt."

But how, I wondered, were we going to persuade these people that we were Summer's heirs and assigns after all this time?

Our audience lanced at one another, not sure whether they had heard aright and the shaman suddenly snapped upright on his stool and glared at us suspiciously.

"Before you presume to collect this so-called debt—" (Ky-Lin translating) "—I should first want proof that you are what you say you are . . ."

"Of course!" Ky-Lin and I interrupted. "You could not believe we would offend your hospitality by impersonation? If you will be patient for a moment or two longer we will present our credentials. I must tell you a little more about the girl, Summer, who rescued your prince from a life of slavery and degradation . . ."

Skipping over the awkward bits, Ky-Lin and I told

of how Summer, while with the prince, had been
entrusted with a fabulous dragon's egg—gasp from
the audience—which, after she had seen the prince
safely back with his people, she had carried to the
dragon's lair in a certain Blue Mountain.

As she attempted to return the egg, it had been
stolen by a traitorous companion, and she had lost
her life in consequence. (Sympathetic groans from
the audience.) For many moons the egg had been
lost, but it had now been found, and the dragons
wanted it back. They had given my brother and me
and our two servants until the next full moon to
return the egg, otherwise they would issue forth from
the Blue Mountain and lay ravage to all the lands
within their reach, carry off the young women and
children, kill the men and the horses.

We had been abandoned by our guide, who had
run off with food and transport, so we needed their
aid to reach our objective in time, before the dragons revolted. . . .

How were Ky-Lins allowed to tell such awful whop-
pers, I wondered? Perhaps they crossed their hooves,
like we crossed our fingers behind our backs.

Our audience were impressed, no doubt about
that, but the shaman hadn't finished with us.

"And where is this fabulous egg?" he demanded,
rattling all his bone decorations. "And how is it that
you came into its possession?"

Ky-Lin had obviously thought about this one,
because the answer came pat enough. "Because I
inherited from Summer the ability to recognise it for
what it is, and also because I can converse with
animals, as she could, and as your prince will have
told you."

The shaman could obviously neither confirm nor
deny this last, but demanded to see the egg, so off
Toby went once more and fetched it back wrapped
as usual in my shawl. As he unwrapped it I could
see just how much it had grown since the last time

I saw it. It must now weigh at least twelve pounds, and seemed to be glowing slightly. There was a definite warmth there too.

I invited the shaman to come forward and inspect it. He walked around it, leant over and peered at it closely then finally, very gingerly, poked out a bony finger and touched it, then snatched it away again, obviously surprised by its warmth.

I/we invited him to listen to it, see if he could hear anything. He knelt down with a rattle of bones and applied his left ear to the Eg. At first he shook his head, then suddenly stiffened, touched a finger to his own heart and then leant forward again, only to shoot back in a surprisingly agile somersault, his mouth an O of amazement and awe.

"I added a hiss or two," murmured Ky-Lin. "And a very little roar . . . Don't worry: he was the only one who heard it."

I turned my chuckle into a cough. Surely now we had convinced everyone! The shaman, however, wanted one last try.

"You said that this—Summer?—could converse with animals? And that you have inherited that gift?"

I nodded, panicking. How to prove it?

"Beau . . ." murmured Ky-Lin.

"But he's—"

"Here," said Beau-cat, nudging the back of my knee. "Been hiding."

I knelt down and whispered. "That silly old wizard over there wants proof that we can communicate. It's very important. Could you forget your dignity for a moment and, say, walk in a circle, sit up and beg, and lie down and roll from side to side?"

He looked at me with those beautiful blue eyes. "What's it worth?"

I blinked. It was unlike him to ask for favours. "What do you suggest?"

The answer, when it came, was so unexpected that I almost forgot where we were.

"How about a kiss?"

I was scandalised. "One doesn't kiss cats."

"Oh, well: worth a try . . . Now, what was it you wanted me to do again?"

Strolling into the middle, he gazed around the audience with that haughty air that some cats seem to be able to summon at will. The people shuffled back, obviously not used to such a large animal—he certainly had grown since I had rescued him: almost twice as big, I reckoned.

He looked back at me. "Now?"

"Please . . ."

He went through the routine with an air of the utmost boredom, as if humouring a group of children, and when he had finished he sat down and washed his face, to some applause.

The shaman hung on, however. "How do I know this is not a well-established routine?" He rattled his bones menacingly.

"Then you choose something you want him to do, and I will instruct him . . ."

"Tell him, then, to jump over the brazier. And back again."

This would not be easy. The brazier, on its tripod, stood perhaps four feet from the ground, and it was glowing with heat.

I explained to Beau. "Can you do it?" I asked anxiously. "I don't want you to hurt yourself."

For answer he stood up, backed away a little, eyed his target and then leapt, not once but four times: twice there, twice back. The audience burst into spontaneous applause and Beau-cat retreated to my side.

"Satisfied?"

"Not bad—for a cat," said Ky-Lin. "Now, Miss Sophy, let's finish this with some fireworks of our own. Raise your arms above your head, bring them down slowly, then point your index fingers at the fire."

The resultant display of coloured balls, stars, ribbons of smoke and tongues of fire almost emptied the yurt, but to their credit Toby, Danny and Claude stayed where they were, with the cat.

I looked around for the scorch-marks on the rugs that lined the tent but there weren't any.

"Pure illusion," said Ky-Lin. "They saw what they wanted to see. And now," he added briskly, "I think some luncheon is in order!"

Pancakes, cheese and milky tea later and we were ready to go. We had fresh, tough-looking little ponies, extra food, fuel and blankets, and two guides, only too anxious to get going.

Ky-Lin reminded me that we shouldn't need any of Makub's hashish or opium anymore, so we left the majority for the shaman, keeping some back for our guides.

We didn't see the shaman again; I think he had retired to bed with a headache. Of one thing I was sure: he was glad to see the back of us.

Later that night after we had made camp and had eaten some more of the delicious blood-sausage I had warmed up, I congratulated Ky-Lin on his strategy, and Beau-cat on his bravery.

"I knew we were all right if we survived the initial attack," said Ky-Lin. "All children love a story, love to be frightened by tales of dragons and such-like, and adore fireworks. And that's all they were: gullible children."

"Well I, for one," said Claude, "will miss their delicious food. The milky tea was most refreshing."

"I prefer less milk in mine," said Danny. "But these sausages are the best I've tasted in an age."

"Good," said Ky-Lin. "You'll probably get offered some more before this trip is over. The pack-ponies are mares, and the other ponies have already been cupped more than once."

Toby and I understood at once, I think, but the other two had to have it explained to them.

"How else would they get fresh milk and blood, except from their horses?" said Toby, though he was looking a bit green. "It obviously doesn't harm the horses, otherwise they wouldn't do it."

I remembered something I had read once. "I believe they prefer their milk fermented: they say it's a nice refreshing drink . . ."

Without a word the other two got up and disappeared in different directions, not coming back for some time . . .

Our guides didn't believe in wasting time. They hurried and harried us from dawn till dusk, determined to be rid of us as soon as possible.

They were probably scared that the Eg would hatch out while we were travelling, and woke us up before dawn, curtailed our lunch-break and had us on the move until long after the sun had gone down.

The little ponies were more than equal to the task, and even Claude didn't fall off so often. Rapidly the mountains drew nearer, and fearsome they looked, with sharp inclines, jagged tops, steep cliffs and great icicles hanging hundreds of feet up.

It was much, much colder, and we were glad of the extra blankets at night. We were already wearing most of our winter gear, and Beau-cat's fur was growing longer and thicker.

On the sixth day we left the plains for good and started to climb through increasingly dense forest of pine and fir, their thick, resinous smell with us all day. It was also getting difficult to breathe again with the increased altitude. Their was no definite path to follow but our guides were adept at finding the easiest way, sometimes having to hack a gap for us with their little axes.

We all felt a little odd: Claude had a couple of nose-bleeds, Danny started talking to himself and I had a slight headache, but Ky-lin told me that this was just a touch of mountain-sickness, which affected different people in different ways, and it would pass as we became more acclimatised.

We climbed for three more days, more slowly as the ascent grew steeper, and Ky-Lin worried as to how we would carry our food and gear once our guides had left with their horses. Toby suggested that we try to build a sledge, so for two nights we laboured, with the aid of the guides and their efficient axes, who chopped pine and spruce, until we had a reasonable enough sledge, capable of carrying at least our food, fuel and any extra gear. All the rest would have to be carried in our haversacks.

At last we reached the head of the pass and made camp in one of the most bleak and exposed places I had ever seen, open on all sides to the weather.

"They should call this Four-Winds Crossing," said Danny, shivering like the rest of us as we huddled round a sparse fire. What he said was true: wherever we sat or crouched, there was an icy wind at our back. I crossed over to the guides and handed them some hashish and a couple of pellets of opium for helping us. They accepted with grunts, but I could see all they were waiting for was their departure in the morning.

In the event they didn't wait for dawn, but were packed up and gone without a goodbye by the time we had struggled awake.

"Right," said Ky-Lin. "Now for it!" and he stretched and creaked and popped until he was once more pony-size, which still made Danny and Claude nervous. "Told you I would pull my weight. Load up the sledge then, and let's get going. It's all downhill from here . . ."

Chapter Twenty-two

River of Ice

What Ky-Lin didn't say was that going down could be quite as painful as climbing, for you were using completely different muscles; also falling upwards wasn't as perilous as falling down a slope—in fact some of that first descent was so steep that we had to hold the sledge back rather than pull it behind us.

That initial way down wound irritatingly between interlocking spurs of the mountains, so although we moved as fast as we could, as far as losing height was concerned it was a slow business. We stopped for a quick mid-day snack, cheese and dried fruit, and then pressed on. Later a few flakes of snow drifted down, and the sky was a greyish yellow.

Ky-Lin looked anxious. "There's a lot more snow up there—we'll need shelter tonight. These hills are mainly limestone, so there should be caves further down."

By sundown we had managed to find a small scoop in the hillside, surrounded by boulders, with an overhang of rock. I made a fire and boiled up enough rice and fish to last until the following night and, at Ky-Lin's suggestion, put the pan outside to catch any snow for filling our water-bottles.

It was a miserable night. Quite apart from the moaning wind that seemed determined to seek us out, both with noise and cold, and the rattle of stones intermittently falling from the rocks above, we all ached all over. Ky-Lin touched us all with his healing horn and that alleviated the pains a little, but did nothing for the cold; however I was comforted by the warmth of Beau-cat, who crept under my blankets and snuggled up against my back.

It had been snowing heavily overnight; as we progressed the sun melted most of it away, but the ground was slippery and several times I ended up on my behind. One consolation was that the spurs of the mountains were widening and our course downwards was faster and easier, although the going was very uneven: smooth rock, stony clefts, thin soil.

At last we rounded the last spur of the mountain and there before us, some five hundred feet below, was a wide valley, sloping gently towards the horizon, the midday sun glittering on what looked like a sliver of river, that grew larger as it progressed southward.

"Great! Now we can float the sledge down the water," said Danny, clapping his hands together; he was tired of dragging on the ropes.

"Not on there we can't." said Ky-Lin. "And tell him, tell them all, not to make any sudden loud noises." He glanced up at the mountains on either side. "There's enough snow up there to give us all a nasty shock."

"Why can't we float the sledge?"

"Because that isn't a river of water: it's a river of ice. A glacier."

A glacier! I had heard of them, read something about them many years ago. Rapidly I translated

Ky-Lin's words to the others, who gazed down at it with a wonder equal to my own.

"Well, if it's a river of ice, why can't we slide the sledge along it?"

"Not on that surface," said Ky-Lin. "At least, not for more than a short distance. It is like a badly iced cake, and is rough with stones, rocks, whatever has got caught up with it over the years. Also, it moves, albeit slowly, more towards the middle and the edges tend to pile up with rubbish. You'll see when we get there."

I translated again, and then we began the steep descent, which was quite the most hazardous part of our journey so far; it was far steeper than we had had to cope with so far, and at one stage we were literally clinging to the rocks with the sledge dangling beneath us. All the while Ky-Lin was trying to educate me with talk of moraines, ablation, neves, sublimation, crystallisation, firn and crevasses, but I'm afraid I was too busy trying to get down in one piece to pay much attention. Afterwards I wished I had, but by then it was too late.

The glacier started like a thin tongue of ice, but gradually widened until it filled most of the valley. As Ky-Lin had predicted, it was very difficult to walk upon. Not only was it both skiddy and slidy, it was also gritty, fissured and uneven. The sledge was more difficult to manage than before, because we had to seek out the smoother bits all the time, or lift it bodily over ridges as high as my waist. Of all of us, the terrain was toughest on Beau-cat. Not because he wasn't far more agile than the rest of us, but because of the tenderness of his paws; he could manage stones and rocks, but the gritty surface of the glacier scratched and tore at his pads, so for the most part he rode on the sledge.

The one bonus we had was to realise how we were definitely moving downhill, cheered at our pause to eat at mid-day to see the highest mountains receding behind us.

"Another two or three days," said Ky-Lin.

We took turns with the sledge, generally an hour at a time, although Ky-Lin, pony-size, always did a double stint. After eating that day it was Toby's and my turn, it being easier with two at once, each with a length of rope. Suddenly Toby stopped on a smooth stretch, so abruptly that the sledge ran into the back of my legs.

"Ouch! What's the matter?"

"Quick, over here everyone!" he shouted. "Just look at this!"

"Hush!" said Ky-Lin, sharply. "We don't want to bring the snows down on us."

"What is it?" Claude, Danny and I were over by his side in a moment, for he was pointing downward through the ice.

"Look," he breathed. "Just look at that . . ."

Generally the ice was cloudy and we could not see more than an inch or so beneath the surface, but here we could see far farther by a freak of the glacier's movement. What we saw was like something out of a book of faery. There, trapped beneath the ice, were the antlered heads of two enormous stags, locked in a battle of death. Anywhere else their bones would have long ago vanished, but here they were forever immortalised. We could only clearly see their heads, part of their shoulders and one leg, but they were so large, even at this distance beneath the ice, that I found it hard to believe they had ever existed.

"Giant elk," said Ky-Lin. "Some call them Irish elk, because their remains have been found in the peat bogs of that island. Peat is a good preservative."

"Why the two of them together?" asked Toby. "Did they kill each other at the same time?"

I translated Ky-Lin's reply for him. No, one would die first, but because their antlers were locked solid, the other wouldn't be able to free itself, and would die later of wounds or starvation, as sometimes happens even now with the red deer of Europe.

I shivered, not only because it was cold, with the bitter north wind chasing us down the valley, but also because it was sad to think of death coming that way—the victor becoming the vanquished. Somehow for a brief moment a thousand years, two, three became now and they were here—

I shivered again.

"Come on," said Ky-Lin gently. "We've a way still to go before nightfall. *They* are history: *we* are now. Their reincarnations will have passed through many stages by now." I had forgotten he was a follower of the Buddha.

That night we found a better cave, which seemed warmer, but this, we discovered, was because of the snow which had again fallen overnight. The wind semed to have increased and was pluming the snow on the tips of the mountains into puffs of what looked like mist, and drove icy particles skittering unpleasantly across the ice of the glacier.

All night long we had been aware of the creaks and groans of the glacier as it moved in the centre at an average of one foot per day. Fresh-fed by spring melts it would flow faster, also in the heat of summer, but now it was almost static. Despite this it still made the most weird noises as the ice rubbed against the banks, or thrust up a barrier in the centre.

What happened later was meant to be, perhaps not. All I know is it changed our journey irrevocably. It was a mistake, my mistake, and a costly one.

It was Toby's and my stint to pull the sledge, the last one before our midday halt. We had done a half-hour when Toby went off to relieve himself. The sledge was much lighter now, because of the food and fuel we had consumed and I didn't find it too burdensome, but the Afghan rifle kept getting in the way. Danny had insisted on bringing it with us, saying darkly that "it might come in useful," but so far it had just been a nuisance. For the dozenth time it hit me in the back of the legs and I lost patience.

Tugging it free, I sent it skidding across the ice in Danny's direction.

"If you want this, then carry it yourself . . ."

"Now don't get in a paddy, darlin' girl . . ."

"For the last time, I'm not your darlin' girl!" and I pulled away as fast as I could. Not far to go now: another couple of days or so and our journey would be over. I fell into a reverie of just what I would do when I got back to Hightop Hall, and saw that I was falling behind with my daydreaming. Seeing a nice long, smooth, stretch of untrodden snow, sloping down for at least two hundred yards, I thought: perfect! Why pull when one could ride?

Gathering up the ropes I went to the back of the sledge and gave it a shove, then ran forward and jumped on as it gathered speed. My weight made it go even faster and I waved gaily to the others as I drew level. Toby waved back, but it was with both arms and urgently, while Ky-Lin started to bound across the ice towards me. I waved again, to assure them I was fine—

Then the world disappeared.

One moment I was accelerating along the fresh snow trying to keep the sledge in a straight line, as I had when a child, delighting in whizzing down the slopes near the village, to tumble off at the bottom and be scooped up in my father's arms, the next I was falling into oblivion, my mouth full of snow, blocking out my shout of panic. There was a bump that nearly knocked the breath from my lungs, a knock on my head and momentarily I lost consciousness.

I opened my eyes again to a blur of white, pain, a dragging sensation in my left wrist, piercing cold and complete disorientation. There was a creaking, crunching noise in my ears, the falling of stones . . .

"Stay still, stay perfectly still . . ." It was Ky-Lin's voice in my ears, thought rather than the spoken word. "Just don't move, however much it hurts. We're coming to get you. No, don't look up: just *wait*. Don't try to talk . . ."

I did as I was told, desperately fighting all my instincts to move, to yell out my terror, to wriggle free of whatever held me fast. I was shivering like the leaves on an aspen tree, my teeth chattering like the proverbial castanets. All I could see from my prone position was a wall of ice, layered like a giant sandwich: white, grey, stony, clear, cloudy, thick, thin. Even the strips were wavering before my eyes, for my shivering was growing uncontrollable.

All at once there was a creaking noise above me and instinctively I cowered, fearing a fall of rock, but a moment later I saw a pair of feet followed by the attached legs, and a moment later there came the reassuring voice of Toby.

"It's all right, Sophy: just lay still."

Idiotically I wanted to correct his English. "Lie . . ." I whispered, but I'm sure he didn't hear me.

"Keep still. I know you're cold and you hurt, but for the moment you are best just laying there while I set things up. You're on a ledge—that's why you mustn't move—and I'm going to land just beside you. The sledge-rope is still attached to your wrist, and I'm going to cut it loose so they can haul you up. Meanwhile I shall stay with you." He was speaking in a very low voice, as if he feared he would bring a further fall down on us.

It seemed to take an age. I could feel his feet nudging my body, hear the sawing of the rope, and then suddenly my wrist was free, the pain started to subside and a creaking, bumping noise told me the sledge was being retrieved. I was now so cold my teeth no longer chattered: they felt as though they were glued together, and I was sure that if I bit my tongue I wouldn't feel it.

There was another slithering noise and then Toby was fastening the rope around my waist. He thrust my hands around something, but I couldn't feel what it was.

"Now, hang on and don't struggle. You'll be perfectly safe. Don't look down . . ."

There was a sudden jerk, and I screamed as I found myself spinning and twisting in space. For a long moment I panicked, as the rope slipped from my waist to my chest, and I was afraid of the disgrace of soiling myself, but luckily I had to concentrate on just breathing, for my weight was tightening the rope cruelly. At last I realised I was moving upwards and, risking a look, I saw a ring of faces above me, spinning slowly round.

It seemed like forever, but it could only have been a couple of minutes later that my front was being scraped painfully across the lip of the crevasse into which I had fallen, as I was finally hauled to safety. I was pulled away across the ice to safety, and a moment later Danny was rubbing my arms and legs, and as Toby was hauled to the surface by Claude and Ky-Lin, all joined in carrying me to the edge and wrapping me in blankets, while a warm, furry blanket wound itself round my neck and proceeded to lick at my ears and nose. I attempted feebly to push away Beau-cat's rasping tongue, but Ky-Lin stopped me.

"Let him. Best thing for you: we don't want frostbite."

Ky-Lin pronounced that there were no bones broken, just bumps and bruises and a slightly sprained wrist.

"No more travelling today. Stay where you are, and I'll scout around for a decent shelter." No words of blame for stupid behaviour: if I had been wider awake I would have realised there was some good reason why the rest of the party had been on a completely different course. I was lucky to be alive, I knew that now, and I tried, inadequately, to thank them all.

I felt even worse when I discovered that the sledge was a write-off and that we had lost a lot of the heavier provisions: rice, fuel, honey, the axe and larger cooking-pot. We still had one spare blanket, a small pan, some flour, dried meat and fruit, but it was a pitifully small heap. Thank goodness there were only a couple of days or so to go. . . .

Ky-Lin found us a roomier cave than usual, and once we had everything inside it started to snow again, so we probably wouldn't have got far even without my "accident." Claude and Danny were trying to wrest apart the shattered remains of the sledge, but they needed the missing axe.

"Pity!" said Danny. "It would have made a broth of a fire."

"The wood's damp anyway," said Claude. "No, it's hopeless."

I was still shivering, and there was a tightness in my chest. Ky-Lin glanced at me anxiously.

"Claude is wrong," he said. "Nothing is entirely hopeless . . . Tell them to stand back from the sledge."

Somewhere at the back of my mind I seemed to recall a fragment of Summer's journey: was it something to do with Ky-Lin splitting rocks, or metal, or something?

There was a sudden flash of light, a scrunching noise, chips of wood seemed to fly everywhere, then rearranged themselves into a neat heap of firewood in the corner of the cave.

"Wow!" said Danny and Claude in unison.

"How did he do *that*?" asked Toby.

"Tell him," said Ky-Lin, "that it is literally the triumph of mind over matter."

"Magic?"

Ky-Lin shook his head. "No magic. Just a simple matter of disassociating various elements into their separate constituents and reassembling them into a combination more acceptable to our present needs."

I tried to translate this but failed: I hadn't the slightest idea what he was talking about. I glanced at Ky-Lin and thought I detected the fragment of a smile—obviously he didn't want me to understand, or he was making the whole thing up and it *was* magic.

We lit a small but warming fire and Claude took over the cooking, producing pancakes with the last of the flour and pouring melted cheese over them. Everything else would have to be divided up between us and carried in the haversacks, but we decided to leave this until morning, especially as Ky-Lin had diminished in size, explaining to me that splitting the wood had weakened him somewhat. I made sure he ate part of a pancake and some dried fruit, then he curled up in a corner and slept till morning, when he seemed almost fully recovered.

That afternoon while Claude soaked some dried meat to add to a supper of rice, we played desultory word-games, several times looking out to see whether it had stopped snowing, but it hadn't. The tightness in my chest didn't seem to lessen, and that night I kept waking up with a troublesome little cough.

In the morning everything was covered with a fresh fall of snow that squeaked its protest underfoot and clogged our footsteps. We had parcelled out what remained of our goods, Toby being in charge solely of the Eg, which was by far the heaviest individual burden.

"Take care now," advised Ky-Lin, now nearly back to pony-size. "If we keep to the edge of the glacier, the snow will have cushioned the rough places."

We made reasonable progress, and before long I was perspiring. I looked across at the others: they too were mopping their brows and Danny, now using the long Afghan rifle as a walking stick, had undone his jacket.

Ky-Lin lifted his nose and sniffed the wind, which had swung round to the south. "There's a temporary thaw coming, he said. "We shall have to take extra care. This will activate small streams and rivulets and may well loosen the snow above us. We'd better move out into the centre of the glacier, just in case."

We ate a frugal luncheon under an overhang so we didn't have to sit on the snow, then moved out again. We had been plagued by thin wisps of mist all morning as the sun sucked up moisture from the snow, but suddenly these cleared temporarily and we all saw it at once. There, admittedly at least a day's journey away, was a green valley.

We gazed at it disbelievingly for at least a minute before the mists closed in again, then we all started talking at once.

"Are you sure that wasn't a mirage?"

"We should be there tomorrow!"

"What a relief to see a bit of green again!"

"At last some proper food . . ."

Then what should have been the impossible happened.

Danny, in his exuberance raised the Afghan rifle in the air and mimed what we had seen the tribesmen do in reality: firing a round into the air. He pulled the trigger twice, mouthing silent "Bangbangs."

Then three things happened simultaneously. Ky-Lin whispered an urgent "No!" the Ring gave a tremendous stab, and Danny pressed the trigger for the third time. There was a terrific bang that ricocheted from side to side of the ravine, then a horrible hush.

Danny threw the rifle away, whispering: "I didn't know it was loaded!" and we all glanced at each other in terror. For a moment it looked as though we might have got away with it, but the Ring was still stabbing away furiously and Ky-Lin was herding us urgently towards the edge of the glacier.

"Find us a cave, a large one, Master Beau!"

Then it came.

At first it was a rumble so low that it was almost under the threshold of sound, but it grew in pitch and intensity until it drowned all other sound. We ran as fast as we could, but the clinging snow impeded our progress, and it was like trying to run in thick, dry sand. We were only half-way to the edge when Ky-Lin left my side and went back the way he had come, and to my horror I saw Toby had fallen. I ran a few more faltering steps and then glanced back. Toby was hobbling and Ky-Lin took him up on his back and started back towards us, but at that very moment a huge slab of ice came skating down the glacier towards them.

I stifled a scream, saw Ky-Lin leap aboard the ice, carrying Toby, and then the vanguard of the avalanche was upon us.

With a huge rumbling roar and an icy blast of air the snow bore down on us like huge waves on the sea-shore, turning over and over, curling and spuming, cresting impossibly high. I looked for Toby and Ky-Lin but couldn't see them, forgetting my own danger until hands grabbed me from either side and dragged me away.

I couldn't see for the tears in my eyes. Gone, probably for ever, were Toby, Ky-Lin and the Eg. Not that the last mattered against the lives of the other two: people I had loved, my especial friends. I would have given anything to have them back beside me.

A moment later I was pulled into a black hole, the rumbling and crashing behind me intensified, I was thrown to the ground and then utter darkness . . .

Chapter Twenty-three

The Caves

The dark . . .

Darkness and pain and partial deafness, choking on dust, the rumble of stone, panic of emptiness—

"I'm here, I'm here!" A brush of fur against my hand. "Don't panic! Just get your breath back and sit up. We are in a large cave and are safe for the moment. Claude, Danny, you and I. And nobody's hurt; just a few bruises, that's all. I'm going to leave you for a moment to explore but I'll be back in a few minutes."

It was the longest speech he had made through the Ring: I realised that, even in my distressed state.

A wail came from somewhere to my right. "Jesus, Mary and Joseph! My *head!*"

"*Your* head! It was *my* head you hit with yours!"

"And whose fault was that, may I ask? Where are we, anyway? And where's Sophy?"

"I'm over here, to your left. Stop arguing and come and join me . . ."

Scrabbling, scraping sounds, suppressed swearing

and we were all together. A quick hug all round, and
then the questions. I wanted to know if they had seen
any more of Toby and Ky-lin than I had, the answer
no, and they both wanted to know where we were.

"Sure, and they were together," said Danny. "And
a canny old thing like Ky-Lin knows how to survive."

"He won't let Toby come to any harm," comforted
Claude. "They are probably looking for us now. . . ."

I told them what Beau had told me, and a moment
later he was back, rubbing against my knees.

"No way out the way we came in, I'm afraid. The
fall brought down part of the entrance tunnel, and
it must be blocked by at least twelve feet of debris."

I could hear the panic in my voice. "You mean—
we're trapped? If there's no way out we'll die!" Without thinking I had spoken the words aloud, instead
of by thought-process through the Ring, and immediately I could hear the others muttering hysterically.

"Now look what you've done," said Beau-cat. "I
never said we were trapped."

"We're in a cave, aren't we, and you said the
entrance was blocked—shut up you two—so we must
be trapped . . . mustn't we?"

"I said we couldn't get out the way we came in,
yes, but that doesn't mean there aren't other ways
out. This is a large cave—just sing a couple of lines
of your favourite hymn. Yes, go on!"

"All things bright and beautiful . . ." How inappro-
priate! Danny and Claude must have thought I had
completely lost my mind, but as my voice strength-
ened I understood what the cat had meant. It was
not like singing in an overstuffed sitting-room, far
more like being in church. "You're right . . . But
how do we know there are any passages leading out?"

"Trust me. Stand up and turn around slowly. See
if you can feel any difference in the quality of the
air. No, I'm not joking. . . ."

I did as he said, then repeated the manouevre.
Sure enough I felt a slight difference in the movement

of the air. I pointed to the two directions I thought
it was coming from, forgetting of course that we were
in darkness. But it seemed he could see me.

"Correct. Well done. As it happens I have already
found our first passage and it leads in the right direction."

"How do you know?"

"Because we want downwards and as far as possible east of south. That way we have a good chance
of finding the ultimate way out. And, yes, before you
ask, I do know my south from my north!"

I was quite sure this new, masterful Beau-cat did.
I told the others why I had been singing and the fact
that Beau had found a passage for us to follow, at
which they cheered up considerably.

"Now," said Beau, "retrieve your haversacks and
let's see what we have. Yours is a little way to your
left. I believe there are some candles in there."

He was quite right. There were a half-dozen ordinary ones and four long-burners, plus vestas. I wasted
a couple of the latter before I managed to get a
candle going, then bent to light some more.

"Steady on," said Beau. "One at a time. We don't
know how long those will have to last."

So, by the light of one small candle we emptied
our haversacks and took stock of what we had. It
was a pitifully small heap. We each had a blanket,
mug and water-bottle, the latter full. Then there
were two coils of rope, a quantity of firewood, the
small cooking pot and a ladle. As far as food was
concerned, it was a small quantity of everything. A
little rice and couscous, but not much; a pack of
dates, another of dried figs, a few dried vegetables,
some nuts, cheese and a handful of raisins. I would
have said that would give us one meal, but not much
more.

"Now that we haven't got Ky-Lin with us, it is up
to you to take charge. Those two need leading, they
can't do it on their own. So, I will help you, and you

must be positive and firm. Every day I will scout ahead and find the best way forward—"

"Every *day*? I thought we'd be out of here by tonight!"

"Sorry, Sophy, but I think it will take longer than that. These hills are honeycombed with caves, but they don't all lead the right way; some are dead-ends and others may be too small to traverse. So, come on and give your first orders. Pack up everything except the shorter rope, get fastened together so we don't get parted. I'll lead the way, you follow with a guarded candle. We'll keep going as long as we can on this first stage."

He paused for a moment. "Tell me: how is the Ring?"

"The Ring?" I looked down at it. "It's fine. . . . Why?"

"Then that means we are doing the right thing. Let me know if it starts playing up, won't you?"

I nodded. After that first stab when we tumbled into the cave it had been quiet, so perhaps things weren't quite as bad as they seemed.

I decided to take Beau's advice and be positive, so I organised the others as he had suggested. "What time is it, Claude?"

He looked at his watch, shook it, looked again.

"Just after two in the afternoon, Sophy. I would have thought it later than that."

So would I: just over a half-hour since we had been entombed, because I had checked my fob-watch minutes before the avalanche. "Well, that's a bonus: means we can travel further . . . Right! Off we go! At least it isn't cold . . ."

In fact, after the sub-zero temperatures we had had to endure, it was almost pleasantly warm; I presumed these caves retained more or less the same temperature, like cellars: cool in summer, warm in winter, although it didn't do anything for my cough.

We started out with high hopes, but after an hour

or so of stumbling along a stony, unlit, uneven, twisting passage, anchored only by a rope that we had
to adjust because somebody either trod on
somebody's heels or was jerked forward painfully, we
were all short-tempered and much less sanguine. The
passage was also not uniformly wide, nor did it slope
down evenly. Once there was a sudden drop of about
three feet; once a rock-fall almost blocked our way
completely: another time we had to lower our heads
to avoid bumping our heads on the roof—especially
Claude!

We conversed in whispers—why whispers? Because
it is a known fact that one always whispers in
churches, cathedrals, libraries, museums, catacombs—
anywhere one feels awe, unease or fear. Anything was
possible in these caves; I would not have been surprised if they brought forth all the things which used
to give me nightmares as a child: bats, ogres, witches,
trolls, statues-which-came-to-life and giant cockroaches.

"Rubbish!" said Beau's thought-voice. "Don't you
think that I would sense those things? Stop worrying!" And he rubbed his face against my thigh.
Goodness, he certainly was growing. . . .

"You almost sound as if you are enjoying all this!"

"Why not? Better than giving up and crying! Think
of it as a game, a puzzle, a maze to solve. We'll get
out, never fear, but it may take a day or two. At the
moment we are travelling at a snail's pace, but when
we get into some of the larger caves we should move
faster. Don't forget you have to measure this stumbling around in semi-darkness with what we achieved
in the open. Twenty miles outside, what with twists
and turns as well, will take four times as long in
here."

An hour and a half later we reached the end of
the passage, which debouched into a small chamber,
before splitting into two exits. While Beau searched
ahead we took a well-earned rest, ate a couple of
mouthfuls of nuts and dried fruit, then pressed on

again. This time the going was easier, but there were several halts as we passed other passages which Beau had to scout. At one, tantalisingly, there came a breath of outside air, but the cat reported that it was only a narrow funnel that even he couldn't struggle through.

At last, after we had used three of the ordinary candles, we reached a larger cavern, and I decided that enough was enough and called a halt for the day.

"We're not going to spend the night in here?" asked Claude fearfully.

"You're not going to tell me that you really thought we would be tucked up safe in some cosy inn, are you?" said Danny. "Are you frightened of the dark, then?"

"Of course not," he answered hurriedly. "It's just that . . . that . . ."

"We're all in the same boat, and we're all together," I said. "So be a good lad and help me prepare something for supper."

We made a small but comfortable fire and boiled up the rest of the couscous with a scrap or two of the fish, and finished with some dates. Hardly satisfying, but better than nothing. We were all physically exhausted, but sleep didn't come easily: our bodies were tired, our minds wide awake. Not only was the ground uneven and stony, but everyone must have been worrying the same way I was: how long would we be in here? What would happen if the little food that was left ran out? Worse, how about using up all the candles? Would we wander endlessly until we lay down and died?

Danny sat up suddenly. "This is no use, you know. I'm not a bit sleepy. Why don't we have a sing-song or something?"

"Or a story," suggested Claude, who couldn't sing.

"A story it is then; who's to start?"

"You can, Danny," I said.

To his credit he told us an amusing folk-tale about

how an enterprising Irish family finally outwitted a couple of ill-intentioned leprechauns.

Claude then told one of my favourites, "Stone Soup," how a cunning traveller and his dog conned a fat and lazy cook out of dinner and a gold coin. But of course this talk of food made us feel hungry again, so when it was my turn I steered away from all that and started to tell the tale of the "Princess and the Pea," but before I had finished I had the strong suspicion that I was talking to myself (and Beau).

"They're asleep," I said.

"Five minutes ago. An interesting tale. My governess never told me that one. But normal princesses aren't as tender-skinned as that."

"Cats don't have governesses, Beau. And how would you know how princesses feel?"

"Young princes have tutors or governesses, and they also have princesses as sisters."

"But you're not a prince—"

"Who says? Want to hear my story?"

I hesitated. The Ring was warm on my finger, the candle was out, what remained of the fire a couple of embers, but I was still not sleepy enough and my chest felt tight. What on earth would he invent to entertain? "All right, then . . ."

"Lie down, tuck yourself up, and I'll tell you just how a handsome prince was turned into a lowly cat . . ."

I see: it was one of those. A fairy-tale. At least "Stone Soup" could have had a basis in fact—just with a clever enough man and a stupid enough woman . . . But even thinking about that and my stomach started to protest, so I shut my eyes and concentrated on Beau's tale.

"Once upon a time," I murmured. "All the best fairy tales start that way. . . ."

"Once upon a time," he began obediently, "if that's what you want. But this is fact, not fiction."

"Anything you say . . ."

"This story begins in the country of Siam some few years ago," he began, and I snuggled down to listen through the Ring. "The current king had many wives and innumerable concubines, so there were plenty of royal princes and princesses—eleven of the former and twenty-three of the latter, if I remember correctly . . ."

I found myself drifting.

"The king decided he had to do something about it, as the palace was getting definitely overcrowded. All the royal children had had English governesses, and that is why I speak your language so well, but the king decided to give his sons the chance of further education, and arranged advantageous marriages for the girls. The princes were sent to foreign universities—"

"Oxford and Cambridge," I murmured sleepily. "Harvard and Yale . . ."

"And the Sorbonne, of course. That's where I went, and that is why I was pleased when you called me 'Beau,' the French for handsome."

"But you are a cat, not a prince!" I interrupted, waking up.

"Fiddlesticks, as you English say! You haven't heard the rest of the story . . ."

"Sorry, I won't interrupt again."

"Well, when I came back from the Sorbonne I found that my father had decided it was time that I got married. I was then twenty-four years old and in no mood to settle down. I asked him to send me abroad again for a while, to one of our embassies perhaps, but he was adamant. Until all of his sons had produced a son he would not be satisfied, for he had not yet decided whom to make his heir.

"That might have been acceptable to my other brothers, but not to me. I had always been a rebel, so I took off on my own with a purseful of money and some jewelry to enjoy the fleshpots of the world.

My wild way of life led me into some very peculiar situations, but none so strange as an encounter I had in Spain. It was fiesta-time, and I had watched a very beautiful girl dancing all evening. It seemed she had noticed me too, for when the dancing was over—and very late it was—she caught up with me as I was returning to my lodgings, and invited me to her place for a last drink. I was already stumbling-drunk, so it didn't seem at all unusual that a young woman like that was not chaperoned.

"As it was, I'm afraid I disappointed her, for immediately I entered her apartment I was sick, then fell asleep on the floor. Waking some time before dawn I found I was immensely thirsty, and wandered down a long corridor looking for the kitchen. On my way I became aware of some strange chanting coming from a room to my right, whose door was partially open. I peered in, intending to apologise to my pretty hostess and beg a glass of water, but what I saw drove all thoughts of thirst from my mind . . ."

He paused, and sighed. "We can finish the tale tomorrow. You must be very tired."

By now I was sitting bolt upright and the thought of sleep was far from my mind. "No, no, go on!"

"All right then . . . Where was I? Ah, yes. I peeped into the room, and I couldn't believe my eyes. An old crone, bent almost double with age, was hobbling round a bubbling cauldron on a brazier, muttering spells and charms! At first I thought it must be some ancient relative of the girl I had met earlier, then I noticed she was wearing the same dress, and in her ears were the same earrings! Even as I watched, I could see the spells begin to take effect; from looking about a hundred years old she was gradually straightening, and her hair was turning from white to its previous colour . . .

"I must have made some sound for suddenly she turned towards the door and saw me."

"Couldn't you just have run away?"

"I suppose I could—I cetainly should have! But I suppose it was the residue of the drink talking, but whatever it was I stepped into the room and accused her of being a witch!"

"What did she do? What did she say?"

"At first she was surprised, then she was very angry that she had been found out, and told me to get out and never darken her doors again!"

"And did you?"

"No, I was an idiot. I did the very worst thing I could have done. She looked so stupid half-changed—"

"Half-changed?"

"The top half was nearly the pretty lady again, the bottom half was still the old crone. I couldn't help myself: I laughed at her."

There was silence.

"You don't believe me, do you?"

"I'm just suspending judgment, that's all," I said carefully. "Of course I don't believe in witches—"

"You should! It was she who made me what I am now. Apparently she knew perfectly well who I was all the time, and had some hare-brained scheme of seducing me into becoming her puppet and then persuading my father to make me his heir.

"I said something to the effect that she must be jesting if she thought I would ever agree to anything like that, saying that she was just a silly old woman and I wasn't the least afraid of her spells and curses. I'm afraid that did it."

This was better than the Arabian Nights! He had a terrific imagination. "Couldn't you still have run for it?"

"She had fixed me where I stood. I could move neither hand nor foot. Some kind of hypnosis, I suppose."

"Couldn't you have struck out at her? Shut your eyes and unhypnotised yourself? Yelled for help?" I was getting involved in his fairy-tale.

"One, she was out of reach and I couldn't move; two, I tried looking away, it didn't work; three, who would have heard me? Anyone else in that apartment would have been her creature anyway.

"Then she started to threaten me, everything that could hurt me most—blinding, laming, impotence— but I gathered from her mutterings that these spells lasted only for a specific time, and I reckoned I could put up with any form of disability for a short while. My spirits started to rise, and at last I found a tongue in my head, tried to defy her.

" 'I don't believe you have any powers at all!' I said. 'Why, if you could work any spells, you would have turned me into a dog or a toad or a crow long ago!' A foolish boast to make, for at once she started to circle me, muttering in a strange tongue, and a rhythm I realised was a primitive form of spell-casting.

"Suddenly I felt a horrid shrinking feeling, and realised the floor was coming up to meet me. I found I was on all fours, and that my feet were turning into clawed paws! The room was expanding, my mouth became full of pointed teeth, suddenly I had sprouted a tail, my body had become covered in fur, and there I was, crouched on the ground amidst my discarded clothing. The only thing from my other life that I still retained was the neckace I had been wearing— an insurance against the need for money—which I still wear."

"You mean the one you're wearing now? The tatty one of coloured glass and brass?" I snorted with derision. "I suppose you're going to tell me it is really gold and emeralds!"

"Of course—when she changed me she changed that as well, without realising it. She laughed at me, gave me a lusty kick, and opened the window. 'Out you go, tom-cat; roam the alleys until you die, or else find a virgin who will give you three human kisses of her own volition. And this you must do within the year, else you will turn to dust!'

"I leapt from the window and fled." He paused. "And that's it. That was four months ago; I won't bore you with my aimless wanderings, nor my capture by that stall-holder you rescued me from. You are the one I have been looking for, the one with the Ring, the only one I can explain this to." He paused again. "So how about it?"

"About what?"

"A kiss, freely given. The first . . . Or more, if you feel like it."

I drew away and tucked myself up again. A story was a story, but as to believing it—

"I don't kiss cats," I said. "Sorry. It was a good tale, though. 'Night . . ." And I turned over and went to sleep almost immediately.

Chapter Twenty-four

The Last Barrier

I woke from a wonderful dream, instantly forgotten as I realised nothing had changed, that we were still imprisoned in this maze of caves. But the good feeling persisted, which was just as well, because the others, except Beau, were distinctly querulous and grumpy. It took me time to get them going, to make them believe that a breakfast of a handful of nuts and raisins and a drink of water from a brackish pool was sustaining.

However we made good progress that day, led by the indefatigable cat and heartened by the fact that the passages we followed all seemed to slope downwards and lead in the right direction. Then around five in the evening, we came across an unexpected hazard.

Beau came trotting back to announce that a few hundred yards farther on the passage dropped away some thirty feet after a recent subsidence, and it would be difficult to climb down.

"We mustn't get too near the edge: it's still crumbling away."

"No other way round? An alternative passage?"

"Sorry, no."

We proceeded cautiously, but there was no doubt when we came to the edge of the landslide, for there were still rattles of stone and pebble, and the ground felt crumbly beneath our feet.

"How do we get down?" said Danny.

"Not sure," I said. "Beau is going to take a look . . . Take care," I muttered to him. "We don't want to lose you . . ."

"Give us a kiss, then . . ."

"Shut up! Sorry . . ."

"Apology accepted. Don't worry: cats have nine lives, you know, even if they are princes in disguise . . ."

His fur slid under my hand and he disappeared. Claude, Danny and I huddled together, listening to the slithers still occuring.

"How long has he been?" I whispered to Claude.

"Nearly five minutes," he whispered back, and after that I must have asked him to consult his watch every thirty seconds, until he told me gruffly to stay still and wait. But the waiting seemed intolerable and it was with the greatest relief that I heard a scrabble of claws and a panting Beau arrived back.

I overwhelmed him with questions until he tapped his paw against my thigh. "Hush up! Let me get my breath back . . ." A couple of minutes later he told me what he had found. "Now you won't like it, but it isn't impossible. It's farther than I thought, some sixty feet or so, and it is more or less sheer all the way down. And before you ask, no, none of you could expect to climb down unassisted."

"Then how in the world did you manage it?"

"Have you ever watched a cat climb down from high up in a tree? No, I thought not. They spread out all their claws and come down backwards, paw over paw, back ones hanging on, front ones finding

the best purchase, then, when they reckon they are
near enough to the ground, they twist around, kick
off with their back feet and land right way up."

I translated the essential bits to the others.

"All right for cats, but how do we manage?" said
Danny.

"Find a witch, and we can all be cats." I said faceti-
ously. Beau was the only one who knew what I was
talking about, and he wasn't best pleased.

"Serve you right if I left you to work it out for
yourselves!" he hissed. Of course he didn't mean it,
and between us we planned a viable solution. We had
a rope fifty feet long, which would have to be looped
securely at the top; this would make it too short to
reach the ground at the other end, but if we added
a couple of blankets that should lengthen it enough.
Unfortunately the nearest knob of rock to which we
could attach the rope was some way back down the
passage, so it meant tying our jackets together by the
sleeves to get the extra length. At last Beau declared
himself satisfied with our knots, and I only hoped the
seams in our now rather tatty jackets wouldn't split.

"Well, who's first?" I asked. "Afraid I've never
climbed down a rope before."

"Neither have I," said Claude.

"Sure and I have," said Danny. "Many's the time
my pa and I went—"

He stopped suddenly as if afraid of saying too
much. He shrugged. "I'll go first. Give us a candle
and vestas, and it'll light the rest of you down." He
spat on his hands and rolled the sleeves of his
woollen shirt down over the palms. Grabbing the
rope he swung himself over the edge accompanied
by the rattle of stones and pebbles. He disappeared
into the darkness, and there was only the creak of
the rope and an occasional muffled exclamation to
show us he was still there.

There was an agonising wait, then a *thump* and an
"Ouch!"

"Are you all right?"

"Sure, fine and dandy!" His voice had an echo. "Apart from a broken leg and a lump on my head the size of a duck's egg . . . Only joking. The rope is still about three feet short: difficult to see where you're landing. Haul the rope back and send down the haversacks next, while I light this candle."

Looping the straps through Claude's scarf, which gave us the extra length we needed, this was accomplished successfully, then it was my turn.

My palms were sweating. "I'll never make it!"

"Of course you will," said Beau. "Make a proper loop from the scarf and Claude will lower you down. You're not heavy, and it isn't very far."

After all that it was easier than going to the dentist; there was a moment of utter panic when I was lowered over the edge, but luckily I kept my mouth shut. Claude lowered me jerkily, hand over hand, but as I had my eyes firmly closed it wasn't until I found Danny's hands around my waist that I realised that I was safe. He set me down gently as I disentangled myself from the scarf.

"All right, Sophy?"

I nodded, exhaling a breath I hadn't realised I was holding.

Now it was Claude's turn. The rope started swaying, Danny grabbed the end to hold it steady, and soon enough I saw the soles of Claude's boots by the light of the candle some ten or fifteen feet above me. Then everything went wrong. There was a snapping, tearing sound and he fell the last six feet, bringing the scarf and my jacket, minus the right sleeve, to land heavily with his left ankle twisted underneath him.

He let out a cry as he tried to stand and crumpled back down again. Even by the sparse light of the candle I could see that his face was white and twisted with pain.

"Think I've broken it—swelling up like mad!"

I unlaced his boot carefully, before the ankle swelled up too much to get it off; casting about for something to wrap it up I saw the very thing: his own scarf. Pouring water from my water-bottle I handled the ankle carefully: there had been plenty of sprains and breaks in the school at which I had taught, and I could see and feel that there was no break, but sometimes a sprain was more painful. I wrapped it up tightly until he looked like a man with a bad case of gout.

"Just take it easy. I'll give you a headache powder to ease the pain a bit."

"Always knew his brains were in his feet. . . ."

"Don't be cruel, Danny . . ." although I was smiling to myself. I telegraphed Beau to unhook the rope and send it down, moving us out of the way. It snaked into a neat coil at my feet, closely followed by the cat himself.

I insisted that we carry on, although Claude was in considerable pain. Perhaps I was being hard, but I knew just how little food there was left and God only knew how long it would take us to find a way out. We did stop early for supper and sleep, although both were in short supply.

I lay awake longer than the others, trying to control my troublesome cough.

Next day we moved as fast and as far as we could, although Claude found it difficult to keep up, even though the passage was now mostly wide enough for Danny to walk alongside and hook his shoulder under Claude's. I was really worried; we were down to a mere handful of food, although there were plenty of little streams and rivulets to slake our thirst. Most worrying of all was the situation as far as the candles were concerned. There were only two and a half left, and while we could manage without food for a while, we couldn't stumble about in the darkness.

I was just about to suggest settling down for the night, having turned to see the exhausted faces of

Danny and Claude, when Beau came bounding up the passage.

"Another half-mile and there is a large cavern. No way out, but a glimpse of the world outside."

Intrigued, we followed him into a cave, the largest I had ever seen, stretching away into a darkness too great for our feeble candle. Not only did it stretch away on either side, it also soared up like the roof of a cathedral, and even our whispers were tossed back in mini-echoes. It was awesome and I felt a bit like tip-toeing. It was the sort of place one would expect to find stalactites and stalagmites marching away like the pillars in a church.

We walked along the left side until we found a relatively smooth patch to settle down on. I dished out most of what was left—only a handful of dried fruit for breakfast, and that was it—then renewed Claude's bandage. As soon as we were finished I blew out the remains of the candle, hoping it would last us for a while in the morning.

Then it happened.

There was a glow in the cavern, a soft light that came and went. We all looked up in the same direction at once and there was a collective gasp of recognition.

"The sky!"

"Moonlight."

"Clouds!"

"And the stars—how absolutely wonderful!"

Stumbling in the dark, but drawn irresistably by the light, we walked into the centre of the cavern, and stood under the jagged hole that scarred the southern wall of the cave. No way could we climb up there: it must have been a hundred feet up, but from where we stood we could feel the occasional breath of fresh, colder air. Heavy clouds interrupted the westering moon, now near full, and I felt a sudden alarm when I realised the Eg had to be delivered on the night after the full—

"Reminds me of home," said Danny. "The roof's leaking. Anyone got a bucket?" and he pointed to the shaft of light, down which drifted a few desultory snowflakes.

We awoke to light, real light, day-light.

None of us had passed a particularly good night. There was the uneven dripping of water from some-where nearby; it was colder than it had been and the blankets were not much help; worst of all there were certain cracking and rumbling noises, mostly far off, although the echoes in the cavern were distortive, and my chest felt tight and uncomfortable.

"Sounds as if the whole complex is falling to pieces," I muttered to Beau.

"Nothing of the sort! Every now and again, espe-cially when the temperature changes, or when water has built up and seeks a way out, then you get a rockfall or two: that's what you can hear. Go back to sleep. . . ."

And now, like all mornings in the light, the night fears and dangers were chased away. The dawnlight coming down through Danny's "hole in the roof" was still grey, but quite strong enough for us to see to eat the handful of food left.

"That's it," I said unnecessarily.

Beau, who had eaten nothing for two days, now came and nudged my elbow. "Come and see some-thing that might cheer you up."

He led me over to a spot almost directly opposite the soft light coming through the jagged hole. I peered at the wall: it looked as though there were faint scratches in the stone.

"What is it? Why is it important?"

"It's hope. Our first. Wait a minute until the light grows stronger, then look closer."

I did as he suggested, then I could make out what looked like pictures of animals, but the sort of ani-mals I had never seen before. A long-tusked elephant with a thick coat of hair, a tiger with down-pointing canine teeth, horses with thick, stubby legs and manes, deer with enormous antlers, just like the ones we had seen in the ice . . . And among them all were sketches of fur-clad men with spears and clubs. Some of the animals were pictured lying on the ground, stuck with broken spears—

"What does it mean?"

"It means that once upon a time, perhaps thousands of years ago, men lit fires in here, cooked, ate, slept and raised their children—and they couldn't have done that unless there was a way in and a way out. Those pictures you see were their record of the animals they hunted and how."

"Then why did they leave?"

"Probably an Ice Age, like the one that created the glacier. They were meat-eaters, so would follow the migration of their food farther south. It could have been tribal warfare or disease, but there are no bones. I've looked."

"You said yourself that could have been thousands of years ago! The way could well have been blocked long since!"

"There are signs of more recent occupation, if you move a little farther along—there! Put out your hand: what do you feel?"

It sounded very silly when I said it. "Big toes?"

"Right. Step back some way and then look up."

I saw what looked like six statues, some twenty feet high, carved into the rock. The light from the roof was stronger now and a shaft of sun struck momentarily against one of the eroding faces: slanted eyes, a calm flat face, curved lips.

"The Six Immortals, I guess," said Beau. "This place must have been some sort of temple some three or four hundred years ago. If you look between each pair of feet you will find a niche or bowl for offerings. So the worshippers had a way in and a way out."

"Then why did they stop coming to worship?"

"That I don't know. What I do know is that we cannot be far from the way out now, and the quicker we get going, the quicker we get out."

I told the others what we had seen, we packed up and started off, but it took longer than we thought. Claude's ankle had stiffened up, and we had to adapt to his slower pace, so that it was well past mid-day when we had traversed the full length of the cavern, some two miles, and left what there was of the light behind, lighting our penultimate candle in the only passage Beau could find.

It seemed claustrophobic being in a passage again after the size of the cavern, but we stumbled on as best we could, and I reckoned we had made another mile when the passage turned a corner and widened abruptly. At the same time the sound of running water we had been hearing intermittently suddenly intensified until it almost drowned speech, and the candle-flame bent back on itself. The only encouragement was that there seemed to be a slight lessening of the darkness ahead.

Now the walls on either side of us were dripping with water, and as we rounded yet another turn we saw why: across our path raged a roaring torrent of water, effectively blocking our progress.

We had come to the end of the road.

Chapter Twenty-five

Dangerous Crossing

I sat down hard and burst into tears. Anger, disappointment, frustration and fear: to have come so far and to be finally denied our freedom. A further cruelty were the chinks of light that came through a crack in the roof above, showing us just how impossible a crossing would be. At some time or another water had built up against a wall of the cave until the rock had given way and the water had roared through, digging itself a deep channel over the years, to disappear underground once more.

One by one we retreated to the first bend in the passage, where at least we could hear ourselves speak.

"I—I can't swim!" blubbered Claude, his tears, like mine, mixing with the fine spray that had drenched us. Indeed we were all shivering, and it was this, more than anything, that brought me back to my senses.

"Neither can I," I said. "But there must be some way across."

"Not through that water," said Danny, his usual optimism dampened. "You're not on your own, Claude, you great lob-lolly, so pull yourself together and get that brain of yours working. We'll think of something." But he didn't sound convinced.

I looked around. "Where's Beau?" I wiped my face, ashamed of my earlier outburst.

"Here," he said. "Just been reconnoitering." He was dripping; his fur clung to him in clumps, bare skin showing through the darkened pelt. "All may not be lost." He spoke to me through drying licks of his fur. "This must be the reason (lick) that the cavern was finally abandoned. (Lick) We can't get out at the far end (lick) where the water exits (lick) because there is a risk (lick) that we would be sucked down and lost."

"It's all impossible!" I burst out. "We can't wade or swim across: we'd be dashed to pieces on the rocks. There must be some other way out!"

"Probably, but it might take days to find it (lick) and even then it could leave us stranded (lick) high up on some mountain. (Lick) Besides we have no food and no candles. (Lick) And Master Claude's ankle is not getting any better. (Lick) No, this is the best we can do. Let me think . . ." He continued to tidy himself, finishing with a comb to his whiskers. Right-handed, or pawed, I noted . . .

The tiny bit of candle in my hand gave a flare and collapsed back, a reminder of how little time we had left.

"Could we catch some fish?" We all gazed at Claude without speaking and he sighed. "Just a thought."

"Rod, line, hook, bait, net?" said Danny, his voice heavy with sarcasm. "Besides which there probably aren't any, and if there were they would be uneatable. What kind of fish.live in a cave all their lives?"

Suddenly Beau started to pace back and forth, his tail twitching from side to side. We all watched him, not really in any kind of hope, but with a wish that he would suggest something, *anything*.

At last he stopped his pacing and looked at me. "We still have the rope?"

I nodded. "About forty feet long."

"Should be long enough. Tell them to tie a loop about a foot across at one end." I relayed his instructions, dying to know what he had in mind, but not wanting to be disappointed by some cat-brained scheme that couldn't possibly work. "Now," said Beau to me, after inspecting the knot, "make a bag out of the jackets, one strong enough to hold me, but leave the two ends free."

I was more mystified than ever, especially when he trod around the scoop of leather and declared himself satisfied. "It'll do."

"Do *what*?" I just had to ask. Beau looked up at me, his blue eyes gleaming in the last of the candlelight.

"The only thing we can do," he said. "You are going to catapult me across to the other side!"

It sounded like complete madness, stated like that, but once Beau had explained a bit more to me, I could see that there might, just might, be a glimmer of hope, although it was an awful risk for him. All his calculations had to be exactly right, and if he failed the consequences for all of us were too horrible to contemplate.

He sensed my reluctance. "What alternative is there? Come on, let's get it over with. The others understand what they have to do?" I nodded. "Your job is to hang on to the other end of the rope and pay it out: *don't* lose the end!"

"What happens if . . . ?"

I couldn't say it.

"Then you will have to pray—ask the Ring to help you, if I cannot."

That was a strange thing: the Ring wasn't jabbing a warning. It seemed as cool as ever. Perhaps it was because I wasn't yet in any real danger. I gave it a quick rub, praying it to help Beau.

He led us back to the roaring waters and in moments we were all soaked once more. The path alongside was neither even nor of uniform width and very slippery underfoot; at one moment we could walk two abreast, the next we were hugging the wall, terrified lest we slip, the weak illumination from above making it even more difficult as we slipped from light to shadow almost step for step.

At one point a large chunk of rock broke away behind us: glancing back I saw it had taken the path with it and shivered with fear: no way back!

Beau, who was leading the way, stopped and looked at me. This was the spot he had chosen. Although the torrent was not at its narrowest here, still some twenty feet across, at least the ledge on which we stood was wide enough to swing a cat—what an awful expression to think of, given the circumstances!—and on the other side was another, not as wide but at least clear of obstacles.

Beau indicated that Claude and Danny should spread out his "sling" on the ground; he climbed in and settled himself comfortably, shaking himself first like a dog to rid his fur of excess water. I knelt down by his side.

"Are you sure?"

His only answer was: "Going to wish me luck?"

"All the luck in the world!" and without thinking I leant forward and kissed his wet muzzle.

There was a sudden gleam of light, blue light, as though a spark had been lit behind those beautiful eyes.

"One down, two to go . . ." He nodded at Claude and Danny. "Tell them to start swinging; not too fast at first, but higher and stronger bit by bit, like a child on a swing."

My mind momentarily confused by having actually kissed an animal, a thing I thought I would never do, afeared by the dreadful position in which we found ourselves, numbed by the terrible cold, dazed by the roar of the torrent and nursing the thoughts of everything that could go wrong, I found it difficult to start everything off. I remembered at the last moment, thank God, to wrap the other end of the rope around my wrist, ready to pay out the rest. The loop I settled around Beau's neck and stepped back. All was now ready. I muttered a swift prayer for all of us, my heart beating like a hammer, and making my breathing more difficult than it had become over the past few days.

At last, still reluctant, I nodded at the other two.

Slowly at first they achieved some sort of rhythm. Beau was now about the size and weight of a large dog, and it took some time to get the swing effective, back and forth, higher and higher. I could see the cat was clinging with all his might to the cloth, to avoid being shaken off too early; he must be feeling pretty sick.

The sling went higher and higher, until eventually at its highest it reached the height of Claude's shoulder. Suddenly on the next outward swing there was a flash of fur and in a seemingly endless arc Beau sailed through the air, a blur of movement against the spray. I followed his progress with agonised attention: like all such moments, it seemed to be happening at half-speed. As I automatically paid out the rope all I could think was. "He isn't going to make it, he isn't going to make it—he couldn't!"

For an agonising moment he landed and then teetered unsteadily on the ledge on the far side, then he gained ground and with a surge of relief I saw him safe and upright on the ledge he had chosen. The boys let out a cheer, which I doubt he could have heard, but I was too busy with my tears of relief to join in. At least one of us was safe. . . .

"Congratulations, dear Beau!" I thought across to him.

"It was the kiss that did it!"

I was glad to see that he still had a sense of humour.

"Listen, Sophy: I think I can smell fresh air. I'm going to go to the end of the passage and find out. In the meantime put a loop on your end of the rope and move a bit farther down. I'll loop mine over here."

Beau stopped some fifty feet farther on, shucked off his loop and passed it over a pinnacle in one easy movement. He then looked through the spray at me.

"Find something similar over there, and get the rope as taut as you can. Back in a bit."

When he did come back, some ten minutes later, he was still soaked through, but he held his tail at a jaunty angle. "It's there," he called out to me. "The way out. About half a mile farther on. So let's get going. Send the first one over!"

We had discussed this before. Danny, being the most lithe and agile among us would be first, so he could help anyone in difficulties from the other side. We had the rope stretched as taut as we could, so it didn't dip into the water.

I relayed Beau's good news. "So, just a quick hand over hand," I said in a shout to make myself heard. "Ready, Danny?"

"Easy as fallin' off a log," he shouted back. "When it comes to your turn grasp the rope firmly, cross your ankles and hang upside down. One hand at a time and don't look down. Just concentrate on getting across as quick as you can."

"Wherever did you learn all that?"

He leaned close, his curls flattened against his head with the wet, and spoke in my ear. "From me da'. And wasn't he the best housebreaker in all Ireland?"

At least that's what I *thought* he said. But I might have been mistaken.

A moment later he was off, swinging across the

gap like a monkey, although he was soaked through in a second, and I could see the spray was getting in his eyes. It took about two minutes to cross the twenty-foot wide chasm, but he stepped off the other side safe and sound. He checked the loop their end, then gave us a cheery wave, meaning: "Next one!"

I had already decided this should be Claude, because I knew that if he was left until last, he would never have the courage to start out. It wasn't his fault: he was just like that. He would always need someone to pull him and someone to push.

Just before he set off Beau thought to me: "Now we've found the way out we won't need the haversacks, so leave them behind. Just get anything you want out first." I knew Danny would have nothing, but had a look just in case. A pack of cards, some of those silly photographs, a couple of dice: I tucked the first and last into an oilskin pack in which I kept my sewing things, fob-watch and Bible. At the last moment I tucked my monthly rags and clean handkerchiefs into my pockets: they would dry out. Claude retrieved his notebooks, also in oilskin, and tucked them into his jacket, together with his chronometer and photograph of his mother.

Then I took at least five minutes arranging him on the rope. His legs were so long that he didn't seem to have grasped the concept of hauling himself across with his ankles hooked over the rope. First one then the other fell off, and when I had got them properly aligned I found he was hugging the rope to his chest instead of hanging by his hands. In the end I got quite cross with him, and told him I would go myself and he would be left on his own if he didn't pull himself together.

At last he started off at a snail's pace, his eyes tight shut and a sort of moaning noise coming down his nostrils. As he got farther across the rope sloped downwards, aiding his progress; at last he seemed to be getting the hang of it. I checked the loop at our end: it seemed to be holding all right, although his slow, swaying progress was threatening to fray the edges a little.

If only he would just hurry up! He was now two-thirds of the way across, and I was just beginning to think I would have to steel myself to follow him very shortly, when it all happened.

His feet became unlocked and slipped down, until he was only hanging by his hands from the rope. He was making no attempt to right himself, and his mouth was open in a silent yell for help. I started forward, but Danny was quickest. In a moment he was back on the rope inching his way towards Claude. By now the whole thing was swaying wildly and I knelt down to hold it steady, hoping to God that it would hold, but it was swaying and jerking so much with both men on it that there was little I could do.

Eventually Danny reached the panicking Claude and leaned down to place his feet and ankles round the rope again and tried to tug him forward, but Claude wasn't having any. He doubled his arms around the rope and just hung on, making no effort to go either forward or back. I could see Danny was shouting at him, getting more and more exasperated, tugging at his collar and his belt. At last he jerked one of Claude's arms free and placed it forward on the rope, and pulled at him again. This time he moved, but only fractionally. Danny repeated the process again and again until he backed up on the ledge and inched Claude up as well.

Then he kicked him good and hard, on the behind—

In the meantime I could see Beau pacing anxiously back and forth. As soon as Claude was safe, he thought-yelled at me to hurry up. "And check the rope," he added.

I turned and saw to my horror that a couple of the strands had snapped, due probably to the extra weight of Claude and Danny together. But there

looked to be plenty of thickness left, and I was now
so cold that I couldn't have re-knotted the rope. I
said a quick prayer, then lowered myself over the
edge, pulled my sleeves over my hands, grasped the
rope by guess rather than feel, because I was so
numb, hooked my ankles over the rope as Danny had
instructed and started to haul myself across.

He had made it look so easy, but I found it very
hard. The weight of my body made it a real effort
to pull with my arms, and my feet didn't help at all.
All at once the Ring started to throb urgently, even
though I had hardly any feeling in my hands. For a
moment I gazed back, dreading that the loop was
about to give way, and saw to my horror that the
piece of rope to which Beau must have alluded was
the one that hung over the river; it had sagged so
much it was now badly frayed, and even as I looked
a strand snapped and curled towards me.

For a moment I was frozen with fear, then the
urgent pricking of the Ring got me going as fast as
I could towards safety. Halfway there, at the lowest
drop of the rope, almost touching the roaring waters
beneath—

The rope broke.

Half a second later I found myself in the water.

This was not water as I had always known it, this
was a battering ram, a great thumping that drove the
breath from my body, bruised my arms, legs and ribs,
banged my head with great cuffs, poured itself down
my mouth as if it had forced my mouth open and
then held it in a dentist's vise. My screams were literally washed away, and I was a piece of flotsam that
wasn't sure which way was up and which was down.

Suddenly I was brought up by an agonising jerk
round my waist, and for a second or two my head
was above water. I took great gulps of air and
promptly vomited before being sucked down again,
frantically trying to rid myself of the constriction
around my waist, only to find that it was the frayed

end of the rope that had snapped and whipped around me.

I realised that this rope was possibly my only hope. It was firmly looped at Beau's end, so if I could hang on perhaps, just perhaps, I could pull myself towards the far side. I wrapped the loose end as tightly as I could around my arm. My mind was starting to blank out, and in another few minutes I should start to lose consciousness forever—

Another kind of painful jerk almost pulled my arm from its socket: had the rope snagged? Another jerk, I swallowed another mouthful of water, got a sudden gasp of air, choked, vomited again. Now I was dragging across rocks, my head took a painful blow, then at last my head was above water and the roaring pounding waters were receding. My shoulders were clear, my waist, my hips; my legs were being scraped against something and suddenly I was in a different dimension, flat on my stomach on the rocks on the far side where the boys had hauled me. Anxious hands were patting and pummelling me and my ears ringing and bubbling with water and distorted voices.

I tried to sit up, but firm hands were pressing me down, pumping the rest of the water from my lungs. I dribbled for a bit and then tried again. "I'm—I'm fine," I managed at last. "But so cold . . ." Somebody's jacket was put round my shoulders and I was helped to my feet, shaking and trembling, Danny on one side and a limping Claude on the other, and led away from the roaring torrent.

There was a faint mew ahead. "Follow me," said Beau. "The light from behind will guide you to the turn in the passage, and then you will be able to see where we get out of here. Just take it easy: there's no real hurry right now."

I was crying however, and couldn't seem to stop, and the three of us stumbled along that ill-lit passage like a trio of drunks leaving an inn at closing-time. I was still shivering, my head ached, my chest

hurt so much I wondered whether I had cracked any
ribs, and I was still coughing up what I supposed was
water.

It took us an hour, that last half-mile, but at last
I could smell fresh air, sharp and cold, and see a
patch of daylight ahead, growing bigger as we
stumbled and swayed towards it.

A moment later and I blinked: something was
obscuring the light, something that grew larger and
larger until it filled my vision. A creature radiating
warmth and comfort and reassurance—

"*Ky-Lin . . . !*"

BOOK THREE

"Journeys end in lovers' meetings."
—Wm. Shakespeare

Chapter Twenty-six

The Return
of the Eg

He seemed to fill the passageway, bringing with him a sort of aura of light, I flung my arms around his neck and hugged him convulsively.

"Ky-Lin! You found us! Is Toby all right? Where's the Eg? Where are we? Where's the Blue Mountain?" I was stopped by a convulsive fit of coughing and a pain in my chest, the worst yet.

He leaned forward and touched me with his little horn, and instantly the pain abated somewhat.

"Dear girl, you are soaking! Here, climb up on my back and I'll carry you outside. Master Claude with an injured ankle?" He bent forward and touched that, too. "Better? I cannot carry you both, but make your way outside and I will arrange for transport. Come, Miss Sophy . . ."

"But where is—"

"Just do as you are told. Answers as we go."

Off we trotted towards the widening oval of light,

with it coming the first intimation of ice, cold and snow, but Ky-Lin radiated heat and I snuggled down against his warm hide as he bore me down the passage and out into the open.

Once outside I opened my eyes to their widest and breathed in the sharp air as deep as I could, although it hurt my chest to do so. We were at the foot of the mountains among the broken rubble of the outermost rim of the glacier, among what I believe Ky-Lin had referred to once as a "moraine."

And there, a basket at his feet, all bundled in scarves and a cloak, was Toby!

He helped me off Ky-Lin's back, exclaimed at my damp clothing and wrapped me in his cloak. I hugged him happily and started off with all my questions, which had so far remained unanswered.

"Let the lad tell his own story," said Ky-Lin as he turned back to help the others. "It'll be quicker!"

Ky-Lin was gone about ten minutes, but during that time it seemed that Toby never drew breath. Apparently the avalanche that had nearly cost us our lives was the most exciting thing that had ever happened to him. "Awesome," he called it.

They had initially outraced the front of the avalanche on their slab of ice, but as it caught up with them Ky-Lin had taken Toby and the Eg on his back, managed to steer them closer to the side, then given an almighty leap that landed them safe on a ledge away from the rolling, boiling mass of snow. Once everything grew quiet again they had made their way down to the valley, and a small Chinese village some three miles from where we now sat. They had made this their headquarters, coming back every day to try to find us. They had even already explored the passage we had emerged from, but had decided that the torrent of water would have been too difficult for us to cross, after going back to the spot where we had disappeared and satisfying themselves that we couldn't escape that way either.

They had examined every exit they could find, mostly farther west, but Ky-Lin had insisted they came back to this one that morning. "I reckon he had this sort of sixth sense, being a sort of magical creature."

I guessed the Ring might have had something to do with it, but didn't say so.

I gazed around; the sun was already setting towards the west, and I couldn't help my shivers. Our goal, the Blue Mountain, couldn't be so far away. I switched my gaze to the south, and there it was! It should have been tinged by the setting sun, but it wasn't. It held a cold blue light of its own. I suppose it had once been conical, the cone of some extinct volcano, but the top had caved in years ago—wasn't there something about that in the long-ago journal of Summer?

I sprang to my feet, or tried to, yielding to a bout of coughing.

"That's it! Where is the Eg?"

"Here." He pointed to the bundle at his feet. "Heavier than ever."

"We must go there. Now!" I coughed again. "We must have wasted so much time wandering around those wretched caves. I must take it *now*! Help me to pick it up and carry it—"

He rose to his feet. "Be reasonable, Sophy! You're in no fit state to carry anything. You can't just run off like that, anyway. The mountain is miles away!"

"I must! Don't you understand? This is what we all came here for—"

"You're just not well enough! And it'll be dark soon. We'll never find our way for starters . . ."

"Well, Ky-Lin will just have to carry me, or something . . ." I sat down again and burst into tears. "How can we be so near and yet so far?"

"Now then, what's all this about?" Ky-Lin was back, with Beau. I explained as best I could, and to my surprise he fell in with the idea without any

objections. "If you are set on it, I will help you all
I can. I have left the others at the entrance to the
cave, where they will be sheltered from the cold, and
will send back litters for them both. We shall go
down to the village, where you will get something to
eat and a change of clothing. It will take a half-hour
for me to get you to the village, and then you must
rest. We'll set out for the mountain about three hours
before midnight, then you will have fulfilled your
quest. You're sure it must be tonight?"

I nodded. "I've got this sort of urgent feeling . . ."

He nodded. "Let's get going then." He looked at
Toby and Beau. "Can you two make it? If you fall
behind, Toby knows the way . . ." I translated quickly
to Toby, and he nodded.

"We'll go at our own pace."

Then Ky-Lin and I were off. I was still shivering
but, as he promised, within a half-hour I was snug
in a village house, supping a bowl of chicken-noodle
soup. Strangely enough, even after so many days
practically starving, I didn't really feel hungry, but
I drank three bowls of fragrantly scented pale tea,
and felt much better.

The villager's wife gave me hot water to wash in
all over, plus clean my hair, and then she took away
my tatty, torn clothing and provided me with typical village wear of padded blue jacket, trousers of the
same material, felt slippers and a cap with ear flaps.
I should have felt warmer, but I still shivered, so she
tut-tutted and led me to a small pallet. Making me
lie down, she covered me with a coarse blanket,
bringing the brazier which heated the house nearer.
Putting her finger to her lips she mimed sleep and
carried the lamp—a wick floating in a stone jar of
oil—farther from my eyes.

I must have dozed off, because the next thing I
knew was the arrival of the others, about an hour
later. Toby and Beau must have been fed and rested
at one of the other houses, because they turned up

a few minutes later, yawning and stretching, but otherwise looking ready for anything. I wished I did.

Within minutes Danny and Claude were guzzling large bowls of chicken and rice, and slurping their tea, belching politely afterwards, which I suppose I should have done also.

Ky-Lin breezed in and asked if I was ready, asking me to tell Danny and Claude that washing water, dry clothes and beds would be ready for them shortly.

"Why, where are you going?" asked Danny.

"To return the Eg, before the time runs out. I have a sort of feeling it's got to be done tonight."

Claude frowned, and glanced at Danny. "But I thought you said—" to receive a sharp dig in the ribs.

"Never mind, never mind," said Danny hurriedly. "We'll talk about it later . . ."

Claude rose to his feet. "Are you sure you're all right? You look a bit pale to me."

"So would you if you had nearly drowned! Now, don't try to stop me, because I have to be there before midnight." But they still looked uncomfortable.

A couple of crude litters stood outside; basically they were just hammocks suspended from bamboo poles, with lanterns slung at either end. Toby looked dubious, ready to argue, but I told him, from Ky-Lin, that he had done enough running about already, the Eg needed safe transport, and anyway he would have to help me once we got to the mountain.

Beau joined me in my litter, but before long I think we both felt it would have been better to walk, apart from the fact that it was too far. The combination of both jogging unevenly at the same time as swaying from side to side made me feel slightly sick, together with the dancing of the lanterns. In spite of that I dozed off again, but Beau excused himself to run alongside for a while.

I seem to remember disembodied dreams with no sense to them: a huge clock ticking away the minutes

at an astonishing rate; a calendar whose pages flipped
back and forth at the bidding of a wind I couldn't
feel; rocks falling all around me and bouncing at my
feet soundlessly; a gargoyle spouting water detached
itself from a wall and marched towards me, leering;
trees burst into bloom in the snow and died in the
sun.

"Hey there, wake up!" said Ky-Lin, touching my
face with his antennae. "This is as far as they will
go."

I climbed stiffly out of the litter, the nasty taste
of the dreams still in my mouth, coughing a little
with the effort. Bright moonlight, piercing cold, and
in front of me a dark mass rising smoothly from the
plain, crowned with a gap like a broken tooth.

The Blue Mountain.

"How do I get up there?" I was shivering again.
It looked very forbidding, dark and threatening, and
I couldn't see any way up. And I had to carry the
Eg, and presumably the lantern as well. "And—and
what do I do when I g-get there?"

"You just leave the dragons their egg," said Ky-Lin
gently. "Summer told us there was a cavern up there,
remember? Just get up there and come straight back."
He nodded at Toby and Beau. "They'll go with you."

Obviously Toby had picked up the sense at least
of what Ky-Lin had been saying, for he held up the
sack in which he was carrying the Eg. "I have this
safe, and we'll take a lantern and go slow. Any idea
where we start off?"

"Around the other side," Ky-Lin explained to me.
"I'll carry you as far as I can, but I'm not allowed
to go any further; our people do not deal with dragons—it has always been so. Each of us pretends the
other doesn't exist. It is easier that way."

Around the other side the moon illuminated a
steep and rocky climb leading to a sort of path that
snaked around the mountain. Ky-Lin carried me as
far as the beginning of the path and promised he

would wait as we set off, Beau in front in case of hidden obstacles, then Toby with the Eg and the lantern, and me bringing up the rear, stopping now and again to catch my breath.

I had thought that the climb would be difficult, but in fact it was surprisingly easy; the path was more or less smooth and the gradient not particularly steep. I suppose it took us about a half-hour to reach the end of the track and the mouth of a dark passage. I shivered again: surely I didn't have to go into the unknown darkness of a cave so soon after our escape!

Toby started forward but I grabbed his arm. "Do we have to go in there?"

He turned and gave me a grin. "Sure, it's the way in, isn't it? This was the way Summer went in, and I bet she was scared, too."

"But the whole place was supposed to have blown up: how do we know the passage isn't blocked?"

"Only by going in and finding out. And if it *is* blocked, then we give the dragons a shout and tell them where we've left the Eg."

I was sure he was joking. "What if there aren't any dragons left?"

"I don't believe it really matters if there are or not. All your uncle wanted you to do was bring the Eg back to the Blue Mountain wasn't it? Well, here you are, and you've carried out his wishes. If the passage is blocked and there are no dragons, we'll just tuck the Eg up snugly and it can hatch itself. Come on: five minutes and the job's done and we can all go home again!"

"I'll go first," said Beau to me. "I don't sense any danger. What does the Ring say?"

Just a steady throb: nothing life-threatening. A warning, but not a definite danger. "Right," I said. " 'Lead on, MacDuff!' "

After a few yards we turned a sharp corner and at once there was a different quality to the light. A

sort of phosphorescence seemed to be seeping from
the walls; it was like the luminosity you get from
decaying plant life, but without the stench. But there
was a smell ahead: a sort of cindery, sulphurous stink
that made me pinch my nostrils. We turned a couple
more corners and then stepped out into what
resembled an arena.

It had once been a large cavern, but now the roof
was gone, leaving the jagged edges looking like the
overhanging eaves of a decayed mansion. The high
moon showed that where we stood the ground was
smooth, but on the other side of a central chasm was
a jumble of rocks and stones, like a giant's play-
ground.

But there was no sign of any dragons . . .

It was warm in there, but not a healthy heat; it
was like the embers of a fire not quite out. We
moved forward until we stood on the rim of the
chasm, from where the heat was coming. Gazing
carefully down, we could see, far, far below, what
looked like the ruby heart of sullen coals, with a
spark travelling now and again from end to end.
Obviously if this had once been the heart of a volcano, then there was still life down there.

There was a sudden puff of heat-laden air from
below, with the rotten-egg smell of steam-trains and
we retreated rapidly, gasping and choking.

"Let's get out of here," said Toby in a low voice.
"You're coughing badly."

"But—but where do we put the Eg?"

"Don't know. Perhaps we can find a place where
it won't roll about."

"Why are you whispering?"

"I'm not . . .   Dunno. Anyway, you are too."

I shrugged. "Let sleeping dragons lie is my motto."

"There's a sort of egg-shaped dip over here," called
out Beau. "Look as though it would be a good fit,
too."

On my instructions Toby carried the Eg over to

where Beau was sitting, and sure enough there was a depression in the ground that looked as if it were made on purpose. Taking the Eg out of the sack, he made a kind of bed for it with the same and then laid it down like putting it in a nest.

I gazed down at it. It was even bigger than I remembered, and must weigh at least fifteen pounds. I wondered how much larger it would be before it hatched, and when that would be. . . . In the moonlight it still held its own sparkly radiance. I patted it gently.

"Good-bye Eg, and good luck. May your hatchling be something very special. . . ." It ought to be, I added to myself, after all these years! "I've carried out my part of the bargain: now it's up to you." I stepped back. "Right. Time to go."

Beau nudged my knee. "Hadn't you better say something polite to the dragons?"

"What dragons? There aren't any."

"Are you sure?"

"Of course!" I had forgotten about whispering and gestured all round the cavern. "Nothing but a jumble of old stones and a few embers. How can I talk to things that aren't there? I'd just feel silly."

"I still think you should try. Just tell them how you came to undertake this journey and that the Eg has now been restored to them."

Toby looked at me with surprise as I gazed out over the chasm to the jumble of rocks which was the only place where dragons could possibly hide, and gave a potted version of why we had come and what we had brought. I finished on a bout of coughing, but decided on one last attempt to find out whether I was talking to thin air or something solid.

I looked back at the stones. Was it my imagination, or had they rearranged themselves a little? I was suddenly afraid. "Listen here, dragons," I said. "Of course I don't necessarily believe there are any of you out there, but if there are, it would be polite to show yourselves and perhaps say thank-you. . . ."

Nothing.

I turned to go, but at that very moment there was a strange kind of hissing noise, like the noise a gas lamp makes when it is turned on too high, and a hot choking blast of air; not air from the chasm, this smelled quite different, more like an overdone roast. At the same time Toby's lantern dimmed right down, so we could hardly see a thing, only being able to distinguish the entrance to the passage with difficulty by its darker outline, as the moon was also temporarily hidden by cloud.

As we gained the beginning of the passage I glanced back one last time, to print the memory firmly on my mind. The moon was now westering and a beam touched the rocks and struck off one— no, two—points of red. And surely there were two more? But those were green—

Another blast of burnt-fat air nudged us down the passage and once again the lantern burned low. We reached the entrance to the path outside and I took deep breaths of the fresh air, or tried to, as my lungs felt stuffed up.

"Come on, Sophy, let's get you—" but Toby never finished his sentence because there was a sudden clap like thunder directly above us. I glanced up and was sure I saw the silhouette of a dragon above us. Not that I had ever seen one before, but it looked just like the ones in my children's books; huge sweeping wings, four taloned feet, a twisted tail and a coruscating flight. It could be nothing else.

"Look Toby, Beau: a dragon!"

"Where, where?" They gazed around, but it must have been in the wrong direction, because they shook their heads.

"Up there! Above us . . ." But even as I spoke the dark shape drifted away out of sight. "It *was* there," I insisted. "I *saw* it!"

"Yes, yes I'm sure it was," said Toby soothingly. "Come on, Sophy, you are not at all well. You look a bit feverish to me."

Indeed I now felt dreadful. I had been artificially buoyed up by the incentive of getting the Eg to its destination, and now we had succeeded and no further effort was needed all I wanted to do was lie down and sleep, for a week if necessary. My chest hurt, I had the shivers again but my head felt as if it was on fire. I followed them down the path, my hand on Toby's left shoulder, because my feet had suddenly developed a tendency to wander off in the wrong direction.

Finally I made it to where Ky-Lin was waiting; he took one look at me then touched me briefly with his horn, as usual alleviating the pains a little. I don't recall any of the journey back to the village in the litter, though when we dismounted I looked back at the Blue Mountain and quite clearly saw two shapes like outsize bats wheeling above the moutain.

"Look, Beau! Dragons . . ."

He gazed up into the sky. "Yes," he said. "Dragons . . . Come and lie down Sophy: you'll feel better in the morning."

I thought I was so tired I could have fallen asleep on one of Toby's mother's clotheslines, but it wasn't as easy as that. I was hot, I was cold, tossed and turned, couldn't get comfortable, and at one point got up to see if the dragons were still there.

Ky-Lin apeared at my elbow. "Back to bed Sophy, and I'll give you something to help you sleep . . ."

As I lay down again he breathed over me gently: a scent of spring, a breath of autumn, stimulating and soothing at the same time. I closed my eyes and slipped into dreamless sleep.

Chapter Twenty-seven

A Day Too Late?

I don't remember much about the next few days: ten, to be precise, as I was told afterwards. During that time I drifted in and out of consciousness, never quite sure what was reality and what was dream—or nightmare.

Once there seemed to be an interminable, jolting journey; I was either burning hot or freezing cold; there were bitter brews to drink. Sometimes there were voices whispering in my ear, words I could not understand; at other times it sounded as though a crowd was shouting somewhere in the distance, and always, always there was the struggle to breathe, as if I were running a perpetual race I couldn't win.

Whenever I opened my eyes there were shadows: the sun chased them across the white walls, the candlelight made them rear and sway like demented devil-dancers. Then there were the dreams. Once, when I was so cold I couldn't bear it, I went for a walk and found myself at the back door of the little cottage I used to share with my parents and they were there at a wicker table under the apple tree, just as I remembered them.

My mother looked up and smiled. "Come and join us," she called. "We've been waiting for you!" But then my father put his hand on her arm and shook his head. It was all in slow motion, as it sometimes is in dreams. His voice, when it came was oddly distorted. "It's not time yet," he said. "Go and check the clock." I started to move towards them, but he held up his hand, palm forward. "Go and check the clock!" I turned back into the cottage and there beside the door was a clock I didn't remember having seen before. I looked at the face, but instead of the usual hours and minutes and numbers of one to twelve there were figures of one to seventy-five and a single hand, which pointed to twenty-two, just my age.

Was this supposed to measure my life-span? I turned back to ask my parents, but they were gone, just a few petals falling from the apple tree, to remind me of what I had once known. . . .

That was the only dream I remembered clearly, but there were others, less pleasant.

Once I awoke, or thought I did, to hear Claude and Danny arguing outside. I didn't know what it was all about, but I thought I heard Danny say: "If you won't tell her, then I will! You can't go on letting her believe she's won!" To which the reply was: "You're not to tell her! If it's anybody's task, then it's mine!" and "But you know how much it means to her—"

I don't recall any more, but I do remember wondering who the "she" was they referred to.

I didn't "come to" apparently for a few more days, but one morning, after a particularly restless, sweat-soaked night, I awoke to diffused moonlight on white-washed walls, a clear head and the ability to breathe without wheezing and choking. A woman was bending over me and I indicated that I was thirsty, and a couple of minutes later I was gulping the best drink in the world: a cupful of ice-cold, clear, pure, mountain water. Five minutes later I was chair-lifted by two of them to the bathroom, where I relieved myself, and was then given a warm bath and hair-wash and dressed in a clean shift. My bed had been changed and re-made as well, and the women fussed and twittered around me in their own language, until I pointed to my mouth and rubbed my tummy, indicating that I was hungry.

Five minutes later there arrived a bowl of warm gruel; it tasted of nuts and honey and I spooned it down eagerly, not realising just how hungry I had been. I tried to ask where the others were, but it wasn't until I repeated the name "Ky-Lin" a couple of times and they nodded, and one of them spread her fingers a couple of times to indicate twenty minutes, that I knew she had understood.

I fell asleep again while I was waiting, to wake to the dissonance of bells and the sound of distant chanting, to find Beau at my side, purring.

"You awake? Feel better?"

I yawned. "I think so—to both questions . . . Where am I? How long have I been ill?"

"We are being cared for in a Buddhist monastery some ten miles from the Blue Mountain. It is high up on a hill, and it is where Ky-Lin normally lives. And yes, you have been ill, very ill for quite a long time. They said it was pneumonia. At one stage we thought—even Ky-Lin thought—that you wouldn't make it."

I felt very uncomfortable. It doesn't help to be told that one had been near death. "I suppose it was getting wet in the caves?"

He nodded. "Apparently." He padded up the bed towards my pillow. "But now you're better!"

I hugged him. "*Much* better! Where are the others?"

"They'll be here in a minute." He pushed his wet nose against my cheek. "Give us a kiss . . ."

I pushed him away, laughing. "I told you, I don't kiss cats!" He was even bigger than I remembered.

"You have done already—"

But he was interrupted. The door was flung open and in came Claude and Danny, the latter clutching a bunch of wild chrysanthemums. I was embraced, congratulated on my recovery, told how much they had missed me, and then subjected to a detailed account of the monastery, where they had been, what they had done.

"For six days we weren't even allowed to tip-toe in to see you," said Danny, "and when we did you looked half-dead already! And now here you are, sitting up and taking notice, just as if nothing had happened at all, at all!" He had gone Irish. "Ten days it was since you went up the mountain and you were all but lost to us!"

Lying back in bed I tried to calculate. "Then it must be the eleventh of November . . . We missed Bonfire Night, boys!"

There was a sort of uneasy silence, and then Claude blurted out: "Actually, it's the twelfth."

I stared at him. It couldn't be. Even I could count. There was another even more uncomfortable sort of silence, broken eventually by a crimson-faced, embarrassed, uncomfortable Danny.

"What he's trying to tell you," he said heavily, "is that you were one day late depositing the Eg."

"And I'm telling you I'm willing to lie and change my notebooks," protested Claude. "You won't lose out, Sophy. I'll tell the solicitors—"

I burst into angry, frustrated, hopeless tears.

"Hey, what's all this?" Ky-Lin came bouncing into the room, his antennae as pink as raspberries. "Welcome back to us, Miss Sophy! But why the tears?"

There was a flurry of explanations.

"Well, well, well. Just sit back and think before you all jump to conclusions. Don't you have some sort

of nursery rhyme about how many days there are in
every month?"

In a sort of ragged chorus Danny, Claude and I
recited the following:

> "Thirty days hath September,
> April, June and November.
> All the rest have thirty-one,
> Except for February alone,
> Which hath but twenty-eight days clear,
> And twenty-nine in each leap year."

"Excellent!" said Ky-Lin. "Now then, what year is
it in your Western counting? Well, Master Claude?"

"Er . . . Eighteen-eighty-four." He ventured.

"And is that number divisible by four?"

He nodded.

"Then this year was a leap year, wasn't it? So, Miss
Sophy was in time after all!"

"I was? I am? I did it after all?" In spite of my
weakness I bounced up and down on the bed.

Claude went red, then white, then red again.
"Apparently yes, Sophy. All my fault," and then he
disappeared, presumably to alter all the dates in his
little black books, from the twenty-ninth of February onwards . . .

Danny raised his clasped hands above his head.
"Glory be!"

"Knew it would be all right!" purred Beau.

Completely forgetting my previous vows I leant forward and on impulse gave him an exuberant hug and
a kiss, to feel a strange constriction in my stomach,
a sort of breathlessness that had nothing to do with
my recent illness. His lovely blue eyes dilated, then
he let out a sigh more human then feline.

"Two down," he said clearly. "One to go . . ."

After that it should have been easy, and home
again before Easter, but Ky-Lin, the nurses who had

been tending me and the monk who made up the noxious potions I had drunk, all insisted that I convalesce for a while longer, until all traces of congestion were gone. So I twiddled my thumbs through the rest of November and into December, when of course the snow and the icing up of the rivers made travelling impossible until the spring thaw.

During my extended stay at the monastery I spent a great deal of time on the balcony-garden outside my room. A set of steps led down to a tiny paved garden, full of button-chrysanthemums and bonsai plants, protected at night by straw matting. When the sun shone it was pleasantly warm out there during the day, but at night I was only too glad to snuggle down under my feather-filled coverlet.

On one such day I was sitting outside with Ky-Lin and Beau; Claude and Danny had walked down to the village that nestled at the foot of the steep hill on which the monastery stood, because it was market day.

I shaded my eyes against the strong sunlight. "Ky-Lin, what's that lump?"

"Lump? What lump?" He had shrunk a good deal because, as he explained, being larger was hard work; he was now about the size of a small terrier. "I don't see any lump . . ."

I laughed. "Perhaps it isn't a lump then." I pointed. "Over there: that piece of stone on the rail of the balcony."

He leapt up to the two-foot rim and nosed what I had referred to. "You mean this?"

I nodded. "What is it?"

"This—this *lump* you referred to—this is a memorial to my friend, my dear friend Growch, Mistress Summer's travelling companion."

"I remember! In the translation my uncle made he was meant to stay behind when she went to the mountain. Did he disobey?"

"He did, and he got badly burnt when the mountain blew. I nursed him back to health, but the damage to his emotions I could not cure. He loved Mistress Summer and served her well, and could never forgive himself for not being there when she—disappeared."

"The account never mentioned what happened to her afterwards . . ." I hesitated. "Did she—did she die with her lover?"

"No-one knows. Some say they both escaped and flew away to a far-away island, but I must admit I did not sense her presence later. But then, of course, I was busy caring for the dog."

"You loved him?"

"Ky-Lins do not 'love,' as you understand it. We are capable of affection and respect, and for Growch I had a great deal of this. He was an amiable companion and we talked much of many things. When he passed away to another plane I was very sorry, but one of the monks, a devoted admirer of his, carved a stone statue of a dog asleep in the sun. This is what you see, but hundreds of years have softened the stone and rounded the statue."

I reached out and touched it, warm from the sun.

"I wish I had known him . . . And Summer."

Ky-Lin seemed to have recovered his composure. "I was glad to know them both. He was a real 'character' as I think you would put it. He taught me a great many words that I am sure my Master would not approve of, but with him they just seemed natural."

I moved forward to lean over the parapet: to my left was the Blue Mountain, ahead the valley stretched away towards the river we should take on the first part of our journey, and towering above us to the right were the mountains.

"What will you do when we are gone?"

"Wait here for my Master. He will decide whether I have expiated all my sins, or whether I have to stay here a little longer, to be of use to someone else."

I tried to question him about his "sins," but he shook his head, only murmuring something about "careless-ness" and "pride." It seemed it was very difficult for a Ky-Lin to become, and stay, perfect. . . .

The proposals came a few days after that. I had noticed both Danny and Claude behaving oddly dur-ing the last few days—arguing in fierce whispers, going into corners with pieces of rice paper, brush and ink, nudging each other and looking at me and then away again. The first time this latter happened I thought I was blemished in some way because of my illness, but a mirror reassured me. Thinner-faced perhaps, but otherwise unchanged. So, when I came across them tossing best-of-three, then best-of five, then best-of-seven, I decided to leave well alone. If they wished to behave like a pair of overgrown school-boys, that was up to them.

So, one afternoon when Claude tapped on the door of my room and asked if he could have a word, I thought it was some kind of advice he needed about his acne, perhaps, or a request to mend his combinations, which he still insisted on wearing. Whatever it was, it was clear he was highly embar-rassed, red as a turkey-cock's wattle and perspiring profusely. I offered him a cup of water and led him out onto the balcony, where there was a welcome breeze and we could stare out over the scenery instead of having to look at each other eye to eye.

"How can I help, Claude dear?"

At first he hemmed and hawed, then all at once the words came tumbling out like a string of broken beads, and as difficult to match together. Apparently I would never be fulfilled until I had known the joys of married life with all it entailed. I needed a hus-band to care for and protect me. Money was no object, because two could live as cheaply as one. He said, obliquely, how much he had always admired me etc. etc., that I was the only one, true, suitable mate to share his life with, so would I accept his hand in marriage? He was sure his mother would find me acceptable, he added, only I must never reveal I had ever worn, er, trousers. . . .

"No, I won't," I said firmly, "because the situation will not arise. I am both grateful and honoured by your proposal, but I have to tell you that marriage plays no part in my future plans, at least for the forseeable future." I stifled my giggles with a fit of coughing. During his declaration I had veered between surprise, repulsion and amusement. The latter was winning, but I was glad to see he looked relieved, not tear-stricken.

"Well, if you're sure . . . ?"

"Absolutely." I felt an imp of mischief ready to jump out from the corner. "Did you toss for who should be first?"

He half-rose from his chair. "How did—how did you know?"

"It didn't take much! Don't tell him I know, just say you failed in your endeavour." I relented, rose and kissed him on both cheeks. "Claude, this doesn't mean I'm not immensely fond of you, and will never forget your company during our expedition. Go and find a girl more worthy of you—and your mother—and be happy!"

After that I didn't have to wait too long for Danny. Perhaps encouraged by Claude's failure, he appeared on the scene only a few minutes later.

This time it was quite different. He came armed with a bunch of flowers and a mouthful of Irish exaggerations, his tongue making the words flow like a lively stream over rolling pebbles (and as near unstoppable). Apparently I was the most beautiful, talented, desirable creature on earth, and the best prospect a man like him could hope to find. He even went down on his knees to propose, but this time the amusement couldn't be held back.

He sprang to his feet. "You're laughing at me!"

I shook my head, tried to stifle my giggles. "No, my dear, not at you, just the methods you use! I'm very flattered that you asked me, but I'll tell you what I told Claude: I've no plans to marry for quite a while."

At first he looked cross, then as relieved as Claude, then finally he laughed too. "Worth a try, girl!"

After they had both gone I turned to Beau, a silent and hidden witness to both proposals.

"Did I deal with them properly?"

He yawned and straightened luxuriously. "Of course. Neither was right for you."

I laughed again. "And I suppose the prince-you-are is?"

"Of course. Wait and see."

When I had fully recovered we left the monastery, after a well-deserved donation of a couple of pink pearls, and rented a small house in the valley below until the spring. It was really one large room with niches for sleeping, a primitive stove and a large brazier. There was a well outside in a little square, a woman to do our washing, an annex that served as a bathroom, and a market twice a week, so we did pretty well, with frequent visits from Ky-Lin.

Of course we couldn't celebrate Christmas as we would have wished, but we did the best we could, with paper streamers, chicken stuffed with what we could get—rice, nuts and dried fruit—and we let off some firecrackers. Afterwards we decided to sing a couple of carols, so the boys stood outside and serenaded me through the the open door. A heavenly choir it was not, although it awakened in me all sorts of nostalgia. Some of the villagers came out of their houses to listen, and the dogs *loved* it, joining in with enthusiasm. . . .

Once we heard that the ice was breaking up on the river, we knew it was time to go. Ky-Lin accompanied us. He was back to figurine size and I carried

him either in my pocket or on my shoulder. We
decided to walk rather than ride: walking was the way
Summer had done it, though in the opposite direction. As we left I took a last look at the Blue Mountain; in the daylight it looked like a harmless, bluish
lump rising from the plain, and I found it hard to
remember that terrible trip to restore the Eg. I hoped
it was all right.

On the way I looked in vain for the deadly swamp
that had nearly ended Summer's expedition. We were
walking along a paved causeway at the time, with neat
fields of rice, vegetables and fruit on either side.

Ky-Lin anticipated my question

"This is it," he told me. "A lot can happen in a
few hundred years. Gradually it was drained, the
land was fertile, the population grew, and now it is
as you see it today. There are still some outlying
patches that remain to be treated, but they will be
done, in time."

Ky-Lin acted as translator when we arranged for
our passage downriver, also when we sold off a few
more pearls to see us on the first part of our long
journey. I would have dearly loved him to come with
us, but as he explained his part of the story was over
and he had to return to the monastery to await his
Master, the Buddha.

"How will you get back from here?"

"A pocket here, a pouch there. I shall wait till
someone goes in the right direction."

He bumped his knobby forehead against mine, a
sort of goodbye, I supposed. "Don't worry about me.
Good luck attend you and your Prince of Purloin-
ers." But before I could ask what on earth he was
talking about, he was nodding at the middle finger
of my right hand. "I don't believe you will be needing
that any more."

I looked down at my finger where the little ring
of horn, the Unicorn Ring, had been getting looser
and looser over the past few days. In fact I now had

to screw up my fist or trap it with my thumb to keep it from falling off.

"It *is* a bit loose . . ."

"Which means you no longer need it. When you relied on it to help you with this expedition you couldn't take it off. Now it is ready to await its next wearer, one who will need its magical powers to help them on another worthwhile adventure. The Ring chooses its own wearer, you know that. Why don't you take it off and put it round my neck? I have been involved with it before and we trust each other. What do you say?"

I hesitated; it had been so much a part of me for nearly eighteen months . . . But I knew I had no permanent right to it. "But—but how will I understand animals, how will I know when danger threatens?"

"Your own common sense and the new life you will lead makes both these needs superfluous."

"What about understanding Beau?"

"He will make his feelings known to you, with or without the Ring. You two have grown close enough not to need words. Trust me . . ."

Slowly, reluctantly, I drew the Ring from my finger. Once off, it seemed to have a life of its own, for in an instant there it was nestling round Ky-Lin's neck. All at once the world seemed a duller, greyer place, birdsong muted, the bales of silk waiting to be loaded a paler colour, the sun behind a cloud. Momentarily I closed my eyes on the disappointment, something brushed against my eyelids and when I opened them again everything was back to normal. Everything that is, but one. Ky-Lin had gone. . . .

Chapter Twenty-eight

"Prince of Purloiners"?

After that it was a leisurely voyage home, by sea when we could, by coach when we couldn't. We swapped a river-barge for a bouncy junk, a smoky coaster, a dhow (not much room in this), a river-boat, and finally the cross-channel ferry. During the long days and gradually warming nights I washed and mended all our clothes—what there was left of them—bought pen, paper and ink and wrote down an account of all our adventures so that perhaps one day my children might read it.

Once we were in "civilisation" again I had to go back to wearing a skirt, and I found I had enough to refit us all cheaply, and to give the boys a little pocket-money. Danny promptly bought packs of cards and small, smelly cigars, Claude some more handker-chiefs, although his permanent sniffles were now minimal. He had already, with the money he had managed from the little I had given them before, bought a length of purple silk for his mother. Toby saved his money right until the last, when he came across a very good second-hand compass in a shop, just before we joined the cross-channel ferry that would take us on our last lap.

My purchases were books, of course; second-hand copies of Mr. Browning's poems—and a real delight they were: it was almost as if he was talking to you, acting out the part of Fra Lippo Lippi, for instance— and a very tatty copy of Mr. Verne's *Around the World in Eighty Days*, another interesting tale.

During our voyage home, Danny and Claude had become close friends, as though the trials we had been through had done much to smooth over their differences in lifestyles and outlook. Perhaps it was more accurate to say that that they accepted the differences, and tried to assess how they could work to their mutual advantages. So much so, that they ventured to me that they were thinking of combining their talents and opening a detective agency.

"If Danny does the detecting, then I'll do the books and the housekeeping," Claude told me. "He's got lots of good ideas. . . ."

I was sure he had. . . .

Having exchanged the few pearls I had left—apart from the half-dozen most beautiful: a huge pink one and five perfectly formed blacks, guessing that I would probably get a better price in London—we still had enough to telegraph Mrs. Early of our imminent return, the price of a hired coach and two cabins on the ferry. The boys shared one, Beau and I the other, although the captain had looked askance at Beau.

"No wild animals," he had said dismissively.

I could understand his hesitation. Already Beau was the size of a panther, and appeared to be expanding every day. I assured the captain that he was perfectly tame, and that I would pay for any damage he caused.

It was true what Ky-Lin had said: we got along fine

without the Ring though of course we couldn't converse the way we used to. I talked to him, though,
and he appeared to understand everything I said, so
we were a comfortable couple; I was going to say
there were no disagreements, but I had learnt enough
about cat body-language to understand what a lash-
ing tail meant!

We had dined well, the sea was smooth and it was
a warm, early June night, with a thin silver moon
curving up from the sea through our open porthole.
Although I was excited at the thought of our long
journey at last coming to an end and thought I
wouldn't sleep, in fact I succumbed within minutes
of lying down on my bunk, leaving Beau gazing out
of the porthole. It seemed only minutes later that
I woke—in fact the moon didn't seem to have moved
at all—to find Beau padding back and forth across
the cabin from my bunk to the porthole and back
again, obviously with something on his mind.

"What's the matter, Beau? Can't you sleep? It won't
be long now; when it gets light we should see the
White Cliffs, and before you know it we'll be on our
way home!"

"*Your* home . . ." I thought I heard him say.

"And yours to share."

"Not the same . . ."

I sat up. Yes, I was sure he had spoken. Right, so
I was dreaming: no wonder I thought I had only been
asleep for a few minutes. Well, dreams could be interesting, and it was nice to talk properly to Beau. His
head was on my pillow, and the moonlight, thin
though it was, showed me a beloved face whose every
change of expression I had become used to; the angle
of the ears, line of mouth, depth of cheeks, attitude
of whiskers, arrangement of fur, the set of the eyes,
the dilation of the pupils—the whole look now was
one of misery, depression and resignation.

"Of course it won't be the same as your beautiful palace in Siam," I said, pretending to fall in with

his absurd stories. "But I will try to make it as comfortable as I can for you—I promise you will eat well and have the run of some lovely countryside. Lots of rats and mice . . ."

"Princes don't eat mice," he said. "All I want is that kiss you promised me, before it is too late."

"I didn't promise you anything of the sort," I said. "I told you, one doesn't kiss cats. The fact that I forgot a couple of times has nothing to do with it!" But I was angry with myself, just for being angry. I paused. "What do you mean: 'before it is too late' ?"

"Because my year is nearly up. If I cannot receive that kiss then I am condemned to spend the rest of my life as a cat. And that I could not bear, however kind you would be to me. I am a *man,* not an animal!"

Because I was still angry with myself I hit out at him.

"You know perfectly well I don't believe that rubbish you told me, don't you? Princes and palaces, witches and spells—a load of rubbish!" I had forgotten I was still dreaming. "And that story of that tatty collar of yours being made of precious stones . . . Pah!"

There was a little silence. "I thought it might come in useful with that orphanage you were planning," he said at last.

How did he know that? I had never discussed it with anyone, even Toby, although it had been much on my mind on the way home.

Somehow that touched me as nothing else had.

I was beginning to realise just how much I valued his comradeship, his company, his constancy. Would it hurt me so much to kiss him once more? Of course it wouldn't! But there was a reason for not doing so, I realised. What would happen if it didn't work? If he had been wrong all along? Supposing that third kiss left him as he was—a cat? What would he feel like? Wouldn't it be better that he blame me, rather than face the humiliation and distress of defeat?

If it meant I could guarantee that he would turn back into the prince he thought he had been, then I would kiss him all over, for as long as it took. . . . But I just couldn't risk it.

"Listen my dear, I just can't do it. I don't want to disappoint you." I patted the bunk. "Don't let's spoil our last night's travel. Come up and have a cuddle!"

Suddenly there was no room to spare; I was surrounded by cat: warm, furry, purring. This latter was a deep-throated rumble, in-out, in-out, on different notes, a semitone in between, and a trifle more *forte* on the breath out. It was soothing, soporific: I closed my eyes . . .

"Of course it may be that you are afraid of being confronted by a prince," said Beau, as if continuing a conversation we hadn't had, and effectually jerking me out of my doze. "What would you say if I told you I was not the scion of a noble house, but rather the bastard son of a waterfront woman, and a thief as well?"

I sat up. "What on earth are you talking about?"

"I am saying that perhaps I should have told you the truth right from the start, instead of trying to romance it up a bit, but I thought you might accept me more readily as a suitor if you thought—"

"A suitor? How on earth could you have thought—"

"That you would countenance a cat? But I keep telling you—"

"You keep telling me about a witch and a ridiculous spell—"

"But that was the only part that was true! The rest I made up, just to impress you!"

It took me a minute or two to digest all this, but once I realised I was still dreaming I decided it wouldn't interrupt the dream if I heard what he had to say.

"Perhaps you had better tell me the truth then," I said. "Not that I will necessarily believe you, of course. And not that it will make the slightest difference to my decision," I added.

He nodded. "Understood. But I will feel better to have told you. . . . The story begins before I was born. In the country of Siam there lived a rich widower, a merchant, with one child, a beautiful girl with hair the colour of the night, eyes the brown of autumn leaves and a skin like ivory—"

"How do you know she looked like that? You said this was before you were born!"

"Don't interrupt! All will become clear . . . Being a rich merchant and trader her father had several warehouses and a counting-house down by the waterfront, and his daughter, who was also gifted with figures, helped her father in the latter.

"One day her father was attending other business and his daughter had occasion to do business with an English ship which was carrying a cargo of tin. During her supervision of the unloading she noticed a young sailor, a handsome young man with fair hair, blue eyes and a smile to melt one's heart, so she told me later. Apparently over the next couple of days they fell deeply in love, and by the time the sailor had to rejoin his ship some couple of weeks later, she was already pregnant. By the time her condition became obvious, she swore to her father that the sailor had promised to come out on his next voyage to marry her, and that he had already sent a letter ahead to his parents telling them of his decision. But her father was so angry and humiliated that he threw her out of the house.

"She waited in vain for her lover to return, for his ship foundered on the voyage with all hands, but her son was born before the news reached her."

"How cruel! First being thrown out of the house and then losing her lover! How did she survive?"

"Although her father refused to see her again, he

gave her a small annual income, enough to keep her
and the boy from starvation. He also gave her a
necklace that had belonged to her mother, a mag-
nificent example in diamonds and emeralds . . ."

Where had I heard that before? "You were that
boy?" In my dream . . .

"Yes, that is how I can remember how beautiful
she was. She told me that if she had been on her
own she would have cast herself into the sea to die
as her lover had, but that I had given her something
to live for. She taught me all she knew about book-
keeping and mathematics, and managed to save
enough to hire me an expatriate Englishman to teach
me to speak, read and write in my father's language."

He paused. "And so it went on until I was about
fourteen or fifteen years old. . . ."

"Go on . . ."

He sighed. "The next bit I always find difficult to
even think about. My grandfather, the merchant, married again, a wicked woman who tried to persuade
him to cut off my mother's allowance. When he
refused he became ill, and was dead within a year
of his marriage. Our allowance was stopped, my
mother became ill and my wicked step-grandmother
sent round the police for the necklace, saying my
mother had stolen it. She had bribed them, of
course."

He sighed again. "Those were the hard times. My
mother needed medicines, and the care of a doctor.
I applied for job after job, but always my applications
were turned down—my step-grandmother again."

"So what did you do?"

"The only thing I could do: I turned to thievery."
He saw my look of shock. "What else could I do?
And I was good at it; it wasn't too difficult, with all
the goods passing through the port. I was quick and
agile, and I was never caught. I found a couple of
fences willing to buy whatever I could not take
home—jewellery or clothes—but food and delicacies

I bought for my mother every day. I don't know whether she realised what I was doing, for I told her I had a good position, though she must have marvelled at the strange hours I kept—but perhaps she just didn't want to know.

"She was only thirty-five when she died; I believe she was longing to be re-united with her English sailor, reckoning that I was now old enough to take care of myself: her death hit me hard. For a while I had no wish to live myself. I grew neglectful of my appearance, forgot to eat or wash. Eventually though I pulled myself together and, not wanting to continue a thief and waste my life, decided to follow my father's profession and went to sea. This was a big mistake: I'm afraid I hated every minute. Businessman, yes, given the chance: sailor, no.

"I reckoned my mother had left me two things she wished me to do. My father had told her of his parents address in England, and she asked me to visit them some day; the other was my determination to retrieve the necklace. To this end I took to spying on my step-grandmother in her villa, and it wasn't long before I discovered that she was a witch; I watched her cast spells to entrap young men and make up the most subtle poisons and potions.

"I waited one night until I reckoned she was asleep, then used my thieving skills to enter the villa and steal back the necklace. Once found I put it on, and was just leaving the villa when my step-grandmother jumped out at me. Apparently her powers had told her I would come."

He stretched, quivered, and settled back. "The rest you know, more or less; there is no need to go over it again. She used her powers to bewitch me into what you see now, and laid the curse of the three kisses on me. Since then I have spent months of my life trying to escape capture, starvation, degradation, and it was only when you rescued me from that murderous stall-holder that I began to hope once more.

"But now my time is running out. It took a great deal out of me learning to eat and hunt like a cat, and also to avoid capture. A couple of times it was only my tough claws that got me out of trouble. I was trapped a number of times by the enticement of food, but luckily my captors had to sleep and I remembered the ways to open doors and unlatch windows."

I knew I was dreaming, I must be, but why would someone like Beau alter his story, so that the desirable prince became an undesirable thief? Surely if anyone was going to be idiotic enough to believe his story they would rather look forward to a princely suitor than a commoner!

I had one more thing puzzling me. "You said you liked it when I called you Beau, but you never really explained why. Was it a pet-name?"

"Depends on how you spell and say it. My father's name was David Bowe and my mother named me after him—only she called me 'Davey.' "

"I *see*!" I thought for a moment. "Can I go on calling you 'Beau'?"

"Of course. Well?"

"Well what?"

"Does it make any difference to your decision? The truth, I mean."

"How can I be sure it is the truth?"

"You can't. Any more than you can tell whether a kiss will turn me back into the man I once was. You'll just have to trust me . . ."

I turned to him, hugged him, stroked him. "Look, I'm quite happy with you as a cat. Why do you want to tempt fate? I love you. . . ."

"I love you too, but I'd rather love you as a man. . . ."

I sat up abruptly. I had never thought that if he really was a man— But I was dreaming, and silly thoughts do come with dreams.

"You aren't, you know," said Beau. "You are as

wide awake as I am. Look, if you are so convinced it won't work, I promise to absolve you from all blame if anything goes wrong—but it won't."

So, tired of arguing, and praying against all reason that he was right and I was wrong, and that I wasn't dreaming, I leant forward and kissed him full on his mouth.

Chapter Twenty-nine

The Wedding Gift

"Told you so," murmured Beau, a.k.a. David Bowe. He took off the emerald and diamond necklace and clasped it round my neck. "There you are: my wedding present. We can use it to finance the orphanage, if that's what you want." He leant over and kissed me, a proper, human, deeply satisfying kiss. "And now, if you don't mind moving over a bit, my darling?"

Chapter Thirty

A Year Later

My husband and I leaned on the gate that led to the playfield, the baby asleep in a basket at our feet. A year after our return another June breeze riffled the corn in the farmer's field next door and stirred the waist-high bracken on the hill, bringing with it the scent of summer flowers, honey, lime-blossom and the richness of warm pine trees. The children, eight girls and three boys so far, although Toby would be bringing us more the next day, were chasing a soft ball across the grass and, judging by the shrieks of laughter, thoroughly enjoying themselves.

Behind us in the old stable-yard, drying linen flapped and cracked in the wind, and through the kitchen window I could see Ellen and her widowed sister Jeannie were making the final preparations for luncheon: cold chicken and summer salad, with fresh, warm bread and milk pudding to follow. All the produce was from Hightop, apart from the flour and yeast, for we now had two dairy cows, were fattening a couple of pigs and had increased the numbers of ducks and chickens and extended the kitchen garden by half as much again, and Mr. Early was busy carpentering a see-saw and swings for the children.

The choice of children we had left to Toby—he knew better than any who needed help—but at first I had been full of worthy schemes for their education—globes and improving books in the room we had designated as the schoolroom. But it was Ellen—who had left the school and Miss Moffat after being accused by the headmistress of not being economical enough with the poor fare the children were offered, which was absolute nonsense, as well I knew—who had put me on the right path.

"Listen, miss—sorry, missus, but it's difficult to think of you as a married lady—you ain't teachin' in a school no more, you're goin' to run a Horphanage. What them children need is food, more food and lovin' care, not books, leastways not at first. Once you've got them clean and tidy and rid of the bed-wetting and have taught 'em to use a knife and fork proper and say yes please and no thank you, the next stage is bedmakin', dustin' and polishin', layin' fires and blackleadin'. Then into the kitchens to prepare vegetables and learn to wash up. After that comes simple stitchery, which my sister can teach 'em, 'cos she earned what she could as a seamstress. Then you can teach 'em enough to follow a receipt, sign their names and add two and two so they aren't cheated when the tradespeople call."

She saw the dismayed look on my face, and I could see she was trying not to laugh.

"Oh Missus Sophy, don't look so worrit! They'll come to your learnin' soon enough, but first things first! Now, the first thing is what they's to wear. It's summer, so vests and cotton shirts and leggings for the boys, and vests, short dresses and pantaloons for the girls. Something cool, comfortable and easy to put on and take off. As this is a Horphanage, perhaps it would be better if they all wore the same colour: how about brown for the boys and blue for the girls? That way there won't be no nonsense about one wearing something better than someone else . . . And that's another thing: they'll have to learn washin' and ironin' as well. And I forgot the butter and cheese makin'."

"But Ellen, some of them will be only five or six years old!"

"Never too young to learn. Fact, the younger the better. Now, when we've got them to rights, the boys can help Mr. Early with the kitchen garden and the animals, and I'll have the girls in the kitchen. Tell you what, you have them in the mornings and we'll take them for the rest of the day. Don't forget, you're not teaching future Prime Ministers and lady librarians, you're trying to make the girls fit for service in good positions and the boys 'prenticed well. That's all. If on the way you find someone to take further, like Master Toby, well and good, but don't expect it!"

She was perfectly right, of course, but I found it difficult to absorb, no more so than on the day we welcomed our first arrivals and I watched horrified as the new arrivals were taken out into the yard, stripped bare, had their heads shaved, girls as well as boys, and were then dumped, one by one, into a large tub of warm water and scrubbed with carbolic soap until all the London grime had gone for good. Two of them were too cowed by their earlier life and the newness of their surroundings to do anything but submit, but the other three yelled and shrieked and fought all the way through and Mrs. Early, Ellen and her sister had their work cut out. Bathed and disinfected, they luckily fitted into the clothes Jeannie had already sewn. They were then fed—outside—just to see about their manners which were, mostly, nonexistent. So that was the first chore . . .

Play-time was before luncheon and before supper. In the winter months we had to spend a good of time indoors, and at those times we used the schoolroom, which I made as bright and welcoming as possible, to hear many stories and play games of blindman's buff, hunt the thimble or musical chairs from the old piano, together with the quieter dominoes, draughts and hands of cards. Two of the downstairs smaller rooms were turned into indoor privies and washrooms. We bought new beds, put up hooks for clothes, provided cutlery and crockery and hung curtains. After we had just about become used to our first arrivals, Toby brought six more, and we started all over again, luckily helped by the first lot, determined to show their superiority.

We had decided that about thirty children was about enough to cope with, replacing after that those who got good positions. We had sold the pearls in London for an excellent price, and the necklace had been bought at our inflated asking price by a certain "Royal Personage" for his mistress! That money was invested in railways, cotton and munitions, which Beau said people always need, and were paying good dividends.

He himself had found a position as consultant with a city Merchant Bank dealing with the Far East, and went up to town two or three times a week. We had given Claude and Danny a hundred pounds each to set them up, because they were still determined on the detective agency.

We had found Beau's grandfather and grandmother living quietly in Plymouth, and although wary at first they had soon accepted their grandson and his wife as welcome additions to the family, and were delighted to learn they were soon to be great-grandparents.

As for Toby, we had offered him a lump sum but he wouldn't take it, asking us instead to put a bit aside whenever we had any to spare and invest it, so he would have a bit put by when he kitted himself out for his first expedition. He was still determined to become an explorer, and to this end was studying every book he could find on the subject, besides searching out the most deserving cases for the orphanage. With the five he was bringing us tomorrow, it would bring the count up to eighteen, with Jeannie's two little girls. He explained that we would always have more girls than boys, because the latter were better able to look after themselves on the streets, and adapted readily to being part of a gang of young thieves.

Another piece of news was that Miss Madeleine from the Charity School was planning to join us next week. Apparently Miss Moffat had found a rather attractive young lady to fill my post, and Madeleine wrote that she was just twiddling her thumbs and would I take her at a low wage? Between the lines I could read that she was desperate also not to end up as an old maid, and immediately bethought myself of the young curate at the village church, who came faithfully every Sunday to lead us in prayers and tell the children Bible stories. Beau was happy for her to come, saying I would have more time with our daughter if I had someone else to do the teaching.

We three lived at the "Temple," as I still thought of it, looked after by Mr. and Mrs. Early. Our bedroom was the one I had first occupied, the baby's Night Nursery next to it, the Day Nursery the room in which I had prepared for our journey, which still left three bedrooms for guests. If Madeleine had one of these, Toby could have one and Claude and Danny double up, if they all arrived for a visit together.

Thinking of those two made me grin, and Beau turned to look at me.

"Share it?"

"Just thinking of that first success of 'Cumberbatch and Duveen.' "

"Typical Danny . . ."

Indeed it had been, but it had opened all sorts of doors for them, so now they had moved from their original lock-up to an office with a room behind for eating, cooking and sleeping and an outside privy, with two let floors above, from which they collected rent. Their first "scoop" had been, as Beau said, "typical Danny." As I saw it, it was ten out of ten for opportunism.

It appeared that he had witnessed an accident in which an expensive-looking carriage had overturned, discharging a small beribboned dog who yapped and dodged between the legs of the passersby. Danny seized his chance, grabbed the dog and bore it back to their lodgings. In spite of Claude's protests he fed it and cleared up its messes and bore its petulant barking, until he could study the papers the next day, and saw as he expected, a reward of ten pounds. He waited until the next day when the reward had risen to fifteen pounds, then had visited the bereaved dog-owner, a hysterical dowager, and offered his services to "find" the dog, hinting darkly at a dog-stealing gang, and the dangers of trying to penetrate their fastnesses, and had been offered the reward, plus five pounds per day if he could return the dog. Obviously he had been successful, but it had taken him five days. . . . Forty pounds to the good, plus the recommendation of a grateful dowager! Danny had a lucky touch, or a four-leaved clover.

Behind us the bell clanged outside the kitchen door and the children ceased their play and streamed for the gate, which Beau swung open. Ten minutes until luncheon, time for the children to wash their hands and tidy up. Beau closed the gate and dropped a kiss on the tip of my nose.

"Saturday afternoon, sweetheart . . ."

"So?"

"So the children are going on a nature ramble this afternoon with Mr. and Mrs. Early. Neither of us will be needed between, say, two and five. I suggest we—" and he bent and whispered in my ear.

I blushed. "In the open?"

"Why not? The sun is good for you, and I like to see my wife in daylight. You are beautiful in any light, my sweet, but the sun is something we can't often take advantage of . . ."

I adored him, of course. Strangely enough, his cat-colours had come through to his human body. His skin was the creamy-beige of his cat-coat, his hair the chocolate of his mask and paws, and his eyes the same startling blue; his body was as lithe and strong as his cat-body. And he loved me too . . .

I nodded down at the wicker-basket, where Serena had just opened her eyes and was stretching and yawning her toothless mouth. Her fist went to her mouth, obviously ready for *her* luncheon. "What about her?"

"Go and feed her, and then let Ellen have her for an hour or two. You know she dotes on her. . . ."

Serena opened her eyes, the same blue as her father's, and yawned again, and my heart turned over with love for them both, my husband and my daughter. Just now, life was good. Doubtless there would be hard times, bad times in the future, but our love would see us through, of that I was sure.

Beau put his arms about me. "Any regrets, my darling?"

"None at all." But then I remembered something that was still nagging at me. "Well, yes: I suppose there is something . . ."

"Tell me!" He kissed me again. "I'll cure it if I can."

"You can't, nobody can . . ."

"But what is it?"

"Well, it's just that . . . Sounds silly I know, such a small thing really . . ."

"What?"

"I just wish I knew what happened to the Eg . . ."

Epilogue

Ky-Lin could have told her . . .

As soon as the Travellers had left, the dragons flew, one by one, across the chasm to where the Eg, their Eg, their long-lost treasure, lay in the niche in the ground long reserved as the official Hatching-Ground. They flew in order of precedence; first the senior Master-Dragon, the Brown, followed by the Orange, the Green, the Grey, the Purple, the Yellow and finally the Blue, his mere twelve hundred years making him the most junior.

One by one they approached the Eg reverently, muttering a suitable welcome, until all seven were grouped round in a circle, admiring, longing to touch, to examine more closely, to guess the weight, estimate the date of hatching. It was for the senior dragon to make the first move, followed by the others in order of seniority. Although it was not encouraged, there were inevitable side-bets; these were safer than quarrels, and they only used trinkets as stakes: a silver platter or two, a small string of pearls, an amethyst brooch—the sort of wagers they laid in their endless games of chess, checkers, Mah-Jong etc.

The dragons' colours glowed with excitement. Although naturally of a neutral colour, the lozenges of scales on their chests reflected their "true" colours, which only dyed their skins when they were excited, as now, or were injured or ill, when the colours seeped into the neutral patches and dyed the whole dragon with a paler shade of the original. This had happened hundreds of years ago to the Blue, at a bad time when he had temporarily mislaid the jewels that would make him a Master-Dragon.

The dragons were more or less agreed. The hatching would take place around Middle-Year, and the weight was about fifteen pounds at present, of which three pounds were the shell. It would be a large baby dragon.

In the meantime there was plenty to do to prepare for the new arrival.

Firstly the Eg must be kept warm and comfortable and turned regularly. One after the other the dragons provided comforts. Yellow filched a padded quilt from the bush where it had been drying, though when he had tried to accelerate the drying process with a puff or two of dragon-fire it was not quite as it should have been, although the scorched bits didn't show once the quilt was folded. Blue concentrated on a layer of dried grasses for the floor of the Nursery, Green fashioned a beautiful teething-ring from bone and coral, Purple picked out the finest jewels for the baby's first toys and Orange wove a basket to hold them, while Grey fashioned wind-chimes from the smallest bones in their collection.

As senior dragon, Brown was in charge of the arrangements and supervised the rota for the weekly turning of the Eg and the continual Hatch-Sitting.

Winter passed, spring brought new life to the crops and countryside and the dragons did their annual Turd-Out, as they called it among themselves, although Brown frowned on this and preferred it to

be referred to in his hearing as Spring-Clean. This
year it was more important than ever that the whole
cave was as pristine as possible, pending their New
Arrival, so they all set to with a will, using their wings
to sweep all the debris down into the accomodating
chasm, so that detritus, dried faeces and general
rubbish went up conveniently in a puff or two of
greasy smoke and a couple of sparks. Their Hoard
was sorted, examined, cleaned, stones polished and
arranged to their best advantage; the silver and gold
on stone shelves at the back, the jewels each in their
own piles of colour: rubies, garnets, beryl, blood-
stones, rose-quartz, carnelian and fire-opals; topazes,
agate, amber and tiger's eye; emeralds, peridot and
jade; sapphire, aquamarine and amethyst; diamond
and crystal; pearl and moonstone and opals, and all
set off nicely with bands of jet.

    Now all was ready, and only three months to
go . . .

    Unseen and unregarded, the Travellers who had
returned the Eg started their long journey home, and
at the monastery Ky-Lin welcomed the spring sunshine and spent much of his time snoozing on the
parapet of the balcony where stood the stone rep-
lica of his friend Growch. Some time soon his Master would arrive and take him to his rest, although
He had so much to do it might be later rather than
sooner. After all, he, Ky-Lin, was one of his Master's
most unimportant servants, and must wait his turn.

    Truth to tell he had rather enjoyed his extended
time on earth. Without becoming too puffed up with
pride, he had at least helped both Summerdai and
Sophronisbe to attain their goals. He, too, wondered
what had become of the Eg. He couldn't miss the
fact that there was more than usual activity among
the dragons, some of them flying by day, which was
most unusual.

    He wondered, too, how far his friends had

travelled homewards, and whether that rogue of a
Beau-Cat had managed to persuade Sophy that he
needed a final kiss to transform him, when he knew
perfectly well that the spell only lasted a year anyway. . . .

It had been a long journey for all of them, as had
the earlier one with Summer: he hoped this one
would have a happier ending. He had thought the
Eg would have hatched earlier than this; there was
certainly life in there, even after all the vicissitudes
it had been through; both he and the boy had heard
the somewhat puzzling sounds from within. Still, he
felt that everyone would be left in no doubt once
it had hatched.

Not that he knew much about dragons. They were
creatures of another, earlier time, some of the sur-
vivors of the Great Darkness he had been told about,
when the Black Star fell on earth and shut out the
sun for aeons. He and his brethren were of a later
time, direct creations of their Master, devoted to the
preservation of life in all its forms, unlike the careless, fire-setting, meat-eating dragons—although their
reputation as man-eaters was erroneous. Perhaps this
one would grow up differently, although if Growch
had been there he would have said: "No chance,
mate. Once a dragon, always a dragon . . ."

March had gone, April and May came and went,
and now the days had lengthened until it was no
sooner time to go to bed than time to get up again,
or so it seemed to the peasants toiling on their land,
although in the monastery the monks enjoyed the
indulgence of the sun on their shaven skulls as they
moved from one duty to another.

Up in the Blue Mountain the dragons jostled one
another for the privilege of Eg-Sitting now the time
was drawing near for the hatching, sometimes only
giving their predecessor five minutes before shoving
him aside and taking over. The Eg grew warmer and

larger, and now it weighed over eighteen pounds.
What a baby it would produce!

As Middle-Year appeared to accelerate towards
them, all the dragons vied with one another to provide their baby with the very best. Orange scorched
his tail down in the chasm while smoking the
tenderest pieces of meat for the baby dragon's first
meals; Grey almost choked on the fluff he collected
from plants for bedding; Yellow was badly scratched
searching for shards of glass to reflect the moonlight;
Green was nearly exhausted when he arrived back
from the south with a length of the finest silk for
covering while the baby's scales hardened; Purple
blunted his claws tearing out suitable white stones
from the moraine to fence in the Hatching-Ground
and Blue took one of the silver spoons and filled
several golden bowls with the finest spring water for
drinking and washing. Of course dragons used to roll
in dew or snow for their twice-yearly bath, but the
baby would be too young for a while even to be
flown out for this.

Nobody cared for bumps and bruises. Their baby
dragon hatching safe and healthy was all that mattered. The years since the last hatching were legion,
and the surviving dragons were not growing any
younger. There must be other dragon eggs scattered
throughout the world but these were in forgotten
places and might never have the right conditions to
hatch, but this one was here, it was real, it was live
and it was about to hatch.

The sun rose higher in the sky, the air grew
warmer, and at last it was the eve of Middle-Year-Day.
There was an overnight full-moon which bathed the
Hatching-Ground and the waiting dragons in silver
light. It seemed that the moon was reluctant to miss
the hatching, for it was still a pale disc in the sky
when the sun rose in the east, and now all the dragons were gathered in a circle around the Eg, most
of the side-bets having been paid out already.

One hour before mid-day the tapping began.

At first it was so faint that the dragons had to hold their breath in unison to hear it at all, but then the noise gradually grew in volume and faster and faster, until it was perfectly audible. Tap, tap, tap; tap, tap, tap.

But the shell of the Eg resisted. The tapping grew more frantic, punctuated by what sounded like tiny thumps, as if a small fist was joining in with the disposable egg-beak attached to the jaw of the baby dragon. The noise crescendoed, and then gradually died back as though the creature within was exhausted, was losing both strength and heart. The dragons glanced anxiously at each other, then turned to the Senior Dragon, Brown.

He thought for a long moment; all sounds had ceased. Then he nodded slowly. "Show claws . . ."

One by one the dragons raised first their left then their right front claws, which were carefully examined by Brown. All the dragons were supposed to keep their claws sharp on the specially imported granite Sharpening Stone, but some of the older ones skipped the chore, so consequently it was the youngest, Blue, who was chosen to help their baby out of his prison of shell.

Brown indicated where he wanted the cut made. "But not too deep; just halfway through. Be very, very careful . . ."

All held their breath as Blue extended the middle claw of his right front foot and held it poised over the Eg. They noticed he was trembling. He took a deep breath, then as delicately but decisively as a glass-cutter etching the thinnest balloon glass, he traced a fine line two-thirds around the breadth of the Eg.

For a moment there was no response, and then the tapping started again, louder this time, the accompanying thumping as well, and now through the crack in the shell a thin mewling sound. Like a

miracle the crack widened fractionally until there was
a minute glimpse of movement. By now all the dragons' heads were circled above the Eg, a living dome
of bony heads and hissing breath.

Noon, and the sun at its zenith on this Middle-
Year-Day. A shaft of light suddenly burned down on
the dragons' skulls and they all drew back as if
scorched. They believed that the sun's rays were
harmful, would burn through their skulls and
scramble their brains. Now the rays of the sun shone
on the cracked Eg and the noise and activity within
increased a hundred per cent. The membrane which
divided the outer shell from its contents stretched
and stretched, thinner and thinner as the crack in
the Eg widened until suddenly with a ripping *pop!*
it burst apart, the Eg-shell opened into two distinct
halves like a two-petalled flower, and its contents were
revealed . . .

Ky-Lin heard the roar from where he lay in the
mid-morning shadows among the bonsai trees on his
little balcony. He sprang upright, thinking for a
moment that the fires in the Blue Mountain had
erupted again, but recognised immediately that the
noise came from the harsh, cacaphonous voices of
the dragons. Whatever it was, they were clearly upset.

Gradually the noise subsided, rising once more
into a brief crescendo every quarter-hour or so, but
this merely increased Ky-Lin's sense of unease. He
could not imagine what could have occasioned such
an uproar, audible so clearly across the miles that
separated the monastery from the mountain. Had
something happened to the Eg? If it had hatched
normally he would have expected something other
than this howl of both anger and bewilderment. Was
there something wrong with the baby dragon? Could
it be malformed? Sick? Dead? And if it were any of
those things, wouldn't the dragons blame both him
and the Travellers for not taking enough care with

it? If so, what could they do? Would they take to the air and pursue Sophy and Company and wreak a terrible vengeance? Or would they seek him out and pulverize him, raze the monastery to the ground?

No, he couldn't let that happen. He must journey towards the mountain and meet them half-way, try to undo whatever damage had been done before it was too late. Accordingly he did a quick transformation into pony-size and made his way through the monastery, down the track to the village and turned north onto the plain. He trotted along in the afternoon heat, carefully avoiding damaging any living growth, his hooves throwing up little puffs of dust.

He made good progress, and as he neared the Blue Mountain the dragon voices grew louder and more discordant. He wished he could understand just what they were shouting about—

He skidded to a sudden halt, realising all at once what an utter idiot he was. Because of the unspoken ban against any congress between his people and them, they had always ignored that the other creatures existed, and of course there was no way he could communicate with them if they came face to face. They were such primitive creatures that thought transference was out, too.

He sank down on his haunches, in his misery shrinking down a size or two. He could not remember ever feeling so miserable, even when . . . But no point in remembering that. He and his brethren were not supposed to feel sadness—nor anger, hatred, love, pride or impatience. Perhaps he had been in the world too long, for he knew he had felt all these emotions at one time or another, most of them only momentarily. His downfall had originally been his pride, and luckily he didn't really know how to be impatient; but he had felt affection for Summer and Sophy, and for the boy Toby, but probably the greatest had been for Growch.

There was only one thing to do. He closed his

eyes, bowed his head, gazed inwards and sent a
prayer to his Master—not a request for direct aid, that
would be wrong, rather a prayer for guidance on
what to do next. One had to rely on oneself for
action.

He was deep in meditation, sinking into that limbo
where the body no longer mattered or responded to
outside influences, when he was jerked back into the
real world by a sudden clatter of leathery wings above.
Claws seized his shoulders and he was borne upwards
into the air with a whoosh! and a sinking lurch in his
stomach. All his senses returned with a rush as he saw
the plain beneath him disappear with alarming speed.
Whatever in the world was happening?

He realised that he had been pounced on by one
of the dragons and was being carried higher and
higher towards the north-east, but to what purpose?
Was he to be dropped from a great height, to be
smashed to smithereens? Made into a snack for the
dragons' dinner? But perhaps they had something
less violent in mind: to show him something perhaps?
To demonstrate why they were so angry?

Whatever the eventual outcome they had obviously
seen him coming and decided to collect him,
although it was unusual for them to fly in the heat
of the sun, so it must be urgent. Lifting his head a
little he saw they were approaching the Blue Mountain, swinging back behind it to the shady side, but
when it seemed they must literally brush the rocks
his carrier-dragon shot straight upwards, making Ky-
Lin dizzily wish he had not indulged in those few
extra grains of rice that morning. They must be all
of three thousand feet high . . .

The next moment they started to drop like stones,
plummeting down so fast that Ky-Lin was thrust back
momentarily against the dragon's bony chest. Beneath
them the black maw of the mountain rose up with
frightening speed: a dark blot, an inky puddle, an
ebony lake—the mouth of Hell itself!

The dragon braked sharply at the last moment, then did a neat landing in the middle of a circle of six scaly others, dropping Ky-Lin unceremoniously to the ground. All around was the stench of cinders, old bones, stale air, sulphur. Ky-Lin choked and gagged and his eyes started to run. Something shoved him in the back, propelling him forward; blinking he tried to clear his streaming eyes, conscious of the dragon-voices grumbling and growling all around him.

His eyes clearing, becoming used to the dragon-stench, he peered ahead of him. He was in a small enclosed space surrounded by a fence of stones and—yes—there was the Eg, or rather one of the neatly bisected halves. Moving nearer without hindrance, he peered down and there, cradled in the egg, its tiny claws clutching a strip of smoked meat which it was attempting to chew with its razor-sharp baby teeth and making contented little mewling sounds, was a baby dragon.

Its blue eyes gazed up at him curiously. Blue eyes? Did they change as the dragons grew, like puppies, kittens or human babies? He peered closer. It seemed healthy enough: four legs, claws present and correct, two vestigial wings, tail, nose, eyes and ears all looking in the right places. Just for a moment it bore a fleeting resemblance to a little piglet, especially as its tail was tightly curled.

And it was pink . . .

Presumably all dragons started that colour, together with the blue eyes, and they lost that ridiculous tuft of blond hair like chicken-fluff that grew on top of its head as they matured.

He was saved from further guesswork—if the baby dragon was healthy and happy then what was all the fuss about—by a violent nudge, one which knocked him sideways out of the ring of stones and onto a bare patch of ground, on which lay the other half of the Eg.

Now all the dragons were hissing, instead of the
crooning-growl they had made over the baby dragon,
but suddenly a thin, angry wail cut across all other
sounds, pitched as it was at a higher frequency; rapidly it grew into a horrendous, ear-piercing screech,
a sound compounded of anger and despair, grating
on the ear like a giant chalk on a giant blackboard.
Ky-Lin moved over to the other half-egg and gazed
down. And there . . . ? There was a baby.

A *human* baby!

The little girl, tufts of black hair sticking up all
over her scalp, eyes screwed up in temper, toothless
mouth agape for another wail, arms and legs pumping, was quite obviously not a dragon, although she
was behaving like one. So, the Eg had held its surprises after all—twins! one dragon-baby, one human
one.

No wonder the dragons were so upset. At last Ky-
Lin had an inkling of why he was here. He realised
that the dragons thought he was partly to blame for
this mess: after all hadn't he helped first Summer
and later Sophy to deliver a flawed Eg? Sure, they
had their baby dragon, but here was a lively, lusty
reminder of their renegade dragon, Black Jasper, who
had broken all the rules and fathered an Eg with his
human love.

Now he was left in no doubt as to his role. He
glanced over to where the baby dragon lay—no eye
contact with his captors, kidnappers, hostage-takers,
hijackers, whatever they were: this only incensed
them, apparently—and he saw the baby dragon lifted
tenderly from his half of the Eg and cradled in
blunted claws, while a padded quilt was ripped in half
by another, sharper claw. Half was tossed across to
land at his feet, a scorched, charred half, while the
other, unmarked half was the dragon-baby's new
cradle.

Another dragon tossed the half-shell with the baby
girl onto the damaged quilt then brought the corners

together into a rough knot, and moved back. Another
pushed him forward again till he was standing over
the bundle. So, he was expected to carry it away. He
opened his mouth, took the knot into his mouth and
tugged, but the cloth slipped away. He tried again,
but once again his ruminant's teeth could not get
a grip, and he that even if he grew to pony-size he
would never be able to carry the bundle away. He
stepped back and shook his head, was nudged forward again, attempted it again, but only succeeded
in trying so hard that he merely let go too quickly
and landed with an undignified bump on his rump.
And if dragons could be said to snigger, they were
sniggering now.

The baby had been quiet for the last few minutes, but now she started up with another piercing
wail, rising to an indignant shriek. The dragons
shrank back, and he realised that the noise actually
hurt their ears, accustomed as they were to their
own much deeper voices. There was hissed conversation above his head, then suddenly he was grasped
once more by strong claws and borne aloft; out of
the corner of his eye he saw that a second dragon
had grabbed the baby-bundle and was bearing it
aloft also.

Once more the vertigo, the churning stomach, the
rush of wind over his hide, but now he was surprised
to see it was already dusk and that there was much
cooler air in the upper reaches, although the further
they descended heat from from the baked earth
beneath came puffing up like an open oven.

Ky-Lin looked down, expecting to find the plain
rising up to meet them, but they appeared to be
swinging further south-west. He saw the monastery
looming up, and already he could see the twinkling
lights of the cooking-fires and lanterns in the courtyard. What were the dragons doing? Almost immediately there was that sickening drop of hundreds of
feet and then a lurch as his dragon pulled up just

short of the balcony. So they knew just where they could usually find him . . .

A moment later he was dropped unceremoniously beside the bonsais, and the bundle followed, a little more gently, to lie in front of him. Above them the dragons hovered for a wing-beat or so, their drown-draught flattening the hair on his plumed tail and smelling of cinders, then they were up and away, their raucous cries fading away as they swept back towards the Blue Mountain.

The bundle beside him stirred. Awkwardly Ky-Lin worried the knot loose until the baby girl lay revealed, wriggling uncomfortably, her mouth squaring itself for another gappy yell. Soon someone would come to investigate, on the excuse of bringing him his supper or lamp, but before then he would have to seek help, make a plan.

Despairingly he nosed the lump of stone that represented his old friend, Growch, and let his thoughts wash out over the stone. "What shall I do next? I've never had to deal with a baby before. . . ."

He didn't expect an answer, but at once, in his mind, he heard a voice: a hint, a murmur that sounded so like Growch that he shook his head in disbelief.

"Come on, mate? Think . . . Babies is no different from pups. At this age they needs milk, warmth and a lick or two to keep 'em clean. Once they starts to grow, then they needs training, care, an' lots of love. Start 'er off right: after that it's up to you . . ." The phantom voice faded, died away.

Of course! A wet-nurse from the village to care for the babe until she was weaned. That took care of the next few months. But then? The voice that had seemed to be Growch's had said "after that it's up to you . . ." but there was always a choice, wasn't there? And if his Master came for him soon . . . But if he didn't?

He glanced down at the baby girl again. She had decided to calm down, but she was still frowning, sucking at one of her fists; then she stretched out her other hand towards him and for a moment her face smoothed out and she was still and there was a sudden fleeting resemblance to . . .

He sighed. Yes, there was always a choice—but then he had just made his.

Hadn't he?